LAST DESCENDANT

Frank Emili

Copyright © 2014 Frank Emili
All rights reserved.

ISBN: 1495248372
ISBN 13: 9781495248375

To my girls, Liana, Sabrina and Rina

PROLOGUE

The twelve black-robed figures stood in a wide circle within the cavernous room, their faces hidden from view under large hoods.

All brought palms together in supplication.

"Father in heaven, heed our prayer!" they recited in unison.

One of the hooded figures, the leader, known as the Master to the others, continued alone in a booming baritone: "Oh God of the most high, we, The Brotherhood of The Rapture, ask for your strength and guidance to find and destroy the bloodline of the Betrayer."

Once again, in unison, they repeated: "Father in heaven, heed our prayer!"

The lone baritone continued once more: "Holy Father, let us be your sword that destroys the Descendant, the cursed bloodline, from the face of the Earth."

"Father in heaven, heed our prayer!"

"Holy Father, guide us to help you bring forth Armageddon as it is written in the Holy Book."

"Father in heaven, heed our prayer!"

The words echoed into dead silence.

The prayer had ended.

All waited for the Master to speak.

"The time is near, Brothers," said the Master. "We have found the Descendant. The bloodline will soon be destroyed and Armageddon assured."

A thin lecherous smile appeared under the hood of the Master.

"A new age of Mankind will be upon us."

CHAPTER ONE
HUNTER

Stephanie preferred to jog in the early morning hours, pounding the suburban sidewalks of Boston between four and five o'clock. Everyone, and everything, asleep at that time of day, that pre-dawn time just before the blackness morphed into dark grey then quickly lighten, bringing clarity to the surroundings that were, just a moment before, mere shadows in the gloom. She considered the early dawn her favorite time of day, when the solitude felt peaceful rather than lonely. Smiling inwardly as she ran, the late autumn air felt cool and clean in her lungs.

At twenty-nine years old, Stephanie maintained her body at a physical peak envied even by professional athletes.

Her familiar route brought her through a narrow lane between the wooden fences of two rows of houses. Less than half a mile away from the end of her run, she picked up speed to increase her calorie burn. As she reached the lane's midpoint, she felt a slight pressure on her neck, like a breeze going through her vocal cords. She did not see, nor feel, the blade that effortlessly sliced through her neck, severing her head from her body like a hot knife through butter.

Her head came away cleanly, fell forward, and took its first bounce on the pavement's gray, hard cement. The initial impact on her chin caused an instantaneous but brief metallic taste in her mouth. Her head then bounced back up and somersaulted in the air on a weird, wide spiral along an invisible axis. Stephanie remained conscious and experienced disorientation at a level never felt before as the world blurred out of control around her. Reaching the peak of its trajectory, her head came down for the last time and rolled across the pavement, finally stopping and facing back towards where her body lay crumpled on the ground.

Stephanie could not comprehend what had happened. She thought she had tripped, fallen, and taken a weird tumble. It took a moment for her mind to take in what her eyes were seeing, her body lying headless several feet away.

Her headless torso continued to spew its lifeblood in fast rhythmic pulses out of the open neck. The spurting slowly ebbed as the massive blood loss reached the critical point where the heart no longer has adequate thick fluid to pump through its chambers. Within seconds, the bloodletting stopped and the body gave a final twitch, a slight, almost orgasmic, convulsion as if fighting to stay alive.

Stephanie saw all of this with her eyes wide in horror. She opened her mouth and tried to scream, but nothing came out. She felt surprisingly little pain in those final moments, just a mild burning sensation at the end of her neck. As the last of her brain's oxygen dissipated, Stephanie's vision faded around the edges and her thoughts less coherent. The last thing she saw, as the darkness embraced her, were a pair of army boots that stopped right in front of her eyes.

Funny, I have a pair just like those, were her final thoughts as her eyes closed for the last time.

The man belonging to the boots wore a black formal overcoat over a black nondescript suit, complete with a white shirt and a black thin tie. A tall, muscular, white man with a rich orange and thick crop of hair kept short, military style occupied the black clothing. His face betrayed a white freckled skin that made him look boyish even at twenty-eight.

The man gracefully sheathed the samurai sword under his coat and carefully picked up the head, holding it between his gloved hands. Turning the head side to side, he carefully scrutinized every part of it with his piercing wild eyes. Apart from a few scratches from its tumble, the head looked perfect and serene as it began to turn grey in color. Sweat still rolled down the face. It trickled to the end of the severed neck and mingled with the blood and saliva dripping to the ground.

He finally turned his attention to her right temple and saw the mark that had sealed her fate. He knew it was there, but he looked for it as a final confirmation, a justification, for what he had done. He had caught site of the mark several times while observing her, unseen, over the last week.

Walking over to the torso, he bent down and delicately placed the head near the body. Quietly and with care and respect, he turned the torso over on its back, straightened the legs and positioned the arms against the side of the body. He now placed the head facing upwards against the severed neck as if trying to put a head back on a doll.

The man stood up and looked down at her. She still looked beautiful to him, even in death.

The act of killing had caused a sexual heat to rise up from deep within his groin. He did not get an erection. The experience more like the sweet pain mixed with pleasure that he used to get as a child when shimming up the swing poles in the orphanage playground. The more he had pulled himself up on the pole, the more he felt the tentacles of pain/pleasure shoot out from the center of his groin, pressing himself even tighter to the pole to increase the intensity to the point where he no longer had the strength to keep his legs wrapped around the pole. Slowly and reluctantly, slide down to the hard, compact ground, regretting the loss of that pleasurable pain.

This morning, though, that feeling had lasted only seconds and quickly supplanted with a feeling of guilt. Not guilt for killing her, for she had the mark and the killing ordained by the Master, but guilt for the pleasure he felt in the act of taking a life, for the total superiority he felt over his victim, the victim's total sense of submission and offering up of life, be it involuntarily. The power over someone's life gave him that sweet pleasure in his groin that filled his whole being. The sense of self-worth it gave him. Later, he thought, he would have to cleanse himself of such mortal feelings.

God had a plan for him. The Master had said so.

Soon after his arrival at the orphanage at age nine, the Master had told him he was special, not because of his Orphan Annie-like bright red hair and freckled face, but because of his destiny. His life before the orphanage had been a test, the Master had explained to him. The beatings and sexual abuse from his stepfather simply part of God's plan to ready him for the way of the holy warrior he would soon become.

"From this day on you will be known as Gabriel, in honor of the avenging angel," the Master had ordained that first day, and the boy, now known as Gabriel, flushed deep red under his freckles.

The Master sent him to a training camp somewhere in the mid-west along with a dozen other boys. The name and location kept secret from the pupils. Training for his calling started immediately and he became a star pupil. Soon he no longer remembered his birth name for he was now Gabriel.

Gabriel remembered very little of his life prior to the orphanage and the monastery, his mind blocking most of the memories of those horrible early years with his mother and stepfather in New York.

"You....are....a bastard!" his stepfather used to say looking down at him in a drunken haze after dragging him upstairs into his bedroom. "But you will have to do," added the beefy, sweaty man who seldom washed, stinking of beer, scotch and cigarettes. "Your mother is out earning her keep, whoring on her back or on her knees. She doesn't even know who your father is, you little prick."

Gabriel would struggle to escape without success against such a big man.

Soon after he turned nine, his mother died from a heroin overdose and his stepfather declared too incompetent by the state to take care of him. The now parentless young boy belonged to the state and sent to a government run orphanage.

It was there that Gabriel first met the Master.

During those early years at the monastery, Gabriel looked small compared to his peers, but he shot right up after puberty. Now at six foot four and two hundred and twenty pounds of muscle, his long dead stepfather would not have dared to treat him as he did in that horrible house.

There were times he yearned to dig up his grave, grab the body of his stepfather by the coat collar, and yell in his rotting, moldy, worm eaten face. "Who's the prick now, dad? Huh? You wanna take me upstairs now, you son of a bitch?"

Now, almost twenty years later, Gabriel had a purpose. God had given him strength, talent and an unflinching dedication to the cause, God's cause, God's will, pre-ordained long before the beginning of Man's reign on earth. He did not know what that cause was but the Master told him he would know soon enough.

When everything fell into place, the whole world would know. In just over a year, every soul on Earth would know, the master had said. He smiled in the comfort of that knowledge. Gabriel trusted the Master. Everything about Gabriel, everything that he held dear, desired, dreamt, came from the Master. The Master would reveal God's plan at the appointed time.

Gabriel preferred killing his victims up close and personal. He had hidden behind a bush in the lane and simply waited for her. As she ran by, with a quick and easy motion he had decapitated her from behind. The sharp edge of his katana sword sliced easily through the neck. With her speed, it required precise timing but his training ensured success.

Satisfied that he gave the body due respect Gabriel quickly and quietly walked down to the end of the lane. He needed to go another two blocks to where he parked the car.

He walked in an easy pace, not concerned over any intruders. At just after five A.M., the houses around him were still dark, their occupants still asleep. Only early risers lit the odd second floor bedroom window but he did not anticipate anyone coming outside anytime soon. He had scouted these streets over the last several days and knew the habits of the residents.

Gabriel got to the vehicle without incident and started the engine. He put the car in drive and slowly drove away, being careful not to rev the engine much more above idle. After a couple of blocks, he turned the headlights on and slowly accelerated to the speed limit. He took out his cell phone and dialed a number.

"Yes," a deep male voice answered at the other end barely after one ring. The Master had answered.

"It is done, oh Holy One," Gabriel said without introduction.

"Good. Continue as planned," replied the Master and the line went dead.

Feeling a quiet satisfaction, he pocketed the phone and continued driving. As the morning light began to appear in the horizon, he recited in his mind his favorite line of chapter twenty-one from the Book of Revelation of his well-worn bible, 'Then I saw a new heaven and a new earth. The former heaven and the former earth had passed away, and the sea was no more.'

"The coming of the Rapture," Gabriel ecstatically whispered to himself, "and Armageddon."

Yes, God has a plan for me, he thought.

Gabriel drove with a quiet satisfaction as he smiled to himself.

CHAPTER TWO
INVESTIGATION

Detective John Bernard slowly awoke to the shrill of the cell phone next to his bed. He slowly turned over and reached for it, noticing his partner's name on the display. He also saw the time: five-thirty in the morning. John winced. It could only mean one thing.

"Shit. It must be another one," John said to himself with a sigh. "What?" he asked abruptly into the phone.

"John. It's Rashid. You awake?"

"No it's the answering service. What do you think?" John replied in a sleepy guttural voice.

"Well, partner, I think you need to tell the young lady lying next to you to stop playing with you under the sheets so that you can get your ass out of bed," Rashid said playfully. You could almost hear his smile on the other end.

"I don't have a girl with me."

"What, you got a stud with you? I didn't know you went that way."

"Oh shut up. I'm half-asleep and you're joking with me? I'm alone."

"Poor baby, all alone. Shit, if I was single again, I'd have a revolving door to my place. There are lots of women in this town, buddy boy."

"Yah, Yah. If you were single your parents would've disowned you by now."

"Ooh that hurts. They're just traditional Arab folks. They want to make sure I carry on the name, man. Not like you."

"Ok, ok. I'm awake. What is it?" John no longer sounded irritated. They were the best of friends and they knew each other well.

Rashid's tone immediately became serious and the consummate professional, "Looks like we got another one."

John sighed, rubbing his eyes with his free hand. "Tell me where and I'll meet you there within the hour."

"It's at the new suburbs, the Kings Cross Estates, Blueberry Street."

"Got it, see you there." He hung up. John lay back for a moment, trying to clear his head and become fully awake. He had gone to bed at two A.M. and still needed a few more hours of sleep.

He finally got out of bed and, wearing only a pair of wrinkled boxer shorts, made his way through the clutter of his bedroom towards the bathroom where he stepped into a cold shower to jump-start his body.

John Bernard had been on the force for nineteen years and finally made detective two years ago at age thirty-seven. He wondered if he would ever make it to retirement. Not because of the risks or the physical demands but because of the mental and emotional strain inherent with the job. The divorce rate for law enforcement officers sat above 50% and he had already one notch on his belt.

Within a half hour, John left his apartment in downtown Boston and grabbed a coffee at a small diner across the street before retrieving his car, an unmarked police issue, from the underground parking. He then headed for Kings Cross Estates. He knew Rashid would be there before him. His partner had moved into that estate and into a new home last spring within an earlier completed phase of the new development. Rashid Ahmed had been his partner since John made detective two years ago. At forty-two and four years older than John, Rashid had made detective three years before.

John liked his partner Rashid. He seemed happily married and with four children still of school age. It gave John hope that marriage did indeed work for some people. Maybe Rashid's attitude made the difference, John thought. Known for his humor, Rashid seemed to let the darker side of life drip off like water off a duck.

When John arrived at the site, there were over a dozen uniformed officers patrolling and guarding the scene and several plain clothed, including his partner talking to another man. Within the laneway, two forensic experts, wearing protection suits to avoid contamination of the crime scene, meticulously scoured the site. A plastic sheet outlined in the shape of a body within the laneway.

John got out of his car with coffee cup in hand. He pulled out a cigarette pack, took one out and lit it, the first of the day. He took a deep drag before heading in Rashid's direction. "What you got so far, guys?"

Rashid looked at his partner. "The Lieutenant here said a man walking his dog found the decapitated body of a woman jogger in the laneway there." He turned and motioned towards to the lane as he flipped open his notepad and began to read aloud. "At approximately five ten this morning a Mr. Ralph Mayer of two thirty eight Blueberry Street took his German Sheppard for a walk. When he came to the laneway, he spotted what looked like a female figure lying on the ground. Mr. Mayer and his dog walked up to within several feet of her and called out. When she did not respond, he walked closer to get a better look. The dog went to nudge, or lick her in the face, and the head rolled over to the side a few inches away from the body. When Mr. Mayer realized what he saw, he ran, with his dog in tow, to the nearest house and asked the, until then, sleeping family to call 911." He paused, turned the page of his notebook, and continued the narrative while John took a drag from his cigarette. "The first pair of officers, responding to the scene at five fifteen, called it in as a possible homicide. While waiting for the crews to arrive they covered the body with the sheet. I called you as soon as I received it from dispatch."

John looked across to where the body lay. "Alright, let's go take a look and see if she has the same mark as the others," he said.

When they got to the victim, John put on a pair of surgery rubber gloves he pulled out of his coat pocket, bent down, and raised one corner of the sheet. It revealed the head facing away from them and clearly separated from the body. With his hand, John carefully rolled the head over exposing the right temple. Just in front of the hairline and in the middle of the so-called soft spot of the temple behind the eyebrow he noticed what appeared to be a crescent shaped dark brown almost black beauty mark about an inch and half long. John lowered the sheet back over the body.

He got up and looked at both men next to him. "Exactly the same birth mark as the other two women," he said solemnly.

They spent the rest of the morning going over the entire murder scene and canvassed local residents. By noon, someone from the coroner's office removed the body and a cleaning crew called in. In a few hours, very little evidence remained of the events of that early morning.

John reflected on what they had so far. Twelve days ago a woman, white, single, age twenty-three, found stabbed to death in her apartment with a single wound through the chest – probably killed with some kind of sword. There were no signs of a struggle. Her younger brother discovered her at around eleven the next morning after he failed to get a hold of her the night before. The autopsy showed she died the previous evening between ten and midnight. The autopsy also showed a crescent shaped beauty mark in the exact location and configuration on the right temple. This didn't cause much curiosity until another homicide victim showed up three days later with exactly the same birthmark. Her husband found her dead after work in the backyard of their home. With no clearly visible wounds, her husband called 911 yelling that his wife had a heart attack. The autopsy showed that a sharp long metal, stiletto like, object, shoved under her chin and pushed up into her brain caused the death. The penetration reached almost up to the back of the skull.

They had discovered no obvious motives in any of the cases. Nothing stolen, nothing destroyed, and now this one, more gruesome but with the same mark.

They had a serial killer on the loose.

John and Rashid headed back to their precinct. As they walked in, one of the other detectives told them that their captain wanted to see them as soon as they arrived. They walked past their desks and straight to the frosted glass door marked CAPTAIN WESTELL, HOMICIDE DIVISION.

"Come in!" a baritone voice responded sharply to their rap on the door.

"We were told to come see you as soon as we got in," said Rashid as both he and John walked in.

"Close the door behind you and sit down," said the Captain. He did not look up from the paperwork in front of him.

A burly man of African descent, Captain David Westell, had very dark, almost black skin, that could still flush with a deep red when angered, especially around the eyes. Aged in the mid-fifties, his short, cropped, black hair showed some gray from the stress of his job.

After a moment, Captain Westell looked up without expression. "Give me the details."

John began quickly and to the point, the captain didn't like to waste time on niceties. "It looks like it's the same killer. The victim is another female, twenty-nine, jogging in the early morning hours, decapitated on the last leg of her run. She has the identical birth mark; a crescent shape on her right temple."

"Decapitated, how?" the Captain asked.

"Forensics is working on it."

"What else you got?" asked Captain Westell.

"Still too early in the investigation," answered John. "We will go through the same procedures as before; check her background, family, friends, lovers, work associates. Even down to the mail carrier of her building and the dry cleaners she uses. We will also do background checks on everyone attending her funeral when we finally release her body to the family."

"Go for it, and keep me posted. Release a statement to the press that we appear to have another related killing but, like the others, keep the beauty mark out of it. We don't want everyone with any kind of beauty mark to panic. Nor do we want to show all our cards to whoever is doing this, though they should have figured out that we know by now. Only the killer or killers would know this. All right, thanks," said Captain Westell dismissively as he resumed his paperwork.

John hesitated. "Captain, the whole affair shows a fairly high level of sophistication and planning."

"What do you mean?" The Captain asked settling back in his chair, not hiding his annoyance that the men ignored his dismissal.

John said thoughtfully, "This is off the cuff but how would someone go about tracking down women with that distinctive beauty mark? Does he randomly walk the streets and other places where people gather and look at their temples, and how about women who wear their hair long? No, it doesn't make sense that a single person is doing this. The fact that he managed to find three of them, unknown to each other, and spread out across the city shows that the search must be methodical and well planned by a group of people. I can't even fathom how they would go about it, but one person can't do it on their own. There has to be an organized group behind this."

The Captain said firmly, "Then I suggest you guys start thinking along those lines. If you had to search out women with a crescent shaped beauty mark on their temple, how would you do it?"

"We'll look into it, Captain," said John as both he and Rashid walked out.

Forensics released the body after a few days to Stephanie Long's family. Since both her parents were dead, and being a single child, the funeral arrangements were left with her only surviving relative; an aunt on her father's side living in a small, out of the way, town, south of Boston.

The aunt, a large woman in her mid-fifties, did not exactly need any solace. Childless and married for thirty years to a brutish man now in his sixties who ran a used car lot, Mr. and Mrs. Watson seemed initially put out for having to arrange and pay for their niece's funeral. They could legally have washed their hands of the whole affair but they soon changed their minds when the media furor put them in the spotlight as the only surviving relatives of a brutally murdered innocent young woman.

Never one to pass on an opportunity, Mr. Watson spent a significant amount of effort exploiting his dead niece.

The used car dealer gave the media and public full access to the funeral. Next, he insisted that they replace the trailing vehicle to the Hearst, normally a limousine caring the family members, with one of his lot vehicles splattered with advertising signs across most of its surface, complete with a 1-800 number in bold on both front and back bumpers. He also demanded that he drive it himself with his wife riding gunshot. He actually had the nerve to smile and wave to the public as the procession snaked its way from the church to the cemetery.

For several weeks, Mr. Watson had special 'funeral' prices for anyone who had signed the funeral home attendance book or brought in one of his specially marked business cards he had placed in a stack next to the casket.

The funeral not only paid for itself but he also made a tidy sum that year. He wondered if there were any other long lost relatives destined for such a famous ending.

John could only look on in disgust as the funeral circus unfolded. The Watson's were not breaking any laws or local ordinances but, damn it, he thought, these hick-town, vulgar people trashed every decent moral value. The media, not exactly the best moral compass themselves, didn't dare criticize. Sensationalism is all that they wanted. It's what sold papers and they certainly got that from the Watsons.

Things died down close to Christmas. With the short attention span of the masses fed nightly with brain numbing vomit across the airways, the sordid event soon forgotten. People went back to their predictable game shows, pre-school intelligence level dramas, and fear mongering news. Sales at the used car lot of Mr. Watson slowed down to its normal pace once again.

The last John had heard Mr. and Mrs. Watsons went on a vacation that early December. They had a hell of a great time while the niece began her slow rot in the ground.

During the funeral, John's team took pictures of everyone that attended. No small feat since the funeral home, church and cemetery were all at capacity. The team also managed to acquire copies of every picture and video taken by the media covering the funeral. Though a long shot, they hoped the serial killer or killers would miraculously show up and spotted among the faceless crowds. Even if they did not know what he...she...they...looked like.

The team did a background check of every person they could identify. To no one's surprise, they found a whole assortment of social outcasts and trash. Pimps, pushers and thieves, to name a few, all made an appearance; all trying to make a fast buck. The whole debacle reminded John of a pack of wild dogs tearing apart and devouring an injured member of their pack. At least wild animals do it for survival. Humans seemed to do it for pleasure.

December came and still no progress and, fortunately, no additional similar murders.

They were at a virtual standstill until one morning, Lieutenant James Collins, leading the team doing the background checks on all the people at the funerals of all the victims, approached John's desk. He had a folder in his hand. Looking at John and Rashid sheepishly, he said softly, "I think we may have something. Can we go to the conference room to discuss?"

"Sure," said John picking up his coffee cup and leading the way.

They found the conference room free.

"Tell us what you got, Jim," said Rashid casually.

The lieutenant opened the folder he had carried in with him and spread out some papers. "Well, huh, I have been looking to see if I could find any patterns between the three homicides that could help us out. As expected, there were several reporters, camera operators and other media crew members that were at all three funerals, and even at some of the crime scenes. We investigated these individuals and all proved to be in other locations at the time of the murders. But we found one curious individual that attended all three funerals that seemed a bit out of place."

Collins paused for effect and both John and Rashid leaned forward in their chairs, eyes staring intently at the Lieutenant. Having received the desired effect, he continued. "A catholic priest by the name of Father Sebastian currently assigned to the Church of St. John on Straw Street." Lieutenant Collins brought out several pictures of the priest and laid them out in front of both of them.

"What's so odd about a priest at a funeral?" asked John as he looked down at the pictures.

Father Sebastian appeared to be in his sixties or early seventies, about six feet tall, thin, almost gangly, with a severe, wrinkled face that looked like it never cracked a smile for fear of breaking. The look in the man's eyes showed fear, or guilty of something.

"Nothing, except that two of the victims was Jewish," answered the lieutenant.

Rashid asked, "What did you find out about him?"

"It wasn't easy," said the Lieutenant. "The office of the Catholic Bishop of Boston is not in a habit of giving out background info on their priests. We had to threaten them with a warrant, and the resulting unwanted public curiosity it would cause, before they became more cooperative." He paused and turned to another page. "Father Sebastian became a priest at twenty-one. Now semi-retired, he helps with the Catholic Masses on weekends and weekdays at seven in the evening. He also helps with other daily activities at the church. Prior to that, he had stints at a number of churches across the world before finally settling in Boston for the last fifteen years. The only thing of interest, as far as I can see, is that he spent seven years in Jerusalem back in the early seventies and a two year stint at the Vatican in the late seventies."

"Any info on what he did in Jerusalem?" asked John.

"He, huh," the lieutenant hesitated while he looked for and brought out another sheet of paper. "He was assigned to help in the preservation and study of the Saint Anne's Church in that city."

"Alright, so he likes archaeology," said John, "and the two years in Rome?"

Again scanning the same paper in front of him before answering, the Lieutenant said, "He went there to document and present his findings from Jerusalem. Apparently, the paper never made it through the Church's publishing process. The Church had concluded the report had nothing of relevance to the faith of the Catholic Church so opted not to publish."

"Even though not related to the Catholic faith, why not release the findings anyway for archaeological interests?" asked Rashid.

"We didn't ask," said Lieutenant Collins.

"Anything more?" inquired John.

"We are still searching for more info on what he has been doing here in Boston, but we haven't approached him yet so there may be more when we do."

"Hold off on bringing him in. Does he know we are investigating him? Has anyone else approached him?"

"Not that I am aware off."

"Good. Keep it that way for now. I'll let you know when."

"No problem. That's all I have for now," concluded the lieutenant.

"Ok, great. Thanks for the hard work, James. Rashid, stick around for a sec," said John as the lieutenant got up to leave.

After he closed the door, John said, "That whole thing with the paper and not publishing it just doesn't make sense." He slouched down on the chair with his feet stretched out under the table and looking at the fingers of his right hand as they were tapping on the table.

Rashid looked at him across the way deviously. "Maybe we should pay him a visit ourselves instead of bringing him in."

"I'm not sure if we both should," said John thoughtfully. "I'll swing by tonight. According to Collins, there should be a mass at seven and the priest will be there. And, Rashid, let's just keep this to ourselves."

"My lips are sealed," said Rashid emphatically.

"I'm going to take the rest of the day off," said John as he got up from his chair.

"You are?" Rashid said lightly with a smile. "If my guess is right about where you're going, you should take confession tonight while you're at it."

"Maybe I will," said John smiling back. "But if I do, I'll be in the confession box a long time."

●●●

John rang the buzzer to the apartment.

"Yes?" answered a female voice from the small, high-pitched speaker on the panel lined with numbers.

"Hi, it's me," said John casually into the speaker.

"Come on up," the voice replied.

John heard a hum from the glass door at the entrance of the buildings atrium. It opened to him as he pulled on the long metal handle.

A modern structure built near the business district of Boston, the building design stayed true to the modern glass square architecture, or lack thereof, that have been sprouting up in most American cities over the last ten years to meet the demands of white-collar professionals wanting to live in the busy downtown business districts. The building had a sterile feel to it with its clean lines, smooth terra cotta large floor tiles and beige concrete wall panels

John headed for the bank of elevators at the center of the well-lit atrium. He had been here many times before and the guard recognized him and only gave him a casual glance as he walked by. He rode up alone with an almost tuneless piano music playing in the background.

John knocked and the door opened almost immediately by a petite Asian woman who flashed a smile at John as she looked up at his face. She leaned sideways with one hand against the doorframe and the other on her hip.

"Come on in, sweetheart," she said in a feminine but not too high of a voice.

The woman stood about five foot four with a trim almost athletic build. Her straight black shiny thick hair fell just past her shoulders and she kept it cut Egyptian style across her forehead just above her eyebrows. The black hair framed her very exotic and beautiful, oval, porcelain looking blemish free face that held cat like oriental black eyes with a small nose and small but thick lips. Her petite and sensual frame covered in a tight fitting gray cashmere one-piece dress reaching down to the middle of her thighs. The lack of lines under her dress made it apparent she wore no undergarments of any kind.

As she turned and led him inside, he caught sight of the V-cut in the back of her dress that exposed her bare back right down to almost the crack of her tight behind that swayed in an exaggerated way, signaling her eagerness.

John smiled with anticipation and his green eyes gleamed as they drank in her beautiful form. Yes, he did like the dress, and the woman inside it.

He followed her into a small but immaculate apartment.

She went straight to the mini-bar and poured two glasses of scotch and water.

"How are you, baby?" asked John smilingly as she handed him one of the glasses.

She took a sip from her glass as she looked up at him. "I'm doing fine, now that you're here. I'm glad you called earlier. I missed you. It's been almost a week"

John had met Winnie Tse, almost a year ago to the day, at the Mayor's Christmas party. She had been there with her sister who worked as an administrator for the City Clerk. John had bumped into her at the bar and struck up a conversation.

Winnie soon mentioned her husband during their conversation and it disappointed John immensely. While attempting to bow out gracefully, she caught his intentions and soon made it evident that it would not hamper any amorous rendezvous if he so desired. She did not have to ask twice. If she was ok with it, who was he to judge?

John and Winnie clicked right away. It did not mean that they were deeply and madly in love, for they had the same beliefs and aversion towards relationships. They had kept it light and tried to maintain it only at the physical level, though inevitable that some feelings would come out after almost a year, but they kept it under control. Both were fiercely independent and did not want any major changes in their lives.

Six months ago, she decided it would be safer and more convenient to simply rent an apartment for their weekly, and sometimes more frequent, rendezvous'. She had found this very place, which she paid and furnished herself. John couldn't ask for a better arrangement.

He took a sip from his glass and looked down at Winnie, who placed her arms around his neck while still holding onto to her drink.

"I missed you too, sweetheart," he said softly while looking into her eyes. "I didn't know if you would be available at such a short notice."

"I cancelled all my afternoon meetings," she whispered as she brushed her lips lightly against his.

She stood on her tiptoes but she just managed to reach and press and grind her crotch against his. He felt her mound against him. He could simultaneously feel her hipbones against his and it gave him a sexual thrill. He began to react to the grinding and she smiled as she felt him respond, and rise, to the occasion.

"It feels like you're getting a little crammed in there," she deviously said breathing the words through hot breath into his mouth.

She pressed even harder against him.

"Yeah, and it's starting to hurt," he whispered with a smile.

He clamped his lips around her mouth and they just managed to put down the glasses on the table before they fell on each other on the carpeted floor. A long while later they both lay exhausted and sweating. Their clothes lay strewn about the kitchen and dining area.

John went to retrieve a couple of bottles of water from the fridge and snuggled back down next to her. She drank half of the bottle he gave her in one pull.

Winnie looked over to John and said, "One of these days we are going to pull a muscle or something."

"I know what I want to pull, he said as he reached for a nipple.

She gently slapped his hand away. "Stop it. I'm sore as it is because of you," she said with a smile.

"You are?" he responded, his eyes widening in mock surprise. "You usually tire me out before you're done. Then I have extra work ahead of me."

"Work, is that what you call it?"

"Just a figure of speech, baby," said John smiling, "because it always gives me an excuse for a second round."

"Let me rest a bit and then we can talk about round two," said Winnie taking another drink.

John laughed but soon they were reclined quietly side-by-side.

She didn't get a lot of rest before the second round.

CHAPTER THREE
SEBASTIAN

John sat in the back of the church and tried to act non-descript. About a dozen people waited for the mass to start.

The Church of St. John, built during the post-World War II era, boasted very little in the way of medieval architecture, or the less extravagant but no less impressive grandeur of the churches of the seventeenth and eighteenth centuries. Built with meager funds from the lower and middle-income urban dwellers of the surrounding neighborhoods the church contained the basic minimal requirements of a catholic church.

The mass soon started. To be more exact, he actually heard it when the organist began a soft hymn on the second floor balcony.

As the priest came in from behind the Alter in a ceremonial robe, all the people in the pews got up and John followed suit but he saw that the man was not Father Sebastian.

The priest, much shorter and younger, began the mass on his own. An hour later, near the end, as he was about to leave, John spotted his quarry. Father Sebastian came out to assist the attending priest with the final communion.

John locked his eyes on the old priest from the moment he came out. Father Sebastian went about the ritual at hand, seemingly engrossed with his solemn duties. Only at the end of the mass, when the attending priest bid the small crowd good night, did Sebastian look up. While slowly scanning the crowd with his eyes, as if giving his own blessing to everyone in attendance, he suddenly caught site John.

He did not first appear to have recognized the Detective. After a brief moment, his eyes widened slightly betraying his stony demeanor with a flash of recognition. He quickly looked away but John caught it.

The mass concluded and Sebastian and the other priest walked behind the Alter and through the door to the church offices and living quarters. John headed in the same direction. As he opened the door and walked through, he caught sight of the two priests. They had removed the robes and now sported simple black pants, jacket, and priest collar over a collarless white plain shirt.

The younger priest looked surprised by the intrusion but not alarmed. With a slight smile, he took a small step towards John while asking in a calm and inquisitive voice, "May we help you?"

Sebastian stood behind him.

"Yes. I'm sorry to bother you, Father," began John addressing Father David in a soothing calm voice and a slight smile. The detective walked closer while pulling out his badge. "My name is Detective Bernard. I'm here to ask if I can have a word with Father Sebastian."

Father David lost most of his smile when he saw the badge. His eyebrows furrowed as he turned his head away from John and looked back at the other priest as if looking for an answer. Sebastian looked back at him without expression.

"I hope it is nothing serious. May I ask what it is about?" asked Father David as he looked back at John pocketing his badge.

"I'd rather discuss that with Father Sebastian, if you don't mind," John answered with reverence and a smile, trying to make the priest feel at ease.

Father David looked at Sebastian and then back to the detective. "That is up to Father Sebastian," he finally said.

Sebastian stepped forward and said with a smile to John as they shook hands, "I am Father Sebastian and it would be my pleasure, Detective Bernard." Turning to the other priest he asked, "Don't worry, Father David, I have done nothing wrong. May we use your office?"

"Yes, of course," said Father David with a bow to his brethren but still showing some concern on his face. "I will meet you at dinner when you are done." He turned to John. "Good night, Detective." He turned and walked down the hallway and around a corner in the direction of the kitchen.

Sebastian and John were now alone. The old priest turned towards the detective with a calm demeanor. "This way please," he said as he turned around. They entered the office where he motioned to one of the two chairs in front of a wooden desk. "Please take a seat."

As John sat down, Sebastian reached for the bookshelf behind the desk and opened a door cabinet revealing a bottle of scotch and brandy next to several glasses. "May I offer you a drink?" he said without looking up. The priest picked up the brandy and began to pour into one of the glasses.

"I am not officially on duty so, sure, I'll have what you're having," answered John.

Sebastian poured the brandy into another glass and handed it to the detective. The priest took his glass, closed the cabinet and sat down in the high leather chair behind the desk.

"It is a monastic life we have chosen but this is one of the small luxuries I allow myself," said Sebastian. "May God bless you and grant you peace and happiness," he added as he raised his glass in a toast and took a long stiff drink from it.

John raised his glass in acknowledgement and took a sip.

"So, Detective Bernard," Sebastian began as he reclined back in his chair and looked at his guest, "though it is always with pleasure when we see a new face in our church, I would assume that you are not here to discuss matters of faith. I seem to recall seeing you in the news and having something to do with the serial killings in our great city. Am I correct?"

"You are correct and may I compliment you in your deduction skills," replied John casually.

"And how may I be of service?" asked Sebastian.

John shifted in his chair and said, "You were in attendance at all three of the women's funerals. I would just like to ask the reason?"

Sebastian stared at John without any hint of fear. "I am a priest," he said without apology. "We naturally sympathize for the victims and the members of their family; especially for the ones of the Catholic faith. I went to provide assistance in any way that I could, as far as spiritual guidance is concerned, of course. Surely, you are not suggesting any ulterior motive?"

"No. Not at all, Father," answered John without hesitation. "I apologize, if I gave you the wrong impression. I can understand, with my intrusion tonight, how you would be concerned…"

"Good," interrupted Sebastian. "I can assure you that the Holy Catholic Church has nothing to do with, or have any insight into, what has happened, and," he paused and said with a slight smile, "you are not intruding,"

John sat back in his chair and asked, "How would you know that?"

"How would I know what?" replied Sebastian with a question.

"How do you know that the Church knows nothing about the killings?" asked John.

"Look," began Sebastian, glancing down at his hands. "The Church knows nothing of the murders. My superiors would have informed us if the Church had any valuable or relative information, or at least instructed us on what to say publicly. No Detective, there is nothing of any relevance for you here."

"And you know nothing of the beauty marks?" asked John.

Sebastian paused for a moment and finally asked, "What beauty marks? Just because they had the same beauty marks, what does that have to do with the Church?"

John caught the mistake. "Who said they were the same?"

Suddenly the office door flew open. A middle-aged man stumbled in reaching for the empty chair. His faded light green shirt soaked with blood in several places. Gasping for breath, he looked up painfully and spotted Sebastian and his guest.

Both men jumped to their feet.

"They shot Father David," the injured man said in a raspy voice. "I think Martha's dead too." The wounded man sat heavily on the chair.

"Oh my God!" exclaimed Sebastian as he stepped forward to assist.

John reached for his gun and chambered a round as he jumped towards the door, leaning against the doorframe. He sneaked a look down the hall but saw no one in sight.

"What happened, Jim?" asked the priest compassionately as he crouched down on one knee in front of the man.

"Two men broke in the back door as I was helping Martha set the table. They pulled out guns and started firing at us. I saw father David go down and then Martha next to the stove. I only managed to get away when they shot me twice and the impact pushed me out of the kitchen and out of their sight. They seemed to be interested in Father David. The guns only made puffy sounds like an air hose." Jim stared at Sebastian with pleading eyes. "Father, it hurts," he whispered as he held his stomach.

From the description, John knew the killers were using silencers. That's why he didn't hear anything.

"Where were you hit, Jim?" asked the priest scanning the front of the bleeding man's shirt.

"In my left shoulder and stomach, Father," Jim answered painfully.

"Hang on, Jim. You'll be alright," said the priest with little conviction.

Sebastian pulled the edge of his white shirt out of his pants and ripped out a piece, using it to stem the flow of blood from Jim's stomach without much success. Dark, purplish blood flowed heavily from the wound.

The shoulder wound didn't seem as bad.

"Who are you?" John asked, keeping watch down the hallway.

"He's the caretaker of the church," the priest answered.

"John, is that you?" a voice called from down the hall. To John it sounded like Lieutenant Nick Mancuso from his precinct. He saw him last at the crime scene of the latest victim talking to Rashid.

What's he doing here? John asked himself. It didn't matter, he concluded. The important thing was that he was here. Maybe he got the two killers.

John answered back anxiously, "Nick, yah, it's me, what the hell happened? Did you get them, there are two shooters!"

"Yah, we got 'em!" Mancuso replied loudly. "Come on out, John. The area is secure."

John furrowed his eyebrows. We, who's we? Nick has someone else with him. Besides Rashid, no one else knew he was coming here tonight, and what was Nick doing here to begin with? Only he, Rashid and Lieutenant James Collins knew about this church at all and Sebastian's possible connection to the killings. Did either Rashid or Collins tell anyone?

"Something's fishy here," John whispered to the priest.

Sebastian turned back to Jim's wounds and noticed his head slumped over, his chin on his chest. The priest felt for a pulse on his neck and failed to find one.

"He's dead," whispered Sebastian sadly to no one in particular. He crossed himself and began administering the Last Rites.

John sneaked another look down the hall. The light around the corner of the hall, where the other priest had gone before, cast a shadow of a man holding a gun, a gun with an extra long barrel, a silencer.

It all felt wrong. John wasn't taking any chances.

"Here I am, Nick," said John, feigning a move into the hallway.

Nick jumped out from around the corner and fired two shots. The bullets flew past the office door near where John crouched and hit the door to the main church.

Keeping his body in the office, John leaned out with his gun and fired back.

Nick had managed to jump back without been hit.

Sebastian finished the Last Rites and crawled over to John. The priest asked anxiously, "What's going on, Detective? Do you know him?"

"Yah, he's a police officer," John replied in a hoarse whisper. "This is crazy."

"He must be who shot Jim, Martha and Father David. What are we gonna do, Detective?"

John looked at the priest. Sebastian looked scared. He could see it in his eyes. John thought it ironic how so many people believed in an afterlife, a better afterlife, but were still scared to die.

"What the hell's going on, Nick?" John yelled without looking down the hall.

Another voice called out to him. "It's too bad you had to be here, John." John recognized the voice as Captain David Westell.

John's mind felt numb. Nothing made sense. "Captain?" he yelled out. "Jesus Christ! What's going on?"

"I'm sorry, John. I really am," Captain Westell said in a truly sympathetic voice. "I assume you have Father Sebastian there with you? We want him, John, and because, as little as you know, you already know too much, we can't let you get away either, John. It's too bad. You were a good man. As the saying goes, just at the wrong place at the wrong time."

John felt a cold bead of sweat trickle down the middle of his back. His own Captain had referred to him in the past tense. Nothing made sense. The two men down the hall were men he knew, men that he worked with on many assignments, and now they wanted to kill him and the priest.

"You have got to tell me what the hell's going on," John whispered through clenched teeth to the priest. "You know more then what you let on."

"There isn't time," replied Sebastian. "We've got to get away from here."

John had to get whatever Sebastian knew out of him, but he agreed with the priest that they had to find a way out of this mess.

"Father, try the phone. Call 911." He turned back to the hall and yelled, "Can't we talk this over, Captain?"

The Captain said, "Sure, John. Just throw your weapon out here and let's talk."

Sebastian had quietly gone to the desk, picked up the phone and pressed it to his ear. He listened for a second and tapped on the handset switch on the phone a few times. He looked at John and slowly shook his head as he put the handset back. They had taken care of that.

"I can't do that, Captain," said John.

"Come on, John," said the Captain, "I can't talk to you when I have a gun pointing at me."

"I know the routine too, Captain. Nick, are you there?"

"Yah, I'm here, John," Nick replied.

"Good. I just wanted to make sure you weren't trying to sneak around behind us."

"No, John. I wouldn't do that. Just do what the Captain says and let's talk."

John looked for an escape route but, with the window barred, the only way out remained through the door they had come in. He whispered to the priest, "Father, I'm open to suggestions. Do you know of any way outta here?"

The priest looked at John with wild eyes, like a trapped animal desperately searching for an escape. Suddenly, his eyes betrayed a revelation. His head snapped around towards the closet door. "Yes, I think I do," he said.

Sebastian quietly walked to a second door in the room that John had earlier assumed to be a closet. John's hopes began to rise with the hope that his assumption may have been wrong.

The priest opened the door and John's heart sank when he saw he had not been wrong after all. The closet contained a rod with several black jackets on hangers. On the floor lay several stacks of books. John concluded the priest had lost his mind and acted out of desperation.

The Captain yelled out again, "So what do you want to do now, John?"

"Stay alive," whispered John to himself.

The priest removed the stacks of books from one side of the closet. He reached down to the parquet floor and pulled out a section of the floor. A trap door! John had trouble keeping his excitement down. The priest hadn't lost his mind after all.

A moment later, John could hear liquid pouring on the floor down the hall, a lot of liquid. He began to smell gasoline and suddenly realized what they were planning to do; with a stalemate and no apparent exit, they were going to burn the place down with them inside.

John turned back to the priest who motioned at the detective to follow him as he began to crawl down through the trap door.

John sneaked another look down the hall and fired another round. Just then, he glimpsed a hand toss a bottle with a lit rag stuffed in the neck. He watched the Molotov cocktail arc in a summersault fashion through the air in his direction. It looked surreal, like a slow motion film. As the bottle began its downward trip, it looked like it trajectory to be near the door of the office where it would inflict the most damage.

John dived for the closet as the bottle crashed to the floor. He heard a 'WOOSH!' sound and a wave of heat hit him as he slammed the closet door shut.

The closet was pitch-black despite the flames on the other side. On his knees, John felt for the opening in the floor and almost fell in head-first when his hand met no resistance.

"I'm down here." Sebastian whispered from the darkness below.

John reached in his pocket for his lighter and flicked it on. Dancing shadows from the flames moved around him against the closet walls. He looked down and saw the square black hole in the floor.

Reaching down with his lighter, John caught site of the priest's face peering up at him looking pale and shiny with oily sweat.

"Quickly, climb down," Sebastian whispered hoarsely, "and be careful. There's no ladder."

John could hear crackling sounds from the consuming flames on the other side of the door. Black smoke seeped through the crack between the bottom of the door and the floor.

He flicked off the lighter and put it back in his pocket. Slowly his eyes adjusted to the darkness and he began to make out a thin line of yellowish light coming from the bottom of the door. The smoke got thicker making it harder to breath.

He crouched as low as he could and reached down with his right leg through the opening. He then dangled his other leg down as he held himself up at chest high with his arms against the closet floor, still finding no firm foothold.

"Jump down. You are only four feet from the bottom," whispered the priest. How he knew this in the dark, John didn't know.

John let go and landed on his feet on a floor that felt and sounded like dirt. He almost lost his balance but managed to stay on his feet. He took out his lighter again and flicked it back on.

He saw a low ceiling room about six feet high. On one side, a solid wall made up of irregular stones. John surmised it must have been the outside wall of the church, the other three sides were not visible in the area illuminated by the small flame of the lighter.

A brownish-black compacted dirt floor gave the place a moldy earthy smell. Construction debris lay strewn around the dirt floor and above covered with wide dark planks over thick wooden beams.

They could actually start to feel heat emanating from the floor overhead. The crackling sound loud and steady as the fire took hold.

"Where are we?" asked John.

"We're in a crawl space under the church," began Sebastian. "No one ever comes down here. I had completely forgotten about it until just now. The trap door is the only way in from inside the church." He turned around and began walking along the outer wall towards the front of the church. "Come, there's a way to the outside," he said.

The lighter started to get hot in John's hand but he kept it lit as he followed the priest.

The two men came upon a steel grill approximately two by four foot square closing an opening on the upper part of the wall to the outside. A dim light from the outside streetlights illuminated what looked like a window well surrounding the grill. Sebastian pulled on the bottom half of the grill in order to pry it loose.

It did not budge. The grill caked in rust and dirt. John looked around and found a number of rusted rebar rods about four feet long lying close by.

He pocketed the lighter and picked up one of the bars. The light coming in from outside provided just enough illumination to see what he was doing.

He wedged one of the ends under the bottom right corner of the grill and began to try to pry it open. He heard the grill squeak but still it didn't budge.

"Pick up another bar and try the other side of the grill the same time I do, Father," said John.

Sebastian picked up another bar and wedged it in the other side. Both pushed down on the bars at the same time.

The hinges complained with a rusty squeak but the grill gave way and began to open. John grabbed the bottom of the grill with his hands and pulled up. It slowly rose and he propped up the grill with the bar he had just used.

"I'll go first to make sure it's clear," said John.

He climbed through the opening under the grill and into the depression of the window well. He took out his gun and stuck his head above the rim.

John saw no one in sight. The street was not a main thorough fare and car traffic appeared sporadic with no pedestrians. He looked up and could see smoke beginning to seep through roof vents and from a small window on the second floor.

"Come on up," said John without looking down.

Sebastian climbed into the window well as John climbed out onto the grass. The priest followed him into the open air.

"My car is parked a block down the street to the left," whispered John. "Come on."

They quickly walked down the sidewalk trying not to look too conspicuous. John had put his gun away.

They had escaped.

The detective's mind began going in all directions trying to figure out what happened and what to do next. He kept looking back at the church as the smoke bellowed out noticeably, surprised none of the few cars driving by saw it, but the calm, almost none existent wind allowed the smoke to rise straight up and blend in with the dark, cloud covered night.

John caught no sign of the Captain and the lieutenant. They must still be waiting for him and the priest to come out of the office, or ensuring they would not come out alive.

Soon someone would notice the fire and the two men still in the church would have to either leave or explain what they were doing there.

John was still trying to figure out his next move when the priest spoke up. "I know a place we can hide out until we figure out what to do."

The detective could see that Sebastian had calmed down considerably since their ordeal. The wild, cornered look in his eyes, replaced with one deep in thought, his eyebrows furrowed.

"What do you have in mind, Father?" asked John as they reached his car and both got in.

"Head east on I-90. A friend of mine has a small cabin about three hours from here. It's just north of Somersville, near the border of the Adirondack Park Reserve. No one knows about the place and it's safe. Just head for Somersville and then I'll guide you from there."

"How do you know it's safe? If my captain figured you out, how do you know this place is not already staked out?"

"Trust me. No-one knows about this place or of my friend."

"Alright," John sighed, "There isn't much choice is there? Since I don't know about it, chances are they don't either."

Once on I-90 and heading east, John pulled out his cigarette pack. "Want one?"

Sebastian looked over. "It's being a long time since I quit, but this looks like a good occasion for one. Thank-you," he said and took one.

John took one and offered the priest a light before lighting his own. They smoked silently for a while.

"Father, you need to tell me what you know," said John.

"Alright, son, you deserve that much," said the priest wearily.

Sebastian looked at John closely for a moment, scrutinizing him and finally said, "I'd probably be dead by now if you hadn't shown up." He looked tired. "My head hurts and I need some sleep. Wake me up when we get close to Somersville and, when we get to the cabin, I'll lay it all out for you." He curled up and nodded off before the Detective could object.

John pulled out another cigarette and kept driving. It would be a long several hours.

CHAPTER FOUR
STRUGGLE REVEALED

They passed a signpost that read 'Somersville - 15mi.'
The time-display on the dashboard showed ten minutes past midnight. The sky overcast, no stars or moon visible.

The December snow hadn't arrived yet. The temperature remained above freezing even during the night.

Darkness pressed in around them as John drove but he didn't suffer from drowsiness. He kept repeating the events of that evening in his mind; the unbelievable fact that two senior police officers could do such a thing, men that he knew and worked with.

He had many unanswered questions. How did they find out about Father Sebastian? Why did they want the priest dead? He understood why they wanted him, John, dead, since he was, in a way, a witness. He did not actually see them kill the other priest, the cook or the caretaker, but it would not be too hard to prove. Why did they do it in the first place and what did it all have to do with the serial killings and the mysterious beauty marks? Could the Captain and the Lieutenant have been involved in the serial killings as well? And the motive, why? Why became the illusive question he could not answer but the man sleeping next to him in the passenger seat said he would 'lay it all out.'

Well, he better, John thought. There were several dead people tonight and he had no idea why. He needed to hear some convincing explanations for what happened.

John kept his ear on the radio for any news on the church fire but he heard nothing. He kept his cell phone off, being all too familiar with the technology to track down the location of an active phone.

Soon a dim glow began to appear just over the horizon. They were getting near the town.

"Hey, Father, wake up," John gently called out.

Sebastian began to stir. He raised his head and looked around trying to get his bearing. "Where are we?" he asked.

"We're coming up to Somersville," answered John.

"Take the Humber Street exit and go north and right through town," instructed Sebastian.

The view in front of them depicted a quaint, small, sleepy town.

John kept the car at the speed limit so as not to attract any undue attention from the sheriff or any of his deputies on patrol for speeders at night. The drive through town turned out to be uneventful and exited through the north end passing the sheriff's office. Then, even the streetlights disappeared.

Once out of town, Humber Street became a rural road and the ride a little rougher. A few miles down the road, the priest told John to turn right into a gravel secondary road. For the next half hour, they snaked their way through a maze of gravel and dirt roads. John lost his bearing long before they got to the cabin but the priest seemed to know exactly where they were going.

They came to the last lane, or driveway, lined with a maze of low hanging skeleton-like branches from large elm trees. They proceeded at a snail's pace through this web with no way to see beyond the thick brush. The branches slowly parting as the car sliced through. Night dew, thick and oily, covered everything in a sickly sheen, accentuated from the lights of the car's beams. A light fog rose up as they drove deeper into the woods.

The lane opened up into a clearing a few hundred yards around, surrounded by high evergreens. They could just make out a rutted path, overgrown with grass and weeds, an indication that the path had not been used for quite some time, if at all, that year. The night remained calm with no perceptible wind but the clouds were slowly starting to thin out uncovering a full moon that blanketed the landscape beyond the reach of the headlights with a grayish hue.

As they continued down the path, the fog became a little thicker, the headlights shooting out two cones of light. Once they got to the other end of the clearing, a cabin gradually materialized out of the mist first as a grayish outline and then a more detailed, solid structure. They drove up to it and stopped twenty feet from the entrance.

The completely unlit building wasn't exactly the small, simple cabin that Sebastian had alluded to earlier. It rose up as an impressive two-storey chalet built out of logs on top of a natural stone base raised three or four feet off the ground.

He must have some well-heeled friends, thought John.

"Do you have a flashlight somewhere in here?" asked Sebastian.

"Of course," replied John. "I'm a cop."

He lifted the lid of the armrest between the front seats and pulled out a police issued black flashlight. He turned off the engine, got out and turned on the flashlight as the priest got out from his side.

"Here, give me the flashlight," said the priest as they met at the front of the car. "Follow me around the side. There's a shed with a generator that provides electricity for the place."

They walked towards the chalet in single file with the priest leading. As they came up to the flagstones and under the deck, they headed for the back of the building. The shed stood about twenty feet from the chalet. The priest opened the unlocked door. He aimed the flashlight inside and to the left where he spied a green button protruding from the center of a metal box. Sebastian pushed the button and the generator turned over a few times before it caught and started to rev up. A few seconds later, some main switch clicked on and the chalet became awash in light. Most of the outdoor and indoor lights were on.

The building glowed like a yellowish jewel in the middle of a coal pit.

"The lights are purposely left in the on position when the generator is turned off so that there is light, as much as you need, when you first arrive," said Sebastian after he saw the look on John's face.

"I'd say," said John. "It's like a beacon in the night. Advertising our presence isn't exactly what we need right now."

"Don't worry," answered Sebastian. "There's enough high forest canopy out there that we're hidden from view from anyone on the ground. From above, it's just another cottage."

"If you say so, Father," said John.

Sebastian reached back into the shed and pulled out a key hanging next to the power switch he had just pressed and led the way back.

When they reached the front, the priest unlocked and opened the door and entered into the main room. John followed and closed the door as he looked around.

The chalet splendor showed in the inside as much as it did on the outside. Not a large place but well designed. The great room, or living area, located at the front center of the structure with an open ceiling to the second floor. A stone fireplace squatted at the center with the chimney stretching up and through the ceiling. The fireplace already stocked with paper, kindling and wood. The large wooden plank floor covered with scattered rugs and various luxurious couches and armchairs flanked by rustic wooden coffee tables. The first floor designed as an open concept except for the bathroom in the back.

Sebastian went to the fireplace, checked that the flue was open, and lit the fire with a box of wooden matches he found on top of the mantle. He then went to the kitchen and found a bottle of scotch and a couple of glasses. He brought them over to the coffee table in front of the fire, sat down at an armchair and poured from the bottle into both glasses without asking. John sat down opposite him in silence. They soon had a warm heat growing both in the chalet and in their stomachs.

"All right, Father," said John, staring at the priest. "I have a million questions, both about this place, about what happened today and how you are involved. But I'll hold back and first let you explain it in your own way and at your own pace without interruption." John sat back and took a sip from his glass. "I am all ears."

"What I am about to tell you," Sebastian began while staring into the fire with a faraway look, "will sound too fantastic to believe, but it will be the truth and I will show you proof that it is so."

"I belong to a secret organization called 'The Protectors of the Truth.' Our organization goes back two thousand years, to the time of Jesus Christ. Our purpose is to protect the descendants of Judah Iscariot – infamously known as the betrayer of Jesus."

Sebastian paused for a moment to let what he said sink in. He looked at John for any reaction. He saw none. John stared back at the priest and took another sip of his drink.

"Look, Father," John finally said as he began to pull out a cigarette from a crumpled pack inside his jacket. "You can't expect me to believe such a crazy statement without anything to back it up. You must know that. I am merely keeping an open mind and letting you explain it. When you're done, we can discuss as to whether I believe it or not."

Sebastian stared back. "Fair enough. Let me explain it and then we'll see. To continue, our sole purpose is to protect the descendants of Judah Iscariot. The Holy Catholic Church, or any other well-known religious order, does not sanction us, but the Church is aware of our existence. What is important to understand, is that another movement, another organization, exists that want us, and the Descendant, eliminated. That is why those women were murdered and why your police friends, who belong to this other organization, were trying to kill me.

"Father David, our cook, Martha, and caretaker Jim happened to be in the wrong place and time, and they were not the only ones eliminated. There have been many others killed around the world that you are not aware of."

John stared at the priest without any reaction.

"Look," the priest continued, "it is best for me to start at the beginning, to the time of Christ. Only then can you comprehend what I am saying and what this means to the world, to Mankind. Judah was not the betrayer of Jesus in the true sense of the word. Judah followed Jesus' command so that the final prophecy of his resurrection would happen, and Jesus trusted no one but Judah to help him achieve it. Jesus loved Judah more than he loved any of the other disciples, and Judah, in return, loved him more than life itself. The Holy Bible even hints at their close relationship and to the fulfillment of the prophecies."

"So, let's say that is true," interrupted John, unable to keep his promise to wait until the end. "A lot has been written about their relationship and your alternate theory. What does that have to do with everything that has happened?"

"What you don't know," continued Sebastian with a gleam in his eyes, "is that several months before the crucifixion, Jesus asked Judah to marry and father a child and Jesus promised that the child would be female. Jesus prophesied that the female child would bear the sign of the moon as proof of who she is. She in turn, would bear a female child as her first born with the same mark and so on down the ages until the time would come when the last of the female descendants would bear a male first born. That male child will be the second coming of Christ."

"Now you're getting into Never-Never-Land, Father," said John with a slight chuckle.

"You promised to hear me out, Detective," said Sebastian seriously. He leaned back in his chair.

"Yes, your right, Father. I'm sorry. Go on," conceded John, no longer laughing.

Sebastian continued, "As I mentioned before, we are an organization that has been successfully protecting the female descendants of Judah for two thousand years and exist only to help fulfill the promise of Jesus' second coming, but there are others that don't see it that way. These others believe that Armageddon must occur only as prophesied in the Book of Revelations and anything that stands in the way eliminated. These others call themselves The Brotherhood of the Rapture in honor of the Rapture, the rising into heaven of the chosen few just before Armageddon. They have been after Judah's descendants for as long as we have existed. For two thousand years."

"Ok, Father," interrupted John with a smirk and shifting again in his chair. "This is almost too corny for even a religious horror flick. 'The Protectors of the Truth,' 'The Brotherhood of the Rapture,' what are you trying to do, create new video games? I need another drink." John picked up the bottle and poured himself one.

"And how do you explain what your friends did back there at the church?" asked Sebastian.

"I don't," said John. "But the line that you're giving me is nuts. You have to do better than that, Father."

Father Sebastian stared at the other man for a moment. "What I have told you is the truth. Make fun of the names, if you will, but the people involved are very serious, and we are locked in a struggle for survival."

John took another sip from his glass as he looked away.

"I see that I will need to show you proof," said Sebastian. He got up and went to the fireplace. At chest high, he reached towards a stone about a foot square in size. It came loose when he pulled and he set it aside as he reached in and pulled out what looked like a number of loose papers, a small bible and leather bound book.

"What I have here are a number of documents and a book that I want to show you," Sebastian said as he brought them over to John. "These are not originals, of course, but copies. The book is a translated copy of a journal written by a Roman friend of Judah. The loose sheets are parts of a translated copy of a recently found Gospel of Judas, and the last is a normal Bible."

He laid the documents out side by side as if trying to organize his thoughts. "You must have heard about the Lost Gospel of Judas found a few years ago?" asked Sebastian.

"Yes I have," said John, "but is it Judah with an h or Judas with an s?"

"Many people are confused about that but the answer is simple," began Sebastian in a practiced voice. "The original Hebrew spelling is J-u-d-a-h and derived from a word meaning 'praised.' In Greek, its written J-u-d-a-s and because many of the old religious documents and gospels are written in Greek, you will see it as such, but since it originated from Hebrew, I prefer using J-u-d-a-h."

"How ironic that it means 'praised,'" said John.

"Or is it?" said Sebastian. "I hope to change your mind."

Sebastian took a drink from his glass and sat back to gathered his thoughts. He reached into his coat pocket, brought out a pair of reading glasses, and put them on.

"Alright, John," the Priest began, getting comfortable, "now, there are four pieces of information I want to show you. The first two are quotes from the Bible."

John felt like back in Catholic school again. The priest was going to give him a religious lesson.

"Bear with me," Said Sebastian, spying John's restlessness over his glasses as he flipped through the Bible to the sections he wanted. "The first is a quote from Matthew 24:29 '- Immediately after the Tribulation of those days shall the sun be darkened, and the moon shall not give her light, and the stars shall fall from heaven, and the powers of the heavens shall be shaken: And then shall appear the sign of the Son of Man in heaven: and then shall all the tribes of the earth mourn, and they shall see the Son of man coming in the clouds of heaven with power and great glory. And he shall send his angels with a great sound of a trumpet, and they shall gather together his chosen from the four winds, from one end of heaven to the other.'"

Sebastian looked up at John as he said, "These are the first of several quotes that are in the Bible with respect to Armageddon or the 'end of days'."

He flipped to another section and said, "The next one is from the book of Revelations and I will only refer to the relative parts '...shortly after his second Coming, down from the sky will come the great hosts of Heaven with Him in the lead to destroy the Antichrist and his one-world empire in the Battle of Armageddon. ...It will mark the end of man's rule on earth. ...So begins a period known as the Millennium, a thousand years of peace and plenty and paradise on Earth.'"

Sebastian put down the Bible and said, "What I have quoted to you are references to the end of the world as we know it today. Both The Protectors and The Brotherhood believe it to be true and that Jesus' second coming will coincide with it, but that is where the agreement ends. For we, the Protectors, believe Jesus will return from the lineage of Judah, whereas they, the Brotherhood, believe that it will be the Antichrist, or Satan that will be reborn from the descendants of Judah."

"So far you have given me quotes from the Bible," said John, still not convinced, "and that's fine. I am familiar with them myself. I did go to Catholic school. There are many interpretations of what you just quoted. How do you know that this, so called, Brotherhood of The Rapture is not right?" asked John.

"Two things; one is this book," said Sebastian as he picked up the leather bound book, "which is a journal, or record, kept by a friend of Judah and, the second, the Lost Gospel of Judah recently found and depicts Judah as an accomplice of Jesus rather than a betrayer as per our beliefs."

John began to fidget again and Sebastian saw it.

"Found only a few years ago, the Lost Gospel has been proven to be authentic and created about 200 years after the death of Jesus, and of Judah, of course. This document is the only surviving copy of what is believed to be the very words as written by Judah himself," said Sebastian. "Let me read a few excerpts of the document, which is not very long to begin with.

"It is Judah, who wrote as the third-person as follows '...Knowing that Judas was reflecting upon something that was exalted, Jesus said to him, "Step away from the others and I shall tell you the mysteries of the kingdom. It is possible for you to reach it, but you will grieve a great deal. ...For someone else will replace you,' and here is another one, '... Judas said, "Master, could it be that my seed is under the control of the rulers?" Jesus answered and said to him, "...but that you will grieve much when you see the kingdom and all its generation." When he heard this, Judas said to him, "What good is it that I have received it? For you have set me apart from that generation." Jesus answered and said, "You will become the thirteenth, and you will be cursed by the other generations...and you will come to rule over them. In the last days they will curse your ascent to the holy generation."'"

Sebastian paused and looked up at John. "Think about what Jesus said to Judah. That Judah will be cursed by all men but in the end he will rule over them all through his seed."

"And you base your believe on this document?" asked John.

"No, of course not, this merely supports what we have believed for two thousand years," said Sebastian. He picked up the leather bound book and continued, "Our belief comes from this journal. Written in Latin and translated to English decades ago, a journal written before, during and after Jesus' crucifixion, a journal that gives more insight in the relationship between Jesus and Judah than any other document. It's a journal, not written by Judah but written by a Roman friend of Judah; a man who realized the enormity of the events that occurred around him, someone who understood the awesome burden of the truth and the importance of the words that he had written. It has some of the identical words as written in the lost Gospel of Judah. We knew the words long before they discovered the Lost Gospel. And it describes the request from Jesus for Judah to marry and father a child," the priest paused for a moment.

"The entire truth is detailed in this document. It is the foundation of our belief and our reason for existence. This Roman became the first Protector," he concluded.

"Why hasn't the Brotherhood of the Rapture been swayed by these findings?" asked John. "Why haven't you convinced them of your beliefs and that theirs is wrong?"

"Because they believe that we, the Protectors, forged these documents ourselves."

"You're saying they don't believe you?"

"I am saying that their religious fanaticism blinds them to the truth."

"And you are not?"

Sebastian looked at John. "I suppose, my son, that you must rely on your own judgment, and your faith."

"Yes. I suppose so, Father," said John with a sigh.

"There is one more thing, and that is the date of the second coming."

"You're telling me you have a date that Jesus and/or Satan is supposed to come back?" asked John incredulously.

"Yes – and the date is December 21 of next year." Again, Sebastian paused for effect. "On the winter solstice of December 21 of next year, the sun will be aligned with the center of the Milky Way for the first time in 26,000 years. We believe it is a new era of Man brought on by the second coming of Christ."

"Father, this is a lot to take in and I'm tired," said John rubbing his blood shot eyes, partly from the weariness from the day's events and partly from the alcohol.

"We both need to get some sleep," said the priest, taking the hint. "It's after one. Take any of the three bedrooms upstairs and we can talk in the morning. When you get up, I want you to read the journal. It will explain many things."

The priest rose and began to make his way to the second floor. He stopped and turned back to John.

"There is just one more thing I want to leave with you," said the priest. "Though the world commonly believes that Judah hung himself soon after the crucifixion, this is not correct. Judah had a farm in the outskirts of Jerusalem to live with his wife and raise a daughter, just as Jesus had ordered him to do. We believe someone killed him while attending to his field. The Bible even contradicts itself and refers to the farm in the Acts Of The Apostles 1:18. Though it states he fell down and split his stomach open, we believe the first members of the Brotherhood of the Rapture killed him and left his body in the field."

John looked at the priest and got up. He had enough for one night. "I need to rest. It will give me a chance to sort this out in my head. Hopefully, it will seem a little clearer tomorrow morning."

Both men headed for the stairs.

John hadn't made up his mind whether he would call the Boston District Attorney in the morning to tell him the whole story or not. He wanted to tell him everything, especially about Captain Westell and Lieutenant Mancuso. How they murdered several people in cold blood.

I am not a fugitive, John said silently to himself. Even though tonight, he felt it.

It had been a long night for the both of them.

•••

John's thinking became much clearer the next morning, especially after a good strong cup of coffee. He had asked about the place and Sebastian indicated that it belonged to the Protectors of the Truth.

John didn't feel much like having breakfast, just coffee. At seven in the morning and still too early to call the District Attorney, he decided to read the journal handed to him by the priest. After placing a few more logs in the fire, he grabbed the journal and sat down in a comfortable lounge chair next to one of the many windows. He looked outside before he began to read.

Even though snow had not yet fallen that December, the trees were bare and the grass had turned mustard yellow. When he gazed at the overall scenery, he saw a weird mixture of beauty and desolation. Autumn always took on a sort of death like feel to John. The shorter days did nothing but re-enforce that feeling. Never the less, the scene outside showed a clear day and the sun shining.

John lit a cigarette and looked at the front cover of the leather bound book. The leather cover engraved in the center with the half moon symbol he had seen on the murdered women. Other than that, it had no writing or any other markings anywhere on the cover, spine or back. The book wasn't that thick either. It appeared to be about only forty pages long.

It shouldn't take too long to read, he thought to himself.

He prepared to read it in one sitting. After that, he'd figure out his next step.

Sebastian had told John that the journal would make many things clear for him. That it would answer many questions and convince him of the truth. Personally, John thought the priest had a few screws loose and he thought likewise of both of the organizations. If they existed at all, they were just two more fanatical groups involved in yet another crazy holy war between two opposing views, with no basis in reality. John believed in a higher being, but this whole 'battle between good and evil' thing, he saw as a human creation of the imagination rather than a real spiritual struggle. Throughout the history of Man, it is for such reasons that battles occurred, or for greed, but that remained a distant second and, finally, John thought it the most ridiculous that both sides of a war called on God for victory. Both side believed that they were on the side of right. As if preying one way over another would make a difference to God, or one set of rituals over another set of rituals would make you more favored in God's eyes and why would God care or play favorites to begin with? John had always felt that, as long as you had some basic respect for your fellow human beings and the world around you, that you would be the better for it. Not that you would somehow, be awarded a kind of prize if you followed a certain set of rules. Only that you would achieve a sort of emotional satisfaction or intellectual pleasure in knowing that you left the world a better place than when you came into it. Though raised a catholic, he believed on only one rule: Do unto others, as you would have them do unto you. One of the Ten Commandments said as much, or something to that effect. He felt that, whatever you believed, follow that one rule and the others would fall into place.

Unless you were a masochist, but that was an exception, John smirked to himself.

As for an afterlife, well, everyone would find out eventually.

When thinking about these heady, philosophical matters, John's mind always went back to a little book from Plato called the 'Apology.' The book detailed Socrates trial for not being pious and corrupting the minds of the young and his eventual execution by poison. Before taking the hemlock, one of his friends in attendance asked whether he believed in an afterlife. Socrates stated something to the effect that, it would be one of two things: either an afterlife existed or it did not. If there were, then he would meet all his heroes in the afterlife and, being one who loved to discuss philosophical matters, he would have some of the best debates with some of the most famous figures in history. If there weren't, then he would have the best dreamless sleep that he had ever experienced. Either way, he did not see death as a negative thing. The only drawback was leaving family and friends behind.

That, at least, made a good and logical argument to John.

Whatever his own beliefs, the journal, at the very least, would tell him more about the struggle between the two opposing groups.

He settled comfortably in his chair and opened the book to the first page.

CHAPTER FIVE
PROTECTORS

Protectors of the Truth

Originally written in Latin by Marius Sestus in the year of Our Lord 53 Anno Domini.
Translated into English in 1937 Anno Domini

Note to the reader:
During the translation of the document, it became apparent that references to measurements and other mathematical nomenclatures would be confusing to the modern reader and thus changed to contemporary units of measure. In addition, various phrases and words, that have subtle meanings, inflections or idiosyncrasies other than their literal meaning, were altered to reflect the true intent, or thought, of the writer. For example, in today's terms, 'I am mad about you,' is not referring to any ill temper towards an individual but quite the opposite, it is referring to deep fondness and even love. Likewise, there are revisions of similar ancient references in modern terms to reflect the true meaning.

My name is Marius Sestus. I am the first Protector – and, if Mankind is to survive, there shall be more Protectors like me throughout the generations to come.

Our one and only purpose is to protect the holy lineage of Judah, the most blessed of the Apostles. The one set apart from the rest for a most holy purpose. The one scorned throughout the ages until his true purpose is revealed by God in the new age of Man. His one true and blessed destiny is that his seed has been ordained to fulfill the prophecy of the return of the Messiah, Our Christ the Savior.

My name is Marius Sestus. I am the first Protector.

I write this as an old man near the end of his life, a life that started carefree but later given a purpose, a most serious and important purpose. Soon I must pass on this purpose, this mantle, to a new generation and to many generations after that.

It is with this in mind that I write these words, the words that must guide the generations of Protectors for many centuries.

The Protectors of The Truth hear my words...

I am the one and only son of Bromius Sestus, a successful and wealthy Roman merchant who lived in Judea during the rule of Emperor Tiberius.

I was born in Rome on the twenty-seventh year of Emperor Augustus' rule of our Roman empire. We moved to Jerusalem just after I turned fourteen years old. My father had decided we needed a change soon after my mother died giving birth to my brother who had also died only hours later.

Emperor Tiberius had just succeeded his stepfather, Augustus, after his death. During the transition, the government in Rome went through a tumultuous period. My father decided to be out of Rome until the political unrest settled down. He had realized that he could make money by importing goods from the fringes of the empire. He proved to be right, since he made a very good profit buying rare goods and spices from the Far East and shipping them back to Rome

Soon after we had arrived in Jerusalem, my father had enrolled me in the local university where I spent several years of joyous and leisure learning, a privilege of the rich. There I decided to become a poet and a playwright. My teachers had said that I had a talent for the written word and I did indeed receive pleasure creating my own forms of literature. There is a certain vanity in its pursuit. Athletics were also a favorite of mine. My Roman breeding gave me excellent physical stature and adept coordination.

At the university is where I first met Judah Iscariot.

What first struck me the most about Judah was his height and his penetrating blue eyes, both rare in the Jewish population for they are a much shorter people with dark brown eyes and olive skin. He stood at six foot high, a trait more common in Roman stock. The blueness of his eyes, reminded me of my mother, eyes that could see right into you without leaving you feeling violated or exposed. They shined into your being like a clear sunny day and, when he added his smile, left you at ease.

Judah's manner of dress indicated wealth and leisure. Jewish clothing is usually much more elaborate than the simple white Roman tunic and colorful sash that we Romans downed. Judah always wore brocaded coats or cloaks, brilliantly colored sashes and matching sandals. He kept his black hair long and well groomed. He maintained the traditional Jewish beard but kept it very short.

My first encounter with Judah occurred at a lecture from a Greek philosopher recently arrived in Jerusalem. There were about fifteen of us in attendance at the late morning lecture and we sat in a half circle around the podium of the outdoor auditorium. Halfway through the lecture, I caught the eye of this well dressed man sitting across from me. He returned my gaze with a friendly, quick smile and turned his attention back to the discussion at hand.

A debate raged about gods and myths between the Greek philosopher and several of the students. The philosopher did not seem to be winning and this appeared to amuse the well-dressed man for he gazed at the opposing sides with a slight smile that seemed permanently fixed on his face, the spell quickly broken when other students began to heckle the philosopher. He subsequently stormed out of the outdoor auditorium in a huff. The rest of us burst out in a loud laughter and all agreed that day's lecture turned out to be worthwhile. My empty stomach dutifully announced the time of the mid-day meal after which normally followed a visit to the bathhouse.

The man I spied earlier approached me.

"My name is Judah Iscariot," he said while looking straight at me with friendly eyes and ready smile. He extended his multi-bracelet covered arm to me.

"I am Marius Sestus," I replied, and we clasped each other's wrist in the formal Roman greeting. He exuded an air of simultaneous friendliness and confidence.

"I would be honored, Marius Sestus, if you would join me for lunch," said Judah as we released our grip.

Since the Jews did not normally fraternize with the Romans, this surprised me somewhat. After all, we were the occupiers, even though this land saw more peace and prosperity now than any other time in recent history. However, there were those of the educated class that understood the benefits of the Roman rule and accepted it more readily. I concluded that this man came from that crowd.

"It would be my honor as well, Judah Iscariot. I accept your offer," I answered.

"Excellent!" said Judah. He nodded to a man who appeared to be a servant. The man ran off as soon as he saw the nod. "My rooms are just a short walk from here. I have sent my servant ahead to notify my staff and ready the meal."

From that moment on, we were inseparable friends. We went to the games together, to the plays together, and attended the same lectures.

I soon learned that Judah came from an upper class Jewish family from Karioth, south of Judea. His father, Simon Iscariot, had moved to Jerusalem with his wife, two years before Judah's birth.

His father owned several tenant buildings and a market specializing in cloths and silks.

Discussions around philosophy and religion became one of our favorite pastimes. Judah was a devote Jew and I, on the other hand, mildly followed the pagan rites of the Roman Gods. Romans did not completely immerse themselves (ourselves) in religious fervor or beliefs. Rome and its government system were sufficient to satisfy a citizen's need for a higher intelligence, rules of living and social governance. This, until then, dominated my belief system. Judah showed me more, much more.

He first introduced me to the Jewish holy writings called the Tanakh. He said it consisted of three sections: the Torah also known as the Five Books of Moses, the book of Prophets, and the book of Writings.

What intrigued me the most about the Tanakh was the focus on the human condition and the betterment of the individual and Mankind. There were things that just made sense. It talked about loving oneself and others, about ones place in the world and respect for everything around us. Most importantly, it provided the purpose of our lives and even the suffering of Man. It explained that there could only be one God and the same for all Man no matter how he worshiped God. With the assistance of the Tanakh and the instructions from Judah, I slowly began to understand. I began to open my eyes and believe.

My father, Bromius Sestus, followed these developments with only mild curiosity. He believed a man must experience all aspects of life and define who he is within himself. If I joined a new religion, then so be it. He would respect my decision as a man. For this reason, I have always had the highest regards for my father.

●●●

The defining moment in Judah's and my life was when we met Him.

After completing our studies, I began my not too successful career as a playwright.

Judah had decided to go into government work and received a position as a tax collector. He did not think it as an ideal job, but he saw it as a stepping-stone for the senior positions he craved.

With money not an issue for either one of us, we yearned for a meaningful and fulfilling purpose in life. About six months later, we both felt we had made wrong career decisions for ourselves and decided to take a vacation together to sort things out and plan our next move. On the recommendation of a shared acquaintance, we headed north to a resort located on the eastern beaches of the Sea of Galilee. We found it to be an idyllic and luxurious spa right at the edge of the water and decided to stay a month.

One day, as Judah and I were drying off quietly in the sun at the water's edge after a long, leisurely swim we heard a number of voices heading our direction from up the beach. We looked up simultaneously.

We had heard from the other patrons at the resort of a man, a preacher, travelling the surrounding area. They said that this man named Jesus, a common enough name, was no ordinary man himself. A revolutionary thinker and preacher, he knew the sacred Tanakh and could quote every word and verse, and the most extraordinary thing was that he could work miracles. Some thought him a magician, and some even the devil, but those who met him in person believed him blessed by God, proclaiming the message of the Almighty One as taught in the Tanakh.

That day, as he stopped in front of Judah and me, a feeling of elation and calm came over us that we had never felt before in our lives. Judah and I immediately thought him more than a man. We knew, and felt, God had sent him. The Messiah stood before us in all his glory.

From that moment, our lives changed forever.

His followers stopped behind him and uttered not a word but looked at each other and then back at us. The crowd numbered roughly twenty, including a handful of women. They were somewhat an unruly crowd, excited by what they were experiencing but most appeared only curious.

Judah and I looked briefly at each other, understanding each other's thoughts. Could it be that we were the only two that understood the nature of the being in our midst?

Looking back at Him, I saw the same stock as Judah, olive skinned and dark haired, and tall at six feet and with a strong build. The man had known manual labor. I later learned his original profession to be that of a carpenter.

His eyes darted between Judah and I, and we realized that Jesus knew our minds and hearts. We were certain of it.

He looked at Judah and said, "Come, Judah. Follow me. You will be one of my disciples."

Judah immediately got to his feet, picked up the clothes he brought with him to the beach, and stood ready to follow him.

Jesus then looked at me and said, "The Roman protector of Judah. You shall not come with us. There is another destiny for you, Marius. A task much longer than one lifetime and just as important as Judah's, but not right now. First, you must learn and come to understand. You will know when the time comes."

That he knew our names though neither Judah nor I had uttered a word did not surprise me. It also did not surprise me when he went on his way up the beach that Judah followed behind with the rest of the procession without even a backward glance at me. Nor did I expect him to.

I quickly picked up my things and ran back to the resort. I had to follow along, even at a distance. I paid for both of our bills and, with my servant, two riding horses and three mules for our supplies we began our trek and caught up to them within the hour.

I quickly realized that I wasn't the only one following along. Jesus had a core group, which he kept himself surrounded with, but there were many that followed at a distance and only gathered around when Jesus preached. I quickly became part of this peripheral group while Judah became part of the inner circle.

Within a month, Jesus had named twelve disciples. By this time, the group began to receive money and other offerings of goods by the growing faithful. Judah became the steward and almoner of the then small society because of his educational training. Actually, between Judah and me, we were the major source of income to the group, and we did this willingly, for we believed in the quest.

Judah would regularly come and sit with me for an hour or so after the evening meal. He would tell me everything that he heard and what went on in the inner circle.

Because of his education, Jesus would ask Judah to sit by him at meal times and discuss current events and views on God. Jesus told him in confidence that the other disciples had the faith and followed Jesus' teachings, but they lacked the intelligence or reasoning that Judah possessed and often told Judah that he considered him his favorite among all the disciples.

Judah told me that once Jesus said to him, and to him alone, "Come that I may teach you about secrets no person has ever seen. For there exists a great and boundless realm, whose extent no generation of angels has seen, in which there is a great invisible Spirit."

Judah told me he had never felt such love for another person. He now understood that his purpose in life was to follow Jesus, even to death if necessary. Judah also hinted that not all was well within the group. He mentioned that some were jealous of his position with Jesus, jealous that he controlled the money, and jealous that Jesus confided only in Judah. This manifested itself the most in the disciple named Peter, but Judah did not care, for he exulted within the warmth of the shining light of God.

The days flew by. One season followed another. Jesus' fame continued to grow. Everywhere we went he cured the sick and preached to whoever would listen. The outer group that I belonged to grew enormously. We numbered in the thousands.

On several occasions, he sent his disciples out alone for short periods to spread the word in his name and he gave them the same powers to heal, including Judah. I saw this with my own eyes, and like many of the others around me, I became one of the true believers. I would not have hesitated to die for Him if he asked me to.

It was a great time for us. We believed we were born in the chosen time. The time when heaven would come to Earth and the new era of Man living in the light of God would begin.

Or so we thought.

One night in early spring and less than a day's walk from Jerusalem, Judah came to me in tears. He ran up to me and crumpled at my feet as I sat by my campfire. I had just sent my servant away to attend the horses and mules.

Judah desperately grabbed at my tunic and said he had just learned the true cost of following the way of the Messiah.

"Whatever do you mean, Judah?" I asked urgently.

Judah looked at me with wide, horror-stricken eyes darting around him, trying to assure himself that we were alone.

"Marius," he began in a choked voice, no louder than a whisper, "he has told me what I must do." Tears streamed down his cheeks and into his beard. "He took me aside and said only I had the strength to help him with the final fulfillment of the scriptures. He said I must help in killing him so that he may rise on the third day and prove to all his followers who he really is. He said that I alone understood who he really was, that the others were still blind. He said that God, his father, had told him this must happen for the veil to be lifted from their eyes."

Judah buried his face in his hands for a moment and looked back up to me. I could only look on in horror.

"Judah, you are mad!" I finally said to him grabbing his shoulders. "How can you say such things? You and I both know he is the Messiah. The others must know it by now. Are they that dump, that simple minded, that they have been blind to the truth all this time, all these months?"

"Yes Marius," he said to me. The pain in his tear soaked face still visible. "Hear me Marius, and hear me well, for these are his words to me and someone besides me must help with the burden of this knowledge. He said, 'Step away from the others and I shall tell you the mysteries of the kingdom. It is possible for you to reach it, but you will grieve a great deal. You are one of the twelve but someone else will replace you. You will grieve much when you see the kingdom and all its generation.' I heard and I understood him, but I still had to ask, 'What good is it that I have received it? For you have set me apart from that generation?' and Jesus said to me, 'You will become the thirteenth, and you will be cursed by the other generations of your time and you will come to rule over them. In the last days they will curse your ascent to the holy generation.' I will never forget those words, Marius."

"What did he mean, Judah? What was he saying to you?" I asked urgently, still not fully understanding the words.

Judah continued as if he did not hear me, "He took me even further away from the rest, and when he felt sure we were completely alone, he told me what I must do. He told me that the day would soon be upon us when I must help the high priests of Jerusalem to kill him. He then would be buried and rise the third day, and he would proclaim this to all the apostles so that they would be ready for his Rising. God will then open their eyes to who Jesus really is. He then said that, because of my actions, the other disciples would hate me and cast me away. He told me to have courage for I would be doing his bidding and not to worry, for what I must do will become self evident to me.

"Then he looked in my eyes and asked me to promise to do exactly what he was about to tell me, to follow his orders precisely. He then told me that, after he left this mortal world, I must find a wife and have a family. He predicted that my firstborn shall be a female and that she, when of childbearing age, must marry and will in turn have a female firstborn. This lineage of firstborn females would continue throughout the ages of Man until the time of his return. He said that when he returned, the last female descent will bear a son as a firstborn and that son shall be Him."

He paused for some time, his look faraway.

"Marius," he continued, unable to look at me. "How can I help kill the Son of God? I would die for him without hesitation, but I cannot do this."

I could feel his inner turmoil, the desire to do as Jesus commanded, but to do him harm lay beyond his capacity. It reminded me of Abraham when God asked him to sacrifice his son.

Judah had looked away as if searching for an answer, but soon looked back at me and said in an almost calm voice, "He then told me about you. He said that I must talk to my friend Marius and tell him the time had come. Do you remember what he said to you the first time we met him on the beach? He said you would know what to do. He also told me to tell you that the firstborn will be known to who have eyes to see, for she shall be born with the sign of the moon and so will all her firstborn female descendants."

My mind a whirlwind because of what Judah had just said.

He stared at me.

"What did he mean, Marius?" he asked me, his eyes darting across my face. "What is it that you have to do?"

"I need to think," I said staring into the flames of the fire.

We sat there by the fire for some time, too stunned to say anything. An occasional moan came out of Judah. He constantly grabbed roughly at his ruffled hair, as if trying to pull it out along with the pain he felt. I could not console him for I had my own thoughts and demons to deal with.

Slowly the ideas came together. Slowly I realized what Jesus needed to accomplish, had to accomplish. How else could all of Mankind come to learn of what had occurred in this remote part of the world? He had accomplished all of the predictions in the scriptures. His death and the rising the final climax. He even predicted it when they were in Galilee. Did he not say, 'the Son of man was destined to be handed over into the power of sinful men and be crucified, and rise again on the third day?'

Yes. I now understood, and Judah had a role in this. Because of his love for Jesus, his intelligence and his strength, he was the only one of the twelve who would understand and have the courage to go through with it. In his grief of what he had to do, he needed help to understand. I needed to help him. That was my role: to help Judah do as Jesus commanded and protect him and his family.

Yes. It made sense now.

"Judah, look at me and listen," I said while I grabbed him again by the arms and forced him to look up at me, his eyes red and wet with tears. "I see what he is trying to do. He must fulfill the scriptures and his predictions. Do you remember what he said back in Galilee? That he would be crucified and rise again on the third day. – Do you remember?"

His face slowly relaxed. He did recall and he began to understand.

"He said he would be handed over to be crucified," I repeated. "Judah, you must go ahead of Jesus to Jerusalem and see what is happening. You must go to the priests and find out what they are planning. If there is any way that you can help them, you must. I realize how difficult it is for you. I love him also, but you now understand what has to happen. I cannot do this for I am not part of his inner circle. It must be you, just as he said. He was right about you. You are the strongest of the twelve and love him the most and, therefore, the only one that can help him. At first, the faithful will not understand. They will hate you, but eventually, the truth will come out."

I stared at his face as I said all these things and I saw that he understood.

"Why are you so concerned with what others will think of you, Judah?" I continued. "Don't you see this is the sacrifice that you must make in order to enter the kingdom of heaven. Just as God commanded Abraham to sacrifice his son, so must you sacrifice the Son of God. It is His will."

Judah slowly stood up. I could see the struggle inside him written on his face as he mulled all of what I said over in his mind and slowly the expression on his face changed. Slowly I could see that he began to understand. The pain did not seem to ebb away, but controlled, accepted as his burden. He relaxed now, almost at peace with the inevitable.

"You are right, Marius," he said finally. "There is no other way and there is no other that he trusts as much. It has to be me. I must ensure that the prophecy is fulfilled."

I could see his mind working as he stared out into space, looking at possibilities, at ways that this could and must happen.

"Yes," he said calmly. "I have to do this in such a way that it is convincing and involves the priests. They have wanted to destroy him from the very beginning." He began to get excited. "It has to be done through them. They have the ability to convince the Romans he is a danger to order, for only the Romans can execute a man, especially by crucifixion."

Judah looked back and grabbed me by the collar. He lost his resolve again and the pain came back with a vengeance. "Marius, it is so hard! He is more than a brother to me."

"I know, Judah," I said, "but you are the only one that has the strength for this, and he knew it from the first time we met him."

"I know," he agreed, looking away. "God help me, I know."

He let go of me and looked around. "I must leave now, Marius, while I have the strength. I need one of your horses. I must go to Jerusalem tonight and return before Jesus and the others awake. For I must be with them when they enter the city."

"Of course, Judah," I replied as I led him to the horses. The servant lay asleep in his cot so I helped Judah saddle the fastest horse I had. When done, I hugged Judah and said, "God be with you."

"And with you too," he replied emotionally as he mounted.

He rode off into the darkness toward Jerusalem.

•••

I did not see Judah again for eight days.

After Judah had rode off into the night I laid down on my blanket next to the fire and tried to get some sleep. I knew he would be gone the entire night and would most certainly go straight back to Jesus' camp after he had talked to the priests in Jerusalem. I sent my servant there to wait for Judah's return and retrieve the horse I lent him. I tried to get some sleep that night and only managed to doze off for an hour near dawn.

The next day, my servant returned with the horse. As I suspected, Judah had rode back in the early morning hours and joined Jesus on his trek into Jerusalem.

I did not go into the city that day, nor did I attend the crucifixion. I had seen men die on the cross before and I could not bear to see Jesus die that way.

Something kept me out of the city. Looking back now, I should have gone in right away, but I knew then that the events needed to unfold as Jesus had predicted and I did not trust myself to stand by and let them happen.

Though I felt compelled to stay back at the camp for the next five days, I needed to know what transpired in Jerusalem. To that end, I invited various travelers coming out of the city to share my camp from which I received news of the events occurring there.

No one mentioned Judah and his actions. It seemed to me only the inner circle knew the details surrounding the events the night of the arrest of Jesus.

One guest made an interesting observation. A merchant from India, the dark man had joined me at my camp on the third day after Judah left for Jerusalem with Jesus.

During our various topics of conversation over the meal, I casually asked about whether he knew anything about some prophet, which I said I heard from others. About a prophet that had been prosecuted back in Jerusalem. He mentioned that he had heard about a man considered a great prophet by his followers. So popular that there were rumors that some declared him the Jewish Messiah. He said that the Romans gave him a trial, on the behest of the priests, and subsequently crucified. He also mentioned that he had personally witnessed one of his disciples deny knowing the prophet, not just once but several times. I later discovered the disciple to be none other than Peter, the one most jealous of the relationship between Judah and Jesus.

Judah identified Jesus to the men that took him, thus, as expected, branding Judah a traitor. Jesus rose three days later and showed himself to the eleven apostles before rising to heaven.

All just as Jesus promised.

I only summarize here because the eleven apostles have spoken about nothing else since. Whoever reads this will be familiar with those epic events. I do not have to describe them here, for this is not the story of Jesus, but the story of Judah.

Within a few days, everyone coming out of Jerusalem began proclaiming Jesus as the Messiah, when, before his death, only a few had known. Jesus had prophesied this when he said, 'The veil shall be lifted from their eyes.'

The time finally came for me to enter Jerusalem.

We packed all my belongings early in the morning and rode towards the city. We entered the gates in late afternoon.

I found Judah several days later at an Inn at the edge of the city frequented mostly by Romans and foreign merchants. His clothes were haggard and dirty and it seemed he hadn't bathed since the last night that I saw him so it didn't surprise me as he sat alone at a small wooden table and single bench at one corner of the room. He had a pitcher of wine and cup. I grabbed a bench and sat down next to him.

"Judah," I said with relief in my voice. He slowly looked up but seemed not to recognize me. "It's me, Marius. Thank God I found you."

"Leave me alone," he said without emotion, looking back down at his cup.

"Come," I said quietly getting up and grabbing him by the arm. He offered no resistance and got to his feet. I threw some coins on the table and led him outside. "I rented a house not too far from here."

I led him to a carriage I had purchased earlier that week. He climbed in and I drove him to my home. I had my servant bathe him, apply ointment and put on a new set of clothes.

I watched close by.

Judah remained unresponsive throughout but did not resist. He merely kept looking down at nothing in particular. At dinner, he ate sparingly. I did not ask what he had been doing since the night he rode off into the night towards Jerusalem. Nor did I try to make any small talk. He said not a word the entire day.

After the meal, I put him to bed and he went asleep as soon as he closed his eyes. He slept through the entire night and did not rise until the afternoon of the following day.

I usually spent the afternoons sitting among the garden at the back of the house under a canopy to get out of the already hot spring sun. That's where he found me, reading a manuscript of a play an acquaintance of mine had written and asked me to critique. It wasn't any good and I had trouble staying focused. I put down the manuscript as soon as I caught sight of him.

Judah had been dressed in some of my clothes by my servant and no longer looked liked a homeless beggar. He looked clean and refreshed but his eyes still showed the anguish that consumed him.

He sat down in a lounge next to mine and looked around the garden with no real interest.

He did not say a word.

I called for my servant and asked to bring food and drink for both of us.

While waiting for the refreshments I decided to tell Judah of what I had seen and experienced since we parted company outside Jerusalem. How I had waited back at the camp and received news from travelers coming from the city.

Our meals delivered, we were alone again. Judah told me what he had done in a garden after the final supper with Jesus and the disciples. How he had identified Jesus to the soldiers and priests with a kiss. How he had run away in shame for what he did, even though he followed Jesus' command.

Like me, he did not attend the trial and crucifixion.

"You did as commanded of you by Jesus himself," I said to Judah. I continued in a low but stern voice, "We talked about this the night you rode into the city."

Judah picked up his cup of wine and stared into the blood red fluid for a moment. "Yes, I know," he said in a resigned tone, "but it doesn't make it easier."

We sat quietly under the canopy. The high walls surrounding the garden kept the noise of the street to a bare minimum. The place exuded serenity. The birds sung to each other among the trees. Crickets played their songs within the shade of the flowers. Looking around at that moment it became clear what I should do. I decided to purchase the home and stay in the city. This would be an ideal base for me to tend to and watch over Judah.

"Judah, we must talk about the future," I said looking at him.

"What of it?" he asked solemnly, refusing to meet my gaze.

Still looking at him I replied, "Do you remember what he ordered you to do once he left this world? What you repeated to me that night?"

I didn't expect an answer. I merely stated or asked the obvious. He looked at me for a moment and looked away again.

"Marius, I appreciate what you are doing," he said sincerely. "I realize I have to move on, and I will. I will also do as he commanded me, but you have to understand that it will take time. That I must greave, greave for someone that I loved more dearly than anyone else in the world."

"Yes, I know, Judah," I said, relieved that he responded at last. "I am glad that you are thinking clearly, despite your pain." I sat up and refilled our cups with more wine. "Let's leave it for a few months and then we will begin to make plans."

I raised my cup in a toast with restrained joy. He acknowledged without enthusiasm, but he acknowledged nevertheless. That display, that simple act of acceptance, a great leap forward for us all.

•••

The next three months went by without incident, as far as Judah was concerned. Though he stayed in the house and only ventured outside to the garden, I went about the city of Jerusalem.

I devised two main objectives that I needed to accomplish.

First, to become an important resident of this place I needed to identify and then establish myself into the ruling class. I am a Roman and with money so what better way to protect Judah then my using every means possible at my disposal?

Second, I wanted to track the antics of the eleven remaining apostles.

In an attempt to achieve my first goal, I began to frequent various Roman dominated spas and drinking establishments throughout the city proper. Apart from a number of enterprising Jewish merchants, the bulk of the natives tended to stay away from these places. The clientele consisted mostly of Roman citizens sprinkled with visiting well-to-do travelers and merchants from other corners of the world.

Through careful inquiries, it did not take long for me to find the core of the upper social caste within Jerusalem. The Roman Governor, Pontius Pilate stood at the center of this little universe within such a remote part of the great Roman Empire. It also became quickly apparent that, to make my way to him, I needed to go through the Governor's personal Secretary, Virgil Crassus. Virgil came from an outer branch of the family tree that seemed not to benefit physically from the Roman stock. His keen mind though, more than made up for the physical shortcomings.

The Governor relied heavily on Virgil Crassus for the day-to-day management of this remote part of the empire and also the comings and goings within the Praetorium, the Governor's residence, where he wielded his power.

Most important to me, Virgil also heavily influenced the social circle around the Governor.

One of the most effective and easiest ways to get discreet but important facts on influential people is through their slaves. I used my servant, though no longer my slave as I gave him his freedom but agreed to continue to work for me for wages, to inquire about the Secretary's general habits and activities.

I soon found the spa and the times that the Secretary frequented. I timed my visits to his schedule and soon spotted him within the establishment.

I introduced myself as the son of Bromius Sestus. Virgil Crassus, knowledgeable in all the old and rich Roman families, immediately knew my family name and it guaranteed an invitation at the next weekly social gathering at the Praetorium.

I showed up at the appointed time with my servant in tow.

I spared to expense. My chariot was of the finest craftsmanship and pulled by a majestic and spirited black Arabian horse in a gold plated fine leather tack glimmering in the sun. I wore the traditional white Roman tunic but trimmed with the finest embroidery, red sash and sandals and with gold bracelets on each forearm. I also, of course, wore my family ring that identified my status. Over my tunic and across my shoulders I wore a silk gold colored cloak.

I made an impressive figure when I rode into the grounds and walked into the banquet hall with an air of importance.

Secretary Virgil Crassus immediately introduced me to the Governor. Pontius Pilate stood at five foot ten inches, olive skinned with a lean, almost muscular build.

He looked me over quickly and offered a warm greeting, obviously impressed with my attire and aristocratic demeanor. Something sorely lacking in this remote part of the world, he later acknowledged in confidence.

He asked about my family, which told me his secretary, Virgil, had briefed him before our meeting. The Governor honored me by asking that I be by his side the rest of the evening. I graciously accepted and sat to his right the rest of the night.

The banquet was a lavish affair. Complete with multiple courses of exotic foods and wines. Musicians, dancing girls, magicians, and acrobats entertained us.

The wine flowed until the coming of dawn. I left before the traditional raping of the servant slaves, boys and girls, began. I no longer took part in that detestable practice.

From that moment on, I received invitations to all ceremonies, banquets and gatherings of the select few.

Occasionally I had the opportunity to meet Herod, King of Palestine, but he tended to keep his own company outside Jerusalem.

With my ingratiation into the upper class now complete, I obtained security for Judah by acquiring the services of the Roman guard, for a modest fee of course.

LAST DESCENDANT

With security out of the way, I could now start to make some inquiries into the activities of Jesus' eleven remaining apostles. I hired a team of servants to act as spies around the city of Jerusalem and I began to gather news.

The eleven apostles had elected a replacement for Judah in order to maintain the so-called sacred twelve. The newly appointed twelfth disciple, Matthias, came from the original crowd that followed Jesus from the very beginning of his mission. I often saw him during those early days when I followed along with the same group.

An unimpressive figure by any stretch of the imagination, Matthias was a short, young Jewish man not yet betrothed, and somewhat of a nervous fellow but very dedicated to the cause.

I also found out that the Apostles lived in a communal arrangement. They, and their families, stayed in one large common home.

They numbered roughly one hundred and twenty by the time the eleven apostles elected Matthias as the twelfth, about two months after Jesus rose to heaven.

Through aggressive recruitment and preaching, they quickly grew to three thousand and after only three months, the common home began to get crowded.

All new followers were required to sell all their properties and possessions and hand over the proceeds to the Apostles who would evenly distribute it among all the communal members. I recall a story that began to circulate about how one couple who had held back selling one plot of land and lying to Peter about it had suddenly dropped dead in front of everyone. Unfortunately, I never did have a chance to confirm it to be true.

This community had one firm belief: that Jesus would return in their lifetime and a new age would begin in earnest, ignorant of the covenant between Jesus and Judah and that it would be many generations before He returned.

The new community's aggressive manner caught the attention of the high priest Caiaphas and the rest of the temple authorities. Caiaphas notoriously remembered as the high priest who first questioned Jesus after his arrest and tore apart his own garment when he accused Jesus of blasphemy. The authorities began to threaten the new community with charges of blasphemy if they refused to cease. To avoid persecution and possible death, the apostles moved themselves and their entire community to the city of Antioch in Greece.

Antioch is a city on the eastern side of the Orontes River. Founded just over 300 years ago by one of generals of Alexander the Great named Seleucus I Nicator. This city became their base from where they began to spread the word of Jesus to all the corners of the world.

While all this happened, Judah began to be more responsive. He started to join in on conversations at dinner times and actually managed an occasional smile.

We began to make plans for his marriage.

It is also important to note that the general Jewish community did not consider Judah a traitor. On the contrary, they considered him a dedicated and noble Hebrew that assisted the priests in identifying a heretic. It was, therefore, not difficult to find him a suitable wife. Judah may have given most of his money away but I still had plenty and there were many agreeable merchants looking for the right men of affluence for their daughters.

Of course, we followed the correct Jewish customs.

Using an intermediary, or agent, we received his recommendation on a suitable wife. Judah showed actual interest and even agreed to the candidate once he had an opportunity to get a glimpse of her at the fountain where she retrieved the family's water.

Her name was Mariel, a dark eyed beauty with olive skin common within these parts.

We completed the correct Jewish protocols, as tedious as they were.

First, the Match: contact the intended bride's father and negotiate the price. Since the Iscariot family enjoyed a much higher social status than the family in question, and with my money, it wasn't too difficult to settle on a price considered very generous by their standards.

Secondly, Judah gave appropriate but very generous gifts to the bride in the proper manner, the bride's family in attendance of course.

Next, the bride's father provided a dowry and, through the agent well paid by me, I discreetly and delicately made it clear that it could be modest, but not to the level to have the father lose face.

We then completed a very generous marriage contract that detailed the rights of the bride and the promises of the groom, all heavily in favor of the bride to expedite the process.

The betrothal came next sealed with a toast of cups of wine that involved all concerned. The tradition referred to as the 'cup of acceptance.'

Finally, we came to the Nuptials and the Marriage Feast that we kept at the appropriately impressive standard for the merchant class.

As a wedding gift, I bought the newlyweds a plot of land to farm just outside Jerusalem. It had a modest but more than adequate farmhouse where Judah and his wife could have a very comfortable life.

The bride and groom settled in.

Judah insisted that there be no servants or guards. Though I respected his decision, I asked for and received increased patrols around the area.

I felt concerned for Judah's well being for two well-founded reasons; the first from thieves and petty criminals that seem to roam the outskirts of all cities; the second from vendettas the Apostles might attempt. They did preach forgiveness, but human nature and strong emotions can get the better of a man.

I had no ill feelings towards Peter and his ministry and actually became impressed with their success. They were spreading the word of Jesus just as he had commanded them to do. As a Christian myself, how could I disagree with that? Behind the scenes, I cheered for their success. I saw this as a perfect complement to our Savior's plans. Peter would lead the charge to spread the word of Jesus and his return, while Judah would secure the lineage until the appointed time.

I made a decision then that I would regret the rest of my life, I decided to search for and tell Peter about Judah and his quest as ordered by Jesus so that we could all work together for the common goal of His return. To achieve this I went to Antioch soon after Judah settled into his new home with his bride. After reaching Antioch via a merchant ship, and after careful inquiries, I soon discovered that Peter and his flock had settled into a small group of buildings near the town square. I took a room at an inn across the square and waited for an opportunity to meet Peter.

In the early afternoon three days later, as I sat at a table outside the inn and having some horrible wine, I spied Peter across the square dressed in a white but very dusty woolen tunic and sporting a mighty wooden Sheppard's staff. Behind him followed three men I did not recognize. Anyone looking at the four immediately knew who the leader was. Peter had an air of nobility, his stride showed a purpose, almost impatience. Looking straight ahead, he did not see me. I called out to him by name. Peter and his entourage stopped and looked my way and he recognized me immediately. After a moment, he turned to his comrades and spoke a few words in a low voice that did not allow me to hear the conversation. The three men then continued in the same direction they were heading, while Peter stood his ground, all the while gazing at me. After what seemed like an eternity, he walked in my direction. He stopped in front of my table but did not sit down.

"Hello, Marius," said Peter coldly, without a smile. His religious fervor did not allow any untoward emotion. His dark brown eyes, common in his people, stared down at me unblinking. His chin stuck out in pride, a pride further accentuated by his long beard, his staff still in his left hand. For the first time since my decision to seek out Peter, I had misgivings about telling him of Judah. I should have listened to my intuition then, but I did not.

"Hello to you too, Peter," I replied with a warm smile in greeting. "Please sit down and join me in some wine. It is not too good, but still refreshing in this heat."

He looked at me for a moment and glanced at the table and its contents. His shoulders relaxed slightly, reached for the chair and sat down opposite me without saying a word. I poured him a cup of wine and refilled mine.

"How are you, Peter?" I asked as I took another sip.

"Thanks to God, I am well, Marius," he replied in a clear voice. He picked up the cup and said a toast, "To our Lord, Jesus Christ from Nazarene, and to the salvation of your soul, Marius." He took a sip and placed the cup down on the table.

"Amen to that," I acknowledged and took a sip myself.

Peter's gaze remained steady as he said without hesitation, "It cannot be an accident, Marius, that we should cross paths in such a town in another country. I suspect that you have searched me out for a purpose. I also assume that you will now enlighten me on what that purpose is."

Surprised by his directness but not by his deduction, I replied, "You are absolutely correct, Peter." He sat with his back straight, holding on to his staff with his left hand and meeting my gaze steadily. "This is not a chance encounter. I heard you were in Greece and I came searching for you. I must first tell you that I completely support your ministry and your mission. I am one of you and believe in our Savior. You are indeed fulfilling the role passed down to you by Jesus. As he once said, 'You are Peter. The rock I will build my church on.'" I paused for effect.

"I am merely fulfilling my destiny," he interjected with a slight nod, the compliment having little, if any, affect.

"What you may not know," I continued, "is that Judah is still alive and well taken care of. He also –."

"As far as I am concerned Judah is dead!" he interrupted raising his voice and slamming his staff against the packed dirt. "He acted as a guide to the men who arrested Jesus. He took money for this terrible deed and now cursed by all men. And when he is judged by God in heaven he will be judged accordingly and cast into hell everlasting."

"Peter, listen to me," I said holding my hands out to him. "Judah loved Jesus as much as any of you. He simply followed Jesus' command. He did not –"

"No!" Peter interrupted again with a still louder voice as he stood up. "Judah acted out of spite! He will die for his sins and I will do whatever I can to hasten that day. For, as I said, as far as I am concerned Judah is dead. His body continues to breath but his soul is dead." He looked down at me and I saw a slight sneer behind his beard. His eyes also gave him away. "You see, Marius, I have also been kept informed of Judah's whereabouts and what he has been up to. He thinks he has entered a new life of domestic leisure. But that is not his fate, for a man like him does not deserve to live." He got up and began walking in the same direction as his friends.

"Do not search me out again, Marius," said Peter without looking back. "You are aiding the spawn of the devil himself. I will not be so sociable the next time."

I sat there unable to speak.

What happened to the Peter that I knew while Jesus was alive? What happened to the warm and open man like a sponge thirsty for knowledge, and gentle and kind to his fellow man? The Peter I just saw carried himself with an air of authority, of pride and aloofness, a man tempered to a certain cause and no longer bending.

How could this have happened, I asked myself?

Then it came to me.

Jesus had thrust this responsibility to Peter. He had said that Peter would build on the foundation that Jesus started, and Peter took on the mantle the only way he knew how. For Christianity to flourish, he had to show authority and strength to his new community of followers. If Peter failed in maintaining the momentum, in maintaining the growth of the movement, it would die out before it even started. It would become just another footnote in history. Christianity's foundation, its main theme, is the return of Jesus Christ the Messiah and getting ready for that return. Peter refused to hear Judah's role in that return. Judah needed to fulfill his own destiny in order for Peter to fulfill his. Both had a critical role in the return of our Lord, Jesus Christ and Peter wanted to destroy Judah.

I had to protect Judah without hurting Peter. I had to get back to Jerusalem immediately.

● ● ●

I looked for the first merchant or Roman war ship, any ship, heading to Palestine. In two days, I boarded a Jewish merchant vessel making its way back without any stops along the way.

I prayed to God that I would arrive to find Judah and his bride, Mariel, well. Despite his past objections, I would insist on a team of armed slaves to provide constant protection for him and his wife.

When we came into port, I left my servant to deal with the luggage. I hired a team of guards with instructions where to go, purchased the fastest carriage I could find, and rode straight for the farm. I left the guards to find their way as best as they could.

I felt confident I would find Judah alive and well.

I was wrong.

When I rode in to the entrance of the farm, I found several of his wife's family members trying to comfort her. When Mariel saw me, she ran up and crumpled on the floor in from of me, and, between sobs, told me what happened. I stood there feeling numb and not saying a word. I only stared at her prostate figure as she told me the story.

Only two days ago, Judah had gone out in the early morning to begin the plowing of the field. He harnessed the mule and began from the farthest reaches of the farm, over a rise and out of sight of the house. When he did not appear by noon, she had ventured out to bring him his midday meal. She found him lying dead, disemboweled, beside the plow. The mule standing and patiently waiting for the command to pull that never came. Birds were already attempting to feed on the entrails.

Mariel had run screaming back to the house. Neighbors had heard the commotion and had come to her aid and they called the Roman guards in to investigate.

The sight showed no sign of a struggle. In fact, the plow had remained erect as if Judah had stopped it, perhaps to do something or talk to someone. With his stomach ripped open cleanly, he seemed to have tried to put his entrails back in but died quickly in the effort. They could not tell how this could have happened, but with lack of any witnesses and with Judah considered no one of importance, they guards reported it as an accident and left it at that.

Mariel's family held the funeral the following day and just one day before I arrived back in port.

I had trouble grasping the tragedy that befell us all. Not only had I lost my best friend, but also the destruction of the lineage and the ultimate return of Jesus Christ, Our Savior. The numbness I felt so great I couldn't shed any tears.

The now useless team of guards finally arrived in several carriages to the farmhouse. In my haste at the port, I paid in advance for one month. I asked them to simply post sentries and I sat down to collect my thoughts, my mind racing.

An accident, I asked myself? How could it have been an accident? A person doesn't just fall down and split open. That's ridiculous. Someone killed Judah, I thought. Murdered by an acquaintance, someone he knew, or expecting. That's why the guards saw no sign of a struggle. Peter's hand must have been involved in this. Who else would care or would have bothered? Judah had come out shirtless and with nothing but the mule and plow and they had not been stolen either.

The day started to grow late and Mariel's family made plans to leave. Only her mother elected to stay behind to comfort her. I did not know what else to do but I knew one thing, I could not leave the two grieving women by themselves. I ordered the guards to gather them up and, using their carriages, we headed back to the city to my larger and more secure home. I settled the women in one of the guest rooms and I took a bath. My servants laid out a fresh clean robe and refreshments for me. I dressed but I could not eat with my stomach in knots.

As far as I was concerned, Mankind was doomed. Peter had inadvertently destroyed our future. The Messiah could no longer return. How could God have allowed this? I failed to comprehend His plan. Had He turned His back on us? Could this be part of the freedom of choice He gave us, the choice to destroy ourselves? How could one misdirected man choose for all of Mankind, are we not all, individually, given that choice? To choose a path for ourselves? Nothing made sense.

I slept very little that night. I no longer had a purpose in life. The destiny I once saw clearly in front of me suddenly gone, shattered into a thousand fragments, like a delicate crystal dropped on a hard stone floor.

My heart no longer had room for revenge. Although an outsider of the Christian community lead by Peter, I still believed in the same teachings of Jesus.

With a heavy conscience, the next morning I asked one of my servants to extend an invitation to dinner for that evening to Mariel's father. I needed to arrange for the return of Mariel to her family. A financial incentive would make that transition easier. It would also not hurt to contribute to a dowry for a second marriage. Still young, she would make a good wife to some other man.

Mariel's father, Samuel, arrived at the appointed time dressed in his best. I did not hate the man, but I also did not like him as he always looked for an opportunity to fill his bottomless moneybag. This evening seemed to be no exception.

"Good evening, Sire," he said as he entered following behind one of my servants. He bowed formally and added, "May God bless this house and everyone in it."

I returned the greeting without a smile, "Blessings to you too, sir. Please sit down and join me for some dinner."

We made small talk while my servants fed us quite well. He knew exactly why I called him and he carefully stayed away from the subject to allow me to make the first move. At the end of the meal, I broached the subject.

"Samuel, I asked you here for a reason," I began. "Though it has been only a few days since Judah's death, we must make plans for your daughter, Mariel."

"You are quite right, sire," he began with a slight bow. "It is only proper that we find her a new husband."

It did not surprise me that he said 'we' in order to imply I had some responsibility in the matter and therefore, financial assistance.

"What is the appropriate amount of time for mourning before a search for a new husband is made?" I asked, confident that the larger the dowry the shorter the mourning period.

Samuel said, "There is no real fixed time. I suggest it not be too long, though. Since she is with child, I think the sooner the –."

"What did you just say?" I interrupted looking up from my cup of wine.

He stared at me for a moment with that stupid smile. "She is with child," he repeated. He saw my surprise. "I see you did not know. Normally a brother or another family member would marry her but Judah had no brothers and he has no family members in this vicinity who would consider such an arrangement, so we must look outside the family." He paused and took another sip of wine to allow me to absorb the information. Soon he continued again. "Of course, the larger the dowry, the easier it will be to find a suitable husband."

I could not believe what I just heard.

She was pregnant! That meant that the lineage remained whole after all.

Of course, I thought to myself, once the lineage has started with the pregnancy, the focus turns to the mother and then the first-born daughter. As cold as it may sound, once Mariel was with child, Judah became irrelevant.

I stood up and paced the room. Samuel misunderstood my actions and thought me distraught because it would cost me more for the dowry.

"Kind sir," he began soothingly. "I am sure that the dowry would not have to be too extreme if we act fast."

With no real social responsibility on my part, he thought I simply acted out of love and concern from my friendship to Judah but that I had reached my limit of compassion. His eyes betrayed his fear. I did not respond. I turned my back to him and stared out into the garden, into the warm night air.

My mind full of elated wonder and relief with the knowledge that the lineage had not being lost forever. The Messiah would return just as he predicted. God had not forsaken us. I still felt the pain from loosing Judah but regained my hope for Mankind. Hope renewed. Despite my elation, I maintained my composure for I did not want this weasel, Samuel, to know my thoughts.

I whirled back facing him and said, "No, Samuel. That would not do."

Samuel's smile dissipated considerably but he managed to hold on to some of it. "But sire, if we are to ensure she is properly wed, a dowry of a sufficient size –"

"What I have in mind, Samuel," I interrupted with an air of importance, "is something different." I took a few steps forward and looked straight at him. "You know that I loved Judah like a brother. Though I am Roman, I continue to have a sense of responsibility for him, and his traditions feel to me as if they are also mine. As far as I am concerned, and many of our mutual acquaintances would agree, he is my brother. You know that I converted to Judaism some time ago. I, therefore, claim my right to make Mariel my wife and raise her unborn child as my own."

"Sire, you do our family honor, but are you sure this is what you want?" asked Samuel while doing his all too frequent bowing, no doubt seeing this as a financial tragedy to his moneybag.

"It is not only what I want, dear sir, but also my duty. Your daughter will be well cared for. She will be a queen in her own household. And her child will enjoy all the privileges that can be afforded by my wealth and position." Sensing that some appeasement would again expedite the process I provided some enticement. "Naturally, her maternal family will also benefit from such a union. My connections and Roman citizenship will undoubtedly open opportunities for the family in areas such as preferred trade routes and reduction in taxes and border duties."

Samuel's smile instantly returned and his bow even more severe. "Sire, you are most generous," he said.

"But let's leave this for some other time," I said. "We have some family matters to deal with and wedding arrangements to make."

•••

Mariel did not object to the arrangement and voiced no concern to a quick and small wedding. After all, she was a widower and with child so it made sense to her to have a low keyed wedding.

On the pretext that I wanted Mariel held in the highest regard within her community, I asked Mariel and her maternal family not to advertise her pregnancy from her first husband. Though common for a male family member of the deceased husband to wed the widow, the tradition came from a sense of duty rather than any feelings of love, so the groom often treated the new wife as second class. I did not want that for Mariel. Nevertheless, my true motive was to keep Peter and the Christian community ignorant of the fact that Judah had a descendant. Vengeance has a long reach.

We had the wedding at my home within a week.

By this time, Mariel estimated that she had been pregnant for about two months so the child would be born seven months into our union. Any outsider would assume that the child was born premature.

The wedding guests consisted of only a few of my Roman associates and the immediate family of my new bride, along with the appropriate Jewish priests that officiated the wedding, of course.

By the wedding day, I had already hired permanent guards to patrol the entire property and the perimeter upgraded with higher walls and strong metal gates. I began to feel more at ease with the safety of my new bride.

I did not consummate the marriage. Not while Mariel carried the lineage that would eventually include Jesus Christ Our Lord. I saw no reason why we could not have a normal marriage after the birth, so I waited until then. I wanted a loving family environment for both Mariel and the child, and matrimonial intimacy and harmony I considered a crucial part of that.

I kept Mariel ignorant of the destiny of the child that she carried. Judah and I had decided when we were making his marriage plans not to pass on our knowledge to his bride to be. For one thing, the bride would inevitably be Jewish, since no Christian woman would even consider Judah, and someone not Christian wouldn't even believe, let alone, agree that her first born would lead to the return of Jesus Christ. I therefore continued with that strategy.

Having done my best to provide security for my bride and me, I focused on my next concern, that I alone now knew the true destiny of the child growing within Mariel. I alone knew about the lineage of Judah and the destiny of his descendants. Who would protect the lineage if a calamity would befall me? Who would know the truth?

I also feared that, with only one female descent per generation, the risk of a break in the lineage remained a high. Protection or not, disease and other life dangers made it almost a certainty. I had to rely in my faith in God to help in this but I also meant to use all the earthly means available to me.

I resolved to ensure that I not be the only one to carry the knowledge of the necessity that both Christianity and the Judah lineage both survive and flourish. It became clear to me that I needed to create an organization, no, more than that, a community, a religion, a life purpose for a chosen few like myself, to protect the lineage and pass the knowledge of its place in the destiny of Man.

I next did something that I said I would never do once I became a Christian. I went to the slave market and purchased a dozen slave boys no older than ten years and as close in age as possible. The group ranged between the ages of eight and ten.

I hired two maids to tend the children's physical needs but I became their instructor in all things. I wanted to become their authority figure and father.

My purpose was simple: raise the boys to have a single-minded purpose of protecting the lineage. That is, indoctrinate them to be the protectors of Judah's descendants and the protectors of the knowledge. I would raise them Christian but with this additional life goal, a solemn pack for the chosen. I would later provide them with their freedom but, if I were successful, it would make no difference to them. Their destinies set to carry the burden of Mankind throughout the ages.

Therefore, I created the Protectors of the Truth.

I spend the remainder of my years molding the boys for their destiny, ensuring the organization would continue long after my death, that it would survive to ensure the safety of the Descendants.

I developed rituals and rites shrouded in reverence and mystery, all in an effort to instill a religious fervor in a team of men who would lay down their lives for the cause, without hesitation, without regret.

The Protectors must and will incorporate themselves into all levels of society. Their numbers are to grow but at a controlled number so as not to attract undue attention from the Christians who need to remain ignorant of the existence of the organization and the Descendants. I made sure all my wealth was available to the Protectors and invested in such a way that it existed for the cause as long as the organization endured.

Mariel gave birth at the expected time to a female child with a mark as predicted on the right temple the shape of a crescent moon. I let Mariel name the child. She chose the name Zipporah, after the wife of Moses, who led the chosen out of Egypt and appropriate, in a way.

I had taught the boys enough of their mission in life that they were in awe of the event, and they kept it to themselves as instructed. I told

Mariel that I obtained the boys as guards for her child as she grew up. It actually wasn't far from the truth. She merely saw my actions as from an overly protective father. I didn't see any reason to let her think otherwise.

Zipporah grew up to be a fine woman and the boys into strong men.

To allow Zipporah a reasonable chance of a normal like, they learned to guard her without intrusion. They perfected ways to stay close but out of sight as much as possible. Of course, she knew they were there, but, knowing no other life, both she and the men quickly adapted to each other.

Mariel and I had another child. A boy I named Bromius, after my late father, who died soon after I met Judah in those early years. My son, Bromius, would follow my footsteps and become one of the Seniors. The position based on authority within the organization and not on advanced age with only three allowed to hold that position at any one time.

•••

I am now sixty-eight years old as I write this document.

Bromius, my son, is in his thirties and, along with myself, is now one of the three Seniors of the Protectors of the Truth, and has made the organization larger, stronger and wealthier. Its purpose as steadfast as can be.

Zipporah, the first descendant of Judah, has long married and given birth to a girl with the same beauty mark. She named her after my wife Mariel, who died ten years ago. The Protectors marked the birth with a great festival though kept as a private affair and time for confirmation of their cause and a sign that God would keep his promise to us, to Mankind.

Mariel is now almost eighteen and betrothed to the son of a Jewish merchant in Spain. We are careful not to allow one of the Protectors be chosen as a husband to the Descendants. Though we protect it, the lineage must flourish on its own.

The Protectors of the Truth remain as discreet as possible. The leaders of the organization present themselves as distant wealthy family members of the Descendants and gently influence the ebb and flow of the life of the women. As far as Mariel is concerned, Bromius is a loving uncle to her. So much so, that he has decided to follow her to Spain, and, of course, his large 'family' and 'servants.' The love that Bromius feels for Mariel is very real indeed and in a way that is more complex then she realizes.

He has purchased two estates close to each other; one for Bromius and his 'family,' and one for Mariel and her new husband to be.

There is a great amount of activity these days in our large household. The Protectors have put into action a series of plans to follow Mariel to Spain. An advance group has already moved and has begun to make ready for the rest.

Before I close off now, for I will continue my writings in Spain, there is one more thing that I must mention. There has been no attempt on the life of the Descendants from Peter and the new Church. It seems that we have been successful in keeping the lineage a secret from them and from the outside world. I am most relieved since, I must confess, it remained one of my greatest worries for a long time.

The Protectors of The Truth must remain vigilante, must remain on guard for any attack.

My hope is that Peter and the new Church will remain focused on spreading the word of Jesus Christ. Peter must place all his energy in spreading the New Gospels throughout the world.

The world must be ready for the Second Coming. This could only happen through Peter and the other apostles.

It is an odd alliance, but we need the Church as much as it needs us – even if it does not know it.

End of translation

CHAPTER SIX
BROTHERHOOD

"End of translation?" John curiously asked himself aloud.

He turned to the next page but saw he had reached the end of the book. He put it down and lit a cigarette, confident that the priest would complete the story. As he smoked, he stared out the window into the clear morning day.

The document opened up an entirely new perspective for him on early Christianity, that's for sure, but it also created a new set of questions.

Was the document real? Who was the current descendant? Where was she? How could the lineage, through a single individual, have survived two thousand years of disease, violence and accidents? They would have to live in a bubble. How could the lineage be linked to the solstice of next year?

Yes, there were plenty of questions that needed answers.

Sebastian had cleaned up the place a bit while trying to keep any noise down to a minimum so as not to distract John from his reading. From time to time, he had looked at John's direction for any sign of a reaction but did not see any. It took John only about an hour to read the entire book and still early morning when he put the book down.

When he saw John light a cigarette, Sebastian poured two cups of coffee and took a seat near him.

John looked at the priest. "Where's the rest of it?"

Sebastian looked at John and answered, "There isn't any. Marius Sestus, the author, died of a high fever on the sea voyage to Spain."

"I assume you are going to pick up where he left off and bring the story up to the present?"

"That's right."

John settled back in his couch. "Alright, let's hear it."

Sebastian also visibly relaxed a little in his chair. "As I have just said, Marius Sestus died on route and buried at sea. The family and the respective organization continued on to Spain where they settled into their new homes. The then current Descendant, Mariel, married and had a female child, again with the same birthmark.

"Life went on uneventfully until an attempt on Mariel's daughter's life occurred when she just turned six. Marius Sestus had organized the Protectors well for she escaped without harm. Mother and daughter were in the market place with two servants in tow. The Protectors discreetly out of sight. In the middle of the crowd, two men pulled out knives and lunged at the Descendants while crying out their devotion to Jesus. Four of the Protectors were on them before they could thrust the fatal blows, both stabbed with a thin stiletto type knife straight through the heart from behind. They were dead before they hit the ground. The mother and daughter whisked away by the servants and the Protectors blended back into the crowd before anyone noticed what had happened."

"Just like that?" asked John.

"Just like that," echoed the priest. "The organization began an investigation. They soon discovered that one of the Christian Apostles, Matthias, the one that replaced Judah to maintain the number at twelve, planned the attack. Now at an advanced age but still alive, Matthias had discovered that Judah fathered a child and Marius had tried to hide it."

"How did he find out?" interrupted John.

"We don't know," replied Sebastian. "Matthias became consumed with destroying the lineage of Judah, not because he wanted to stop the second coming, but because he thought the lineage cursed."

"And what of Peter, did he know and condone it?" John asked.

"We don't know whether Peter knew anything about this," answered the priest. "Attempts were made by the Protectors of the Truth to contact Peter and the other apostles but to no avail. No amount of reasoning could open their eyes. It seems that Jesus had accurately predicted this as well ...'You will become the thirteenth, and you will be cursed by the other generations of your time and you will come to rule over them. In the last days they will curse your ascent to the holy generation.' To this day, the eyes and minds of the Church remain closed to the truth.

"You must understand, John, that Christianity has long awaited the Second Coming of Christ. They attacked or destroyed anything seen as a threat to that belief. We were...are...in that category.

"Matthias and his successors created, supported and still maintain a clandestine organization to search out and destroy what they see as the evil descendants of Judah. What they think is out to stop the Second Coming. Matthias created what he called The Brotherhood of the Rapture. It was, and is, an organization with a single purpose: search out and destroy any threats to the Second Coming. And the Protectors of the Truth are at the top of that list."

"And the Vatican, are they aware of this?" asked John.

"The Catholic Church, and all of the Christian offshoots, may know about the Brotherhood of the Rapture but do not appear to support the group," answered the Priest. "Though, in their silence and lack of action to stop them, they seem to condone the organization. And your Captain and the Lieutenant are part of this organization."

He paused for a moment and took a sip of his coffee.

"Getting back to the history," continued Sebastian. "The Descendants and the Protectors of the Truth eventually left Spain. Over the generations, they moved all over the then known world. The Sestus line also changed their last name to a modernized version: It is now Sesti.

"The two rivals, the Brotherhood of the Rapture and the Protectors of the Truth, have been in a constant cat and mouse game, but the lineage has survived, right to the present day.

"Every few years, the leaders of our now global organization search for and recruit fifty orphans no older than ten years old. The screening process is very comprehensive in order to ensure we choose only boys with the proper aptitude and intelligence and sent to training camps located in several locations around the globe. At twenty years of age, when their training is complete, we assign between two to twelve

Protectors to a Descendant either just before or after she is born. Some are not assigned to directly protect the Descendants but responsible for the logistics and financial aspect of the calling.

"The most successful strategy by the Protectors is to create decoys. Orphaned baby girls obtained and tattooed with identical marks on their right temples. We do not inform the Protectors assigned to these girls that they are protecting decoys. Only the inner circle of senior members is even aware of the practice. It may today seem cruel to these girls but, in previous centuries, their fates would more than likely have been a life of slavery and prostitution. Instead, they lived the life of leisure and wealth. They are targets, but overall, they live longer and more comfortable lives."

"Except for the unfortunate ones like those killed in the U.S.?" asked John. Without waiting for an answer he added, "How many more were sacrificed for your cause?"

"Too many, I'm afraid," Sebastian answered with a deep sigh. He looked at John and, after a pause, continued. "It is not how many we sacrificed, for that is not our intent. You should be asking how many of the decoys The Brotherhood of the Rapture has killed. In almost two thousand years, the numbers are in the hundreds. Over the last several decades, advancements in tattoo techniques have allowed us to mark babies right at the hospitals and without the knowledge of the mothers and the hospital staff. The women in the U.S. were just such individuals.

"So we come to the present day; just one year away from the second coming. So close that we can almost taste it, as they say."

"Where is she?" asked John. He did not have to explain whom he meant.

"She is in a safe place, far away from here and she doesn't know of her lineage or how important she is to Mankind," answered the priest.

John needed time to digest this newfound knowledge. Even if he did not believe any of it, at least two groups did, and they were in a life and death struggle with each other while killing many innocent people along the way.

"So why did you tell me all of this?" John asked.

The priest looked intently at John and answered, "For a couple of reasons: one, that you just happened to get caught up in this when you visited me last night and, two, there are only a few of us Protectors left alive in North America. I need all the help I can get to find the Descendant and ensure she remains safe."

"I happened to be in the wrong place at the wrong time and you're desperate," reiterated John.

"That's putting it bluntly but, essentially correct," said the priest. "For security reasons, I have not been told where she has been for the last twenty years. She is in Europe, but that's all I know. The Brotherhood has killed our European head of the Protectors and no one else seems to know where she is. In a way, that is good news, since the Brotherhood probably also do not know, but we have to be sure."

"I got it," said John. "There's a lot for me to think about. First thing first, let's check if there is any news on the fire and the killings at your church. I'd like to see how they explained it away."

Father Sebastian found the remote for the television and turned it on. He switched to a Boston news station currently reporting on a possible garbage strike. They both sat down in front of the TV. After a few minutes, the Anchor introduced a female reporter at the scene of the fire.

The screen showed a flurry of activity at the church still emitting white smoke that framed a petite, black woman reporter as she began, "This is Connie Stevens for BT11 News reporting live and on location at the Church of Saint John on Straw Street. At around 8:45pm last night, Police, Ambulance and Fire Crews responded to a call about smoke coming from this church behind me. When they arrived, they found a fire burning out of control at the back of the church and in the living quarters. The team at the sight called the Fire Marshall after they managed to put the fire out just before sunrise. They soon discovered three bodies within the remains of the building. The police have since ruled the fire as arson and the three bodies as murder victims.

"Captain Westell from the Homicide Division of 73rd precinct has this morning put out a statement that they have identified one of their officers, a Detective John Bernard, as the culprit behind the killings and also set the fire in an effort to hide his crimes. Captain Westell indicated that the officer suffered a nervous breakdown and went on a killing spree of who he believed to be behind the serial killings that have taken place over the last several months. The Captain and one of his Lieutenants had cornered Detective John Bernard at the church but he managed to escape and took a hostage with him. The hostage identified as one of the priests of this church, a Father Sebastian. The police are actively searching for the renegade officer and the hostage, and expect to make an arrest soon. This is Connie Stevens reporting live for BT11 News. We will return with more details as events develop. Dave, back to you at the news room."

John sat and stared at the television set unblinking, with his mouth open and in shock. 'Dave' cut to commercials and Sebastian put the TV on mute.

"It seems we have a problem," said the priest in an even tone.

John looked around at Sebastian. "No shit!" said John, sounding a little more excited than the priest. He ran a hand through his hair. "My God, these bastards move fast."

The priest looked severely at John and said, "Yes, well, they have been around for some time. I am sure they have picked up a few tricks along the way."

"If I try to call the District Attorney now, they will trace the call in no time and I'll be as good as dead. It will be hard to turn the tables on them now," said John with a sigh of resignation. "It's a good thing we checked the news before I made the call."

"Have courage, my son," said Sebastian with increased strength in his voice. "The Brotherhood is not the only organization that is well organized. I have a phone connected to a secure landline that we can use. I will convene a meeting with some of the key members of the Protectors and we will formulate a plan that will get us out of this. We must get to the Descendant!"

John looked at him closely. "You are one of the leaders of the Protectors of the Truth, aren't you?" he asked already knowing the answer.

"Yes, I am. And I'm also a direct descendant of Marius Sestus."

CHAPTER SEVEN
MARIELLA

Mariella Amaya stepped gingerly to the edge of the snow-covered cliff and looked out into the deep green valley below. The air cold, just above freezing, but a clear, sunny, December afternoon with only a hint of a breeze. She normally came to visit this spot early in the morning several times a week but for some unexplainable reason, drawn here today in the afternoon.

The view was exquisite.

Known as the 'Parco Nationale Della Majella,' the panoramic view looked across and up the barren snow-covered mountains bordering the miles long valley and the Orfento gorge of the Italian peninsula. The peaks of these mountains stretched so high into the atmosphere and above the tree line that they remain barren of any plant matter and covered with snow year round. Lower down these mountains, sporadic vegetation clung to the bare rock face below the snow line. At the halfway point, the walls literary became vertical and completely bare again. The exposed rock began as a band of grey about one hundred feet in vertical depth, suddenly turning into a tan, almost reddish hue, for several hundred more feet, before it ended at the beginning of a gentle slope covered with trees, ferns and fauna. Like God had used a large chisel to cut away enormous sections of the mountain, the exposed nerve of dual-colored bare rock travelled across the entire Valley in a uniform pattern on both sides. The gentle slope below this gash began with a light green that gradually changed to a deep hue, almost black color as it reached the Orfento gorge below.

Mariella loved to come to this spot whenever she could sneak away from the all too prying eyes of the monks from the 'Monastero Di Santo Pietro di Decontra,' a monastery outside the town of Decontra in the province of Abruzzi, Italy.

She had lived twenty of her twenty-four years in Decontra. Born in a remote town somewhere in the south of France, the family moved to when she turned four. Her uncle on her mother's side, now a monk at the monastery, had also migrated with them. The family never gave her a good reason why they moved to this small town, only that it had something to do with inheritance of some property but, given how remote and desolate this place was, it could not have been worth enough to justify the move. Nevertheless, here she was. Besides, she really had no clear memories of the other place in France.

Decontra was a tiny, traditional, single-church, village with rustic buildings perched at the lip of the gorge. Once a lively place, this dying village could now only boast a population of sixty-eight permanent inhabitants, Mariella included. Rumor had it that the first residents were outcasts from another nearby village. The law-abiding folks of that village forced the outcasts of this forgotten time to live up the steep hills. These unwanted were nicknamed the De Contro, Contraries as it translates in English, thus the village name of Decontra.

With the average age of the population at sixty-seven, Mariella's twenty-four years made her the youngest resident, and a shining jewel of the town. By any standards, Mariella was a beautiful young woman reminiscent of the Sophia Loren era. Many villagers often wondered if their lineage intersected in the recent past. She stood at five foot six with a very sensual, feminine build of which she seemed to be unaware. Not surprising since the town boasted little to no tourism, she seldom saw any men even close to her age. Her olive skin hinted at an ancestry derived from the Southern European people infused with Arabic blood during the Ottoman Empire conquests.

Mariella stood at the precipice of the gorge, clutching her woolen shawl tightly around her and marveled at the vista at her feet. The view presented a wondrous beauty to her senses but also a reminder of her loss. This vast and gaping maw within the earth took her parents and her younger, and only, brother. The road wound around the mountains, hugging the vertical rock wall on one side and looking out to a vast openness on the other. They may or may not have been going too fast on the downhill side of the road. No one really knew, but her father liked to turn the engine off and let the car coast down in order to safe fuel. They came around a bend and the road suddenly disappeared due to a very recent and unknown washout from the rains. They found the car and all three of the occupants at over four hundred feet down the cliff. All three killed instantly on impact.

Mariella had been in school that day.

The monks, one of them her uncle, took Mariella in and cared for her ever since.

She loved her uncle very much. Known as Brother Marco by all, to her, he remained Zio Marco, preferring to use the Italian version for uncle. The monk became the main force behind her development and education. Though all the monks loved her and equally shared in the day-to-day care giving, everyone considered Marco her guardian and her emotional guide.

Mariella's education continued well beyond high school level. At twenty-four, her daily routine not only consisted of medial chores to provide her with a sense of piety, but also several tutoring sessions. Throughout the years, they included a vast array of subjects such as psychology, world history, mathematics, physics, chemistry and several languages, which she had a particular talent for and became fluent in, such as English, French and Arabic. All in all a better education then most University post-graduates.

"There you are, Mariella," said a male voice in Italian-accented English behind her. "I thought you'd be here. The other brothers are worried sick about you."

Mariella slowly turned her head and saw her uncle walking towards her from out of the winding tree-lined path that hugged the edge of the gorge and eventually led back to the monastery. A portly figure with a rotund belly and pudgy cheeks, Brother Marco would have been a perfect shoe-in for Friar Tuck from the old pre-1950s Robin Hood movies. At five foot six, he stood at eye level with Mariella. His white, shiny face held an almost permanent smile when around his niece. Although only forty-nine years old, he preferred the old ways and his attire reflected such tastes. He wore a simple brown long-sleeved tunic that reached down to his ankles and held close to the waist with a rough hemp rope

"Hello, Zio Marco," Mariella replied in English with almost no hint of an accent and a smile on her face. They liked to talk in various languages, especially English. It made their conversations more private and good practice.

Mariella turned back to the vista while her uncle came up and stood next to her. They were facing south-west and, at this time of day, the sun just to their right and warming their faces.

"It is a wondrous sight," said Marco while his eyes drank in the panorama. "For me, it reaffirms the existence of God."

"Amen to that," said Mariella as she continued to stare out while hugging herself to keep out the cold.

"Let's go back," said Marco, after some time. "It will be dark soon."

She turned without a word and they walked up the path side by side.

Marco and Mariella reached the monastery within a few minutes. The Monastero Di Santo Pietro di Decontra held no exceptional history or architecture. The Cistern monks founded the monastery in the thirteenth century A.D. on land donated by a local count.

The two lone figures entered through the carriage entrance that held two large wooden doors made of simple but solid wooden planks with a small entrance cut into one of the carriage doors. The other three sides of the monastery held several windows overlooking the panoramic view of the valley. The ecclesiastical hall, the presbytery and the adjoining sacristy-chapel boasted arched ceilings with frescoes dating back to the original construction of the monastery. The thirty starkly simple and small dormitories, the kitchen and dining hall located on two floors in the outer wall facing the valley. The original builders used local rock as the basic building material for all of the walls and floors. The roof structures made of wooden beams and trusses from locally harvested trees and covered with traditional reddish terra cotta tiles. Through generous donations from the Sesti family, which Marco heavily influenced of course, they restored the monastery back to its original, though basic, glory. In just the last twenty years, they added electricity, plumbing, and even heating. All considered a real guilt ridden luxury for the monks in residence.

As they entered the great hall, Mariella turned to her uncle without meeting his gaze. "I want to go to the library and do some reading on my own, Zio Marco. I will see you at supper." She turned to go without waiting for a response, a sign that she wanted to be alone.

She cut across the ecclesiastical hall to an arched doorway leading to a large library covered from floor to ceiling with shelves upon shelves of ancient manuscripts, volumes and illuminated works. Leaded glass windows strewn across three sides of the upper most part of the forty-foot high walls allowed direct sunlight to penetrate the room and provided ample light for the readers during the day. The sunlight also warmed the room to a comfortable temperature during the winter months that lasted through the late evening hours. Dust mites danced in the sunbeams, the light currents of air created a random but intricate dance between these snowflake-like inanimate creatures. The place considered a comforting, almost maternal, place to Mariella.

Three monks were the sole occupants of the library when she walked in. Two librarians were restacking a large number of books and causing most of the dust in the air. The third, Brother Pio, pouring over some large book with a tattered leather cover and yellowish paper frayed at the edges. All three briefly looked up and smiled a greeting to Mariella as she walked in. She knew all three well, just like all of the seventeen monks in the monastery. In a way, she considered Zio Marco her father figure and the other sixteen monks her Uncles.

Mariella regularly spent time in this room. Apart from her meditative visits to the valley, she considered the library her other favorite place. Spending many a day with her face buried in any one of a countless number of written works housed in this library. Mariella felt at home in this large cavernous room with the smell of decaying paper and leather, the warmth from the rays of the sun and the view of rows upon rows of books. It all gave her a sense of comfort, of familiarity, and she never felt alone with the ever-present and active monks going about their own work or activities. They all made her feel welcome and part of the large 'family' of the monastery.

Mariella knew most of the ancient written languages of these old documents. Old English, Latin, and Greek were not a problem for her. She even managed old Hebrew quite effectively. Her skills even surpassed many of the monks at the monastery. The documents not only gave her insights into the major religious events of ancient times but also to the everyday life of those olden days that held such fascination for her.

Mariella picked up a book familiar to her and sat down at one of the several empty tables strewn across the library. She opened the book and began to read superficially and will little concentration. She had come here for the soothing effect of the place rather than to read. She felt restless, almost a yearning. Over the last several months, a somewhat alien feeling began to rise up inside her. A primeval desire, or lust, not for just any man, but for a specific man invading her dreams at night. A man standing at a distance, shrouded in a grey mist obscuring his face, a man with an animal magnetism emanating from his very fiber, a masculine desire directed at her. He would open his arms to her as if pleading for her to come to him. Which she tried but the faster she ran to him, the farther away he seemed until eventually the ever-present mist swallowed him up. Lately, she had been having the dream almost every night. Mariella would wake up in a sweat and with a burning sensation deep in her loins. She'd curl up and try to get back to sleep which took some considerable time. Mariella felt this man as the one for her, her love, her soul mate, the one she had been waiting for to make her whole again, something she had not felt since her family died. How it seemed possible, she did not know. Mariella only knew it to be true, and she would meet him soon. Of that, she felt certain. In the meantime, Mariella would dream of him when she slept and thought of him when awake.

Mariella was deep within her daydream when an alien sound reached in and caught her attention. She heard automatic gunfire, about a dozen rapid-fire shots, from somewhere in the Monastery. She remained seated in front of her book and tried to listen for more gunfire to confirm what she had just heard when suddenly one of the monks in the library, Brother Pio, moved so quickly that he seemed to materialize at her side. With surprising strength and without saying a word he grabbed her by both arms, lifted her off the bench and quickly guided, almost dragged her, out of the library. Her feet barely touched the ground. The two Librarian monks remained standing in a stunned stupor as Mariella and Pio quickly crossed the archway separating the library from the hall and headed for the kitchen.

"Brother Pio, what are you doing?" she finally asked breathlessly. "And what was that shooting?" He still held her firmly with his arms around her shoulders.

"Please, Mariella, just come along," he said gently but the tremor in his voice betrayed his calm demeanor. "I will explain later."

Mariella obeyed and let him lead her. She trusted him implicitly. They entered the kitchen where she saw another monk already there waiting for them. With a shock Mariella saw him holding not just one but two black sub-machine guns. One in each hand and facing the opposite entrance to the kitchen, as if guarding it. She barely comprehended the sight. A man in full friar outfit holding a fully automated weapon in each hand. It looked almost comical.

"My God, Brother Nicola!" exclaimed Mariella wide eyed. "Where did you get those?"

Nicola looked back at her, smiled and said, "To protect you, cara mia."

He threw one of the guns to Pio who checked and loaded it just as expertly. Just then, her uncle ran in. "Quickly now!" he said after briefly looking Mariella over for any sign of injury.

Marco ran to the pantry, opened the door and walked in. Pushing aside two large sacks of potatoes, he reached down to the floor and pulled off a small wooden plank. He pulled up on a handle. Invisible until then, a trap door lifted up on hidden hinges. Pio guided the ever more shocked Mariella into the pantry towards Marco. Mariella did not know the trap door existed. She thought she knew every nook and cranny of the monastery. She thought wrong.

Marco turned around and held out his hand to Mariella. She took it and he led her down dust covered wooden stairs and into total darkness as they got beyond the light emanating from the kitchen above. The mixed smell of damp earth and moldy wood rose up from the darkness. At the bottom of the twenty odd steps, Marco switched on a small electric lantern he found hanging on a nail on one of the wooden pillars and held it up to light their way. The trap door above closed without anyone else following. They could hear the sacks of potatoes dragged across the floor and back over the trap door, concealing it once again. They also heard footsteps leading out of the pantry area and the kitchen.

Mariella and Marco were alone.

From the glow of the lantern, Mariella could just able to make out the room; about twenty-feet square with a ten-foot ceiling, the stairs they just came down in at the center of the room and the floor made of packed dirt. It appeared to be an old cold storage room used to house perishable food before refrigerators came into use. The room did not look like it had been in use for some time. It merely held a few dust covered but otherwise barren wooden shelves on one wall and a small pile of planks from what appeared to be fallen shelves in another corner.

"We must be very quiet now, Mariella," whispered her uncle.

"What happened, Zio? Is it a terrorist group? Thieves?" asked Mariella ignoring his request.

Just then, they heard more gunfire and indistinct yelling. Marco grasped Mariella's hand and signaled her to be quiet. He turned off the light. Running footsteps of several men pounded across the floor and stopped in the kitchen. Someone opened the pantry door above and took a few steps inside.

"No one here," said a muffled male voice that Mariella and Marco did not recognize.

The door closed again. The voices and footsteps receded out of the kitchen. Mariella took her first breath since she heard those first steps in the kitchen. Her uncle turned the lantern back on and headed for the pile of wooden planks. He carefully and silently moved them to one side revealing a small wooden door in the wall. He pulled on a latch invisible to Mariella and slowly opened the door, trying to keep the squealing of the rusted hinges to a minimum.

"I always meant to oil those," he said to no one. He reached into the darkness to one side and flipped a switch. A dim light emanating from deep below betrayed a set of circular stone stairs.

"Follow closely," he said to Mariella.

Marco quietly closed the door behind them and led the way down. The staircase wound around the wall of the deep shaft about ten feet in diameter with lights to guide their way set in the walls at set intervals. Above, Mariella could hear gunfire and several muffed explosions. She looked down the center of the shaft but, despite the light, she could not see the bottom.

"Where are we going?" asked Mariella in a hoarse whisper.

"This is an escape route from the monastery," answered her uncle. "It has been here since its construction. Only a few of the monks know about it. It extends down to the bottom of the gorge about five hundred feet."

"What's happening upstairs, Zio Marco?" Mariella asked. "You must tell me."

"They are here for you," he said without stopping.

"For me? For what and why?"

"That is a long story, Mariella. I will explain later. For now, just believe me that we must escape for your sake and for everyone else's."

She grabbed him by the sleeve and yanked him to a stop. "That's not good enough, Zio," she said in a harsh voice. "Tell me what's happening."

"I can't. Not now." He tried to continue down the stairs.

Mariella pulled even harder, preventing him from continuing and almost making him loose his balance. She stared coldly and said, "No! Tell me now!"

"Mariella, please be patient. Now is not the time. If you want to live, please follow me," his eyes pleading. Mariella looked at him and saw his concern and sincerity. She slowly released the grip. His face showed relief as he again continued down the stairs.

Mariella followed quietly

●●●

Gabriel's intense green eyes scanned the scene below him. Dressed in his traditional black suit and overcoat and with his trademark short orange hair, it made him appear strangely imposing and slightly comical at the same time. Standing at the top of the stairs of the dormitory floor, he had a commanding view into the ecclesiastical hall. Strewn across the stone floor of the hall were the blood-splattered bodies of several monks as well as some of his men. Gabriel and his men had successfully killed sixteen of the seventeen monks stationed here, but he paid a heavy price for it. Twenty-one of his twenty-four men lay dead or dying somewhere in the monastery. To make matters worse, the woman with the mark continued to elude them. Gabriel assumed she hid somewhere in the monastery with the help of the last living monk, according to his count of the bodies.

The first inhabitants of the monastery built it as a virtual fortress but Gabriel managed to get half of his men on the roof and rope down and through the outside windows of the dormitories while he and the rest of the men stormed through both the carriage and pedestrian entrances.

Not all of the monks were the evil Protectors, thought Gabriel. He could see that by how surprised some of them were before his men cut them down. He felt some regret but thought he had no choice in the killing of the innocent monks. They were part of the sacrifice needed to keep the secrecy of his mission intact. That, along with the woman, remained all-important, he thought.

The Brotherhood of the Rapture attacked with the element of surprise but the Protectors mounted a defense with surprising speed. Gabriel assumed a coordinated and swift attack from above and below would improve their chances but the Protectors massed in the right locations and killed over half of his men before they could regroup, but once they were in, it was only a matter of time. Within a few minutes, the monks were low in ammunition and cornered in two areas: two men trapped in the dormitories and four in the kitchen.

Gabriel and his men lobbed several hand grenades where the monks were hiding, followed by his men firing as they ran in. As soon as all seemed clear, his men scoured the monastery as quickly as possible.

Gabriel had to find and kill the woman! He needed survivors to force from them her hiding place. He should have thought of that before they killed without discrimination, he thought. The first of his three surviving men came out to the hall from the Library.

"Anything, Jonathan?" Gabriel asked loudly from his perch.

"No survivors or sign of the demon woman and the last monk," replied the tall, muscular, blonde man.

Another of Gabriel's men came out of the kitchen. "No one alive in there," he reported.

The third, and the last, man, a tall dark Jamaican, came up from behind Gabriel on the stairs. "They're all dead back there, too. No sign of the woman."

"Did you check per protocol?" Gabriel asked.

"Yes, sir. Each one," he replied.

Gabriel walked down the stairs and stood among the dead in the hall, now his turn to follow the protocol as he asked from the others. Gabriel approached each of the seemingly dead monks, rolled them over on their backs, and put a bullet in their belly. If they did not stir, he fired a bullet in their head just to ensure they were dead. If the belly wound solicited a movement, he would interrogate the man on the woman's whereabouts. None moved. All received the coup de grace. Gabriel's own men, lying dead or wounded, also received the final death bullet. Without asking, his three surviving men did likewise for their wounded or dead comrades in the other rooms. They could not afford any survivors that might talk.

"Torch the place," ordered Gabriel after they had checked every body.

His three men ran out the front carriage entrance and came back with several canisters of gasoline. One went upstairs to the dormitories while the other two spread out on the main floor.

They soaked everything combustible ensuring the fire would reach the wooden rafters. The resulting collapsed roof inflicting maximum damage.

While his men continued with the preparations, Gabriel reached for his phone and dialed.

"Yes?" came the reply after the first ring.

"She got away with one survivor, Master," said Gabriel without a greeting.

"I am disappointed in you, Gabriel," said the male voice in a flat tone without emotion.

"I am sorry, Master. I will pass my command to the next in line and leave my fate to his and your hands," said Gabriel also in a monotone, almost practiced, voice.

"No, Gabriel. That is not required," the phone replied without hesitation. "Check with the roadblocks. It is unlikely they are hiding anywhere nearby. They are probably trying to escape as we speak. Call me when you get to the first roadblock."

Gabriel hung up and headed outside through the Carriage entrance. He got into one of the four vehicles they had hid behind a rise next to the road nearby. He crashed it through the carriage doors and into the hall, running over several bodies as he did so. He and one of his surviving men retrieved two more of the cars and drove them into the hall with the same indifference to the bodies strewn about. All four men walked out to the entrance and turned around looking back at the devastation they had caused. Gabriel pulled out a flare and lit it with a lighter from his pocket. He threw it towards a pile of gasoline soaked chairs.

The fire already burned greedily through the rafters as they drove through town in the last remaining vehicle. They were out of the town proper in just a few seconds and long before the villagers noticed the fire.

•••

After what seemed an eternity, Mariella and her uncle made their way to the bottom of the shaft and to a low arched entranceway, her legs weak from the long descent. Ducking to prevent hitting their heads on the low ceiling, they walked down the dark winding tunnel for another fifty feet. The still illuminated lantern now guided the way to another wooden door of the same size as the tunnel. Marco pushed and it gave way. A few paces away she could see light penetrating through roots and branches. After closing the door, the monk pushed the brambles aside, making an opening just wide enough for them to get through. He led the way and Mariella followed.

Once outside, Mariella looked up. They were at the bottom of the gorge. Now late in the afternoon they stood in shadow. The air felt cool but not as cold as at the exposed ridge from earlier that day. The base of the gorge extended out thirty feet wide and they walked south upon a worn path on one side.

She suddenly recognized where they were, the gorge Dell'Orfento. At various intervals, the path wove under the valley wall acting like a half dome above their heads. Over thousands of years, the rushing waters of a now dried up river carved out the rock like a spoon carving a gouge out of the side of a brick of soft butter. Mariella and Marco continued down the path without a word between them.

Marco suddenly turned off the path and towards thick brush on the far wall of the gorge. He parted some branches and disappeared into the bush. Mariella raised her eyebrows in surprise, no trace of his entry evident. His right arm shot out with palm up, an indication for her to take it and follow through a large crack in the rock. She held onto his hand as he led her through the darkness. After only a few feet, the crack opened up further. As the monk relit the lantern, Mariella saw that they were in a large cavern at least a hundred feet wide from left to right and the front stretching out into the darkness. The ceiling arched irregularly upwards at least fifty feet high.

In the middle of the cavern, a heavy tarp covered what appeared to be a car. Marco pulled the tarp aside and revealed a BMW sports sedan. He went to the trunk and pulled out a duffle bag that held a pair of jeans, shirt, leather bomber jacket and running shoes. Mariella looked away as her uncle changed.

"Get in," said Marco as he got into the driver seat.

Mariella closed the passenger door just as he started the car. They drove to the other end of the tunnel to another crack in the wall. She looked at her uncle and calmly inquired without expecting an answer, "Why am I not surprised that the clothes fit? Looks like you planned this all out."

Marco glanced sideways at her but remained silent.

There is more to this man than I have ever imaged, Mariella thought. When we finally get a chance to talk, he will have to make it good.

The walls closed in to no more than a foot of space on each side of the car and she could not see where the two walls came together above. Marco glanced over and saw the look on her face. Her hands, like claws on the armrests. "Don't worry," he said with a slight humorless smile. "I am very familiar with this tunnel."

"I am sure you are," she said, eyes locked on the view in front.

"We will be out of it soon enough," he said.

They continued down the tunnel for several minutes, only the headlamps of the car guiding their way. Marco slowed down before the gate became visible. He knew the route well. Stopping a few feet from it, he crawled out of the front window, the walls too narrow for him to open the door.

The gate opened out away from them and Mariella saw that branches again covered the path ahead. Her uncle went up to the foliage and pushed the branches aside making just enough room for the car.

Outside, the day began to wane.

Marco came back, got into the driver's seat and drove out into the open air. He stopped the car again just beyond the brush, got out, closed the wooden gate and replaced the branches back, covering the way once again. He got back in the car and followed the dirt road at breakneck speed, heading roughly north. About a half mile through the winding path, they came to a paved road. It soon led to the highway and a smoother ride.

Mariella looked at her uncle once her nerves settled down. She no longer saw the meek monk from the Monastery. He now looked like someone dangerous – not to her but to anyone standing in his way. He remained Zio Marco to her eyes but no longer a monk.

Mariella smiled a little as he drove the car skillfully through the winding road looking like a getaway driver for someone in the mob. Who knows, she thought. Maybe that's what this was all about after all. She would find out soon enough. She would make certain of that.

They headed east as the sun began to set.

LAST DESCENDANT

•••

Gabriel had placed two roadblocks, about a half mile apart, on the only road out of Decontra. They were in place before his assault team had arrived at the monastery. Gabriel, sitting shotgun, ordered the driver to stop at the first one. Four of the six men stationed there dressed as government road workers while two as police officers to stop traffic, one in each direction. Gabriel got out and approached one of the men in worker uniforms.

"Anything?" asked Gabriel looking around.

"Nothing at all," said the man. "We saw only three cars since we set-up, all heading out of town: two cars with only the drivers, both male, the third car with two elderly men, all locals we have on our list. The other roadblock reported the same. Nobody from the monastery got by us. Did you get her?"

"No. She got away," said Gabriel looking around. "She has one of the Protectors with her. It looks like they had another escape route."

"What next?" asked the man looking at Gabriel. When their eyes met, it sent a chill through the man's heart and he looked away uncertainly.

"Stick around for another hour. Call me if you see anything unusual," said Gabriel.

"Yes, sir," said the leader.

Gabriel walked out of earshot, took out his phone and dialed. "Looks like they didn't try to go through the roadblocks, Master. They must have used some kind of alternate escape route."

"Keep looking, Gabriel," said the Master. "Especially near the monastery. They couldn't have gotten far."

Gabriel did as told without question, such was his devotion. He would gladly have given his life for the Master. When in the presence of the Master, he felt only intense love and devotion. Gabriel loved the Master like no other, not a sexual love, but a love transcending the flesh. Gabriel felt that the Master knew this and was pleased and why the Master gave him the most important task of the Brotherhood: the task of finding and killing the last of the evil descendants of Judah. After completing this final task, the Rapture and Armageddon would happen, just as written.

This responsibility given to him showed how much the Master loved him and trusted him. It made him want to serve the Master even more.

He got back in the car and ordered the driver to proceed to the next roadblock. His phone began to ring. He had it to his ear before the second ring. "Yes, Master," he said.

"Gabriel, I have placed Zaneer in charge of the situation there in Italy. Go immediately to the private plane. I need you back in the U.S. as soon as possible. The pilot already has his instructions."

"As you command," said Gabriel. He hung up only after he heard the click from the line disconnecting on the other end.

Gabriel instructed the driver to head for the airport and they were airborne within the hour.

•••

The day turned to night by the time Mariella and Marco had reached the Adriatic Sea on the east coast and headed south. Not long, they reached an old marina with a single streetlight near its entrance. The gate leaned open and seen better days. Marco drove slowly down the drive, the headlights guiding their way. After a few hundred yards, he stopped short of one of the piers.

Marco reached across to the glove compartment and pulled out a police issue flashlight. When he shut off the car, the darkness closed in around them.

"This way, Mariella," said Marco switching on the flashlight.

He got out and slowly headed out onto the pier. Mariella followed closely behind, her uncle constantly glancing back to check on her.

They soon reached a white and blue modern cruiser about thirty feet long, moored near the end of the pier. Marco gingerly jumped on board and swung around to help Mariella. He flashed the light down at her feet and showed her where to step. Holding her hand, she got onboard.

"This way," said Marco. He opened the door to the wheelhouse and entered inside followed by Mariella.

Marco went to the cockpit and began flipping switches like a seasoned captain. He soon had the engine started and went outside to untie the mooring lines and push away from the pier. He came back in, engaged the drive to the propeller, and slowly revved up the motor. Soon the vessel moved away from the pier and out to sea. With the exception of the glowing dash lights, all other lights, in and out of the boat, remained off. When he got approximately a half mile out, he turned right and headed south. Only then did he turn on all the running lights and the internal cabin lights in the wheelhouse and below deck.

Their destination was Malta, the small island nation south of Sicily where a member of the Protectors waited for them, preparing the safe house. Marco still kept his cell phone powered off to avoid detection, turning it on only when within sight of his destination.

Mariella positioned herself behind the captain's seat and hung on to the backrest as her uncle steered the boat out to sea. Marco sailed visually blind and relied solely on radar and other instruments. He turned on the heat and the cabin began to get warm.

Mariella felt overwhelmed with everything that had happened that day. She sat down at the table and bench in the wheelhouse and tried to make sense of it all. That very afternoon she had been peacefully reading a book in the library. Now she and her uncle were in the middle of the Adriatic Sea running for their lives. The events, from the library to this very spot, ran like a well-choreographed movie script. Obvious to her that the escape route, the car and the boat, all planned in advance, and the monks, the men that she knew so well, all worked together without a word. Instead of pandemonium, they worked like a team.

Where were they now, she asked herself? Brother Pio, Brother Nicola, and all the others; were they dead?

She had known most of them since she had moved to Decontra. They were like her family. They *were* her family. And who did the shooting? She had also heard explosions. Were they bombs? She buried her face in her hands and closed her eyes. As strong as she was, she still felt the tears coming. Things were just too confusing, too horrible. Mariella looked at her uncle for any sign of an answer and the blood from her face drained out. She spotted a man standing at the bottom steps to the lower deck looking at her. She began to rise in panic when her uncle noticed her agitation.

"It's okay, Mariella," said Marco, reaching out to her while keeping a hand on the wheel. "He's a friend."

Though only slightly mollified, Mariella sat back down as the man walked up the stairs to the wheelhouse.

"Who is he, Zio?" asked Mariella, staring at the man now at the top of the stairs smiling down at her.

He looked about seventy years old, six feet tall and lanky with a hint of a paunch, dark skin, of African descent, with large black freckles at the top of his cheeks. His slightly receding peppery hair kept about one inch in length and brushed back. The eyes looked kind and made his smile look sincere. His dressed normal for this location and time of year with jeans, boots, and a dark brown, almost black, leather jacket over a grey turtleneck sweater.

"His name is Jonathan Koite," said her Uncle as he continued to guide the vessel through the dark night. "I have known him for many years. I trust him implicitly."

During the introduction, Jonathan had briefly glanced at Marco but quickly looked back at Mariella.

"Hello, Mariella," said Jonathan in a baritone voice and with perfect English. He had not moved from the top of the stairs. "It is indeed an honor and a pleasure to finally meet you in person."

"He will explain all about what happened today, and why it happened," said Marco. "He will tell you some things that you will find hard to believe, but he will tell you the truth. He will tell you about an organization that is almost two thousand years old, an organization that he is a senior member of and that I also belong to."

Mariella had looked at her uncle as he made his little dramatic speech. She now looked back at the man standing next to him.

"May I sit down?" asked Jonathan with a slight bow of reverence.

Mariella motioned him to the bench across from her without a word.

"Thank-you," he said.

Jonathan Koite gingerly sat down at the small table. His hands together in front of him, fingers interlaced.

"Your uncle is correct," he said. "The tale is extraordinary, and it involves you."

While Marco piloted the boat, Jonathan told Mariella about her lineage to Judah. He told her about the Protectors of the Truth and their role within her family. He told her about The Brotherhood of the Rapture but he left out a crucial part, he left out her family's destiny and the final birth, the Second Coming, and the date of the event. Jonathan told her only about her lineage. He let her assume that The Brotherhood of the Rapture wanted her family dead because of Judah's role in the death of Jesus.

About the Second Coming, that would have to wait for another time.

CHAPTER EIGHT
ESCAPE

Father Sebastian began making telephone calls as John Bernard lit another cigarette

The priest had just told John that the Protectors had to move to the next stage of their plans; find Mariella, the last Descendant, and make sure she was safe and stayed that way for the second coming. They were so close, he had said. Only one more year left. The Protectors of the Truth had to consolidate their numbers, he added, and surround the Descendant in a cocoon of safety, but first they had to get to her.

The priest had also confessed that he lied to John when he said he didn't know the location of the Descendant. He did not want to take any chances with such important knowledge on someone he hardly knew so he kept it to himself until now.

John saw the concern on Sebastian's face when, after the third of a dozen numbers he had did not answer.

"The lines are all supposed to be manned 7/24," said the Priest. "Something is wrong."

He continued down the list of the twelve numbers he had memorized a long time ago. He had success with the seventh.

"This is....David, who....is....calling?" whispered the tenor male voice riddled with pain.

Sebastian held the phone out for both he a John to hear. "David. This is Sebastian. Sebastian Sesti. What has happened?"

"It is good to hear... your voice, Senior," said David with renewed energy when he heard Sebastian's voice. "We were attacked yesterday.

We….managed to hear from….the team in Iceland soon after. They were also….attacked at the same time. A coordinated attack….by the Bro…..» Multiple gunfire cut off his words.

"David! What's happening?" asked Sebastian.

"Only two of us….left. We are again under….heavy fire. Senior, you must protect her. Most of the others….are dead. You must not let them find….her. They say they know wh…." A single shot rang out at what sounded like close range. The phone clanged as if dropped on the floor. Sounds of steps and then a new male voice came on.

"Hello! Who is this?" said a deep, authoritative voice.

Sebastian quietly hung up the phone as the voice began to repeat the question.

"My God!" said the priest staring out into space after he hung up the phone.

"What happened?" asked John anxiously. "What's going on?"

"They have attacked the other cells. The Brotherhood, they have attacked all our teams," said Sebastian as he stood up. "Yesterday, when we were ambushed at the church, it was not an isolated case but a coordinated effort on a global scale."

"All of them? How many are there?" asked John.

"Once all of the North American teams were killed, we had only twelve left, one of them the real one, of course." Answered Sebastian as he began to pace. He pointed at the phone. "That last one was the seventh team that I tried. The first six didn't answer, and the lines are supposed to always be manned." He sat back down quickly next to the phone. "I must try the last five."

He began to dial. None answered. Not even the team guarding Mariella. Sebastian slowly put the phone down, eyes downcast. "No one has answered," he began. "But this may not mean that the Descendant is dead. Chances are, the eleven teams guarding the fakes have been destroyed, or at least compromised. But the team with the true Descendant could be following the emergency protocol which is to get to a safe house." He looked up at John. "John, it is time for plan B."

"You have a plan B?" asked John without humor.

"I don't know where the safe house is," began Sebastian. "But I know how to find out." He squared up his shoulders and said, "John, we are going to Italy."

John started to smile sarcastically, "Sure. Let's just stop by my apartment to get my passport on the way to the airport. I'm sure we would just breeze through security. After all, I'm only wanted for multiple homicides."

Sebastian looked at John, smiled back and said, "Give me credit enough to know how to deal with those types of logistics."

"And how would you do that?" said John doubtfully.

Sebastian picked up the phone once again and began to dial as he replied, "Don't worry about that. Go check the rooms upstairs for some change of clothes, there should be some that'll fit you. I will make some calls and I'll come right up to find some for myself." He still wore his priest outfit from the night before.

A few minutes later, they were both upstairs searching through the rooms. The closets had an assortment of clothes of various sizes. Obvious to John that someone had done some careful planning.

Sebastian had made a call to an international shipping company that flew planes out of New York's La Guardia. A member of the Protectors owned the company, explained Sebastian. This member would sneak them on a freight plane scheduled to leave for Rome that evening. At the other end, a car would be waiting for them. It would take four to five hours from there to get to a city called Pescara on the east coast.

"And what will we find at this city of Pescara?" asked John.

"That's close to where the real Descendant has been living for the last several years," began the priest. "Her name is Mariella, or Mariel, in honor of the wife of Judah. You may recall the name in the ancient journal."

John looked at the priest. "So the cycle would come full circle," he said. Then added, "And would she have a virgin birth as well?" He regretted the comment as soon as he said it.

Sebastian looked at John with a slight smile while checking the size of a couple of pair of pants. "You're lucky I have a sense of humor, John," he said. "No. It's not what's expected. She's to choose a mate, a husband before then, but we cannot tell her the destiny that awaits her or when the event is to occur. She will be told about her lineage back to Judah and that some people are trying to kill her because of it, and that we are protecting her, but we are not to tell her that she will be the mother of the Messiah's second coming." The priest dropped the pants on the bed and looked at John. "That will have to happen by God's will alone," he said.

"Then you and your brethren have a lot of faith. For that is a big assumption that you are making," said John.

Sebastian did not reply.

"What if she does not choose a mate, as you put it, and not have a child?" asked John. "What then?"

"Only God knows His plan," said the priest. "We are mere mortals and can only do as we are guided."

John remained skeptical.

"Have faith, my son," said Sebastian, reverting to his priestly ways.

"Yah, have faith," said John as he found a shirt his size. "All I know is that there are several women who have been killed by a fanatical religious organization that some of my colleagues are involved with and are now trying to kill me. You have also told me about many battles across the globe, all resulting in many deaths. And finally, we know of one more woman that's targeted and we will be going on a wild goose chase looking for her before they find and kill her first." John put on the shirt as he finished his rant. He seemed satisfied with how it fit. "As far as faith is concerned," John added, "that remains to be seen."

"At least that's not a prerequisite for helping out," added Sebastian with a slight smile.

"No it's not," said John without smiling back. "I am merely acting on instinct, and training."

"That's all I can ask for," responded the priest still smiling, "but be on your guard, I may make a true believer out of you yet."

John did not answer.

Sebastian had found clothes that he liked.

The priest made them some sandwiches for lunch before they headed out. John sat at one of the bar stools in front of the raised kitchen counter eating his sandwich while Sebastian made another for himself.

Sebastian finished explaining to John the details of their flight to Italy. Their route would take them on I87 south to New York and straight to La Guardia. The trip by car would take roughly five hours and provide them with plenty of time before the plane took off. They would hide in the plane when they arrived rather than wonder around the city or the airport and risk getting spotted, all too easy to do with the large increase in cameras around the cities and public areas, such as airports, since the 2001 terrorist attacks. Even with hats, the facial recognition software would spot them without too much trouble. "We will go straight to the plane and hide there until take off," said the priest.

"This is your game, Father," said John. "I'll follow the play you call as best I can."

John took another bite of his sandwich when they heard an explosion outside the front of the chalet. He dropped the sandwich, dove across the counter, and dropped down below the countertop. He found Sebastian crouched nearby. The priest reached in one of the bottom cabinets and came out with a shotgun and several shells. He also pulled out two grenades. He handed one to John, pocketed the other and then loaded the shotgun with the shells.

"We made as many contingency plans as we could think of when we built and furnished this place," said the priest after noticing John's reaction towards the cache weapons.

"I can see that," responded John and added, "The glass of the front windows did not shatter. I assume they are bullet proof?"

Just then, a spray of automatic gunfire hit the large windows near the kitchen, the bullets leaving white smudge marks on the glass but it remained intact.

"Scratch the last question, Father," began John. "I just got my answer."

"It's daylight and the lights are off," said Sebastian. "The glass is reflective on the outside which makes it impossible for someone out there to see in, the burst of gunfire on the windows just a shot in the dark, so to speak."

John ran out from behind the counter and towards the fireplace to get a direct view of the car they drove in last night. What he saw barely looked familiar, the trunk, hood and wheels, blown off. The rest engulfed in flames. "Looks like they blew up my car," he said.

Automatic gunfire then hit the front door. They could hear wood splintering, but the bullet did not penetrate inside. A second burst hit the door again, the bullets bounced off metal. John looked at the priest with a curious look on his face. The priest, crouched behind the fireplace with the shotgun in his hands, saw the look.

"The core of the door is half inch steel," said the priest. "This is a virtual fortress. All the windows are bullet proof and the doors steel reinforced." He sneaked back behind the counter and next to John.

They heard more automated gunfire outside aimed at other areas of the building.

"We should be safe for a few minutes," said Sebastian. "But what I would like to know, is how the hell they found us."

"We'll figure that out later, if we're still alive," said John. "Got any other rabbits in your hat, Father?" It surprised John at how little fear he felt. Now that he thought of it, he felt no fear at all, just a slight adrenaline rush but none of the primal urge to flee, to escape the danger. The panic that people describe coming from deep within ones stomach did not rise within him. He felt enough confidence to get out of this, even without a plan. No, more than that, he knew he would get out of it. How strange, he thought.

"Yah, I do," Sebastian replied. "First we gotta find out how many there are, and where."

The priest got to his feet but still crouched low as if not trusting the strength of the windows and doors completely.

"I am going to go upstairs and see what I can find out from a higher vantage point," began Sebastian, looking at the ceiling. "You go around the first floor windows and try to see how many there are from down here." He quickly headed for the stairs without waiting for a reply.

Gunfire continued hitting the Chalet in various locations but none breached the walls.

Moments later, they regrouped behind the staircase.

"All right," began Sebastian breathlessly. "I saw thirteen of them: five in the front, where they suspect we will come out, four to the right and four on the left. They are usually in groups of sixteen so there are three more that I did not see."

"I only saw three," said John.

"They are hiding in the tall grass and you can't see them from the ground floor," explained Sebastian.

"Your organization has trained you well, Father," said John with new admiration.

"All in the name of the survival of mankind," responded the priest. The sporadic shooting had stopped in the last couple of minutes. "Looks like I am going to impress you some more," said Sebastian as he made his way to the small den near the staircase. "Quickly, John, they will storm the house any minute now!"

The den had a single window opposite the door with a desk and chair to one side and a simple bookshelf on the other.

Sebastian went to the bookshelf and reached behind a book on the second top most shelf. He pressed a switch and the entire bookshelf swung silently towards them. The lights came on as the bookshelf stopped opening. The opening revealed a minivan in a room just big enough for it and nothing else.

"Get in the passenger seat," ordered Sebastian as John stared in wonder. Sebastian's authoritative voice broke the spell.

The priest got in after John and into the driver's seat. With a key already in the ignition, Sebastian handed the shotgun to John.

"Now pay attention because this is going to happen fast," the priest began as he reached over and flipped open the glove compartment facing the detective. A panel with a set of seven switches appeared.

"These switches in front of you remotely control detonators connected to several explosives placed in specific location in and around the chalet. When I say 'switch one now' you are going to flip the first switch from the left. When I say 'switch two now,' you are going to flip the next switch, and so on, but only when I say so and not before or after. Got it?"

"Got it," answered John.

"Now, when I start the van, the wall in front of us will lift up quickly and we are going to make a run for it. The explosions will make enough damage and confusion that will increase our chances of making it out of here alive. The van and wheels are also bullet proof, but I will need you to keep an eye out for any of the men out there that try to stop us and, since you're armed, do what you have to do."

John nodded in confirmation.

"You ready?" asked Sebastian, placing his left hand on the wheel and the other on the key in the ignition.

"Ready," said John.

"Ok," began the priest as he crossed himself. "Switch one now!"

John flipped the first switch.

Outside, a set of at least two dozen explosives went off in a circle around the chalet about fifty feet away. The simultaneous explosives were of two kinds: one type, smoke screens, and the second, fragmentation land mines that sprang up at four feet in the air and exploded metal shards or nails up to two hundred feet. They heard screams as the devices hit their mark.

Sebastian turned the ignition on and started the engine. The wall in front of them flipped up quickly. Sebastian floored the gas pedal and the van leaped outside into white smoke. He drove blind as he kept the van in a straight line.

They heard automatic fire from their left.

"Switch two now!" the priest yelled.

John hit the second switch.

A huge yellowish white light flared behind them and the sound of the explosion hit a fraction of a second later. As the shock wave hit the back of the van, the rear lurched up and quickly came down on the dirt. The van swayed but Sebastian kept it going in the same general direction. Where the chalet once stood, a small mushroom cloud started to rise.

"Switch three now!" came the third command.

Five small explosions in a row detonated on each side of the van about fifty feet away. Exploding shards blanketed the area. Shrapnel hit their mark as they heard more screams from falling men.

"Switch four now!" the priest yelled and another set of explosions appeared on each side further up the path they were following. The bombs were acting like protective tunnels as they raced for the brush up ahead. They were not on the original path that they drove on the night before but headed for an impenetrable wall of trees two hundred feet away.

"Do you know where you're going?" asked John.

"Just keep your eyes open," said the priest.

"Switch five now!"

Another set of explosions on each side. They heard no screams this time. Nor did they hear any gunfire. They were now less than one hundred feet from the trees and closing fast.

"Switch six now!"

John hit the sixth switch.

The explosion blew the trees apart, but the blast made the trees fall away from the newly created path, and the van raced for it. An opening appeared where thick brush grew only a moment before. As expected, Sebastian saw that the blast created a crater in the same spot. The van leaped in the air as it hit a dirt ramp just before the blast area. It flew over the crater and came down hard on its four wheels on the other side. They were outside the row of protective trees that surrounded the now destroyed chalet.

"Switch seven now!"

John flipped the last switch

•••

Captain David Westell and Lieutenant Nick Mancuso were sitting in an unmarked police car blocking the path through the trees to the chalet before the first explosion that destroyed John's car. If the priest and John tried to make a break for it, this looked like the most likely path, thought Westell. They saw no other route out.

Their car faced the chalet and commanded a clear view of the entire area. According to their watches, the bomb placed under John's car by one of the Brothers was to go off anytime now. The two men waited patiently.

Westell looked around. All the men in the team of The Brotherhood of the Rapture assigned to assassinate Sebastian and Detective John Bernard were in position. They were to attack as soon as the car blew up. These were his true comrades in arms, thought Westell with pride. They included Mancuso sitting next to him in the passenger seat, comrades not only in arms, but also in life and death.

Westell and Mancuso came from the same training as Gabriel. Their life, dedicated to the cause, but their skills were not the same as the assassins out in the field. Though he and Mancuso trained in the art of war and close combat, they were to serve The Brotherhood among the civilian population. Both Westell and Mancuso applied to the Boston police academy and slowly moved up the ranks, Westell actually making Captain.

Westell saw John's car explode and then heard it a fraction of a second later. Both he and Mancuso cocked their handguns and got ready for any escape attempt. What happened next took him by surprise. A ring of explosions went off around the chalet. Eight of his comrades were in close proximity of the blasts. Westell saw body parts fly in all directions and he could only watch in disbelief. As the ring of smoke from the blast expanded slowly outwards across the field, a van suddenly flew out from the wall of smoke and into the clearing. It sped towards the right and away from where Westell and Mancuso blocked the path. Some of the surviving attackers were regrouping and running towards the van, firing their weapons. A second later, a huge blast erupted from the chalet, sending debris everywhere. A plume of smoke began to rise up in the air, the chalet completely obliterated.

Westell and Mancuso remained in their car staring, mouths open, in shock at the devastation going on in front of them. A series of explosions began to occur alongside the van like a protective shield as it sped towards the wall of trees. The men racing after the vehicle cut down by shrapnel. Finally, Westell came out of his stupor and began to scramble out of the car. Mancuso, triggered into action by Westell's movements, did likewise on the other side. They began firing at the speeding van but neither one hitting their mark. They saw another explosion create an opening in the wall of trees. The van flew towards the opening and jumped through to the other side.

Captain David Westell and Lieutenant Nick Mancuso were turning to get back in their car when the ground around them suddenly heaved up violently. There were several pounds of explosives buried under the twenty-foot path between the trees exactly where the police car sat. The blast shredded the car completely. Metal shards flew in all directions. The two men turned into burned minced meat. When the dust settled, the largest body parts that remained weighed no more than a pound and scattered across more than two hundred feet

•••

John Bernard heard and saw the explosion demolish the path they used the night before, along with a car and two men standing alongside it. In the brief instant between looking at the men and the explosion, he thought the men looked familiar. He did not have more time to think about it, his attention drawn to a second and final explosion going off from where they had just leaped. The explosion destroyed the ramp they had just jumped and replaced it with another large crater. In the end, anyone inside the wall of trees had no chance to get through with any type of vehicle, short of a bulldozer.

Sebastian crossed himself again as they got onto the gravel road and headed back to the town of Somersville. John looked over at the priest. Sebastian no longer seemed so old and helpless.

"Father, you make most movie action heroes look amateurish," said John lightly with a slight smile.

In contrast, the priest responded in a serious tone. "We may not be in the clear yet. Keep your eyes open. We have a long drive." He quickly glanced over at John and added, "As misguided as they were, men have died today."

The statement did not need a response.

•••

Gabriel couldn't believe what had just happened. He had been watching the events unfold from the cover of the brush on the far side of the chalet. He did not think it necessary for him to assist.

He was wrong.

For the second time in two days, he underestimated his enemy. All but two of his men were dead and the priest and the cop had gotten away, again.

Gabriel stood with a machine gun in his right hand over the corpse of Jonathan, the tall blonde-haired one he had with him the day before in Italy, one of his best. From the waist down, blood-covered pinkish intestines spewed across the dead grass. The remaining lower part of the body rested over ten feet away. The torso lay covered with three-inch spiral metal rods imbedded into the flesh. Several had pierced the head. One stuck out of the left eyeball with the eyelid half closed, preventing it from completely closing by the metal spike. Even though Gabriel knew this man as far back as the orphanage, he did not feel grieve.

The Brotherhood recruited Jonathan and Gabriel on the same day. They had come to the training camp at the same time and trained alongside each other from that day forward. They shared a common lifelong dedication to the cause. So did the other recruits, for that matter, but, between Gabriel and Jonathan, they shared a certain camaraderie, a certain link, for they knew each other even before the 'day of enlightenment;' the day when the Master came for them. Unless required to work alone, as he did with the Boston victims, he kept Jonathan part of his team. Now Jonathan lay dead at his feet.

He looked at where the minivan had exited at the wall of trees and saw that it became impassable after the explosion. He looked at the entrance he had blocked with a car before the attack. The explosion had torn through the vehicle, killing the two men inside. With no vehicles and no clear exit, he had no chance for a pursuit.

Out of fifteen men, only two survived, and one severely wounded with his right arm blown off by the explosion that destroyed the chalet.

The two men searched for the bodies of their fallen comrades. They fired a single bullet into their heads as required by protocol.

Gabriel looked down at the body of his friend. He pointed the gun at the temple and fired. Jonathan had long been dead, but the protocol, engraved in Gabriel's mind necessitated the action, 'a bullet for the dead Brothers to ensure their passing.'

The other two had completed their gruesome task and now stood, without a word, a few feet in front of Gabriel as an acknowledgement of completion. They were waiting for his next order.

Gabriel did not relish the call to the Master and report yet another failure. Killing himself would have been his choice, almost a pleasure, a release, but he did not have the Master's approval.

He looked at the man who lost his arm, little remained below the shoulder. Chunks of meat and flesh hung from the stump. An inch of the white bone protruded from the wound. He had lost a lot of blood but remained able to assist in dispatching his fellow comrades and now stood wobbly in front of Gabriel. His face betrayed no hint of pain. Gabriel approached the wounded man. The tall Jamaican, with him in Italy and one of the three survivors from that failed mission, also a trusted Brother like Jonathan. The dark man held Gabriel's gaze steadily. Without a word, Gabriel raised his gun and pointed it at the man's forehead, no more than a few inches away. The wounded man did not flinch. All three survivors knew what had to be done. They knew from the moment he received the serious wound. Any man requiring more than just field dressing had to be dispatched by The Brotherhood. Nothing needed to be said. Gabriel pulled the trigger.

The bullet made a clean hole in the center of the forehead and it exploded the back of the head with such force that it sprayed brain matter, bone and hair more than twenty feet back. A gaping hole remained. The other man had moved further to the side in an anticipation of the spray that he knew would occur, as this was not the first time he had witnessed such an event. The dark man's legs gave way beneath him and he fell to his knees and slowly toppled over to one side. With his legs buckled, he remained on his side and his head came to rest on the ground, eyes remaining open and face expressionless.

Gabriel looked down at the dead man at his feet and stared at his face for a moment. He slowly closed his eyes and leaned his head back facing the cloudless blue sky, arms to his side, right hand still clutching the gun. He took a deep breath. The primordial scream that emanated from deep within him made the remaining man wince and step back in fear. It seemed to go on forever.

When he finally ran out of breath, the echo of his cry reverberated across the open expanse for some time.

•••

John and Sebastian did not stop until the gas gauge pointed near empty several hours later. Wanting to put as much distance as possible between them and the devastation back at the chalet they stopped for no other reason. They turned off at a rest stop on the highway, still some distance from New York and filled up the gas tank, paying only cash.

John spotted several cameras strewn about the rest stop. They kept their hat and sunglasses on, and, being December, were able to keep their collars up to cover most of their faces without too much suspicion. They also feigned severe colds and constantly wiped their noses with tissue paper, further obscuring their faces. The cashiers and attendants were only too eager to give them their other purchases and change, and allow them to get on their way as quickly as possible. The rest of the trip to New York, and eventually to La Guardia airport, remained uneventful.

Sebastian did all the driving and this gave John some time to relax and think.

As the priest had said earlier, many men died at the chalet, thought John. He had seen only three men, but the priest correctly spotted many more. He went over the battle in his mind and counted at least a dozen, including the two men killed near the car blocking the original entrance. Now that he thought of it, all the attackers wore black, except for those two. He suddenly realized who they were, the Captain and the Lieutenant!

He opened his eyes and turned to the priest wide eyed. "Father, I just realized who those two guys were at the car that exploded at the entrance to the field."

"Yeah, I know," interjected Sebastian during the pause. He did not look at John, but kept his eyes on the road. "They were your Captain and the Lieutenant that were so nice to us back at the church."

That seemed so long ago and far away to the detective, almost another lifetime. "That's right. How did you recognize them among all the commotion?"

"I realized who they were when I saw what they were wearing. The assassin branch of The Brotherhood wear only black, all others imbedded in most levels of society wear, so called, civilian clothes in order to blend in. Just like us."

"There were a lot of men out there waiting for us."

"Yes, and well armed too."

"And how did they know we were there?"

Sebastian glanced at John before he answered. "I'm still trying to figure that out myself. They must have known well in advance of the attack, for that took some planning."

Then John realized something. He almost slapped himself on the side of the head. "Of course, I should have known. What a fool I've been!" He looked at the priest. "My car, it's only a couple of years old. It has an onboard GPS device. The Captain must have tracked us since we left Boston."

"Yes. You're right," agreed Sebastian after a moment's pause. "And he sent for the Brotherhood instead of having us arrested. He wanted us dead."

Then another thought came to John. "How about this van?" he asked with worry in his voice.

"No. It's too old," assured the priest. "We made sure of that."

John calmed down but still embarrassed that he hadn't figured it out until now. He had only thought about his cell phone last night but then, he did not usually play the part of the hunted. It's a little harder to reason when you are on the run, he thought.

They arrived at the airport cargo entrance by the early evening. A Protector, working as the guard, waited for them. He immediately recognized Sebastian and opened the gate.

"It is an honor, Senior," the guard said while being careful to look casual to any prying eyes. "There's an employee parking lot to the left. Park the van there and head for the north door in the second building."

He handed a parking permit to Sebastian to hang on the rear view mirror.

"Don't worry about the van," he added. "I'll get rid of it at the end of my shift. Good luck, sir."

Sebastian drove to the designated area and hung the permit on the mirror as instructed.

"Wait here," said Sebastian. "We're expected, but I want to make sure it's safe. I'll come back and get you. I may be a few minutes."

Soon, Sebastian came back out as promised but with another man in tow.

The priest motioned towards the man as he said, "John, this is Robert. He will take us to the plane."

Robert nodded to John, who smiled in greeting, and said, "Gentlemen, leave the van here and follow me. I'll take you to the plane heading for Rome."

He led them to a converted 727 in the company hanger. They entered the aircraft from the rear of the plane via a ramp that led up into the body of the plane. The aircraft loaded and ready to go.

Robert pointed to a large wooden box the size of a small room and said, "See that container there near the front of the plane? You can hide in it when the customs official inspects the cargo. Please go in there now and don't make a sound until the pilot or co-pilot comes to get you in about an hour. You will have the run of the plane after that and until you get to Rome."

John and Sebastian got in and Robert closed and sealed the panel behind them. There were air holes in the back panel near the top. Otherwise, it appeared empty. It looked roughly ten foot square but plenty of room for them to lie down and get comfortable while they waited.

There heard no sound coming from outside the box. They didn't even hear the customs official inspect the plane. Paid off very well that day, he barely glanced at the contents before approving the cargo.

John and the priest waited patiently in the container. They heard the plane's engines start up and it wasn't until the plane began rolling towards the runway and the co-pilot came to release them.

Besides the pilot and co-pilot, no one else remained onboard. They now had the run of the place until their arrival in Rome.

They found eight seats located just outside the cockpit and soon made themselves comfortable as best they could. Sebastian and John had almost seven hours to kill. Upon landing in Rome, it would be early afternoon local time. John thought about getting some rest before they arrived, but he remained too keyed up for sleep.

Their plane entered a queue of planes scheduled for takeoff on the same runway. The pilot estimated it would be at least another half hour before takeoff.

John raised the armrest between his seat and the next and reclined with his feet up. He looked at Sebastian who had done the same in the row of seats behind him and said. "There is something that I have been meaning to ask since you told me of your organization."

"We have plenty of time to talk now, John," said Sebastian. "Ask away."

"Why haven't you gone public?" began John. "I mean, you and your organization are in a strictly defensive posture. In the simplest terms, you are bodyguards to a very old family. Members of The Brotherhood of the Rapture are the ones who are killing people. You should be able to garner sympathy from every human being who values justice and human life, and the Church; they should be able to see how misguided The Brotherhood is and how this actually fits in with what the Church has believed all along: the Second Coming of the Messiah, and finally, the world itself. How the hopes of all are finally within reach, their prayers answered, so to speak. If what you say is true, everyone would be on your side"

Sebastian looked at John and smiled with genuine understanding and patience.

"How I wish that were true," he said to John. "Do you not think that we would have tried? From the time that my ancestor, Marius Sestus, tried to reason with the apostle Peter, we have tried to make others see the light, especially the Brotherhood. And you, yourself, are not entirely convinced of the Second Coming either."

"I didn't say that," said John.

"Not straight out but your words and actions betray you. The phrase you used just now, 'if what you say is true,' it's a perfect example of your lack of conviction. Not only that, if you did believe you would help us without hesitation or concern for your life. After all, it would reinforce your belief in God, in an afterlife, and that the giving of your life would only assure your salvation, but you hesitate, and that shows your reluctance or doubt in believing all or some of what I have told you. In the end, you may just think of us as merely two fanatical groups fighting each other over a misguided cause."

John did not answer. He knew there was some truth in what the priest said. If he truly believed then he would gladly give his life for the cause, but he still had doubts.

Sebastian saw the look in John's face. "Even with everything that you have seen over the last two days, you still doubt."

"But I haven't seen anything that proofs the Second Coming. I have seen men fight for what they believe in, but that is all."

"Exactly! You need proof, and how do you expect the world to believe if I offer only words? Without proof, I, we, the organization, most certainly branded as fanatics. Our exposure, our coming out to the public, would give The Brotherhood of the Rapture a great advantage. It would make it easier for them to track us down."

The plane continued its slow taxi towards the runway as planes ahead of them took off one by one.

Sebastian continued, "Over the last two thousand years we have tried several times to reveal ourselves to a select few of outsiders, including the Catholic Church. We even tried to reason with offshoots of the original Christian Church such as the Protestant Church and many others. All rejected us. All their eyes veiled to the truth, and thought us evil.

"More and more we became convinced of what Jesus had said to Judah, '...and you will be cursed by the other generations of your time...' Only after He has returned, will the world's eyes finally open to the enormity of the situation. Our knowledge of the truth is both a blessing and a curse. Be that as it may, I would always prefer knowing the truth than roaming around in the darkness of ignorance."

John said, "I understand what you are saying, Father, but how about today's generation. Surely they are open minded enough to hear what you would have to say. Is it not worth trying?"

"Are they really ready, John?" asked Sebastian with a sad smile. "Today's generation would be even more skeptical than any of the past. Look at the media machine. It has enslaved the people of this age. People controlled in every aspect of their lives. What to eat, what to drink, what to wear, even what to think. The masses told what they should aspire to and what will make them happy, no matter how ridiculous. Anyone that does not conform considered eccentric at best, a nut, an outcast, at worst.

"Look at the styles of clothing. No matter how ridiculous it is the young always conform. An excellent example is the act of displaying your underwear above the pant waistline and wearing pants halfway down to your knees. Earlier generations associated that kind of behavior with senile old men and laughed at on the street. In the last several decades, that style is actually considered hip, as they say."

"Then why not control the media?" asked John.

"We are not that powerful," said Sebastian. "If we were, we would have destroyed The Brotherhood of the Rapture, or at least made them impotent enough as to no longer be a menace to us."

"At least make your case about how many people have died. You can claim a religious right to exist and ask for protection," said John.

"Now you are being naive," said Sebastian with a smile. "The world teeters between political correctness and a constant bombardment of violence and death on the big and small screen. We may get some to agree and take our side, but most will think us crazy, even though we may legally get the right to exist."

John recalled how just the night before he had ridiculed Sebastian and compared the struggle to a video game. How many people would listen to the news flash about The Protectors Of The Truth? Most would simply open another beer and change the channel, while others would return to their video gaming systems and focus on beating their last score.

Sebastian continued. "Most people are caught up in their own lives. They would only rise up if something affected their little sphere of influence, that is, affected them directly. Tell the masses that gasoline supplies have run out or declare a shortage of pizza and you would have riots on the street. Tell them there is genocide halfway around the world and it doesn't even cross their minds as they devour the pizza while driving their SUVs. If it doesn't infiltrate everyday life, then the masses have an attention span as long as it would take to change the channel. No John, if we went public with our organization, we would just be putting ourselves in harm's way."

John realized that Sebastian was right and the priest had more to say.

"For the sake of argument, let's try a different view point," said Sebastian. "Let's say that the world embraces what we stand for, accepts that Mariella is the final link to the coming of the Messiah." The priest leaned closer to John. "Can you imagine the crazies that would come out of the woodwork? Every fanatic around the world would be clamoring to get at her. I am not saying to kill her, though that would be a major concern for us, but just the onslaught of the devoted would be enough to overwhelm us. We would not be able to stop the flood of people just trying to be near her." His voice rose as he continued. "And the media, my God, they would exploit her to no end. It would be the ultimate reality show. 'LIVE TOMORROW NIGHT, THE BIRTH OF CHRIST, MORE AFTER THESE MESSAGES.' Can you imagine?"

He sat back and looked calmer as he said in a low voice. "There is a reason why Jesus was born to a poor couple in a remote location two thousand years ago. Thus it should be so even in these modern times." He paused for a moment. "Maybe not as poor," Sebastian finally concluded with a quick smile, "but at least just as modest and unassuming."

John pondered what Sebastian had said. John did not have the answers. Who did? "How many people have to die in the name of God?" he finally asked.

"Is it in the name of God?" retorted the Sebastian. "Or is it in the name of vanity of man, from those who believe they are right and just in the eyes of God?"

"How can God allow all the death and suffering to happen?" asked John.

"He doesn't allow just that to happen, he allows us to have the freedom of choice. That is the ultimate gift, but it is also a great responsibility and one that can and has constantly been abused throughout our history." Sebastian looked into John eyes. "We, Man, choose the death, we choose the suffering, not God. Yes, he has the power to stop it, but then, where is the free will? We would be mere puppets and not the greatest creation he has ever made."

John barely noticed that they had taken off during their discussion.

They soon scrounged around the small kitchen and found some sandwiches and soft drinks. John had a tuna sandwich and a bottle of water. He wasn't particularly hungry but felt he had to get something in his stomach before he tried to get some sleep.

To John's surprise, Sebastian had three sandwiches and two cans of soda. The priest explained that he learned early in life that one never knew when or where the next meal would come from and should always consume enough calories to keep going for a while. After he ate, Sebastian got comfortable across several seats and dropped off to sleep as quickly as he had in the car the night before.

John had a little more difficulty settling down, amazed at how quickly the priest fell asleep. He was amazed by the priest period. In his seventies, Sebastian acted like a man in his forties, if not younger still. Only yesterday John considered him a possible suspect in a series of murders, but instead, Sebastian revealed himself to be something else altogether; a man who had a firm conviction in what he did and a purpose in life that transcended his own wellbeing and security. John saw Sebastian as a leader of men but could also appear meek and almost unassuming, two traits of contradiction but also a talent that could be extremely useful.

Today's carnage also showed another faucet of Sebastian, thought John. He saw a man that remained calm under fire. Someone who took calculated moves and did not hesitate to kill when necessary. A bit disturbing since the man was also an ordained priest. When he thought about it, though, the history of the Church did not exclude taking action when required. In ancient times, and even in the last few centuries, it used violence as a necessary tool for its survival. Sebastian, a creature of circumstance and forged by the burden of responsibility. John also thought about how much he himself had changed in the last twenty-four hours as he slowly drifted off to sleep.

John dreamed of men in black suits.

CHAPTER NINE
SEARCH

The plane landed just after one P.M. local time in Rome. John and Sebastian went back in the container and the co-pilot sealed it up appropriately.

The customs process went without any issues and a locally stationed Protector, masquerading as a cargo handler for the shipping company, let the stowaways out of their hiding place.

"My name is Camillo," said the Protector in a heavy accented English. He smiled and extended his hand to both Sebastian and John. "Welcome to Italy."

Sebastian shook his hand as he said, "I am Senior Sebastian and this is John Bernard, my guest."

"I know who you are, Signore," his attention on the priest, "and it is an honor to meet you in person." Camillo bowed slightly to Sebastian and then turned to John and shook his hand as well.

On a box nearby, Camillo had placed a couple of orange vests, the standard issue for airport workers on airport tarmacs. Camillo picked them up and handed the vests to the two men. "Please put these on so you will not look out of place as we exit the plane," he said.

Sebastian and John put them on. Camillo looked them over and smiled. "Good. Good. Please follow me. I have a baggage car waiting just outside the plane. We will take it to the employee parking lot. I have a car and supplies waiting for you as requested."

"Thank you, Camillo," said Sebastian as he and John followed Camillo out of the plane.

They came out to a cool but sunny day in Rome, the temperature well above freezing and comfortable in the light jackets they had on under the orange vests.

Camillo took the two men to a late model four-door dark grey BMW parked in the employee parking lot.

"Here are the keys, Signore," said Camillo handing them over to Sebastian. "There is a pass-card on the dashboard that you will need to swipe at the exit to open the gates. In the glove compartment, there is a map of Italy and ten thousand in Euro Dollars. The car is safe. It has no electronic device that can be tracked." He handed a cell phone to Sebastian. "Here is a phone that you can use. Though easily tracked it is a pay per use type that I bought at the airport so risk to you is minimal. Turn it on only when you need to use it."

"Thank you, Camillo," said Sebastian as he shook his hand again. "May God protect you as you have protected our cause."

"God be with you too, Signore," replied Camillo smiling warmly.

Sebastian got in the driver's side and John took the passenger seat. The priest drove to the exit gate as Camillo looked on.

John opened the glove compartment and found the map and the money as promised. He flipped through the money held together by a rubber band; used bills of tens, twenties and hundreds. "So this is what ten thousand Euros look like," he said.

"Take half and hand the other half to me," said Sebastian. "That way, if we get lost, or need to split up, we each have some money to get by."

John did as instructed and pocketed half the money. He handed the rest to the priest.

They got to the exit and drove out without incident. A mile down the road, Sebastian pulled over to the side of the road. "Take out the map and I will show you where we need to go," said Sebastian. "You will be my co-pilot on this one. I am not very familiar with the roads around here. It's been a while since I've been to Italy."

John took out the map and opened it as they sat in the car.

"Where we need to go is fairly straight forward," began Sebastian. "We are essentially going from west to east to a city called Pescara right on the Adriatic coast. Highway E80 will get us there well before night fall. There is a cemetery called San Pietro in the city that we need to go." He pointed to the route and location of the city on the map.

"What's in the cemetery?" asked John.

"We are looking for a particular crypt in the mausoleum with the name of Maria DiJuda engraved on it." Sebastian pulled back into traffic heading for highway E80.

"A play on words if I ever heard one," said John. "The Di translates to 'of', therefore DiJuda translates to 'of Judah and Mariella is another form of Maria. In short, we have 'Mariella of Judah,' in a cemetery named Saint Peter. How poetically cryptic it all is."

"Yah, I know, and I must compliment you in a well executed exercise of deduction. It must be the cop in you. The cemetery's name only a fluke but it is common and used often and the last name format is very common in Italy as well. DiGiovanni, DiPietro, meaning 'of John, 'of Peter', are widely used. My idea. Sorry."

"So, we're heading for a cemetery in a city on the Adriatic coast. Once we get there, it will probably be closed, so we need to break in somehow and then, in the dark, find a name on a crypt among thousands."

Sebastian briefly glanced at John and said, "You're always so skeptical, John. The cemetery is actually small and easy to get into. I've seen pictures of it. Also, the mausoleum holds a hundred crypts at most. It shouldn't be too hard to find, even in the dark." He paused for a moment and then asked, "You still have your flashlight, do you not?"

John reached in his pocket and said, "Yes. It's the standard police issue, small enough to handle along with a gun." He reached into his side pocket and pulled out a cylindrical black tube about the size of a cigar. "It's a silencer I got from your stash of weapons back at the chalet," said John shyly. "I figured it may be of use in some situations. Always be prepared."

"Indeed," said Sebastian with a slight smile. "Then we have everything we need."

They had a very scenic drive from Rome to Pescara. Highway E80 wound through the countryside providing a panoramic view of the urban life of the country, where not even a square foot of untouched land remained. A country populated by more than sixty million people and with a history spanning thousands of years, could not boast the so called 'wild country' of the new world of the Americas. Everywhere you looked, human presence was evident. Influenced by a time when man tried to tame nature. Vegetation, bent to the will of man. If seen for the first time, the naturalist would be shocked at such a sight, but esthetically very pleasing to the eye to see manicured 'lawns' wherever you looked, only a matter of perspective.

John and Sebastian reached the outskirts of Pescara just before dark and stopped at a small café for dinner. Sebastian, fluent in Italian, asked the proprietor if he knew of San Pietro cemetery and its location. The old café owner provided directions and, checking his watch, added, "But it closes at eight, signore." He spoke in the distinctive dialect of the region. "No, no, you will not make it in time tonight. You will have to wait for the morning, yes? If you do not have a place to stay, you go down the coastal road. There are plenty of hotels there." He waved his arms for emphasis and a smile. "Yes. Yes. Lucky for you it's winter, signore. You should have no problem finding rooms at this time of year."

John and Sebastian finished their meal with an espresso and paid the bill before heading out. They were on the sidewalk heading for the car in the cool night air when a boy no more than ten jostled John as he ran past. The detective thought nothing of it and continued walking when he heard a sudden cry of pain from the direction the boy. Both men stopped and turned to investigate. No more than twenty feet away, an elderly man had the boy by the arm while slapping him on the side of the head and yelling in a language that John could not understand. The boy cried out in pain while trying unsuccessfully to fend off the blows.

"Hey you, leave that boy alone!" John yelled as he began walking in their direction, Sebastian repeating the demand in Italian for good measure.

John discreetly took his gun out of its holster and hid it in his pocket with his finger on the trigger.

The man looked up. He looked at the boy, grabbed something from his small hand and yelled a few more words as he shoved him aside. The boy lost his balance and fell on the sidewalk. The lad looked no more than four feet tall, dark skinned, dark eyed, and hair long and unkept.

He went barefoot and filthy from head to foot. He got up without looking around and ran down the street and out of sight.

The man followed the boy with his eyes until he disappeared. He turned back to look at John, walked over to the detective and opened his hand, palm up. "I believe this belongs to you," he said in accented but good English, removing and tipping his black round felt hat with the other hand. He held out a wad of bills.

John checked his coat pocket and found it empty. The stranger held the change from the dinner bill John had placed in the now empty pocket.

John took the money with a look of surprise and said, "Thank-you sir. You have a sharp eye."

"Not at all," said the man. "I know that boy. Don't judge him too harshly. He is only trying to survive. To be honest, I wouldn't have stopped him if I didn't recognize your companion." He looked over at Sebastian.

Both Sebastian, standing a few paces back, and John looked at their new acquaintance more closely. They saw a shabby looking man in his late fifties or early sixties. Old, worn out clothes that had seen better days and too few washes covered the gangly six-foot frame. His leathery face looked almost timeless and accentuated by a long, hooked nose and bushy, grey, peppered eyebrows over elongated, black eyes. His shoulder length hair grey and scraggly, like his tobacco-stained beard reaching down to his chest and obscuring most of his thin chapped lips.

Sebastian's eyes narrowed. The stranger caught the all too familiar look. "My name is Angelo Petulengro, and, yes, Senior, I am a gipsy," he said without offering his hand, thinking it not appreciated or acknowledged.

Without smiling, Sebastian extended his right hand and said, "I prefer using 'Roma', since that is the proper term for your people rather than the more derogatory term of gypsy."

Angelo Petulengro shook the priest's hand and smiled, displaying an incomplete set of yellow, nicotine stained teeth.

Sebastian smiled back in acknowledgement but John remained wary. "How do you know me?" asked the priest.

"You are Father Sebastian, are you not?" inquired Angelo almost coyly and ignoring the question. "Sometimes referred to as Senior Sebastian?"

"Since you are well informed, there is no use denying it," said Sebastian. He glanced at John. "This is John, a close associate of mine."

John nodded but did not extend his hand out in greeting. He still had a grip on his gun hidden in his pocket. He wasn't taking any chances and stepped around to the back of the gypsy, ignoring the whiff of body odor he received as he did so.

"You haven't answered my question," continued Sebastian. "How do you know me?"

"I became very good friends with one of your Protectors during the many acts of kindness the monks of the Monastero Di Santo Pietro di Decontra bestowed upon my people," replied Angelo. "He showed me a picture of you, and I recognized you when you entered the café earlier. I waited for you to come out. Have no fear that the monk has betrayed you, for if you know anything about the Roma, once accepted in our circle, we guard the trust bestowed on us with our lives if we have to. Our family and community values make us strong. Spiritually, the monk is my brother and I would protect him, and his secrets, with my life."

"Yes, I am very familiar with the Roma, and I believe what you say. Which monk is it that you know?"

"Brother Marco, who is still alive, by the way, or at least I assume that he is, since the mode of escape has been used."

"Thank God," he said with obvious relief in his voice. "We were not sure. Tell me what you know," he said furrowing his eyebrows.

"Except for Brother Marco, you do know that all the monks of the monastery have been killed?" asked Angelo. "God rest their souls."

"Yes. I am aware of what happened. It's a real tragedy."

"A few years ago, Brother Marco and I talked about escape plans in case his hiding place was discovered by your enemies. I arranged for him a cruiser to be available at all times for a quick getaway. The boat taken two nights ago, the same day your enemies attacked the monastery. With a car found abandoned near the pier, I can only assume that he got away successfully with his Charge."

"Where did they go?" Sebastian asked breathlessly.

"That I do not know," said Angelo. "Marco felt that, for my sake, the destination be kept from me."

"I understand," said Sebastian. He looked at John and then back at Angelo. "Thank you for what you have told me, and for the return of the money." Both he and John turned to go.

Seeing that they meant to leave, Angelo took a few steps towards them and said, "Please. Let me help you. I know the city very well and I can assist in ways that you cannot even begin to imagine."

Sebastian and John looked at each other and tried to interpret what the other thought.

Angelo saw the hesitation and continued, "Marco told me about the Descendant and the importance of the Age that we live in. I am Christian and believe what my spiritual brother told me. I only wish to help to see the Son of God reborn."

"What do you have in mind?" asked John cautiously.

"Tell me what you need? What you plan to do?" said Angelo extending his hands out, palms up, in invitation.

"We need to get into a cemetery tonight, but it's closed," said John, testing the waters but not providing more details.

"Easily done," said Angelo enthusiastically, "but it's still too early to break in. Too much traffic still and we will need some help." He paused for a moment while thinking. "My son can be of assistance," he concluded. Angelo did not wait for Sebastian and John to respond. He headed for their car and added, "Let us go. I have a place on the outskirts of the city where my people live. We can wait there, rest, and make plans."

John hesitated for a moment. In such a confined space as the car, the gypsy's body odor he noticed a moment ago would be even more overpowering, but he shrugged his shoulders and got in the passenger seat. He could not come up with any better idea. The priest got in the driver's side. As soon as the gypsy got in, John looked up, glanced back and then looked at Sebastian, who shyly did not return the look. John then turned to his right and slowly began to roll down the window. He stuck his head out to the clean cool air.

Angelo Petulengro grimaced and rubbed his nose with his woolen sleeve soon after he got in the rear passenger seat behind John. He looked at the two men seated in front of him with a slight scowl and looked relieved when John began to open the window. His eyes watered from the overwhelming smell of their cologne and bleach in their clothes. He almost gagged. He too began to open his passenger window. As the car wound through the streets of Pescara following his directions, the cold night air helped to ease the assault of smells Angelo had to endure.

At the outskirt of town, just as they were entering the rural area, they came across a shantytown and Angelo's community. It consisted of horse-drawn carriages and an assortment of shacks. The carriages were in various conditions ranging from colorful, well-kept, roof-covered transports to dilapidated, broken down canvas-covered carts unfit for travel and possibly even habitation. The newcomers spied an assortment of mud-floored shacks nearby of different sizes from a single room to a multi-room structure, constructed from all kinds of materials scavenged, stolen and sometimes, but rarely, donated.

People of all ages huddled around open campfires trying to keep warm and cooking their meals. The numbers at each fire numbered from two to several dozen, but never only one. There were no outcasts here. The whole community of gypsies may have been outcasts to the 'civilized' world but not within their own ranks.

The car slowly wound through this ramshackle town. Everyone turned to look at the vehicle but when spying Angelo sitting in the back seat, quickly lost interest and turned back at what they were doing.

The smell permeating from the settlement nauseated the newcomers. Their noses overpowered by the smell of urine and feces. They did not know which smell was worst, Angelo in the back seat or from the town itself. There appeared raw sewage everywhere and little done to cover the open pits.

Angelo motioned them to pull over next to a wagon in relatively good condition flanked by a single room shack. The wagon itself quite elaborate, with a wooden curved roof and carved wooden walls with a door at the very back, while the shack merely a collection of corrugated metal in a failed effort to build a solid structure.

Several people mingled around the large family fire. John counted about a dozen; An old woman sitting near the fire, two young adult women tending to the pots, two adult men sitting by the fire sharing what looked like a bottle of wine and an intense conversation, and several children ranging from toddlers to preteens running about. None straying too far from the fire like moths attracted to light. Everyone stopped and focused their attention on the car as it pulled up and stopped nearby, apprehension evident on most of the faces, including the children. When they saw Angelo get out of the back seat and wave, the air suddenly grew less tense, especially near the two men who had gotten up, their conversation forgotten.

John and Sebastian got out of the car and went to stand by Angelo as if looking for guidance on what to do next.

"This is my family," said Angelo with obvious pride.

The three walked up to the fire. Angelo's family gathered around the three men. Only the old woman remained in her chair. Angelo began introductions and just the man shook hands. The women nodded and the children just looked on. The old woman introduced as Angelo's wife, the two men his sons, the younger women their wives and the children their brews.

"Please sit down next to the fire and keep warm," said Angelo cheerfully to his guests. He motioned to several empty chairs. "You have eaten but I have not."

One of the young women brought him food without offering John or Sebastian any and it looked like some form of stew. After a few mouthfuls, he motioned to one of his sons who soon brought out a bottle of clear liquid and several glasses.

Angelo began pouring. "Here, have some." He handed a glass to each of his two guests. "It's Grappa. We distill it ourselves from the leftover grape skins when we make wine."

Sebastian and John took a sip. Readily available from any liquor store in the States, they were both familiar with the drink, but they were not ready for the potency of this homemade liquid fire. John coughed while only watery eyes betrayed the effect on Sebastian. It had the taste of fermented grapes. Angelo laughed and his sons let out a chuckle as they drank from their own glasses. Angelo tipped his head back and swallowed the entire contents of the glass in one gulp. He let out a sigh and quickly finished his meal. John Pulled out a pack of cigarettes and offered them to all the men. Everyone took one.

Angelo began the conversation as he lit up. "Which cemetery do you need to get into?"

The priest looked at Angelo's sons and the old gypsy noticed the glance.

"Have no fear of my sons," said Angelo. "They can be trusted."

"We need to get into San Pietro cemetery," said the priest, taking the old gypsy at his word.

"Yes, I know it," responded Angelo. "It has a six foot cement wall as a perimeter with two iron gates at the entrance that is locked every night. It's not hard to get into at all. We can climb over the wall with a short ladder."

"There must be a very good reason why you want to get into that cemetery tonight," said Angelo. "And I think I know the reason. You don't know where Brother Marco went and somewhere in that cemetery is a clue, or a message, as to where he is, or going to. Am I right?"

"Yes, Angelo, you are correct," conceded Sebastian. "In the cemetery there is a crypt. And just inside that crypt there will be something that will tell us where Brother Marco went."

"And then what?" asked Angelo. "They've gone by boat. Which means you will need a boat as well. I can help you there but I will need two thousand Euros. I can have a boat ready by the time we retrieve the directions from the cemetery."

John figured the old gypsy marked up the real cost but he and the priest had an urgent need and saw no harm in the gypsy making a bit of money for his family. He pulled out a wad of bills, counted out two thousand Euros, and handed them to Angelo. Chances were, it would be a stolen boat, thought the detective, but if you came right down to it, still a real bargain. Where else would you get a boat for two thousand Euros, no questions asked?

The old gypsy handed the money to one of his sons and said, "You know who to talk to. Have a cruiser ready in a few hours at the same dock."

The son got up and disappeared into the night. Angelo grabbed the bottle and poured himself another drink. "We have a few hours to kill before its late enough to sneak into the cemetery without been seen by anyone. Anyone else would like another drink?"

John and Sebastian presented their glasses to the old Gypsy who smiled and began to pour.

The traffic turned sporadic after midnight as they drove through the old narrow streets of Pescara. They reached the entrance of the cemetery by a very narrow cobble stoned street in an older part of the city.

Angelo's older son, Donato, came along. He brought along a five-foot ladder to get over the cemetery wall. When they got there, the car's headlights pointed at the entrance of the cemetery and John found that Angelo had described it correctly. The cemetery occupied about a half city block along the coastal road. Its perimeter consisted of a grey six-foot concrete and stucco wall. Two concrete posts about ten feet apart marked the entrance and rose above the wall another 3 feet and capped off with iron round urns as decoration with two black, iron gates, strung across the posts and secured shut with a chain and a heavy keyed lock. An aged iron plaque painted white and with engraved black lettering hung on one of the post at eye level. It read 'Quello che siamo, sarete. Preghiamo per voi.'

Sebastian translated it aloud for John's benefit. "What we are, you will be. We pray for you."

"That's telling it like it is," said John.

"I wonder if the author of the plaque was being humble or had a dark sense of humor," added Sebastian.

"Maybe both," concluded John.

"Park the car next to the wall," interjected Angelo. "And don't use your flashlight unless completely necessary.

They shut off the car and Donato brought the short ladder out placing it against the wall. A full moon shined brightly from the cloudless sky. They could see quite well and kept the flashlights off as instructed. Sebastian retrieved a tire wrench from the trunk of the car.

"What's that for? Protection?" asked John in a whisper. "I have this." He padded his jacket where he kept his pistol.

"To get into the crypt," answered Sebastian.

"I hope not to get at the body inside?"

"If there is one, but we shall see."

For John, the wall hardly presented itself as a serious obstacle, an easy climb over the wall and a short drop on the other side. Not so for Sebastian and Angelo, they both climbed up and sat on the smooth top of the wall while Donato came up and sat next to them. He reached back, picked up the ladder, swung it over to the inside and leaned it back against wall. Donato jumped down on the ground and waited for his father and the priest to climb down.

"That was easy," said Sebastian after climbing down.

"You usually don't have to worry about intruders in a cemetery," responded John who checked his gun and screwed on the silencer just in case.

They all kept their voices down.

"We are looking for the public mausoleum. Do you know where that is?" asked Sebastian, the question aimed at Angelo.

"Come with me," replied Angelo with authority.

The four men walked down a cobble stone path. They left the ladder where it remained for the return trip. To the left and right of the path, sported densely populated burial artifacts, family owned tombs housing several crypts and head stones of various shapes set either vertically or flat on the ground. Evergreen bushes and trees grew all around in an attempt to soften the look of these granite and marble monuments.

The pasty face of the full moon bathed everything with an eerie light creating an old black and white movie atmosphere. The moon shadows carved impenetrable black slices out of anything that they covered. John glanced over to Sebastian walking next to him. Under the moon light, the priests face seemed carved out of marble. The eyes invisible under the shadow of his eyebrows, like two black holes in a death mask. His glance back at John with a slight smile only increased the impression of menace on his face. Even the sounds of their shoes on the cobblestones sounded eerie when accompanied by the grey-white light.

The sound of passing cars and the rhythmic lapping of waves from the distant shore remained just within earshot and created an almost constant static-like background noise to the trespassers. Nothing stirred. Not even the usual night predators that stalked small prey foolish enough to be outside after sunset. The cobble stone path forked in various directions, reaching every corner of the cemetery but Angelo seemed to know where he was going and they reached their destination within minutes.

The mausoleum was a surprisingly low structure. It stood only six feet in height with a flat tar covered roof and a long rectangle shape of about a hundred feet in length and twenty feet deep. Each side along its length held three rows of crypts with thirty in each row. There were ninety on each of the two faces, one hundred and eighty crypts in total. The four men stood on the moon light side allowing the names to be visible on the face of the crypts.

"Angelo, you and your son take this side and John and I will take the other side using our flashlight," instructed Sebastian. "You are looking for the name Maria DiJuda."

They walked to the end of the building and split up as instructed. John switched on his flashlight and he and Sebastian began scanning the names on the marble faces. He ran the circle of yellow light down one column and then up the next and so on down the line. They were only third of the way across when they heard a low call from the other side. Paul and Sebastian hurried over and found Angelo and his son, Donato, in front of the crypt they were looking for.

The crypt on the top row at about chest high looked identical to all the others, the face of the crypt made of grey-veined white marble common throughout these parts, its size about a two-foot square and flush with the grey cement of the opening. A small brass vase, screwed into the marble with a bracket, held several fake flowers. The engraving simply had the name 'Maria DiJuda' and birth and death dates 'N 27 10 1864' and 'M 29 4 1923.' The N for natto meaning born and M for morto meaning died.

"That's the one," said Sebastian. "John, keep the light on it. I'm going to break it open with the tire wrench."

Sebastian swung the wrench at the center of the marble face. It easily cracked the soft material. He swung it again several more times and the face fell off in pieces. Just behind it, they found a slab of cement of the same size held in place by silicone caulking. The priest also swung at it several times and it broke into pieces as well. The flashlight revealed the end of the wooden coffin, sealed well inside the crypt it looked new.

"There's just a coffin, but nothing else," said John.

"That's all we want," answered Sebastian. "There's no body in the coffin and placed here when the Protectors arrived twenty years ago." He stepped closer and peered in. "Near the base of the coffin will be a series of numbers. That's what we're looking for."

They all looked closer and engraved in the wood near the base they saw sixteen numbers, 3593102114481697. Sebastian took out a pad and pen and wrote them down.

"Looks like a serial number of some kind," said Angelo as his son looked on over his father's shoulder.

"Is it a code?" asked John.

"Neither one," said Sebastian turning back to look at the men behind him. "It is the location of the safe house where Marco and Mariella have gone. It's not a code or serial number. It's quite simple actually. It's the la....." He stopped in mid word as a small dart-like arrow hit him between his upper left arm and chest. He staggered back against the mausoleum and sank down with his back against the wall. A grimace of pain appeared on his face as he grabbed the arrow with his right hand.

John swung around in the direction that the arrow came from. As he did so, he instinctively dropped on one knee and pulled out his gun, ready to fire. Another arrow meant for him, swished by over his head, missing him by only an inch. His hair ruffled by the passing of the arrow. Angelo stood directly behind John and did not react quickly enough. The arrow hit Angelo squarely in the chest. John fired three times at two shadows twenty feet away next to an evergreen tree. There wasn't even a flash. One figure went down while the other staggered, raising his left arm as if to fire. Before he could do so, John took careful aim and fired two more shots at the figure still standing. The lone figure staggered back from the impact of both shots and fell backwards on the ground next to the trees. John ran over to where the attackers lay. He flashed the light at them. They were both dressed in black with only their heads and hands exposed. John kicked away what looked like miniature cross bows lying near them. They had carried two each. The last one John killed tried to get a second shot off when John fired first. He checked for a pulse. They were both dead.

John ran back to check on his comrades as he holstered his gun. He found Sebastian where he left him, sitting on the ground, leaning against the wall of the mausoleum holding his arm. The stone expression on his face barely betrayed the pain he obviously felt, the arrow still protruding from his upper left chest region.

"The Brotherhood again," said John to the priest.

"Go check on Angelo," said Sebastian, nursing his arm. "He got hit as well."

A few feet away lay Angelo on his back, his head cradled on Donato's lap. A low continuous moan emanated from Donato as he sat looking down at his father, brushing the old man's wild grey hair back from his face with his young bare hand. Angelo had his eyes closed but still breathing.

"How you doing, old man?" asked John, using the phrase affectionately as he crouched down next to the gypsy.

Angelo opened his eyes and looked at John and then Sebastian. The priest had gotten up and stood over John nursing his arm.

"Not too good, my friends," replied Angelo in a hoarse whisper. He grabbed John's hand as if looking for some comfort and strength. Angelo's breathing came ragged. He closed his eyes for a moment, then opened them again and looked up at his son and then back to John and Sebastian.

"Just rest," said John. "We'll get some help."

"I'm not an idiot," Groaned the Gypsy. "I'm finished, but you two have an important mission. Now that you know where she is, go and ensure that she is safe." He coughed in pain but continued in a whisper, "My son will show you where the boat is docked." He paused as his body shuddered slightly and gripped John's hand tighter. "Good luck, my friends," he said as he gasped his last breath and slowly closed his eyes, his hand going limp in John's grip.

Donato's moan increased in intensity and he hugged his father's head tightly as he rocked back and forth.

John placed a hand on the young man's shoulder. "I'm sorry, Donato."

"Come on, son," Said Sebastian after a while. "John will help you carry your father back to the car."

John hesitated for a moment, picked up the tire wrench and said, "Give me a minute."

He went up to the open crypt and pulled on the coffin enough to allow the end to hang over the edge of the open crypt by a few inches. With the flashlight in his left hand and the wrench in his right, he began striking the bottom edge of the coffin where the engraved numbers were. Wood began to splinter off in pieces with every swing. He stopped only when satisfied none of the numbers remained visible. He then went over to Donato and said gently, "Come, I will help you."

Slowly Donato released his father from his grip and got up. The two men each took one of the old Gypsy's arms over their shoulders and carried him upright as they headed back to the car. Sebastian followed behind, cradling his left arm under his right. When they got to the gate, they found the lock cut by their assailants. They abandoned the ladder and gently bundled the old Gypsy into the back seat. Donato got in next to him while John got in the driver's seat and Sebastian in the passenger front seat. Donato directed them to a marina located less than ten minutes away, the same marina that Marco and Mariella had been only two nights ago. After they entered through the open gate, Donato lead them to the boat.

Before the two men boarded, John turned to the young gypsy and shook his hand. He handed the young man the keys to the car and along with another thousand Euros. "I know this will not compensate for your Father," said John, "but please take the money for your family and do what you wish with the car." Donato nodded his head in appreciation. John looked at him for a moment and before boarding the cruiser.

Sebastian also shook Donato's hand. "I know there is nothing that I can say that will ease you pain," said Sebastian, seemingly ignoring his own wound for the moment. "All I know is that we will remember your father as a man of integrity and justice. He did the right thing by us and

I will always honor his memory." He too boarded the boat as Donato disappeared into the night.

Though John and Sebastian did not know it, the boat was the same model as the one Marco and Mariella took. In the wheelhouse, Sebastian slumped in the bench while telling John to position himself in the cockpit. The priest instructed John how to start it and navigate out of the marina.

"Go out to sea heading east for about a mile," instructed Sebastian. "Then head south and place it on autopilot."

Once on autopilot, John headed down the lower deck and found a basic first aid kit in the galley. He also found at least a week's supply of food and other basic supplies. He even discovered a bottle of brandy in one of the cabinets. The Gypsy had thought of everything.

John came back up into the wheelhouse and poured Sebastian a drink but none for himself, not yet anyway. After a couple of drinks went into the priest, John got to work on removing the arrow. He first cut the jacket and sweater away from the wound. The arrow itself six inches long and with half of the shaft buried in the flesh. The wound had bled but not enough to be of a concern. He looked at it and said, "I should cut the wound further to make room for the arrow head but I don't have any local anesthetic. It's best that I simply pull it back out the same way it went in and I will do so with a quick pull to minimize the pain. You follow me?"

"Yes, I got it," answered the priest in pain and eyes closed. "Do it quick."

John sterilized around the wound as best he could with gauze soaked in antiseptic. Sebastian winced with every touch. He took another drink as John grasped the arrow shaft and feathers with his right hand and braced Sebastian's shoulder with his left. He pulled, but the arrow remained lodged in the priest's shoulder. Sebastian let out a cry at the tug.

"Shit. Sorry Father," said John beginning to sweat.

John braced himself again and pulled harder. Again, it didn't budge. Sebastian let out another cry and almost fainted.

"Jesus Christ, Father, it's really stuck in there," said John, now sweating profusely. He grabbed the arrow again. Before he pulled, he said, "I am going to pull it again as hard as I can but this time I'll rock it up and down slightly to see if I can dislodge it, but it will hurt like a son of a bitch."

"It hasn't been a tickle up to now," groaned the priest.

"You ready?" asked John.

"No, but hurry up before I'm dead."

John pulled but the arrow did not move. The priest let out a moan. Maintaining pressure, John rocked it up and down. Sebastian cried out as the arrow practically popped out of his shoulder.

"God damn, that was a real bitch!" said John breathlessly.

The arrow had four serrated blades for maximum penetration and damage. As he held it up to show the priest, he noticed Sebastian had fainted and slumped down on the bench. John used the opportunity to clean inside the wound and stitch it up. He had him patched up before the priest came to.

"What happened?" said Sebastian groggily. He had been out for almost a half hour.

"You fainted," replied John as he put a sling on the priest's arm, "but that was a good thing because I took the opportunity to stitch you up before you came to."

"How long have I been out?"

"About thirty minutes."

"Where's my note pad?" asked the priest as he grouped around for his jacket.

"I'll get it," said John. He had cut off the jacket and left the parts on the bench across the table and took out the pad with the sixteen numbers written on it.

"Those are coordinates," began the priest grimacing in pain. "Split them in half, the first eight are the latitude and the second eight are the longitude using the decimal degree format. If you don't know what I'm talking about, look it up on the computer built into the dash in front of you."

John did as instructed. Once he understood what they were, he rewrote the numbers.

Lat 39.931021 and Lon 14.481697

He keyed them in the onboard computer and navigation system. It pointed to the island of Malta, Pembroke Village, Fortizza Road. John told the priest.

"That, my son," said Sebastian. "Is where we must go." He got up and began to climb down to the lower deck. "Key it in and keep watch while I get some rest." He barely made it to one of the berths at the front of the cruiser.

John set the coordinates into the navigation system and reset it on autopilot. He then poured himself a drink from the remaining brandy, and lit a cigarette. He didn't know how many of these kinds of adventures he could handle. Only two days had passed since the first incident at the church, but Boston and his job as a police officer seemed like another lifetime. Used to violence, blood and guts had little effect on him but what he had seen yesterday at the chalet reminded him of a war zone.

I suppose it was...or is, he thought to himself. And what of his family? They must be worried sick for him, but he could not risk calling. Most certainly monitored without their knowledge and, as soon as he called, he would give away his location immediately. No doubt about it, he thought. He had used the same tactics himself on many occasions.

And his partner, Rashid? John wondered if his partner believed John could murder someone in cold blood. John knew he had to try to contact him, but he did not know how. Like his family, he knew Rashid must been monitored. He would just have to be patient and leave it for another day.

The sky remained clear and the wind calm. The moon still in the sky although more to the west now and would set in a couple of hours. The view looked surprisingly clear across the calm sea. Even though they were a mile out, the silhouette of land with many points of light scattered across it like stars across the night sky remained visible. Out towards the open waters he could make out odd lights from boats making their way over the Adriatic Sea to their various destinations. The sea remained calm and the boat made easy time.

Consulting the computer John learned Malta to be about fifty miles south of Sicily. Their trip would take them down the back of the boot of Italy, around the heel, past the toe and the island of Sicily. Total trip would be around eight hundred plus miles. Depending on weather conditions, and how often they would need to refuel, it would take a couple of days at a speed of twenty to twenty five knots.

If they took the same route by boat, Marco and the descendant Mariella would be arriving around now, John calculated.

John sat back and scanned the horizon. Everything looked normal. It would be sunrise in a few hours and he needed to stay awake and keep watch, switching with Sebastian when the priest had rested enough. Unless they planned to anchor every night, someone must stay up to pilot the boat.

Sunrise found John still awake and at the wheel. Clouds had begun to form just before sunrise but the wind remained calm, keeping the waves to a minimum. The boat had no problem making its way down the coast at a good twenty-five knots, or just under thirty miles an hour.

Despite the droning of the motors, the detective had managed to stay awake with a steady supply of strong coffee and cigarettes he found among the supplies.

Sebastian came up to the wheelhouse about an hour after sunrise. His face didn't seem as ashen as the night before and that made John feel a bit better.

"How you doing?" asked John.

"Like shit," answered Sebastian, his arm still in the sling.

"Now, now, such swearing from a priest," said John lightly with a slight smile.

"I'm sure God understands, and it wasn't really swearing," responded the priest. He tried to move his shoulder and received a jolt of pain for his efforts and it showed on his face. "I think the cure was worst then the disease."

"Sorry, Father," said John. "It was really wedged in there. I had to get it out. I had no choice."

"Yes. I know, son," conceded Sebastian. "Any more coffee?"

"Yes there is, but let me look at that first," said John as he approached the priest.

John pealed back the gauze. The wound didn't seem infected. He reapplied the bandage and went to get the Priest coffee coming back with a cup and some pills.

"Here," he said, "and take these aspirins. They were in the first aid kit. They'll help with the pain."

Sebastian did as ordered and lit a cigarette. He smoked and sipped on his coffee silently for a few moments, looking out at the horizon. "How's our progress?" he eventually asked.

"Pretty good," answered John. "Considering the tide, we've gone just over one hundred miles since we began five hours ago."

"Good, good. We'll have to check the fuel and the boat's capacity and calculate if and when we have to refuel."

Sebastian went alongside John at the cockpit and checked the computer. "Well, looks like we're in good shape'" he said. "We seem to have enough fuel to get to Malta without a stopover. Angelo and his son's were, indeed, worth every Euro."

"Yes, they certainly were," said John. "Very unfortunate he got killed." He paused for a moment and then added, "That arrow was meant for me, you know."

"Yes, I know."

"Once again The Brotherhood is right on our tail, and once again, we manage to escape by the seat of our pants. We're going to run out of luck one of these days." He checked his cup and poured himself another coffee. "So how did they know where we were this time?"

"I don't think they did," answered Sebastian. "Or else they would have been there full force."

"Like back in the Chalet?"

"That's right."

"And those two?

"They could have been just two scouts checking cars with out of town plates. Pescara is not that large of a town and still close to Decontra. They may have stumbled on the car parked outside the cemetery." Sebastian looked up from his coffee and added. "They may not necessarily have been looking for us either. They could have been looking for Marco and Mariella, and found us instead. It doesn't matter. The important thing is we're out of there and on the move."

John got up from the captain's chair and headed down to the galley. "Want some breakfast?" he asked.

"Some scrambled eggs and toast would be nice," said Sebastian as he slid into the chair in front of the controls. "And get some sleep after that. I can keep watch for today."

"That's the plan whether you like it or not," said John as he rummaged around the galley. "I'm running on reserve as it is. As soon as we both have something in us, I am crashing for a few hours before I take over again."

It wasn't long until their bellies were full, John snoring away and Sebastian piloting the boat.

That day, and the next, went by without incident. The weather cooperated and the sea remained calm. Near dusk of the following day, they spotted the low hills of the northern most island. They had come down from the north, around the heel of Italy, and just within striking distance of Sicily.

That final stretch from Sicily became almost a traffic jam. John was amazed at the amount of boat traffic that travelled the north-south route. They stayed within view of land but came no closer. The boat continued south, past the smaller second island and down to their final destination. The entire eastern coast of the islands of Malta presented a breathtaking view that neither of the two men had anticipated. Even in December, the water remained a clear aqua blue turning into a deep azure as the sun began to set. The shore edged with a thin rim of white foam as the water splashed onto the coral laden rock. The main island of Malta stood between the boat and the sun as it set. Its rays created a halo like affect in a burst of multi hues of violets, purples and pinks.

"I should have visited this island long before this," said John as he took in the vista. "It would have been nice to do some sightseeing."

"I couldn't agree more," answered Sebastian. He pried his eyes away from the skyline and looked down at the shore for a dock. None visible at this late in the day and they had only a few minutes left of daylight and would not make it in to shore quick enough. Without knowing the area at all and having to come in practically blind, they decided it would be best to anchor offshore for the night. Daybreak would allow a better view of the shoreline and a place to moor.

John shut the motor off and dropped anchor. With the engine no longer running, the only sound came from the lapping of the waves against the side of the boat. Even the seagulls that followed them down the entire island cost no longer flew overhead at this time of day.

Sebastian scanned the shoreline during the last few minutes of daylight and caught sight of a handful of boats tied to a few moorings on shore. "We will have to check on those boats tomorrow for any sign of Marco and Mariella, but the odds are they are already inland."

"We might as well make ourselves comfortable, Father. I'll make us some supper."

They ate under a dim light and kept the blinds and curtains drawn. They also shut off the boat's running lights.

After the meal, John checked Sebastian's wound and saw no infection. "You no longer need to keep your arm in a sling but take it easy with it so as not to open the stitches. In a few days they'll be ready to come out." He disinfected the wound and re-bandaged it.

"Tomorrow morning, as soon as the sun comes up, we'll dock and go to the location where the coordinates point to," said Sebastian. He had looked at the satellite view on the internet and it lay squarely on a house only a few hundred yards inland.

That night they both slept to the sound of the waves and the slow rocking of the boat. The next morning found both refreshed and ready to take on the day.

After breakfast, John started the engine, pulled up anchor and headed into shore. They found themselves at a small dock in what appeared to be an out of the way marina. A short man in his seventies came to meet them as they drifted in. Sebastian steered the boat as John got on deck and threw the line at the native on shore.

"Ahoy there!" hailed John, trying to sound like a seasoned mariner.

"Hello. You are English," said the man without asking, his own accent barely noticeable. He tied the line to one of the piers. "Welcome. Welcome. I do not get too many tourists on this side of the island at this time of year. Welcome to my marina!"

"It is a beautiful location, but we will not be too long," said John, taking the lead as both he and Sebastian got off the boat. It took a few moments for both of them to get their land legs back. "How much to keep our boat here?" he asked.

"Only twenty Euros a day, but cheaper if you stay longer," the proprietor said with a smile.

John pulled out a few bills. "Here are forty for now. That'll cover you for two days. We'll be back before then."

"As you wish, my friend," the man replied. "Just ask for Joey when you return." He began to head back to the small building just off the pier.

"Oh, one more thing," said John. The man stopped and turned back. "Have you received another boat about our size with a man and woman yesterday or the day before?"

"No sir," said the old man, "but there are a lot of marinas up and down the cost. They could have stopped at any one of them."

"Thanks," said John.

The man nodded and went on his way.

John and Sebastian headed out of the marina and towards a dirt road that ran parallel to the shoreline. The road ran for a few hundred feet and ended at the start of a paved street running perpendicular to the beach. A street sign on a telephone pole showed it to be the very one they were looking for.

"Fortizza Road," said Sebastian anxiously.

Only a single house stood on the street surrounded by a ten-foot wall. They approached the white limestone building crowned with a red terra cotta tiled roof. The house held a single wooded door as an entrance. They saw no one outside and the gate hung open. Nor did they see any traffic on the road. A single late model small car sat near the front door, hinting that there may have been someone home.

They approached the front door and looked at each other as Sebastian rapped on the door. A moment later, the door cautiously opened and Brother Marco looked out at the two men. "Senior!" he exclaimed as a smile appeared on his face.

"Marco!" answered Sebastian as he stepped forward to embrace him.

"It is so good to see you. I knew you would make it."

"And you have no idea how relieved I am to see you." Sebastian loosened his embrace and looked at Marco. "Where is she?"

"She's in the kitchen talking to Jonathan. He came with us on the boat."

"Good. I am glad he made it too."

Marco glanced over to John. "Who is this, Senior?" he asked.

"Have no fear, Marco," began Sebastian. "He is an outsider but he can be trusted. He has saved my life more than once in the last few days." He let go of Marco and added, "Brother Marco, this is John Bernard, a police detective from Boston, who is now officially on the run because of me."

Marco extended his hand in greeting and said, "If the Senior trusts you, then so do I." They shook hands. "I am honored to meet you. You have done a great service keeping him alive."

"Thank you," said John. "I have heard a lot about you as well, Brother Marco."

"Please, just call me Marco. It is less formal," said the monk with a smile. "Please, gentlemen, come on in."

He led them down a small hall to a contemporary kitchen. At the table sat Jonathan and Mariella.

"Jonathan, I am so happy to see you also made it," said Sebastian warmly.

"Great to see you too, Sebastian," replied Jonathan joyfully, getting up to shake hands.

Sebastian turned to Mariella and his eyes lit up along with his smile. "Mariella, my dear, you have no idea how relieved I am to see you. I am

Father Sebastian. Do you remember me?" He took her hands into his as she got up.

Mariella looked at the Elder and a sign of recognition showed on her face. "Yes, I do recall you," she said timidly, "and thank-you for your concern, but Zio Marco has taken good care of me."

"I am sure he has," replied Sebastian looking back at the Monk. "Marco is a good man." He turned to John and said, "Let me introduce you and Jonathan to John Bernard. He is a close friend of mine who has been with me in these trying days and who I owe my life to." He turned to the detective and added, "John, this is Jonathan Koite, also an Elder member of the Protectors and this is Mariella Amaya, the Descendent I told you about."

John was barely aware shaking hands with Jonathan. What captured his attention, what took his breath away, was the beautiful creature standing before him. He saw nothing else but Mariella, and the beauty and sensuality that emanated from her. Everyone else, mere shadows at the peripheral of her light. His senses overloaded by the powerful presence of her being which the others called Mariella. He had never felt this before. John's throat constricted and his body felt like lead. A knot had suddenly materialized in the pit of his stomach and he could barely breathe, let alone move. He felt heat rise up into his face as his skin flushed red.

John managed to grunt a simple, "Hi."

Mariella had turned her attention from Sebastian to John. As soon as she caught sight of him, she let out a small gasp for here stood the man in her dreams.

The touch of their hands lingered for only a moment but, for John, it felt like an eternity. Eyes locked in a visual embrace, unable to look away, not wanting to look away. Mariella managed a small smile at his guttural greeting. The attraction noticed by the other three men in the room who exchanged glances and a quick knowing smile. John and Mariella reluctantly released their grip of each other's hand.

Mariella cleared her throat and said, "Mr. Bernard, please sit down."

"Please, call me John."

"Call me Mariella."

"Mariella," repeated John, smiling, her name like honey on his tongue.

"John," she said also with a smile.

They both sat down at the table facing each other, unable and not wanting to break the connection.

Marco scratched his head and looked over at the Seniors. "Jonathan, Father Sebastian, can I talk to you two in private?" Without waiting for a reply, he grabbed the pitcher of wine from the table and three glasses. "We can go to the garden in the back."

Without a word, the three men exited to the yard from a back door. Mariella gave a feeble wave without looking back.

The Elders, Jonathan and Sebastian, and the Protector Marco sat at iron benches around a limestone round table.

"Well, that was something to behold," said Jonathan with an amused look.

Marco poured wine into the three glasses and said, "My fears have been for not." He took a sip. "It seems she has found her true love, her mate."

"He looked just as smitten as she," mused Jonathan.

"The saying is so true," said Sebastian with a smile, "God works in mysterious ways."

Marco looked at Sebastian and said warmly, "Father, it really is good to see you."

"Drop the formalities, Marco," said Jonathan, looking at the two men. "He may be a priest but he is also a friend."

"I am not being formal," said Marco without looking away from Sebastian. "He really is my father."

Jonathan had been taking another sip of wine and nearly choked. "Say again?"

"I did not become a priest right away," said Sebastian. "Not till my late twenties. Before then I was married and had a child, a son, Marco. My wife died in a car accident a year after she gave birth to Marco. I placed my son in the care of the Protectors and I became a priest to work within the Church to identify and weed out members of the Brotherhood of The Rapture that infiltrated it." He paused and took a sip of wine. "Sorry for not telling you, Jonathan. I did not want the knowledge to affect your decisions, your leadership, as an Elder of the Protectors of The Truth, especially as it relates to Marco. I thought it best that everyone thought him as another orphan like the rest."

"I did not know myself until in my twenties," said Marco. "And I must confess it did influence my decision to become a monk. It's also fortuitous of me to be among the members who protected the real Descendant."

"I had nothing to do with that," added Sebastian. "I am proud to say that Marco earned that right on his own merit."

"Then let us drink to father and son," said Jonathan raising his glass to the two men.

"To us all," corrected Sebastian and they all emptied their glasses.

When the stories of their adventures were finished, the three sat in silence. Many good men had died the last few days. They all silently prayed for their dead comrades. They even prayed for the souls of their misguided enemies.

"So what do we do with those two in there?" said Sebastian lifting the mood of the others. "The sexual tension was such that you could cut it with a knife."

"Do?" inquired Jonathan. "Why, we do nothing. Let nature take its course. Though it does appear to have been a divine influence in what has happened."

"Have no fear, father," began Marco. "Mariella has had the most intellectual and moral upbringing that can be had and without any outside interference. What she decides will be what she wants and not influenced by the world's modern self-absorbed immoral ways. No self-interest companies have been able to influence her outlook in life, but she is also not trapped by any irrelevant ancient tradition, just as she is not a slave to modern materialism." He looked at the two men. "No gentlemen, she is her own person and has her own mind. She may even be a good influence on that man in there." He concluded with a smile.

"I can believe that," said Jonathan with a quick laugh. "I got a good sense of what she is like on the boat trip here. I don't fear for her, I fear for him."

They all laughed in agreement and soon sat in silence for a few moments, enjoying the implication of the union and what it would ultimately mean for all of Mankind.

"Do you realize, gentlemen," began Sebastian, "that we are only twelve months away from witnessing the greatest promise to Mankind that has ever been made? We are a most fortunate few that know what is to come. For almost two thousand years, our organization has been patiently keeping a promise to protect the lineage and we are blessed enough to bear witness to the end result, the fruit, of that promise."

"You are so right, Sebastian," answered Jonathan. "We are indeed blessed."

"Amen, but these are also very dangerous times," added Marco.

Jonathan saw the shadow come across Marco's face and said, "Gentlemen, it is time that we consolidate our strength. We must gather all that remains of the Protectors right here, to this place. Build an impenetrable shield around the Descendant and her potential mate."

"Yes, of course," answered Sebastian. "I fully agree, and I'm sure Marco feels the same."

Marco nodded in agreement. "Of course I do."

"Good," said Jonathan. "We must begin right away, and let's be careful that we don't inadvertently give away our location while we try to make contact with anyone that is left. The last think we need is yet another attack by The Brotherhood. We have been lucky so far, always staying just one step ahead of them." He looked at the two men soberly. "But not by much."

CHAPTER TEN
LOVE

John propped himself up on his elbow looking down at Mariella lying next to him among the tall red spring tulips. On her back and with her eyes closed, Mariella enjoyed the warm midday sun on her face.

They were married the middle of April and now, three weeks later, his head still spun from the joy of it. The wedding was not an elaborate affair at all, at least not in the traditional sense. Mariella the only female at the ceremony and the rest were all men, members of the Protectors of The Truth. Sebastian, Father Sebastian, did the ceremony while Marco gave away the bride and Jonathan acted as the Best Man to John. They held a simple reception afterwards, attended only by the bridal party in question.

The happy couple did not go anywhere for their honeymoon. They and the entire entourage remained in hiding, of course. Now here they were, in the warm spring air enjoying their time together. They lay on a blanket in the middle of the tulip field near the shoreline, the air warm enough to allow light summer clothes and enjoy the noonday sun.

John couldn't keep his eyes off her. He kept wondering how it could be possible that such a beautiful, intelligent woman could be interested in a man like him. He delicately ran his finger down the bridge of her nose and to her lips and chin, carefully observing every curve of her facial features, marveling at the beauty of her. How it affected him. She still made his pulse speed up and excited him sexually even after three weeks of never losing sight of her. On the contrary, it made him want her even more.

As he caressed her lips, she kissed his finger and smiled slightly. She slowly opened her eyes and looked at his face peering down at her. He felt her eyes on him but he kept his eyes on his finger as it slowly looped around her chin, down her neck and to her cleavage. He stopped and began to undo the top button of her cotton blouse, as she lay there without resisting, still looking up at him. Her pupils began to expand as desire welled up in her. He undid the top two buttons and reached under her blouse, cupped her full breast, her nipple between his fingers, kneading it expertly and causing it to harden.

"You dog," she said playfully while squirming under his touch. "Keep that up and you will have to take me right here, right now."

"Ooh, now you're talking," said John not stopping his playfulness. "You're just like me. You can never get enough, even after this morning, and it isn't even lunch yet."

"Well, I thought that's what lunch was going to be today." She reached for him and found him already hard. "Looks like I was right."

John looked around mischievously and found they were deep enough in the tall tulips and over a rise facing the sea, hidden from any prying eyes. The house stood several hundred yards away and out of sight. Even the four Protectors assigned to guard them stayed at a discreet distance and knew when to give the newlyweds some privacy, such as this particular moment. Later, John would give them a signal when they could come back into view again, but right now, the world consisted of him and Mariella, and the smell of tulips and salt air mingled with the sweet scent of sex.

Satisfied that they were alone, John quickly loosened his pants and pulled them down to his knees. Mariella wore a cotton skirt that matched her blouse. Under her skirt, she wore nothing else. Her legs yielded and he entered her.

"You planned this to happen, didn't you?" he said, his breath hot in her ear. He pushed deep inside her as if trying to lose himself in her.

"I left my panties back in our room, hoping this would happen," she replied hoarsely. "Wasn't that naughty of me, my love?" Her legs locked around his torso pushing him in even further.

LAST DESCENDANT

Within seconds, he felt the pressure build up inside. He could not hold back and he let out a groan as he spent himself inside her like never before. She felt his release like a pulsing bolt of energy that made her gush out in mutual pleasure. Her lips locked on his as she cried out into his throat. They both lay in their embrace; not wanting it to end, but it ebbed as quickly as it came. She felt the last jolt from him as his muscles began to relax. She, in turn, loosened her vice-like grip on him. Her inner thighs quivered with exquisite ache that slowly faded.

Mindful of his weight on her, he slowly rolled over and reclined by her side, looking at her chiseled black eyebrows that framed large, cavernous eyes. He peered into those dark, almost black orbs and saw a desire, a yearning that he had never seen emanate from a woman for him and for him alone.

"I love you," he said to her, meaning the words with every fiber of his being. "Even if we were apart from this day forward, if I could no longer say it, know that I will always love you forever."

She reached up and caressed his cheek. "I love you too, my knight in shining armor."

"Right, your knight in shining armor," he replied sarcastically. "More like a villain ravaging you at every opportunity."

"Ooh yah," she said, her eyebrows wrinkled in feigned horror. "I like that. Ravage me, baby. Spank me hard."

"Whoa, girl," he laughed and looked down at her. "You are going to kill me, but this is why I love you so much."

"Because I'm gonna kill you?"

"Yah and what a way to go."

They embraced and kissed passionately for that's all he could manage this time and she didn't mind, for she too felt spent.

Later they opened the picnic basket, hungrily eating their sandwiches while enjoying the sun in quiet contemplation. A cool breeze rolled in from the sea softly caressing their cheeks. The tulips swayed in unison as if celebrating the presence of the human guests among their fields and doing their best to provide a magnificent sight and sweet smell for the senses.

A week ago, Mariella had told John she thought she was expecting a child. Besides missing her period, all the other signs were there. He was ecstatic at the news, and what a response from the Protectors! They celebrated for two days after the doctor confirmed what they all hoped, but still one thing bothered John. They had yet to tell her their son's destiny, the significance of the child. Everything had happened just as the prophecy had foretold and he went over it in his mind.

Mariella had fallen in love with him. She had married and conceived at such a time that the baby would be born in the final days of December. Again, if the prophecy were correct, it would be the evening of December 21. The child would be a boy, Christ's second coming and a new age of Man would begin. This would all happen, John thought, as long as The Brotherhood of The Rapture did not manage to kill her, and that is what the Protectors of The Truth were there to prevent. That is what the men around them at all times and standing at a discreet distance would gladly lay down their lives for.

I am to be the modern day Joseph, he thought amusingly. Maybe I should take up carpentry.

He had to talk to the Elders, Sebastian and Jonathan, soon and decide how to tell Mariella. She had the right to know what their son's destiny would be and how it would affect their lives. Once he came into this world, he would not just be of their concern, but the concern of all who believed, and the non-believers as well, or at least the ones that would think of Him as evil would try to get at him, try to kill him. He would never have a normal life, even as a child. That worried John. The Protectors would never allow his little family to fend for themselves. John knew he would have little say in the day-to-day upbringing of his son, nor would Mariella for that matter. How would she take it? How would he take it?

After lunch, they remained in their arms for another hour and eventually decided to head back to the house.

Mariella had gone up to take a shower and John looked for the Elders: Jonathan, Sebastian and Marco. The two Seniors elected Marco as the third Elder when the original could not be found and presumed dead, probably killed by the Brotherhood in the bloodbath back in

December. The month of May brought warm weather and John found the Elders in the garden at the back of the house.

They changed the property quite a bit since arriving five months before. They added a barbed wire on top of the ten-foot wall, the front gate replaced with a much stronger structure with sentries posted at all times, and replaced the terracotta gable styled roof with a flat asphalt roof to allow easy patrolling of the walled enclosure. Several guards stood watch from the top of the roof, armed with an array of weapons, and finally, to keep the public away from the area, the Protectors had bought all the properties surrounding the house out in almost a quarter mile in each direction. Including the public road, at a considerable price paid to the government.

The plan called for them to remain at the current location for the birth. Plans did not yet extend past that date.

The three Seniors discussed the latest results of the ongoing search for other members of their organization. To-date, they had successfully contacted and called together at their location almost a hundred men. These men were now scattered around the entire area that they now owned, in the other houses, behind walls, and even in holes, keeping a constant vigil for any kind of danger, or anomaly, no matter how small.

"So, how is the bridegroom today?" asked Marco jokingly when John arrived at the outdoor table.

John smiled back at the three men. "Just fine, gentlemen. Just fine." He sat down at one of the empty benches around the cement table. "Mariella is taking a shower and we should have a quick talk while she's occupied."

"What's on your mind, son?" asked Sebastian.

John got right to the point. "We have to tell her the destiny of our child and who...what...he represents."

"Yes, you're right," Jonathan agreed.

John looked at the three men silently for a few moments and finally said, "I think it best that I should be the one to tell her."

No one spoke.

He continued before any of the Elders had a chance at a rebuttal. "I am the closest to her now and she would listen to what I would say more seriously than any of you." He looked at them closely. "Please don't take it wrong. Our love is strong."

"Yes, you are right once again," nodded Jonathan before Sebastian and Marco could object.

"When will you tell her?" asked Marco, speaking for the first time.

"As soon as possible," answered John with some relief on how easy that went. "Tonight, when we have retired to our room, I'll tell her."

"Why not tell me now?" Mariella's voice called out from the door of the kitchen.

All four men suddenly turned in her direction in surprise. John stood up and slowly walked towards her in shock. He barely managed to find his voice and asked, "How long have you been standing there, my love?"

"Just for a moment," she answered. She had changed into slacks and a shirt. "I washed quickly, wanting to be with you as soon as I could." She took John's hand and led him back to the bench and sat down next to him, snuggling herself into his arms and lovingly used him as a backrest. None of the other men had moved or uttered a sound. Mariella glanced at all of them with an easy smile. "So tell me, gentlemen, what you want me to know?"

With their quickly thought out plan in ruin, Marco spoke first, thinking him to be the one she knew the longest and whose words would carry the most weight. "Mariella, my dear, there is something we want to talk to you about that is of great importance. The – huh –"

"The child in you has a great destiny," interjected Sebastian. A small sly smile appeared on Mariella's face.

"A destiny greater then you may realize," added Jonathan during the slight pause. Mariella did not lose her smile.

John interpreted her smile as one of a mother amused at the attention of loving uncles and added, "Mariella, they are serious. Please don't take this lightly."

Mariella's smile grew even wider and said, "It's all right, babe. I know all about it. I am just amused at how miserably you are all failing in your attempt to tell me."

"What do you mean?" asked Marco in bewilderment.

"You have taught me well, Zio," began Mariella, comfortably nestled in John's arms. "I am not the innocent girl that you think I am, or was, until I met John." She looked up playfully at John as she uttered his name. He remained too shocked to say anything. "I have known since I conceived who I carry inside of me, and what he means to the destiny of Man," she concluded.

All four men stopped breathing at the same time.

"His soul may belong to God, but he is also my son as well as John's," she said. "That I am sure. And that's how it should be." Her voice had a tone of finality.

The men let out their breaths simultaneously.

"But how could you have known?" asked Sebastian breathlessly.

"I heard you men talking on a number of occasions when you thought I was not within earshot, or assumed I was somewhere else. Women are good at that, especially me, growing up among secretive monks. I had to learn quickly how to eavesdrop if I wished to know more about the world. Putting all of the information I gathered the last few weeks together with what you told me, selectively I might add, about my lineage, it all made sense."

"My love, you never cease to amaze me," said John.

"Get used to it, my dear," she said giving him a peck on the chin. "You men have a habit of always underestimating us women."

"I think it is time for a celebration drink," said Sebastian with eyes wide. "I am just not sure if I need it for my nerves, or as an actual toast of celebration."

"It's to a toast," interjected Mariella, "and I will even have a small sip."

Marco wordlessly went to retrieve some glasses and a bottle of wine.

Sebastian interlaced his fingers in resignation and said, "Mariella, there is a manuscript that I think it best that you read. It will give you more of an insight on who…"

"I have already read it," Mariella casually interrupted.

"You have?" Sebastian could only grunt out.

"Yes, I managed to slip away with it for a few hours one day, and I must say I am rather pleased that I am named after Judah's wife, Mariel, and you should be proud of your family's history, Sebastian."

"Yes," replied Sebastian as he stared incredulously at Mariella. "Yes, I am proud of it."

Marco came back with a bottle and glasses. "We need to send some of the men into town," he said. "We are getting low on provisions.

When they needed additional supplies, they were very careful with who ventured into the public eye. Sebastian, John and even Marco did not dare try heading into town, too public and too many cameras around. The other men also avoided visiting the same store and town more than once. It prevented any of the locals from getting too familiar with the new faces in town. Even if the men maintained a very low profile, they kept any necessary risks down to a bare minimum.

Marco poured several glasses of wine and handed one to Mariella. He raised his glass and said, "I for one am very relieved everything's out in the open. We no longer have to worry what we now say or do. Things are going better than we had hoped for and soon, after almost two thousand years of patient waiting, we will be the privileged few who will witness the new dawn of Man, and a new beginning."

Sebastian held up his glass and added, "Let us all pray that your words hold true."

Everyone agreed and they all drank to the toast.

CHAPTER ELEVEN
MASTER

Cardinal Ferdinand Costa took a sip of his unsweetened espresso and pondered how to answer the reporter. How often did the media ask him the same question? Too often, he thought in resigned disgust.

He sat at a table for two in the outside patio of the coffee bar across the street from St. Peter's Square. The reporter that sat across from him couldn't have been more than twenty. The soft, pudgy, pasty, skin of the round, baby face barely knew the blade of a razor.

The young American reporter proved to be typical of today's youth of the world, Costa thought, soft and undisciplined both in mind and in the body.

The senior cleric did little to hide the look of distaste on his face as the young man, not looking up, and oblivious of the reaction he created across the table, devoured the cannoli in front of him while waiting for the answer to his question. White dusty sugar caked the edges of his mouth as more of the snowy confection floated down onto his open notebook in front of him. He casually wiped the sugar aside with the soft edge of his hand, ready to write down the answer. Hearing nothing, he swallowed the remains of the ricotta-filled pastry and looked up. "Your Eminence?" he asked in English.

"Yes?" inquired Costa coming out of his reverie.

"Would you like me to repeat the question?" responded the reporter uncomfortably.

The cardinal looked directly at the young man. The square jaw and military-cut grey hair under the cardinal cap looked very intimidating to the novice reporter from the popular American magazine 'New Generation.'

Costa's face went through a subtle but noticeable change that conveyed his focus back to the subject at hand. "No. That is not necessary, my son."

The cleric finished his espresso and sat back in his wrought iron chair as he formulated in his mind the answer to the reporter's question. He liked the uncomfortable feel of the metal digging into his buttocks and lower back. It was in keeping with the disciplined and Spartan life he believed necessary to achieve oneness with God. This, he believed, was another ruin of these modern times: no discipline and over indulgence. The soft comforts made Man love his earthbound flesh and fear death itself. For death of the flesh, of the mortal body, was the only path to God and everlasting life.

He looked at the young reporter and, trying to keep his voice steady and void of anger, said, "So you think we, clerics of the church, are rich men who partake in all forms of luxury without remorse or care for our souls."

The reporter caught by surprise and taken aback by the abrasive response could only stammer, "No, No, Your Eminence! I did not mean to offend! I truly wish to allow the Church the opportunity to address the question asked by so many people of the world. That is, if Jesus said that it is easier for a camel to go through the eye of a needle than for a rich man to enter the kingdom of heaven, then, when their time comes, how will members of the Catholic Church, one of the riches organizations in the world, be allowed into heaven?" He tried to appear humble but it did not fool Cardinal Costa. "Our readers would be most interested in hearing the truth, Your Eminence."

The cardinal felt anger build deep inside the pit of his stomach. The fool reporter addressed him correctly enough, but the tone of his voice lacked respect. He calmed himself before he began his all too frequent explanation. The cardinal would not lower himself to the same level as the feeble-minded man in front of him.

Costa began slowly and without anger, "All members of the Catholic Church, from a newly ordained priest right up to the Holy Father, the Pope himself, have few earthly possessions. These usually consist of personal toiletries and some mementos from occasions in our lives that are precious to us, such as a watch, an embroidered handkerchief from our earthly parents. And even those are of little monetary value." He paused as he touched and rubbed the center of his chest where his golden cross would normally hang when in official cardinal dress. On this occasion, he wore the traditional black outfit of a common priest, his preferred dress when not wanting to attract attention in public.

Cardinal Costa continued. "Your question is in reference to, of course, the limousines, chauffeurs, Christian jewelry, and elaborate dress so common at ceremonies and other formal gatherings." The cardinal's eyes were severe and penetrating as he mentioned these luxuries. The reporter caught the look and cowed under the glare. "These things are mere tools of office and exist only to solicit the appropriate respect for the position." He leaned in slightly as he added, "Rather than for the man himself."

"Even the limousines and chauffeurs?" asked the reporter with mild audacity.

Costa straightened his back and marveled at the boldness of the man. He may have been soft in flesh and mind, but he showed some courage.

Or was it disrespect for the Church? The cardinal asked himself. Mankind moved farther and farther away from the grace of God.

It took all of his strength to answer with a calm voice. "The limousines are armored cars and the chauffeurs are members of the Swiss Guard, or of the Gendarmerie Corps of the Vatican City State. They exist to provide security for bishops, cardinals and the Holy Father himself. Not because we fear death, but because of what the positions signify within the Mother Church and the respect that they afford." He paused for a moment to search his mind for a similar example to get through this thickheaded child. He found one. "You may have heard of a saying from across the ocean in America that the Office of the President of the United States is greater than the man himself. Likewise, for the senior positions within the Catholic Church, they are greater than the men that hold those titles. The positions themselves are what must be respected, not the men. We, the bishops and cardinals, are the successors of the Apostles, and the Holy Father, the Pope, is the successor of Saint Peter himself. These positions, through the men that hold them, must be protected and respected at all times for what they signify to the rest of the world and, most importantly, to the faithful." With an icy tone while turning his nose up to look down at the youth in front of him, he ended with, "No one must be allowed to violate or diminish these titles through physical, or verbal, attacks on the men who hold them."

Costa had directed the last comment at the reporter. The young man understood immediately.

The reporter tried to shrink more into himself and, looking meekly up at the cardinal who now sat upright to his full height, said, "Yes. Yes. Very good, Your Eminence. I couldn't have put it better myself." He smiled thinly and kept his head down as his eyes tried to look up at the cardinal. Beads of cold sweat began to appear on the young man's forehead. The cardinal merely stared down severely at the soft man and said nothing.

The reporter squirmed in his chair uncomfortably and began to gather his papers together. In his nervousness, he knocked over the paper plate that held the cannoli. Confectioner's sugar dusted the air as the plate softly hit the ground at his feet. The reporter paused for a moment as he stared down at his mishap and smiled another thin acknowledgement to the cardinal, who remained as still as a statue. Only his eyes showed movement, missing nothing.

"Thank-you for your time, Your Eminence," said the reporter, as he got up to leave without waiting for a response.

The reporter brushed by Costa and the steel grip of the cardinal's hand caught the fleeing man by the forearm. The reporter froze in his tracks and the cardinal slowly pulled him down to him, the young man too powerless to resist. Costa looked into the face of the now frightened child and whispered, "May God guide your hand as you write your story for the magazine and," he paused while pulling the reporter closer, "may it tell the truth as I have told it."

The reporter looked into the cardinal's eyes. What the young man saw produced a nervous quiver in his sweaty, bottom lip. Costa saw the effect he had on the other man and felt confident the story would shine as much positive light on the Church as the reporter could muster.

The young man only managed a whisper as he said, "Y-Yes, Your Eminence. You can count on me."

The steel grip loosened as the cardinal blinked once in acknowledgement. The reporter left as quickly as his now shaky legs could manage. He would later sport a bruise on his arm as a reminder of his oath while he typed the story for his magazine on his computer. He would keep his promise.

Costa got up with athletic ease soon after the reporter's exit and straightened out his black jacket as he turned and headed for the door. The dark shadow across his face lightened only slightly. He nodded his greeting to the ever-observant proprietor of the coffee shop as he walked by the counter. The greeting met in kind but with a deeper bow.

The caressing mid-afternoon spring breeze felt warm under the sunny, cloudless sky. Cardinal Ferdinand Costa felt only relief to be outside and away from that flabby and uncouth reporter. As head of the Congregation for Catholic Communication, he knew these interviews were necessary. They were all the more so when you considered the fast declining membership in the Catholic Church. The members of the College of the Cardinals saw these interviews as recruitment opportunities, and rightly so, but he did not have to like them.

The cardinal took out his cell phone and called his secretary, who confirmed the meeting for eleven that evening. He felt relief to hear it so, for he had a lot to discuss with the other members.

Still early in the day, the cardinal decided to go back to his offices at the Papal Palace within Vatican City. The Swiss Guard and the much larger Gendarmerie Corps knew Costa well and he passed through the various gates around the Vatican City with relative ease. He had been a resident there for over a decade and still felt a sense of wonder for the city-state.

Officially known as the State of the Vatican City, it consisted of a walled enclave about one hundred and ten acres within the city of Rome. Since its official creation in 1929, no country had dared to invade it for fear of reprisal from its billions of worshippers. The Vatican City included large areas of gardens, St. Peter's Basilica, and the Papal Palace. The Palace was a large complex housing the Papal Apartments where the Pope lived and included some of the Catholic Church's government offices, a few chapels such as the famous Sistine Chapel, the Vatican Library and several Vatican Museums. To Costa, the gardens were the most beautiful and one of the most tranquil areas in the city-state. They were a perfect setting for personal meditation and renewal of one's faith. Today, he took the long route back to his offices by going through these natural wonders.

Costa encountered several bishops and cardinals during his walk back to his offices. They were also enjoying the gardens on route to wherever their own affairs took them. He made small talk with a few and casually acknowledged greetings to others, but he kept it to a minimum. Costa did not like to fraternize with other members of the Church. He did not consider it necessary. If anything, he found most of the clergy to be lacking in discipline demanded of them by the Church, especially so in these modern days.

Costa regarded the discipline of faith, mind and body interconnected. A flabby exterior hinted at a flabby mind and, thus, a flabby, undisciplined faith in the Church, its teachings and in God. As proof of this belief, he kept his six-foot-one body lean and hard with daily, rigorous exercise while consuming only the most basic and Spartan of foods. Two espressos a day the only luxury he allowed himself, and even then, without sugar, savoring the bitter taste it left on his pallet. He drank only water and did not partake in alcohol or tobacco. He was a ravenous reader in all things religious, and prayed and meditated several times a day.

The cardinal entered the outer room of his offices and found his secretary at his desk. The secretary, a priest in his early thirties with a brush cut and lean, muscular build, much like his superior, rose to his feet and gave a slight bow.

"I will be in my office for the rest of the day," said Costa without a greeting or halting his stride as he headed for the closed doors of his inner office. "Interrupt me only if there is an urgent matter to attend to." He spoke in English and he expected his secretary to respond in kind.

The priest bowed for the second time and acknowledged respectfully, "Yes, Your Eminence."

LAST DESCENDANT

The cardinal entered his office, closed the double doors behind him, and sat at his ornate desk. The office and furniture, inherited from his previous predecessor, was not in keeping with the cardinal's simplistic lifestyle with its large area rugs, decorated high ceiling, fresco-covered walls, and elaborate furniture, but he understood the necessity of appearance that commanded respect for his position.

Cardinal Ferdinand Costa was one of 195 cardinals that served the Catholic Church. As a whole called the College of Cardinals, the numbers tended to vary depending on how many departments and Episcopal Sees that the current ruling pope maintained. Cardinals were essentially bishops who headed such organizations and Costa led the Congregation for Catholic Communication, charged with getting the message of the Church into the mainstream media and the reason why he accepted the interview that afternoon. One of the countless he had agreed to attend throughout the twelve years he held his current position.

The responsibilities of the College of Cardinals included voting in the election of a new pope when the current one died. Costa still felt a twinge of bitterness for failing to win the election the last time this occurred.

He would have made many changes if he had become pope, Costa thought to himself. The Church would have had a more dominant role in the world, and the Order of Matthias would have been leading that charge. Instead, they had to take a more clandestine approach. No matter, later that night, he would know how the search progressed.

The cardinal worked on paperwork required for the Church the rest of the day. He ordered dinner in his office and remained there until the time arrived to leave for his meeting.

He kept on the simple black outfit he wore that day and, with his secretary in tow in a similar outfit, headed out onto the street to hail a taxi instead of using the car and driver he had the right to as a cardinal, wanting to remain low profile.

His secretary directed the driver to a location near the outskirts of Rome. As they did on every occasion in the past, they stopped several blocks from the place where the meeting took place. Walking together through the dark streets, with the secretary walking slightly behind as a show of respect, both men removed and pocketed their white clerical collars.

They approached a large, old, three-story building surrounded by a five-foot, wrought-iron fence. A prominent member of the Roman political elite, also part of the cardinal's Order, owned the house.

They rang the bell attached to one of the double-doors in the front façade. A man, also dressed in black, immediately answered the door. The doorman recognized the two men and stepped aside without a greeting.

The cardinal and his secretary walked to a small room where they found a dozen hooks. Only two still had black robes. Costa smiled to himself in silent satisfaction, they were all waiting for him. The cardinal's secretary helped him with his before putting his own robe on. They pulled the hoods of the robes over their heads and made their way out of another door at the opposite end of the room.

They entered a cavernous room with seventeenth century fresco decorated walls and ceiling. The floor, covered with a checkered black and white marble tile, held a dozen chairs placed in a wide circle. Men, in the same black hooded robes, stood in front of ten of the twelve chairs. No one said a word as Costa and his attendant walked in, but the newcomers felt an air of expectation from the others as they took their place in front of the remaining two empty chairs, the circle now complete.

Costa understood the importance of rituals and traditions better than any man of power and influence. It ensured that the members remained completely dedicated to the cause and would never waiver in their faith of who they were and what they must do.

With the room lighted by only a few wall sconces, it was not possible for Costa to see the men's faces, but he knew each one. The meeting could now begin, but first the prayer.

Costa brought his palms together. The rest did the same.

The congregation began in unison, "Father in heaven, heed our prayer!"

In a booming voice, Costa recited alone, his face hidden within the shadow of his hood. "Oh God of the most high, we, The Brotherhood of The Rapture, ask for your strength and guidance to find and destroy the bloodline of the betrayer of your only son, Jesus Christ."

Once again, all in unison repeated, "Father in heaven, heed our prayer!"

The cardinal continued alone as before, "Holy Father, let us be your sword that destroys the descendants of the cursed bloodline from the face of the Earth."

"Father in heaven, heed our prayer!"

"Holy Father, guide us to help you in bringing forth Armageddon and the preceding Rapture, as it is written in the holy book."

"Father in heaven, heed our prayer!"

Silence fell upon the congregation. The prayer had ended. As the echoes of the final words died down into nothingness within the vast chamber, all sat down, each in their own chair with hands on their laps. All waited for the Master to speak.

Costa finally broke the silence. "So, what is the latest from our brothers throughout the globe in their quest for the search of the final Descendant?"

The first hooded figure to the cardinal's right began. "I regret to report, Master, that our team in Italy have not been able to relocate the trail of the Senior of The Protectors and his new friend. There has been no trace since the last contact in that cemetery close to the monastery, the last hiding place of the Descendant."

Cardinal Costa, the Master, did not respond and kept his silence. When it became clear that no additional information was forthcoming, the next one on the right gave his report. "The Greek contingent has had no success in tracking down either the Descendant or the Senior. The search will continue until instructed otherwise. That is all that I have, Master."

The next hooded figure began. "The American team has been rebuilt soon after the devastation in December. Since we lost the trail back in Italy, we have not found any evidence that they made their way back to North America."

The remainder of the eleven men had little to offer as they each spoke in turn.

The Master remained silent for some time after the last report. Finally he spoke, "We are seven months away from the day we have been waiting for, the day that will end the war that The Brotherhood has waged with the betrayers for almost two thousand years. The Order of Matthias, from which we originate, has ensured that we had sufficient resources, in both money and men, to guarantee our success, and yet our prey has eluded us." He paused and let out a small sigh of frustration. The eleven did not miss it. He began again. "Gather up all the teams and concentrate the search within the Mediterranean Sea and the costal countries throughout."

Costa stood up and the rest followed. "We will reconvene in seven days." The meeting ended. He rose and left with his aide in tow. The others gave a slight bow as he passed and waited for the Master's exit before they took their own leave.

After shedding their robes, Costa and his aide were back on the street and down a few blocks. The younger man was about to hail a taxi when the cardinal turned to his secretary and said, "We are being followed."

Without missing a step or turning around his secretary asked in a low tone, "What would you like to do, Master?"

"Call the Pound and tell them we have a stray dog on our tail that needs to be caught and disposed of, and don't call me Master outside the Chamber."

"Yes, Your Eminence. Sorry for my weakness."

They continued walking as the cardinal's secretary confirmed the sighting without giving himself away. He then took his cell phone out and dialed.

"Fornello's Pizza," answered a male voice on the other end.

"I am returning a library book that is twelve days overdue," said the secretary.

"That will be twelve Euros," responded the voice as a confirmation of the accepted pass code.

"We have a stray dog that needs to be captured. It is a medium male with a light gray fur coat following us at approximately fifty meters. We are just east of the Pound."

"Confirmed. We'll have a Catcher on his tail in five minutes."

"Understood. We're going to walk for several more blocks to lead it farther away." The secretary disconnected the call. "Five minutes," he said to the cardinal.

When they felt they were far enough away from The Brotherhood's meeting place they stopped at an outdoor café and ordered espressos. The pursuer stopped in the shadows of an arched entrance of an old building less than a block from the café.

•••

Corporal Vigilo had followed his marks from the time they had left the Vatican staying several cars back from the taxi that the two men took. When they got out of the taxi, he had parked his own car and followed discreetly on foot. When the two men entered the large mansion, he simply waited a block away and casually smoked a few cigarettes. He was not told what to look for, but only to observe, remain undiscovered, and report back as to where they went and did when they returned to the Vatican.

Probably another sex scandal, the corporal decided. The priests could be having a homosexual relationship and were going to some orgy.

Nothing surprised him these days. He had seen and read enough about such scandals in his relatively short five years in the Gendarme Corps.

He had just finished his second cigarette and starting to get impatient that his marks were still nursing their coffee, when he noticed a man with short, cropped, blonde hair walking slowly down the street towards him with a map in his hands. The man looked at the street sign nearby and back down to his map with a confused look on his face. He stopped for a moment to look around as if taking his bearings and spotted the Corporal. Smiling, he walked over with his map held up.

"Signore, signore, please, can you help?" asked the man with a heavy German accent. "I am a tourist and think I am lost. I am looking for house number 345. Can you tell me which way?"

"You are going the right direction but it will be on the other side of the road," answered Corporal Vigilo, slightly annoyed at been seen.

"Thank-you, thank-you!" said the German as he smiled and extended his hand. The Corporal reached out instinctively and shook it.

"Quite all right. Good night," said the Corporal in dismissal as he looked back at his marks still sitting at the café.

"Good night," replied the German as he walked away.

A few seconds later, Corporal Vigilo felt a sudden tightness in his lungs as if struck with a club. He grabbed his chest in surprise as a second bolt of pain exploded beneath his ribs. Trying to breathe in but unable to do so, his face turned deep red then purple. His facial muscled twisted in agony and his eyes felt like they were going to pop out of his head. He looked at the receding back of the German he had just talked to and tried to scream in pain but only managed a few short gurgles of a drowning man. Corporal Vigilo fell to his knees as he clutched his chest and ripped his jacket and shirt open in a futile attempt to make his lungs work. Failing that, he reached out from the shadows but only managed to topple over and onto his back. The darkness closed in quickly as his heart gave one final twitch and stopped beating all together from the massive coronary it had just experienced.

The German walked by the café as he pulled off the ultra thin glove he had on his right hand. He carefully pealed it off inside out and placed it in a small plastic bag before pocketing it. He gave a quick and barely perceived nod to the cardinal as he went by.

Costa and his secretary got up and walked several blocks before hailing down a taxi. They were back at the Vatican within the hour.

• • •

Commander Daniello Gallo felt perplexed. "How could a seemingly healthy man in his late twenties have a massive heart attack?" he asked the Coroner.

The Medical Examiner, a small bookish looking man in his fifties, held the heart of Corporal Vigilo with both hands, slowly turning it over as he peered down at it through the bottom of his bifocals. The Corporal's body lay naked on the stainless steel table with its chest split open. Blood oozed down the grooves around the edge of the table intended for it and into a catch basin.

"Not only is it possible," casually answered the Coroner, "but I've seen it on several occasions." He nodded towards the body. "Even by such a seemingly healthy specimen as your Corporal there." He put the heart back in the body. "Yup, heart attack all right. No doubt about it."

"Thanks, Doctor," conceded Daniello.

As the head of the one hundred and thirty strong Corps of Gendarmerie of Vatican City, Commander Daniello felt an urge to leave when the Coroner began to staple up the chest right after folding the rib cage back in place. The commander went outside and took a deep breath of fresh air, trying to rid from his nostrils the smell of antiseptic and formaldehyde mixed with the putrid odors of bodily waste and fluid.

Though early morning, he had insisted that the coroner do the autopsy right away but it would be a couple of weeks before the results of the blood analysis came back and he needed to know right away whether there were any other reason for the heart attack like drugs or other substance abuse.

His driver waited for him by the car parked nearby. At a lean five foot six, the commander easily slid into the passenger front seat of the Mini. His lanky driver had slightly more difficulty in easing himself into the driver's seat but the small vehicle remained the preferred mode of conveyance for the Gendarme Corps exactly because of its small size and ease in which it could get through the tight roads of the ancient city of Rome.

"Back to the office," said the commander as he lit a cigarette and eased back into his seat.

"What were the results, Commander?" asked his subordinate, unable to contain his curiosity.

"Heart attack, and keep your eyes on the road," replied Daniello dismissively.

They rode back to the Corps' headquarters in silence.

Daniello did not stop at his office but headed directly to Cardinal Peticlere's office and asked the attending secretary priest for an audience right away. After a quick check by phone with his superior, the priest nodded for the commander to proceed into the main office of the senior cleric.

The commander entered an office much like the office of Cardinal Costa, large and very ornate, and the norm for rooms in the Palace of the Vatican.

A second cardinal sat across from Cardinal Peticlere, who sat behind his desk. The commander recognized the second senior cleric as Cardinal Leary. In white with red trim summer attire, they both stood as the commander walked into the room and closed the double doors behind him.

Daniello approached Cardinal Leary who stood closest to the door. The commander bowed, kissed the cardinal's ring, and said, "Your Eminence." The ritual considered the appropriate protocol by the faithful when approaching a cardinal. The commander did the same with Peticlere.

Both clerics sat back down with Daniello taking the second visitor chair at the front of the desk.

"So Commander, what have you found out?" asked Leary, a tall, portly, red haired Irishman in his seventies who had been with the church from his early twenties.

"The coroner merely suspects a heart attack," said Daniello. "The question is what caused it?"

Peticlere leaned forward and said emphatically, "Poison. It must have been someone from the Order of Matthias. They discovered your man tailing Costa and they made an example of him."

The commander looked at the cleric with mild surprise. He was not used to seeing such outbursts from the cardinal. Like his counterpart, Peticlere was also a man in his seventies but much shorter, lean and with black hair that betrayed not a strand of grey.

"We have no evidence of that, Your Eminence," said Daniello calmly.

"No need to fall back on police protocol with us," said Leary. "You may be the Commander of the Corps of Gendarmerie of Vatican City but you are a Protector first and foremost, just like we are, and our duty is to ensure that the Descendant remains save until the blessed day arrives."

"Absolutely, Your Eminence," said Daniello, "but we are still not sure whether Costa is the Master of the Brotherhood of the Rapture, or if he is even a member, and before we even consider taking any action against another cardinal we have to be absolutely sure."

"Yes, of course, Commander," said Peticlere. "We are all in agreement. For if we are wrong, than our souls are forever damned for killing another human being without just cause, especially such a senior cleric."

"Unjustified killing of *any* human being would be a serious sin," added Leary.

"Yes, of course, Brother Leary," conceded Peticlere.

"And please tread lightly, Commander Gallo," said Leary. "The last thing we need is to lose another of our men, especially you. Don't forget what happened to the Commander of the Swiss Guard back in ninety-nine."

Cardinal Leary referred to the murder of the then Commander of the Swiss Guard.

"I have not forgotten, Your Eminence," replied Daniello, remembering the events of that year.

Unlike the Corps of Gendarmerie who were the police force for the Vatican and tasked with such things as law enforcement, criminal investigations and crowd control, the Swiss Guard were solely responsible for the safety of the pope. They were in essence his bodyguards.

In 1999, an agent of The Brotherhood of The Rapture posing as a junior Swiss Guard murdered the commander of the Swiss Guard who was a member of the Protectors of the Truth. The Gendarmerie quickly managed to track down the killer. Cornered and unable to escape, he committed suicide by turning the gun on himself. The Vatican leaked an unofficial story that it was the tragic result of a homosexual affair gone wrong. The media bought the story and ran with it. With the Church staying mute on the matter, it made it all the more credible.

The circumstances surrounding the event made the Protectors of the Truth believe another agent of The Brotherhood lurked in the Vatican with Cardinal Costa as the prime suspect.

"It is unfortunate that the current commander is not one of us," said Daniello. "It would make our investigation a lot easier."

"That's true," said Peticlere, "but you are a capable man with many talents."

"So what's your next move, Commander Gallo?" asked Leary.

"Well, we will continue surveillance as best we can," began Daniello. "We know that he is adept at avoiding electronic tracking and listening devices. They seem to disappear as soon as we place them, no matter where. Whatever conversations we have been able to capture have not been very informative and are very cryptic. Even his secretary is extremely careful. The priest appears to be cut from the same cloth as the cardinal and we suspect he is also an agent of the Brotherhood, but again we have no proof."

"Given that we have very little evidence, nothing that is substantial really," interjected Leary, "we cannot approach The Holy Father Pope Julius or even the College of Cardinals."

"And if we did we would tell them what?" asked Peticlere, not expecting an answer. "That Cardinal Costa is a member of a radical Order hell bent on killing a woman that they believe is a descendant of Judah. That he is responsible for the death of a member of the Corps. They would think we were mentally disturbed at the very least. The Church is familiar with such a group, but it does not recognize it as a legitimate Order nor would it condone its actions or take it seriously."

"Nor would the Church recognize the Protectors of the Truth as a legitimate entity either, if they knew about us," added Leary. "No gentlemen, we, the Protectors, are on our own on this. As our Savior, Jesus Christ, has said, the veil over their eyes will be lifted only after the Second Coming."

"And that is soon," added Peticlere with controlled excitement in his voice.

The intercom buzzed. The number showed Peticlere's secretary.

The cardinal pressed the talk button. "Yes?" he asked.

"I am sorry to disturb you, Your Eminence," said the priest. "Cardinal Costa is on the phone. He asked to speak to you."

"Thank-you, I'll take the call," said the cardinal, exchanging glances with the other two men.

He pressed the speaker button on the phone for all in the room to hear.

"Brother Costa, it is a pleasure hearing from you," said Peticlere while the other two men in the room remained quiet.

"Thank-you, Cardinal Peticlere." The voice sounded tinny coming from the small speaker, but still recognizable as the voice of Cardinal Costa.

"What can I do for you, cardinal?" asked Peticlere.

"I am just calling to see how the investigation into the death of the officer is going," answered Costa without any inflection in his voice.

"Why ask me?" questioned Peticlere glancing up to the others.

"Because Commander Gallo and Cardinal Leary are there with you now," replied Costa in a casual voice as before.

The three men in the room looked at each other in surprise.

"Come now, Cardinal Peticlere," continued Costa. "Do not lie. It is a sin."

"I have not said one way or the other," responded Peticlere in a controlled voice.

"Then you do not deny it?" asked Costa. The accusation in his voice came through the telephone line.

"What may we do for you?" asked Peticlere without answering the question, leaving it open to interpretation as to whether he used the royal we or answering for all three men in the room, thus not committing himself either way.

"I told you," replied Costa. "I am simply inquiring as to whether the officer died under mysterious circumstances or if it was just an unfortunate situation."

"It is possible that you may know more about that than I," said Peticlere.

"Anything is possible," responded Costa. "It is possible that I know more and it is possible that I know nothing about what happened to the officer of the Corps." Playing with his opponents he continued, "It is possible that you and I are on opposite sides of two great forces completely at odds with each other. In a struggle, a battle for survival from which the outcome of that struggle could have a profound impact on Mankind and change the world as we know it."

The three men in the room sat staring at the phone as if they could see into the face of the man himself. Costa's voice betrayed his enjoyment of the jostling, as he continued. "Each one of us is thinking that the other is on the wrong side, the side of evil, but then, I have the bible on my side and the faith and support of over two billion people, one third of the population of the entire globe." He paused for a moment as if for effect. "And how many believe in your cause, Cardinal Peticlere? One hundred? A thousand? Less?" He gave out a sigh. "No matter, it is only a hypothetical situation, for there is no struggle, no opposing forces and views. Are there Cardinal Peticlere? We are servants of the Church and on the same side, are we not?"

"Of course, Brother Costa," answered Peticlere.

They knew they could use none of the rambling against Costa.

Just a hypothetical situation as he put it, thought Daniello. He knew Costa played with them and Costa enjoyed it.

"In all likelihood the evidence will show it as simply an unfortunate heart attack," Costa began again. "But if it wasn't, it means there is a killer, or killers, on the loose and that you and your friends need to be careful. Think twice about your next move so that no one else meets the same fate. That would be unfortunate, would it not, Cardinal Peticlere? But we need not worry, for we all know the report will show just a heart attack and no other action required by anyone involved. That would be the safest thing to do. Don't you agree?"

Without implicating himself, Costa had just threatened all three men.

Peticlere managed to keep his voice calm and answered, "The evidence will show the truth, whatever that may be, and appropriate action will be taken based on what is reported."

"Then let's hope the report will show a simple heart attack," responded Costa. "Good day to you all," he added dismissively and hung up.

Peticlere hit the release button on the phone to make sure the line disconnected.

"Well, that was an interesting call," said Leary as he physically relaxed back into his chair.

"He did not say anything that could be used against him," said Daniello as he stared into space. He had not moved from his chair the entire time but now he got up and paced about.

"Yes, I know," said Peticlere. "He was careful with that, but he also got his message across – 'stay away or else'."

"So what do we do now?" asked Leary.

"Your Eminences," began Daniello, as he turned back to the two men who remained seated. "Even though none of what he said could be used against him, he taunted us. It is further proof of who he is. He may not be the Master but he must be a prominent member. I suggest that I eliminate him personally and, if caught, say that I had a private vendetta against him so that I could distance myself from the church."

"Calm down commander. You know that's not going to work," said Peticlere. "No, no. Just watch him for now and let him make the next move. The Descendant is safe and we need to take no action for now. Let's just see what he plans to do."

The meeting soon ended but Daniello remained unconvinced. He brooded over this as he walked alone back to his office. He began to develop an idea, and with the idea, he began developing a plan. The more he thought about it the more excited he got. There would have to be sacrifices but the plan seemed sound to him. Yes, he needed to take action, despite what Peticlere said. Besides, the cardinal was equal in rank to the commander in the eyes of the Protectors. There were only three senior to himself and they were all with the Descendant in Malta and he had limited access to them to minimize the risk of been tracked down by their enemies.

Daniello had a plan. It had risks, but the risks were worth taking by the right man, and he knew such a man.

•••

Commander Daniello Gallo entered the foyer of the clinic and headed for the administration office. The patient he inquired about was still in his room. The admitting clerk, a young woman that he had not seen before in his previous visits, corrected Daniello by clarifying that the people staying at the center were guests and not patients. He smiled politely and headed for the stairs instead of the elevator.

The building looked more like a retreat than a detox center. It had all the amenities of a modern complex, complete with a swimming pool, dining hall, fitness center, racquet and tennis courts, and even a spa.

He had come just after lunch and found few people in the halls and, of those, mostly employees of the center. Like the rest of the country, the guests were enjoying their afternoon nap, or at least resting in their rooms.

Lieutenant Viorel Tarney of the Swiss Guard answered the door after the first knock. The lieutenant looked down at the shorter man and instantly recognized his close friend.

"Daniello, how are you?" asked Viorel as a wide smile appeared on his lean, clean-shaven face.

"Good to see you again, my friend," answered Daniello as the two men embraced.

"Please come in," said Viorel, stepping aside and motioning to the other to enter. "I was just reading a book. Unlike the other patients in this place, I like to read rather than sleep in the afternoons."

They sat down across each other at a small table next to the window looking out onto the back garden.

"I thought you were all guests and not patients," said Daniello.

"You must have met the new clerk. That is the official politically correct party line these days but let's not kid ourselves, we here are all addicts of one form or another."

Daniello did not have a reply to that. He had seen his friend crash many times, each one worse than the last, each time closer to the edge, closer to death. The last one could have been fatal, recalled the commander.

Viorel had rented a small room for the day in an old hotel in the outskirts of the city. He did so because he had shared accommodations within Vatican City with another guard and not allowed alcohol, so he rented a room when his affliction got the better of him. On that particular day, he had with him several grams of coke along with two bottles of vodka. He finished the coke and downed both bottles within a couple of hours. If it weren't for a nosy and unusually perceptive hotel manager, he would not have survived. The manager had seen the look of desperation in Viorel's eyes when he checked in, carrying only a brown paper bag clutched tightly to his chest. Two hours later, the manager had come knocking on the door. He had not seen his guest leave and suspected something amiss. The manager used his master key to let himself in and found Viorel naked and unconscious on the floor next to the bed with the sheets wrapped around his legs, an empty bottle on the bed and another on the floor next to him. He would have died of alcohol poisoning if the hospital hadn't been so close by and if they hadn't pumped his stomach as soon as they got him there. The hospital released him a few days later. Viorel knew the routine by then and voluntarily checked himself into the clinic. He had been there for just over four months.

"Are they treating you well?" asked Daniello.

"The last four months have been a slow starvation and merciless exercise regiment, but I am twenty five pounds lighter and more fit than I have been in twenty years." Viorel proudly patted his flat stomach.

"And you look much younger," added Daniello and he told the truth. Viorel looked to be in his mid thirties rather than just under fifty. At five foot ten, he looked lean and healthy. The look accentuated even further by the short black mop of hair on his head. No one would have guessed that he had struggled with alcohol and drug demons most of his adult life.

Daniello had been visiting his friend Viorel once a month since he had checked in. He brought him cigarettes and news of the outside world, especially Vatican politics. Viorel found all of it entertaining and a break from the daily routine of the center.

"How about an espresso?" asked Viorel as he got up and went to the hot plate holding a coffee machine. "I just made it." Along with cigarettes, coffee was one of the few addictive substances allowed in his room.

"Sure," answered Daniello with a smile.

They drank their coffee, smoked cigarettes and made small talk as they always did during Daniello's monthly visits.

"What's on your mind, Daniello?" asked Viorel after a particular long pause.

The keen senses of the lieutenant surprised Daniello, but he shouldn't be, he thought to himself. Though the commander considered Viorel one of the best officers in the Swiss Guard, at least when sober, he just couldn't be relied on staying that way for long. Viorel needed constant attention to remain clean. They both knew it was only a matter of time before one of the crashes would be Viorel's last and, because they both knew it, were always straightforward with each other. That's why Daniello used Viorel for difficult, almost suicidal assignments, even though Viorel did not belong to The Protectors, nor did he know anything about its existence or their enemy, The Brotherhood, for that matter. Viorel could not be relied to keep such secrets for obvious reasons.

Viorel wasn't even under Daniello's command. The former belonged to the Swiss Guard and the latter part of the Corps Gendarmerie, two distinctively different security organizations within the Vatican. Viorel worked for Commander Gallo in a strictly volunteer and confidential basis. It fed into Viorel's taste for intrigue and espionage, one of the reasons why he became a Swiss Guard to begin with, so Daniello used him when required, though the commander hated himself for exploiting his friend, but he considered it for the greater good, and, of course, if caught or killed they could blame his addictions for his actions.

"You never cease to amaze me," said Daniello. "You are very perceptive. Nothing about you is average."

"Neither are my weaknesses," added Viorel.

Daniello looked at the man and did not answer. He didn't have to. They both knew it to be true. "I have another assignment for you," he said directly.

"I haven't been re-instated," said Viorel without missing a beat, sipping his coffee. "The Swiss Guard may not want me back. Besides," he added with a smile, "I haven't been released from this lovely place."

"Like that ever made a difference before," said Daniello smiling back. He then got very serious and lost his smile as he added, "This one will be very difficult, both to accept and to accomplish."

LAST DESCENDANT

Viorel finished his coffee and looked at Daniello gravely. "I assume that I have to agree before you tell me the assignment?"

Daniello used an ominous tone as he answered. "You must agree before I tell you and you must be certain of it." He prayed Viorel saw the seriousness, and the danger, in the commander's eyes trying to tell him that, if he agreed and had second thoughts about it later, he would not live long to regret it. Daniello hoped that his friend understood this for he did not wish to go that route, but would if he had to.

"Sure," said Viorel, "why not? The next crash will probably kill me and there will be a next one. There always is."

Daniello did not answer.

"Yes commander," he added in a serious tone to convey his understanding. "I agree. Tell me what you want me to do."

Commander Daniello Gallo told him.

CHAPTER TWELVE
ATTACK

Mariella had gone for an afternoon nap so John decided to go for a walk down to the beach. No guards followed him for his safety was not their prime concern, only Mariella. This allowed him to enjoy some solitude lost in his own thoughts.

John couldn't help wondering how everyone he knew from his previous life were doing, or what they thought of him. What little news John managed to get from European radio and television did not add much to what he had already heard that day in December at the chalet.

As far as the chalet and the battle that raged that December morning was concerned, nothing ever surfaced in the news as if it never happened. He asked Sebastian about it. The priest had said that The Brotherhood often cleaned up after such attacks, or covered it up with some other more mundane calamity like fire.

They must be very good at this sort of clean-up, thought John.

By chance, he had heard a story that described the death of Captain David Westell and Lieutenant Nick Mancuso. The reports indicated that the off duty officers had shared a ride home when they were involved in a single fiery car crash causing their vehicle to explode, killing both men instantly and beyond recognition. John wondered if Rashid bought that story as well or whether it just didn't fit in with the events surrounding the murdered women. Unless he heard something on the airways, John would never know for he had no safe way to make contact with his old partner. Nor would he try to make contact with friends, acquaintances, or with any of his family. Even contacting his old lover, Winnie, remained out of the question. Certain that the Boston police force, the FBI and, of course, The Brotherhood of The Rapture monitored anyone even remotely connected with him, he knew it best to stay away and off the grid, as they say.

For now, his old life did not exist. Besides, his new life turned out quite well. If anything, a hell of a lot more comfortable and interesting than the old did.

The May sun felt warm on his shoulders as he walked along the narrow sandy beach. Like the first day when they arrived, the color of the water showed a beautiful clear aqua marine blue. As he looked out, he saw the familiar fishing boats from the villages nearby, the men casting their nets to catch the small schools of fish that ventured within these waters.

Further up the beach lay the marina that they had originally docked when he and Sebastian first arrived. The Protectors had purchased it from the old man who had owned it and now staffed by two of their members. To keep the locals at bay, and quell some of the curiosity, the Protectors propagated a rumor that a rich Russian oil tycoon purchased all the land in the area, a common occurrence in other parts of Europe so it didn't raise too many eyebrows.

John enjoyed living in Malta. It was a beautiful place with exceptional weather. With money no longer an issue, he enjoyed a virtual paradise when compared to his old life. He thought about this and smiled. They said money wasn't everything, but that saying believed only by those who had it, not those who didn't. Like air, it wasn't important until you didn't have it.

He saw no point trying to make plans beyond the end of the year for the Seniors had told him when his son was born, all would be revealed, but no one could say what that revelation would be exactly, for no one really knew. He realized he had to have faith like everyone else in this small community but it still bothered him for it seemed only he had any misgivings at all. Everyone else remained steadfast in their faith. It wasn't that he did not have faith as well, he just didn't like not knowing what came next, not having any control of his life, least of all, not having control over the life of his wife and child. In the end, he resigned himself to the fact that these were things beyond his control. Besides, he knew this from the onset, from when he decided to marry Mariella, so he could only blame himself if he and his wife did not have the life of a normal couple. Not that The Protectors had any ill conceived or evil plans that made his life terrible. On the contrary, The Protectors treated John and Mariella like royalty, but royalty did not have the freedoms of the common man. He had reconciled himself to such a life, at least for now.

These moments of perceived freedom and away from the constant attention from the guards allowed him some reflection and he enjoyed these rare times. Looking out to sea and watching the ebb and flow of the waters helped to sooth his mind, his soul. He regularly came out here and watched the sea and the fishermen at their work.

John stopped to rest. He sat on the ground and leaned against the trunk of a nearby tree, enjoying the shade that it provided. As his eyes travelled over the familiar waves, John caught sight of a boat that he had never seen before anchored several hundred yards from shore. It didn't look like one of the fishing boats but more like the boat he and Sebastian had when they arrived. He didn't consider this unusual except that there were two men dressed in black on board scanning the shore with binoculars.

The hairs in the back of his neck rose up.

Could it be? Were they so close to finding us, he asked himself?

The men with the binoculars continued to pan across the shoreline and did not stop to look in his direction. This told him they had not spotted him, not yet at least. John did not get up but crawled around the tree and hid behind the trunk. The foot wide tree provided little cover and he turned sideways to make himself thinner.

What next, he asked himself, as he continued to spy the men on the boat from around the tree? He looked closely and saw that they were no longer scanning the coastline but had stopped to focus their attention towards the marina. Both men were on the top deck to maximize their view.

Then something quite unexpected happened. One of the men suddenly toppled over the railing and dropped into the water and, almost simultaneously, the other standing next to him fell backwards and onto the deck. The man in the water slowly floated back up to the surface, remained face down, motionless and bobbing in the water with the motion of the waves. The other lay flat on his back and did not move.

The guards at the marina, thought John. They must have spotted the two spies and shot them.

A moment later, he saw a speedboat with two men coming from the direction of the marina heading towards the larger boat. At the same time, he spotted a half dozen men running from the direction of the main house towards the shore while two more came running in his direction. John could see all of them fully armed with various automatic weapons. Obviously, he thought, the men at the marina called in to the main house and sent out the alarm.

The two men quickly escorted John back to the house as the men on the small boat came alongside the larger vessel. One began tying the smaller boat to it as the other pulled the body out of the water. As John approached the house, he looked back and saw the larger boat moving towards the marina with the smaller one in tow.

As John came closer to the walled perimeter of the house, he saw that it had turned into a tightly sealed-up fortress. They closed the main gates and armed men stood watch on all sides within the perimeter. John and his escort entered and he headed directly to the kitchen where he expected all three Seniors: Sebastian, Marco and Jonathan, to be huddled together trying to make sense of what happened and what the next move should be. All three men were there.

"Where's Mariella?" asked John without introduction.

Sebastian spoke up first. "She is safe, John. She is in her room with guards on the door and others stationed outside directly below her window with orders to shoot even their own comrades if any venture too close."

John relaxed noticeably as he looked at all three men. "I assume those men out there on the boat happened to be a small contingent of the Brotherhood."

"Correct," confirmed Marco in a calm voice.

"Then we are discovered," added John as he sat down heavily in one of the chairs at the kitchen table.

"Not yet," explained Sebastian. "Our men at the marina spotted the boat as it began to come in from far off shore. It seemed to be in a search pattern rather than a direct approach, so this cannot be an advance attack unit but a search party. We were also monitoring the airwaves and no transmission went out from the boat."

Jonathan interjected, "But it is only a matter a time before their Command realizes this particular search team is no longer reporting in and put two and two together."

"Then we make our stand here," said John. "When they come, we will be ready."

"Not exactly, John," said Sebastian. "When they come, a large contingent of the Protectors will indeed be waiting, but the rest of us will be far away from here."

"And we will regroup somewhere else," added John.

"No," corrected Sebastian. "The team left here will fight to the death if need be, giving us time to flee and hide our tracks."

John looked harshly at Sebastian, unable to contain his anger. "You make a decision that sends men to their deaths that coldly, that efficiently?"

"No, John," replied Sebastian, "never coldly. Men that lead at times have to make difficult decisions. This is one of those times."

"Yes, I know," said John. "That line, that scene, has been played out many times in those John Wayne type war movies." He got up in anger, toppling the chair behind him. Nobody moved. "It is easy for you to give this order while we run away with the second team."

"You forget yourself," said Sebastian with a pained expression of one judged unfairly. "We must think of Mankind as a whole. Better to sacrifice the few to save the many."

"And, I have heard that corny line in second rate movies before too," added John. He looked at all three men staring up at him. They had remained sitting. "How many will remain behind?" he finally asked in disgust.

"We will be almost seventy out of the ninety-seven gathered here in Malta," said Marco. "You, Mariella, my father, Jonathan and the remaining Protectors will leave tonight."

John suddenly realized they had picked Marco to lead the men that were to fight The Brotherhood. The realization of what that meant suddenly sank in. John blushed in embarrassment. What a fool he had been and how small he now felt.

John realized that Sebastian had decided to leave his only son behind to certain death. Sebastian saw the concerned look on John's face. "Do not pain your self so, my son," he said to John with understanding in his voice. "We must do everything we can to convince them we are all here and making a last stand. They will focus their efforts here and buy us the time we need for an escape without leaving a trail." He looked proudly across the table to his son. "He is the most capable of all of us to lead the men in such a critical battle. So it must be so."

"Thank you, father," said Marco, returning the look of affection with an almost embarrassed expression.

John's heart broke. He had known the man for several months now and knew him to be good. He looked at Marco and tried to speak. "But...," was all he could croak out from his now constricted throat.

"Whatever you do," interjected Marco, "do not tell Mariella of these plans. I am the only family she knew before you came along. If she got wind of what we plan to do, she would not cooperate. We will simply tell her we will regroup at another location."

John could only nod. If she found out, when she found out, she would be furious with her husband. She might even find it difficult to forgive him.

•••

Marco and a small escort went along with the group leaving to the small, private airstrip in the middle of the island. The place contained a hanger with three small jets, each capable of holding about fifteen passengers, more than enough to handle the thirty-member group. Among the many skills that the Protectors had, it also included some with flight training and each plane assigned an appropriate flight team. The planes were fully fueled and would reach almost anywhere in the world. Extra fuel tanks on the wings made that possible.

Mariella had understood the gravity of the situation and allowed herself to be guided by the men in charge. She put up a small fight about needing some clothes but they told her everything had been taken care of, the planes provisioned some time ago with everything they needed for just such an event.

During the confusion of the boarding and engine checks, Marco said his rushed goodbyes to all, being careful what he said to avoid making Mariella suspicious. When he got to her, he simply gave her a hug and said not to worry for she was in good hands.

"I'm not worried about me, Zio Marco," said Mariella, returning the hug. "You make sure that you make it out and join us, wherever we are going." The team had not told her their destination.

Marco found it very difficult to hold back the tears but he could not allow them to betray his thoughts. "May God always be with you, sweetheart." He released her and turned away, avoiding eye contact.

"Zio," said Mariella.

Marco stopped in his tracks and turned back to her, "Yes?"

"Promise me you will come back to me."

Marco looked at her and hesitated, realizing that she saw something that made her uncomfortable. He barely kept his composure. He then did something that he never did in his life. He lied to her. "I promise, Mariella. Now please, get on the plane."

Mariella still hesitated but she eventually made her way towards the plane.

Marco turned to the other men. He shook John's hand and simply said, "Take care of her."

John looked at Marco in the eye and replied, "With my life, my friend."

Marco simply nodded and released his grip as his tear-filled eyes looked away. Marco then shook Jonathan's hand. No words exchanged, none needed. He then turned to his father, Sebastian, who had stood nearby watching as Marco said his goodbyes. He now went up to his son and hugged him for the final time.

"My only regret is that we will not meet again until we are reunited in heaven," said Sebastian. He released his hug and grabbed his son by the shoulders as he added, "Go with God, my son."

"I will wait for you at the gates of heaven," said Marco. He gave a slight smile as he said, "Don't worry. I will have a talk with Saint Peter and straighten everything out. He will greet you with open arms." Heaven or no heaven, Marco felt a pain in his chest that he had never felt before.

"I'm sure you will," said Sebastian as he smiled back though his bottom lip betrayed a small quiver that did not escape the ever-observant eyes of his son.

Mariella stood on the first step of the stairs leading up to the entrance of the second plane. Two Protectors were helping her. She stopped and turned back to look at her entire escort a dozen steps away. "Zio!" she yelled.

He looked up at her.

"Remember your promise!" she said.

He looked at her and did not respond. The look on his face remained passive as he raised his hand and gave a small wave. The other men looked back at her. As she looked, both Sebastian and Jonathan remained calm and did not betray what they felt, but when she looked at John, he just didn't have the same discipline. Both Jonathan and Sebastian jumped towards her as she scrambled down.

The Protectors at the bottom of the stairs had their arms out as she tried to jump. "No!" she yelled reaching out to her uncle as they held her back.

Marco stood as stiff as a statue while looking at her and made no move to come closer, knowing that if he did, it would just make things worse.

She looked at him. "Zio, don't you dare!"

Sebastian and Jonathan had reached her and many arms gently but firmly carried her back in the plane. She struggled in vain to free herself, all the while crying out openly.

"No!" she yelled but no one paid attention. "Damn you all let me go!" She looked back at her uncle with tear-filled eyes while she reached out with her arms to him. "Zio! Zio Marco!"

Within seconds, they carried her through the door and in the plane. Marco had not moved a muscle. He simply stood there and watched as they carried her into the plane. He now turned and saw John nearby. He too rooted to his spot. John turned to Marco and simply looked at him. Marco gave a slight nod and walked away towards the waiting cars. John headed for the plane and got in as the door closed. The engines' whine began to increase, getting ready for takeoff.

Marco sat in the backseat of one of the cars as the planes taxied out to the runway. He did not look out as the engines opened up and the planes began their final takeoff. Only when the planes were no longer within sight did the men get in the cars and head back to the compound. Marco remained mute in the back seat for most of the ride back.

Never again will he hear her voice call him Zio.

Before reaching the compound, Marco's emotional state changed as if a switch closed inside his head. One moment he struggled to absorb the final words he heard from his niece and, the next, he became the disciplined leader of a team of the world's best soldiers, methodically planning his next move in the defense of the compound.

Marco's plan was twofold; one, put up such a good fight as to maximize the casualties of the enemy and, two, make the enemy think the descendant remained within the compound. Marco knew it was just a matter of time before he and his men were defeated but he planned to give his friends enough time to make good on their escape.

He ordered the driver to head straight for the main house where men were setting up a command post within the dining room just off the kitchen, so often occupied by him and the other seniors. As he walked in, he saw ten desks positioned against the walls. Five desks each held an audio/video transceiver that communicated to a team of twelve men. Every man in the team wore a headset that held a radio and camera. This added up to sixty men stationed throughout the compound and grounds nearby. The other five desks each held nine video monitors showing every angle throughout the grounds and beyond. One man sat at each of the ten desks. With Marco and his second-in-command, they were seventy-two men in total.

Marco positioned the men in such a way as to have at least two lines of defense before the enemy got to the main compound and the house. As the Brotherhood breached each line, and he figured it would only be a matter of time before they did so, the surviving defenders retreated to the next line to help repel the advancing assault. He figured they'd be outnumbered in the neighborhood of five or six to one, but they had home advantage. It should be quite an edge, he thought.

He assumed the assault would come both from sea and from land simultaneously. He did not expect heavy artillery. After all, Malta wasn't exactly a remote third world country. Unless The Brotherhood wanted undue attention from the country's police force, and even the military, it would have to be low keyed. More of a commando assault than a General-Patton-Give-'Em-Hell tank assault. No, he expected an assault similar to what John and Sebastian experienced back in North America.

Some of the men had removed and were now monitoring the radio from the boat they had captured. A male voice soon called and asked for Beta Two to report in and provide a status. Marco picked up the transmitter, pushed the talk button and said, "This is Beta Two, no change in status. All clear, over." He released the talk button.

Everyone held his breath as the seconds ticked by. Soon the voice came back on. "Beta Two, please provide the code word, over."

Marco looked at his second-in-command, a lean African around his own age, who merely shrugged. Marco did not respond to the request. Soon the voice asked again. "Beta Two, please provide the code word, over."

It was the last transmission they received from the radio.

•••

The evening approached, the sun had just set, and none of the teams reported anything unusual, nor did the cameras show anything out of the ordinary. It now became obvious that the assault would take place at night.

They had shut off all lights outside and inside the compound. They also boarded up the windows of the command post to prevent any light from escaping into the night. Large floodlights scanning the surrounding area would merely advertize their location so they did not use them, night-vision equipped cameras and goggles were more effective, but Marco and his men were smart enough to know that the Brotherhood would most likely have similar, if not the same, equipment.

Two men handed out all remaining weapons and ammunition. Apart from small arms that included automatic rifles, they also had a handful of sniper rifles. Sharpshooters positioned themselves just behind the front lines to pick off any enemy soldiers that managed to get too close to the first line of defense. Lastly, they rationed out the few hand-grenades they had out to the men. Only about fifty were on hand. It had been difficult to obtain a larger cache without raising suspicion.

Marco sipped on his coffee while reviewing a map of the surrounding area and the positions of his men. Everything seemed ready, nothing else to do but wait.

His second-in-command came in carrying what looked like a watch with a thick Velcro type wristband. "I have something for you," he said.

"What is it, Habib?" asked Marco. "A going away present for me?" A bad joke but he got a smile.

"You could say that, Commander," answered Habib showing the device to Marco.

"A watch?" asked Marco.

"Not exactly. We have finished placing all remaining explosives within the building. We have almost a thousand pounds of TNT and several thousand pounds of fertilizer and other common household materials that can be used as explosives."

"Just like the Oklahoma bombing," added Marco.

"Yes," continued Habib. "That was only a van full and it destroyed most of a large building. We have several times more than that. When set-off, there will be nothing left of this building and compound but a large crater."

Marco looked at Habib and added, "Everything in the compound will be pulverized, leaving no evidence of its occupants. The question is will they buy it? Will they assume she was inside with us?"

"We can only hope," said Habib.

"Well, there is nothing else we can do," added Marco.

"Let me place this on your wrist, Commander," said Habib as he moved to do so. "The device is remotely connected to the trigger mechanism of the explosives."

Marco looked at the device as the other man placed on his wrist. "Are you sure this will do the job?"

"What do you mean, sir?"

"I mean, too many things could go wrong. I might not have enough time to set-off the explosives; I could be killed before I hit the switch, blown up, anything."

Habib looked at Marco for a moment before he explained, "Commander, this device doesn't set-off the explosives, it prevents them from going off."

Marco looked at his second-in-command in surprise. "What?" he finally asked.

"The device on your wrist has a button that you can push to turn it off manually. That would cause the trigger device to release, setting off the explosives. Most importantly, the device also monitors your heartbeat. If your heartbeat is no longer detected, it allows the explosives to detonate."

After putting it on Marco's wrist, Habib pressed a small switch on the side of the device. "It is now active. Even if someone tries to take it off your wrist, it will set off the explosives."

"I see," said Marco with a mild surprise, absorbing the information he just heard. The device prevented the explosion, not caused it. "A dead-man's switch."

"Something like that," said Habib. "Instead of stopping a process, it initiates it." Habib thought about that for a moment and corrected himself. "Come to think of it, it *is* a dead-man's switch. It stops the process that prevents the explosion so that it does indeed occur."

Marco shrugged his shoulders in confusion. "That's almost a double negative. Bottom line is, I die and the compound becomes a crater. End of story."

"You got it," agreed Habib.

Marco looked at the display and saw a two-digit number blinking.

"What you are seeing is your heartbeat," explained Habib, looking at the number, "and, at seventy-four beats per minute, you are a man who is very composed and in control of his emotions. Almost too calm, all things considered." He finished the sentence with a smile.

Marco took another sip of his coffee. "Maybe this is decaf," he said amusingly while looking at his cup, "and I thought I was drinking the real thing."

As the night continued to fade from gray to black all the equipment switched over to night-mode and the views on the screens changed to a new green-tainted, alien-like world. Anything that had any resemblance of heat showed up as a lighter color from the rest of the surrounding landscape. Initially everything showed as a lighter color. Almost impossible to distinguish the men from the ground they stood on. The sun had heated up everything but, within an hour, the heat quickly dissipated and the contrast increased between inanimate objects and warm-blooded things.

This transition period would have been the ideal time to attack, thought Marco. He, therefore, assumed correctly that The Brotherhood were still massing and not yet ready.

With a cloudless sky and the moon full, it made it easier to see the enemy but it did not allot any more advantage to one side over the other. Around midnight, Marco took the radio and switched on the general frequency for all his men to hear. He had no qualms that they would fight valiantly, but they deserved a few words from their commander.

"Gentlemen," he began in a somber but commanding voice. "Tonight, we fight for our cause. Tonight, we ensure that our Charge, the blessed Mariella, will complete her destiny, that she be the vessel for the return of our Messiah. We gladly give our lives to ensure we stop the enemy here. Fight valiantly my friends, and do not give up your lives easily but ensure you take as many of the enemy with you. God bless you all for you fight for His cause. Before this night is over, we will meet again at the gates of heaven. It is a privilege to fight by your side and an honor to lead you in this worthy battle. Mankind will remember you for what you are, The Protectors of The Truth!"

He switched off the general frequency transmission. No one made a sound in the room.

"To The Protectors of The Truth!" yelled Habib raising his fist in the air.

"TO THE PROTECTORS OF THE TRUTH!" everyone yelled back in unison, including Marco. If he had listened carefully, he would have heard the same cry all over the compound.

They were ready!

The attack came just after one.

●●●

The compound perimeter consisted of three sides facing inland and the fourth and final part facing the sea. As predicted, the Brotherhood attacked on all sides simultaneously, effectively reducing any opportunity for the defenders to reinforce any sides that became weak and increased the chances that the invading force would break through somewhere in the parameter.

Marco heard the first report of the attack from the men facing the sea. They saw the boats coming from around an outcrop of land to the left of the compound.

"Boats without running lights spotted at sea," called out Operator Five.

"How many?" asked Marco.

"Five – no – six boats spotted, sir!"

"How far out?"

"About six-hundred yards. They will be within range in a few minutes." Operator Five relayed the questions to his team and provided the responses to his commander as he received them.

"Any idea on the size of the enemy forces on the boats?" asked Habib of the operator.

"Hard to tell, sir," replied Operator Five. "Possibly ten to twelve men on each boat."

"Tell your men to fire at will when within range," ordered Marco.

"Yes sir!" said the operator. He relayed the command to his team.

They heard the gunfire on the inland side before the reports started to come in.

"Team Two taking enemy fire, sir!" yelled out Operator Two.

"Return fire at will," ordered Marco. "That goes for all of you," he added.

After that last order, Marco could do nothing but look on.

All the teams knew their jobs.

"Team One taking enemy fire!" reported Operator One without taking his eyes of the monitors.

"Team Three taking enemy fire!"

"Team Four taking enemy fire!"

Everyone's eyes in the room glued to the TV monitors. Each showed flashes of gunfire and tracers as the bullets flew.

The enemy advanced with little concern for their safety. The Protectors mowed them down with return fire. Marco scanned the monitors and estimated at least fifty men of The Brotherhood were down but more appeared right behind them.

The pictures on the screens from the cameras on the men showed a chaotic scene. Some fell over, or showed the sky, indicating to the spectators in the room that they had been killed or at least unconscious and, therefore, out of commission. They heard screams throughout, men yelling out to their comrades, providing direction or asking for help in certain heavily attached places.

"Team Three reporting heavy casualties! Six men down! The rest are regrouping at the next line of defense alongside Team One!"

"Team Five reporting four casualties but they are holding!"

"Team Four reporting seven casualties! The five survivors are pulling back to Team Two line of defense!"

Habib came alongside Marco, neither one taking their eyes off the screens.

"The Brotherhood is advancing faster than we had hoped," said Habib.

"I know," said Marco with a worried look on his face. "We must hold out longer."

Habib took out his black Smith & Wesson 45-caliber semi-automatic and checked the clip, fully loaded with ten rounds plus one in the chamber. He had several clips strapped to the belt of the holster; each held ten rounds as well. Satisfied, he re-holstered his gun. He looked up and saw Marco watching him.

"I just hope I get a chance to use this to exact maximum damage on the enemy before I take my leave of this world," said Habib.

Marco smiled lightly. His mood lifted somewhat. "I hope so too," he said.

"Team Five down to two men. They are pulling back to the compound perimeter!" yelled Operator Five.

The sounds of battle getting louder just outside the command center and obvious that The Brotherhood were getting closer, the Protectors pushed back to the perimeters of the compound.

"Team Three and One are pulling back to the compound!" reported Operator One. "They are down to four men!"

Operator Three simply monitored the surviving men of his team and allowed Operator One to provide status.

Only Team Two and Four remained outside the perimeter, but not for long.

"Three men from Team Two and Four remain and have dropped back inside the perimeter!" reported the last Operator.

"Well, that does it," said Marco in a serious voice. "We are down to defending the compound behind the wall." He paced back and forth behind the operators staring at videos of the men left alive.

Marco counted the number of men remaining. The results were not very encouraging. Within fifteen minutes, he went from sixty fighters down to nine plus the twelve in the command post for a total compliment down to only twenty-one. He had hoped for a better resistance and more time. For the first time in his life, he began to doubt his ability to command. What had he done wrong? Where could his plans have been better? He blamed himself for how quickly the enemy killed his men.

Habib finally spoke up. "We may have lost fifty men but the attackers have paid a heavy price. Rough estimates put their casualties at over three hundred. For every one of our men that died, he took six with him. That's pretty good numbers, if you ask me."

"I know," responded Marco, "but there appears to be over a hundred left out there, if not more."

"We are in a virtual fortress, commander," added Habib enthusiastically. "We can hold out for a considerable amount of time. They have to come to us, not the other way around."

Marco realized Habib was right. Moreover, he realized what his second-in-command tried to do. Habib had seen the doubt in the commander's eyes and provided a word of encouragement. His affection and respect for Habib increased many fold at that very moment.

"Thank-you Lieutenant," Marco responded enthusiastically, using the title as a sign of respect. "As always, you provide effective council and an accurate assessment of the situation at hand. We have, indeed, inflicted heavy casualties on the enemy." He felt more in control as he began to pace about the room. "Now that we are all inside the compound and heavily fortified, we'll be able to hold out as long as needed for our friends to find a suitable haven."

Marco issued a flurry of commands to his men. He began to organize for the final assault. He sent half of the ten operators out to defend the perimeter.

"Habib, you must go with them and direct the men outside," ordered Marco. He wanted to send all the men out but he had to keep a handful to monitor the cameras and maintain a 360-degree view of the compound. He needed to know what was happening so that he could send reinforcements, what little he had, where needed.

"Sir, my place is by your side." Marco could see his lieutenant torn between following his orders and defending his commander.

"No, my friend," said Marco keeping his voice steady, not wishing to lose his control over his emotions. "Your place is to uphold the cause of the Protectors of The Truth. That is best served by keeping the enemy at bay for as long as you can, with all your power."

Habib could only stare at his commander. He finally looked down but did not move, almost rooted to where he stood. Marco went to him and placed a hand on his shoulder. "Habib, you have never disobeyed me. I realize that you are torn but we must all remember our cause. Go and do as I ask. What we do, and what we are about to do, is just and necessary."

After only a second of delay, Habib stiffened in attention as a sign of respect for his commander, nodded his head and said, "Yes sir, just as you ask!" He turned and walked out to his destiny. He halted in mid-step and added in a low voice without looking back, "Sir, it has been an honor to serve under your command." He did not wait for an answer but walked out without looking back.

Marco watched his second-in-command walk away. Once out the door, Marco whispered to no one, "And it has been a pleasure to serve with you."

The battle intensified.

The Brotherhood attacked the fortified walls of the compound perimeter relentlessly. It had yet to breach the walls but it was just a matter of time. The fortification weakened with every hand grenade thrown and with every shoulder-fired rocket that hit the mark but with each hit, The Brotherhood paid a price. Every time the enemy forces exposed themselves to fire a salvo, a defender stood ready with careful aim, hitting their mark more often than not but, to the Protector's dismay, it seemed like an ever-ready supply of attackers took the place of the fallen.

Marco watched it all unfold on the monitors. His men were not being killed as quickly as when they were outside the walls but sharpshooters on the other side looked for anyone careless enough to expose themselves. If it weren't for the constant assault on the walls, it would have been a stalemate indefinitely but the walls were weakening.

Marco checked his semi-automatic handgun in his holster and chambered one round. Satisfied, he re-holstered his gun and checked his submachine gun to ensure the thirty-round magazine was full before he pulled back the action and loaded a cartridge, making it ready to fire on full automatic, the submachine gun his primary weapon and his handgun his second. Finally, he checked that the 'dead-man' device on his wrist remained in order. Satisfied, Marco ordered all his men out and he followed behind shutting off the lights of the room as he did so. Only the faint glow from some of the still functional units on the tables illuminated the room.

Marco needed all the men to defend the wall, including himself. Outside he saw the front gate heavily damaged and therefore the weakest point in the perimeter. He ordered the group that just came out to defend it.

LAST DESCENDANT

The attack continued unabated. Marco looked around in search for his second-in-command. Not spotting him on this side of the wall, Marco assumed that he manned the other side. With Habib commanding the rear of the compound, Marco stayed at the front gate.

The scene looked no different then what he saw on the monitors, his men pinned down by the constant mortars and from the sharpshooters scattered across the countryside outside the wall. They had no choice but to blindly lob hand grenades over the wall in hopes of meeting their targets. The strategy had little effect and the bombardment on the wall continued.

Marco racked his mind for a plan, a plan not to save him and his men, but a plan to buy them more time, anything to buy them more time. He looked into the faces of his men and he saw only determination, courage, and even patience. Patience for an opportunity to take out the enemy, but he did not see fear: the fear, panic, that many soldiers experienced in battle when all seemed hopeless and the will to live burned deep in their bellies. No, these men did not fear death, they embraced it, for they believed death, like birth, as merely another gateway to a new life, a new horizon, another step closer to God, and Marco understood this for he had been raised in the same environment and taught the same beliefs. He felt pride to be part of such a fearless but just group of men, and at the same time, ashamed to have felt doubt in his capabilities and theirs no matter how quickly it had passed. Seeing his men in battle quickly erased those doubts. He fed off their strength by just being close to them and it restored him to the place in his mind where he again felt at ease and accepted their fate.

Marco fought side by side with his comrades. On several occasions, he looked out over the wall and when spotting a careless attacker out in the open, quickly dispatched them with his submachine gun. Twice he had a narrow escape, one bullet nicked his right ear while another hit the wall next to his cheek and ricocheting just past his nose.

Two hours had passed since the first assault occurred and Marco had less than a dozen men left alive. He had no idea if Habib was among the dead or among the living. He had not gone to the rear of the building to find out and he failed to raise him on the headset. The only solace the sound of gunfire from the rear indicating he still had some men alive and defending the perimeter in that area.

Marco had long since discarded his empty submachine gun and now down to his last clip in his handgun. A body of one of his men lay near the front gate less than twenty feet away. He looked over and decided to check the body for any extra clips, or for any other weapon for that matter. He had just taken a step towards the body when a large explosion hit the gates of the compound wall, the concussion so great it threw the body of the dead man into the air and splatter against the house wall. The almost undistinguishable mass of flesh slowly eased down, leaving a trail of blood and bits of flesh clinging to the stucco wall. The concussion of the blast had also hit Marco, thrown backward and somersaulted in the air before falling flat on his back. His ears ringing loudly, the sounds of battle far away, muted. Blood trickled from his eyes and ears as he lay momentarily stunned but he did not lose consciousness. The blast blew the gate in and metal shards lay strewn across the courtyard. Marco looked down at himself and saw a one-foot piece of metal rod imbedded into his left thigh and protruding from the other side. As he slowly recovered from the blast and regained his equilibrium, he tried to get up and his left leg gave way making him fall back on the ground. Only then did he feel the pain. His training allowed him to keep it under control as he tried to pull it out from one side and then, failing that, tried from the other. His leg seemed to have a death grip on the metal rod. He stopped when he felt his consciousness beginning to wane and the resulting blackness closing in around the periphery of his vision. He had to remain conscious. He could not afford The Brotherhood capturing him unconscious and discover the device on his wrist and somehow disabling it.

Marco began to crawl back to the house entrance leading back to the now empty command center. Three of his men had come from around the building to guard the open gate and had killed five attackers trying to storm the entrance. Their guns were blasting away as he managed to crawl inside. Rhythmic blasts of light pulsated from the ends of their barrels as they fired into the night. As Marco crossed the threshold, he crawled to the side and leaned back against the outside wall next to the door. This allowed him an unobstructed view out onto the courtyard and the open gate. He caught sight of the three defenders at the gate get shredded almost in half by return fire, weapons falling out of their now dead hands. The barrels continued to glow red for a few seconds from the repeated firing.

The sounds of battle from outside suddenly ceased. To Marco this could only mean that all of his men were either dead or incapacitated. He figured he had mere seconds to crawl to the back of the room and hide behind one of the heavy desks waiting for the enemy, wanting as many of The Brotherhood within the blast area as possible when he set off the explosion. The longer he lived and resisted the more of the enemy that would pour in.

Marco checked his gun in the dim light of some of the few still functional monitors. Despite the blast, the gun remained in good working order but his leg continued to bleed profusely. He ripped off a strip from his shirt and tied it tight around his leg just above the wound. It did not stop the bleeding but it slowed it down somewhat.

Marco's hearing had returned and he sensed movement from outside. It came closer to the door but stopped short of the entrance and out of view. What he heard next surprised him.

A calm male voice called out patiently, "Commander, do yourself a favor and surrender the Descendant to us and I will ensure that your deaths are quick and painless."

Marco couldn't believe the voice would ask such a stupid thing. Did the man really think he would do so after all that occurred?

"You have got to be joking," replied Marco incredulously. "I'll tell you what, you surrender and I will ensure that your death is quick and painless." As he gave his reply, Marco wondered how his enemy knew him as the commander. Had someone in his team betrayed the cause? He found that hard to believe but the man knew. Did the enemy also know the Descendant was gone? That concerned Marco far more than the pain in his leg or his impending death.

"Come now, commander," said the voice. "Let's be serious. You know you have lost. It is only just a matter of time." When no response came, the voice continued. "Commander, I have a surprise for you."

Marco had come out of his hiding place and stood up on his good leg as soon as he heard the approaching footsteps, gun at a ready. He paused when he saw who it was.

Habib looked bloodied but otherwise in good health. Hands tied behind his back as a man with red hair had a firm grip on him and a gun against his head. Habib looked at Marco and simply nodded as he said calmly, "I'm sorry I was caught alive, commander. They knocked me out from behind in the midst of battle."

"Isn't this nice," began Gabriel with a smile, "comrades in arms meeting for one last time."

Marco had a bead on Gabriel's head. If he fired and hit his mark, the muscles in his enemy's hand would convulse automatically on the trigger, firing the gun and killing Habib.

Still aiming at Gabriel, Marco said, "I should kill you where you stand. You're going to kill us anyway."

"But you will not," said Gabriel. "Because you will always have some hope that you will get her away and somehow save her."

"Who says that I can't?"

"How can you?" replied Gabriel, the smile still on his face. "You are surrounded. You are bleeding from your leg. It's no use. Make it easy on yourselves."

Marco saw the cockiness in his adversary's face, the over confidence of a narrow-minded fanatic. Marco knew what he had to do. He looked at his Lieutenant Habib, into the man's eyes, and saw the acceptance. No, he saw more than that, he saw a soul that wanted it to happen as retribution for all his comrades that died that day. The commander gave Habib a slight knowing smile, acknowledging that he understood. Habib smiled back as Marco dropped his gun and reached with his right hand for the detonation button on the dead-man device.

Marco watched the transformation on Gabriel's face at the realization of the commander's next move. The eyes of the two men locked in a battle of wits as Marco gave him a slight smile and pressed the button.

Marco felt a momentary, but extremely intense, feeling of elation as every cell in his body blasted into oblivion. He would have been happy to know that Gabriel experienced the exact opposite at precisely the same moment in time.

The mushroom cloud, like a miniature version of the atom bomb that exploded over Hiroshima and Nagasaki, expanded into the dark night sky. An orange glow visible on all the islands of Malta preceded the shockwave through the ground felt as far away as Sicily. The crater that remained far greater than anyone could have predicted. Very little evidence remained of the battle that night.

For months, the authorities struggled to understand what had happened. Many theories discussed but none accurate. In the end, because of the earlier rumors of a Russian tycoon on the island, the official report indicated a battle between opposing Russian mafias that ended in a devastating explosion killing many on both sides. It made headlines around the world for days but quickly became last page news by the end of the week.

CHAPTER THIRTEEN
ASSASSIN

Lieutenant Viorel Tarney of the Swiss Guard checked out of rehab the day after the visit from Commander Daniello Gallo of the Corps of Gendarmerie of Vatican City. The commander had laid it out in a very straightforward way; for reasons not made very clear to Viorel but only that, for the sake and survival of the Church, Cardinal Ferdinand Costa needed to be assassinated and done so publicly.

Viorel did not ask why to either the killing or the circumstances in which it must happen. He did not think he would get an answer, nor did it matter to him. A man that he trusted told him that it must be so and he took it on faith that it was necessary.

He arrived with just a duffel bag with him when he had checked in to the rehab center and that's all he left with when he checked out, plus the twenty thousand Euros in brand new one hundred Euro bills and a picture of Cardinal Costa. Daniello had left these things for Viorel at the end of his visit the night before.

"You know you are not ready for the outside world," said his councilor, Italo Mastro, as he helped Viorel stuff his meager belongings in the bag. Viorel had already stashed the money in his jacket.

"I'm as ready as I need to be," responded Viorel without looking up.

Italo did not respond and seemed almost hurt by the reply. The Lieutenant saw the effect his words had on the other man. He stopped packing and looked up at his councilor, regretting his words.

"I'm sorry," said Viorel. "You have been a good friend to me here. Hell, you are one of the few friends that I got." He paused, trying to arrange his thoughts and the words that would ease the other man's concern while not giving anything away. "I have something important coming up that can't wait. What it is will keep me too busy to think of anything else, let alone drinking. Actually, if I'm to be successful, I must not drink until after the next church holiday." He smiled as he added, "So you see, I have a goal, a purpose, and that's what I need in order to stay off the bottle."

Councilor Italo smiled back. "You are paraphrasing me. That's good, it means you were listening."

Viorel resumed packing as the councilor looked on. "I can't stop you from leaving. No one can. You checked in voluntarily so you can check out at your own discretion. Just remember the words that you just repeated back to me."

"I will, my friend. I wouldn't be alive today if it wasn't for you," said Viorel with sincerity as he stopped packing again.

Italo grabbed the half-empty carton of cigarettes on the dresser to hand to Viorel when he noticed a picture hidden underneath. Italo picked it up and looked at it with mild curiosity. It was the picture of Cardinal Costa.

"One of your heroes?" asked Italo humorously.

"Yeah," answered Viorel in a convincing sarcastic voice, taking the picture from Italo's hand. "Just like you."

Viorel wondered how he could have been so careless as to leave such a thing out in the open.

"And Cardinal Costa to boot," said Italo. He shrugged his shoulders as he added dismissively, "Whatever works for you."

Most Romans could identify and name dozens of the cardinals. What with the newspapers brimming over with political intrigue in the Church, this was not surprising. With Cardinal Costa, in the public eye more often than most, Viorel wasn't too worried when Italo identified the cardinal in the picture, but he saw it as a slip on his part, never the less.

The councilor reached into his pocket and pulled out a card. "Here," he said. "My home and cell numbers are on it. I will be at one or the other twenty-four hours a day. Call me anytime."

Viorel took it and looked at the card. "Thank-you for always being there," he said in a low voice, thankful that his councilor had changed the subject so quickly.

"I will always be there, Viorel," said Italo. Pointing at the card he added, "Just a phone call away. Don't forget."

"I wouldn't."

Viorel finished packing after the councilor left. He had a lightness to his step as he came out of the building and into a waiting taxi.

Good to be on the outside again, he thought.

He did not go back to his shared residence at the Vatican City, but rented a hotel room instead. Not only because he hadn't been cleared to rejoin the Swiss Guard but also because he needed the privacy to plan and execute his assignment.

As the cab weaved through the streets of Rome, he got glimpses of the cafes and bars with various signs of their wares; neon signs of all brands of beer, wine, vermouth, you name it. Intimately familiar with each product, each brand, his mouth watered and felt parched at the same time. The desire burned deep within him. His councilor had been right, he was not ready for the outside world, but he didn't have the luxury of time. Daniello had said it had to be on the holy day of Ascension, and, in this current year, that fell on May 17, only one week away.

Viorel closed his eyes and tried to suppress the urges. He had promised himself, and Daniello, that he would stay off the booze, at least until he had successfully completed the assignment. After that, who knows, he said to himself.

To take his mind of his yearnings, Viorel thought about Daniello's request. "Cardinal Costa must be killed in public on the day of Ascension, May 17."

Why, he asked himself?

He went through in his mind what he knew of the Catholic holiday. Though not considered a national holiday in either Italy or anywhere else, it remained important to the Church. The Ascension was, quite simply, the day that Jesus Christ bodily rose up to heaven. According to the scriptures, this had occurred in front of the apostles exactly forty days after Easter, the Resurrection. Viorel assumed there was a symbolic reason for the assassination on this day but he couldn't figure out what. It didn't really bother him, he was simply curious. On May 17, the Cardinals were to be part of a procession outside St. Peter's cathedral and obvious to Viorel that it must happen during that very public ceremony.

The taxi finally reached its destination. He rented a room in an old hotel at the outskirts of Rome. More of a tenant than a hotel, but they asked few questions and did not request any ID, just the rent in advance. He paid in cash for one month.

The room an average size, complete with a small table and chair, and a full bathroom that had seen better days. His only concern was the one entry to the building right by the front desk and under the watchful glare of the proprietor. This made it hard, but not impossible, for Viorel to sneak in anything larger than what he could hide under his jacket. Nevertheless, it was the best he could do under the circumstances.

The first order of business was acquiring a weapon for the assignment. That same evening, he went looking for a long time contact that had provided him with whatever he needed in the past. The contact could obtain a wide variety of weapons to satisfy the needs of the select few involved in activities practiced by men, and women, such as Viorel. He never asked questions, for an inquisitive mind did not last long in this business. Viorel's contact was simply a supplier satisfying a niche market, and a lucrative one at that. Besides, the Swiss Guard gave its undercover officers wide discretionary powers when on assignment. This afforded the organization the farthest arm's length dealings with the men, thus minimizing any backlash in the event that something went wrong or public. What the organization did not know would not hurt it.

The café / bar that Viorel searched for was located near the river Tevere just south of city's airport, Leonardo da Vinci. Out of long practice and habit, Viorel had given the cab driver an address of a café three blocks from the actual one he wished to go. This was not too difficult to do; cafes existed all over Rome on almost every corner on every street.

Viorel walked up to the nondescript building with a traditional canopy over the front window and glass door. The half dozen small tables stationed on the sidewalk in front of the place were empty. The inside held a dozen tables with a simple bar against one wall and a hall leading to the kitchen in the back. An old Gitoni machine, also known as a foosball table or tabletop soccer, stood empty in the far corner. Located within a rundown area near the docks, it wasn't exactly a people friendly location, so it didn't surprise him that it had few patrons, and this was exactly what the proprietor liked. The combination of the close proximity to the docks, while away from the curious crowds, made it a successful front for pushing contraband goods.

Viorel stopped at the threshold of the entrance and quickly scanned the room with his eyes. The air smelled of strong coffee and cigarettes with an undertone of grappa that made his mouth water. He counted only six men in the place, including the bartender. Viorel quickly spotted his contact. Alone at a table for two, in the far corner of the café, sat a shriveled old man who looked up as Viorel entered the café. Recognizing the night's newcomer, the extremely wrinkled ageless face looked in danger of falling off its old skull as it cracked a smile, exposing an extremely white set of dentures that looked out of place within the leathery mask, the smile an invitation for Viorel to take the empty chair across from the old man. The other patrons didn't even bother to look up as they continued their own subdued conversations across the room. The bartender came around the bar and approached the table without a word.

"A double, short espresso," said Viorel, without taking his eyes off the old man.

No one said a word as the bartender turned around and headed for the large espresso machine so common around the country, an absolute staple at any place that served food or drinks.

"It is good to see you're still alive, Ennio," said Viorel.

Ennio acknowledged the comment with a slight smile and shifted his small frame as he reached for the shot of grappa on the table. His old hands, wracked with arthritis, barely managed to pick up the small glass. He drank the clear fiery liquid in one gulp. The face betraying nothing as the burning fluid travelled down his throat. Only his watery eyes showed a glint as the liquid settled comfortably in his belly. The entire motion and experience not lost on Viorel. He could literally taste the grappa as he got a whiff of the sweet and woody smell.

Viorel felt himself at the all too familiar cliff's edge again. The desire for a drink stronger than any sexual urge he had ever experienced in his life. A cold sweat broke out on his forehead as he moistened his lips with his tongue that begged for a drink, any drink, to travel across its surface.

Ennio did not miss the internal battle raging within his guest. All too familiar with Viorel's affliction, his weakness for the bottle, the ceremonious and exaggerated drinking of the grappa an intentional, and sadistic, act on Ennio's part and Viorel knew it.

Ennio smiled and said, "I was thinking the exact same thing about you."

Viorel responded with a simple smile.

"And you look in much better shape than the last time I saw you," added Ennio.

Viorel recalled that day. Over a year ago, Viorel had drunkenly stumbled into the café, not because of business, but because it was the only place that would not refuse him a drink. Ennio agreed to one beer before he told the bartender to take the drunken man to a nearby hotel to sleep it off. The old man did this, not out of compassion for Viorel, but because he did not want any undue attention from the authorities if something were to have happened to him back out on the streets and easy prey in that part of town by the human animals prowling at night.

"Yes, I remember," said Viorel. "Thank you for what you did then. I wasn't ..." He stopped as the bartender brought over the espresso along with a couple of packs of sugar and a glass of water. Having never seen him before, Viorel hesitated.

"No need to worry, Viorel. He's my son, Marino. He can be trusted."

Viorel wasn't so sure. He instinctively had a bad feeling about him. He looked nothing like his father. Where the old man was short, thin and still had a full mop of hair surprisingly dark though peppered with some grey around the edges, the son was tall, husky and had thinning pure white hair. Viorel poured a package of sugar into the espresso and stirred the thick liquid with a spoon without saying a word.

"Seeing that you did not order a correct espresso, am I to assume that you are off the bottle, again?" asked Ennio. The term 'correct' used for coffee spiked with an alcoholic drink, usually brandy or grappa.

"That's right," answered Viorel as he took a sip of his coffee.

"How long?"

"Four months and seven days."

"It is commonly said that youth is squandered on the young," reflected Ennio, changing the subject. "But I believe it is as it should be. As I get older, I grow more and more tired of life. The days become routine and new experiences no longer seem so new."

Ennio paused and drank the last few drops of espresso from his cup. Viorel waited patiently. He knew Ennio long enough to know that the old man needed to chat and philosophize a bit before he got down to business.

"Yes. Life is no longer as exciting as it used to be," continued Ennio as he stared at his guest. "I'll bet that you can still remember your first bicycle, just as you remember your first kiss and the first time you had sex. You remember many first time experiences when you are young, but the memorable times seem to get fewer and fewer as you get older. No matter how new they may be, they become less exciting, and so, we look for other distractions. Failing that, we look for ways to numb our senses and try to push away the feelings of mortality. We each have our own ways to deal with it." Ennio paused and waved for his son to bring him another grappa.

"So you see youth is not squandered on the young. Some may not like it, but life and death follows the path of least resistance," concluded Ennio.

"The path of least resistance," repeated Viorel. He waited for the old man's son to bring the grappa and return to the bar before adding, "I can always count on you for life's little lessons and I say that with all sincerity and humility."

"It is one of the few things that I willingly give away for free," said Ennio with a smile, "but, unfortunately, what you are here for will not be free."

"I would think not," said Viorel.

Ennio took a small sip from his glass. "What are you looking for, my friend?"

"I need a sniper rifle," said Viorel without hesitation and in a matter of fact way.

"How quickly do you need it?" asked Ennio.

"In four days," answered Viorel. That would still give him a few days to work out the remainder of his plan.

"Required effective range?" asked Ennio, continuing his questions.

"Three hundred yards, four at most."

"Any special penetration requirements such as armor piercing?"

"None."

Ennio paused for a few moments. "You said you need it in four days?"

"Correct."

"For something that quick I will have to rely on what I already have in stock."

Viorel smiled knowingly. "I am sure your stock is quite extensive."

Ennio did not reply but smiled back. "I have just the thing. I got a hold of three a few months ago. I have one left and it will meet your needs and then some."

Viorel sat up slightly.

"It is a Russian made rifle not available in the open market," continued Ennio. "They began manufacturing it in 1998 for their army. The SV-98. Very hard to come by outside of Russia. Not as good as some American made rifles, but quite effective and lethal at your requested range, and available now. I could get you something better if I had more time."

"Specs?" asked Viorel. He had heard of it.

"Caliber is .308 Winchester, bolt action, molded fiberglass stock, comes with a silencer, a twelve inch adjustable stand and a 7X scope."

"Weight?"

"Just over six kilos or fourteen pounds."

"How much?"

"Twelve thousand Euros would have it to you tomorrow night," answered Ennio.

"Make it ten thousand and throw in a box of Teflon coated rounds," said Viorel with only a slight hesitation. The asked amount not an issue, but he'd have lost respect if he didn't at least haggle the price down somewhat.

"Deal," said the old man.

Ennio put out his hand and Viorel shook it. The deal sealed.

"Be under the bridge at Via Del Faro on the south side of the river at 11pm tomorrow evening. My son and I will be there with your order."

Viorel finished his coffee and stood up. "I'll be there with cash in hand." He reached into his pocket to retrieve a few Euros for the espresso.

Ennio waved him off. "Don't worry. Coffee is on the house for our best customers."

Viorel headed out into the cool night air. He decided to walk for a bit before hailing a cab.

• • •

He woke up early the next morning. The sun had just risen and it looked like another sunny, warm day.

After freshening up, he dressed and headed for the nearest café where he ordered a cappuccino and cannoli. He took his order to the waist high stand-up counter against the large window near the entrance and had his breakfast, while a dozen other patrons did the same, the ritual a common sight in every city in Italy. Few people ate their breakfast at home. Men and women of all ages and social status lined up at the closest corner café and ordered a coffee and pastry. They either hurriedly ate their breakfast at the counter, much like where Viorel now stood, or devoured it during their morning commute to whatever profession awaited them.

The sun streamed in onto his face, enveloping him in a warm comfort, as he watched the constant flow of people entering and leaving the place. The air filled with chatter between anxious commuters looking at their watches, while many more were talking into their cell phones, juggling their breakfast in one hand and the phone in the other.

Viorel stood back and leisurely ate his breakfast, almost enjoying the controlled melee around him, savoring the fact that he had never been part of that daily stressful routine. As a member of the Swiss Guard Investigation Unit, he either worked within the Vatican City walls or dealt with the fringes of society. Neither one afforded him a mundane daily life.

Viorel waited for the rush to end before starting his day. The crowds usually lasted only a couple of hours, especially outside the tourist areas such as this.

As he walked out into the open, the streets were practically emptying themselves of office workers as they poured into nearby buildings, slowly replaced with housewives who began their daily shopping. Retired men gathered in cool shady corners lighting up cigarettes starting casual conversations of past glories over the noise of a variety of outside workers so common in large metropolitan areas. Viorel walked for several blocks, enjoying his surroundings before he waved down a cab and headed for St. Peter's cathedral. Thirty minutes later, he stood at the entrance of the square.

St. Peter's square wasn't square at all but a wide circle in front of the cathedral. One end contained the main raised entrance of the church, the platform where the Pope and cardinals were to march out in a procession after the mass on the day of Ascension. Viorel's interest lay with the colonnades that stood on each side of the square in an almost half circle. Recalling his extensive knowledge of Vatican City, the Colonnades consisted of 284 fluted columns and 88 pilasters, or half columns, of marble. The columns arranged in four rows and topped with a roof. The structure had one opening at the street end of the square and another at the Basilica entrance.

Viorel made his way across the vast space to the end of the left side colonnades, and to the Charlemagne Wing. Tall dark double doors marked the entrance leading into an exhibition hall on the second floor. Two Swiss guards stood at the entrance. Blood rushed to his head as he walked in the direction of the entrance doors, feeling his heartbeat and breathing speed up. He slowed his pace slightly to allow himself to settle down. He felt in control again as he approached one of the guards in the full Swiss Uniform so familiar to the public. Viorel pulled out his ID.

"I need to get in," said Viorel with authority as he began to put away his credentials.

The guard hesitated for only a second and said, "Yes sir." He nodded to the other guard looking on who acknowledged by unlocking and opening the door while stepping aside. Viorel slipped in as the guard closed the door, breathing a sigh of relief as they boomed shut

The air felt much cooler inside the large foyer. No lights were on, but sufficient sunlight entered the area through large windows on the upper half of the high walls, providing Viorel a clear view of his surroundings. He headed for the marble stairs at the far end of the hall and followed them up to the second floor. Being familiar with the place, he headed for a hidden maintenance door in a remote corner behind heavy curtains. He pulled out a key, one of several given to him by Commander Gallo, from his pocket and opened the door. Viorel made sure the curtain fell back in place as he entered. What little light he had came from a crack in another door at the end of a straight narrow set of stairs. The sunlight that seeped in made it obvious that the door led to the outside. His eyes needed a few seconds to get used to the dusk like setting. The air in the stairwell felt much hotter and stuffier then the main hall as he slowly walked up the stairs. A deadbolt kept the door sealed from the inside. He unlocked it and it opened easily inward.

The harsh sunlight blinded Viorel as he stepped outside on the roof of the colonnades. As his eyes adjusted to the glare, he could see that this vantage point gave him direct view of the square and the front of the cathedral as he had hoped. The edge of the roof he now stood on trimmed with a balustrade, a decorative stone railing that ran around the entire arched roof. The balustrade would give him all the cover he needed. As he looked to the other side of the square, he saw that the colonnades structure there mirrored the one he stood on. Satisfied, he retraced his steps and walked out of the square in a few minutes.

He spent the rest of the morning walking the narrow avenues of the city almost oblivious of his surroundings as he turned his plan over repeatedly in his mind, looking at it from every angle, reviewing its weaknesses, as well as its strengths. Even all the worst-case scenarios showed that he would have favorable odds in eliminating his target. It did not bother him too greatly that they also showed the odds were against him in getting away with it, or living through it.

There were worst ways to die, he thought to himself. Like from alcohol poisoning, all alone in a hotel room, lying naked on the floor with the sheets around his ankles and an empty bottle clutched in one hand.

•••

Viorel ate very little that evening. He worried about the meeting at eleven. It was not like the old man to ask for such a remote and dark location. Past exchanges had occurred behind a warehouse next to shipping/receiving doors.

His son must have something to do with it, he thought. Possibly changed procedures to suit his needs, or settle his fears. The son worried him and Viorel's intuitions, his senses, were usually right. He decided not to take any chances so Viorel brought his gun with him just in case. He had it in its holster attached to the back of his belt, the grip free from its strap to allow quick retrieval.

He had rented a car that afternoon to transport the rifle and to have a ready escape vehicle in case something went wrong. He then bought a large telescope from a hobby store, not for the telescope, but for the packaging. The box and Styrofoam made an ideal concealment and transportation method for the rifle.

At precisely two minutes before eleven, Viorel drove his car just off the road in a flat area beside the bridge. With the structure less than one-hundred yards away he waited in the car with the engine and lights on until he saw some kind of signal.

At exactly eleven o'clock, a set of headlines approached from the other side of the bridge. The vehicle stopped underneath the bridge's foundation and the lights turned off as the car came to a stop. Viorel did the same and got out of his own car.

He did not like the location for it had only one way out. He would have liked at least another escape route, even on foot, but he had no other alternative.

Viorel walked slowly towards the other car. The streetlights from the nearby road allowed some detail but not enough for his liking. He wondered if that was intentional.

The passenger front door opened and the interior dome light came on, exposing the old man, Ennio, as he slowly got out. In the driver's seat, he saw the son staring out at Viorel, both his hands on the wheel.

That at least was a good sign, thought Viorel.

"Hello, my friend," called out Ennio as he closed the door and stood by the car, leaning on his cane with his right hand.

The old man had never called him that before and it made Viorel even more nervous. He did not reply but continued cautiously towards the car as he unbuttoned his jacket for easier access to his weapon.

"Do you have the package?" asked Viorel.

"Of course," answered the old man with exaggerated gaiety.

Something was wrong, thought Viorel. The old man was always more talkative than this. Something had changed sometime between yesterday at the bar and tonight.

Viorel stopped ten paces from the vehicle. The son remained unmoving in the driver's seat while the old man stood unsteadily near the car.

"Show me the package," said Viorel.

"It's in the trunk," said Ennio, glancing back at his son. "Marino, get the delivery out of the trunk."

Without hesitation, the big man opened the driver's door and got out. With his hands at his side, he walked carefully to the back of the vehicle without taking his eyes of Viorel. Neither did his father.

Alarms were still going off in Viorel's head as the son opened the trunk and momentarily lost from view. Marino came out from behind the open trunk lid with an automatic rifle in hand. Things happened very quickly then, even though it seemed like slow motion to Viorel as adrenaline pumped through his veins.

"No!" the old man yelled out too late.

As the son aimed at Viorel and began to pull the trigger, the lieutenant rolled to his right while reaching for his own gun. The rifle fired and the bullet whizzed by Viorel by a wide margin. After one roll, Viorel got up on one knee and aimed with both hands on the gun. He fired a single shot and a small hole appeared just under the right eye of the big man. Brain matter and bone flew out from the back of the head as it tossed back from the impact, the rifle flying out of his hands as he fell backward and dropped on the ground behind the car. Ennio let out a yell as he looked back at his dying son. He reached into his jacket. Viorel fired two more shots, hitting the old man in the chest. The cane flew out of the old man's hand as he too fell backward near his son.

Viorel stood up and lowered his weapon when he saw that both men no longer posed a threat. He walked to where they lay. Marino, the son, lay unmoving with open dead eyes staring up at nothing. The old man lay groaning on the ground, his breath coming out in short gasps. Viorel hovered over the dying man for a moment before he put away his gun and crouched down. He reached down to open the old man's jacket, looking for the hidden weapon that he had been reaching for. He found none.

Ennio looked up at Viorel and whispered, "I was reaching for my inhaler." He clutched his chest and added, "Asthma."

"I'm sorry, my friend," said Viorel with little emotion. He did what he had to do.

Incredulously, Ennio replied hoarsely, "Not your fault." He looked back at his son. "He should have known better. I told him you were an old customer. He was too greedy, wanting to take the money and keep the rifle. Figured you were a lost cause because of the booze."

"If there was any other way, I would have taken it," said Viorel.

"I know," said Ennio in a weaker voice. He looked at Viorel again. "Life...and death...follows the path of least resistance." With those last words, the old man's breath let out for the last time and his eyes fluttered close.

Viorel said a prayer for the old man and got up. Ignoring the son, he grabbed the rifle and ammunition and headed back to his car. He then took out the box with the telescope. Carefully opening the box so as not to damage it, he took out the scope and tossed it in the river. He then put the rifle and ammo in its place, carefully packing the Styrofoam around the rifle before he re-closed the box and gently placed it in the back seat.

Viorel made it to within a few blocks from the hotel when he broke and began looking for an all-night grocery store. He looked for beer, nothing but a beer, two at most, just to dull the edge. The events that evening had shaken him.

He thought about Ennio and his son, Marino, lying dead under the bridge. They no longer breathed, no longer felt desire, or fear because of him. He didn't just take their rifle, he took everything from them, everything they ever had and everything they would ever have. The realization hit him hard, and he began to slide. He had crashed many times before and the despair, the emotional shock, always the same, always the trigger.

He found an open store and quickly headed inside. As he got to the counter, he glanced up and saw the neat rows of bottles; new, unopened bottles of gin, brandy, grappa, and many others, all lined up in attention, calling out to him from behind the counter. His mouth became instantly dry and his throat constricted as he tried to swallow. He grabbed the edge of the counter as vertigo hit him and he closed his eyes, trying to push the image of the neat rows of bottles away. He felt both guilt and emotional pain as he thought of how he had failed everyone he knew; his councilor, the commander, his parents, and everyone he had known in his life.

He was too weak.

The man at the desk said something but Viorel did not hear him. He simply glared at the clerk and motioned to the brandy bottles, two bottles, the beer long forgotten. He paid the clerk without a word, grabbed the paper bag containing the bottles, and hurried out the store.

Viorel parked the car around the corner from the hotel, grabbed the telescope box and paper bag, and hurried to his room. The wife of the owner manned the front desk that night and gave him only a passing glance as he strolled in with his burden, too absorbed in the late night movie playing on the television set sitting on the counter.

He struggled to get the key in the door but finally managed to get it opened without making too much noise. He entered, locked the door from the inside, and carefully rested the box and the paper bag on the small table. After retrieving a glass from the bathroom, he filled it with the golden liquid from the first bottle. He promised himself not to stop until he finished both bottles.

•••

Viorel rose from the dark abyss very slowly but made no effort to open his eyes. When he eventually tried, a sharp pain rattled the nerve endings at the back of his eyeballs. The pain forced out a slight groan from his throat, which solicited an even stronger bolt of pain, this time from the back of his skull. He forced himself to lie still without moving a muscle, without even attempting a deep breath, lest he wake up the dormant but raw nerve endings throughout his body. Still keeping his eyes closed, he felt himself lying on his right side in a fetal position, his right arm numb from lack of circulation. He needed to straighten out and get on his back. He gritted his teeth and straightened out in one slow but smooth motion as his body simultaneously screamed both pain and relief. He gasped for breath at the exertion and felt new pain run through his ribs as the air filled his lungs. The more he moved, the easier it got, until he could actually move his limbs without having the urge to yell out in pain. He swore to himself that he would never drink again, the same promise he made to himself after every crash.

He tried to open his eyes, but his lids were matted shut. He used his hands to pry them open and immediately closed them again as the light coming in from the window began to drill a hole in the back of his eyeballs. He lay there again with his eyes shut, trying to regain his strength. He tried again and this time they slowly adjusted to the daylight though open no more than just a slit.

He sat up in bed and swung his legs over the side. As he did so, an empty brandy bottle fell off the bed and onto the floor. It did not break but a thud-like hammer blow pierced his eardrums. The bottle rolled on the tile floor, the bell sound the glass made on the hard tiles like the church bells of all the churches in Rome clamoring in unison between his temples. The din finally stopped as the empty bottle hit a leg of the table. Just then, he noticed the second empty bottle on the table.

He frowned as the daylight and the clock on the nightstand showed it to be late afternoon. He had slept most of the day and actually surprised that he woke up so soon. There were times when he passed out, comatose a more accurate description, for an entire day soaked in his own sweat and urine.

Suddenly a wave of nausea hit him. He barely managed to crawl to the bathroom and, for fear of missing the toilet, threw up in the bathtub. What came out were the remnants of last night's meal. His body had long absorbed the liquor. The act of throwing up caused his chest muscles to tense up, shooting a new wave of pain through his upper torso, and his head wasn't spared, the top of his skull felt like it was going to explode, as bitter, think fluid shot out of his mouth in spurts. Every beat of his heart made his temples pulsate in agony. His body finally relaxed when his empty stomach had nothing left to throw up.

He leaned over the side of the tub, with his chin on the rim, reaching for the cold tap and tried to rinse out some of the multicolored bile at the bottom of the tub. He tried not to look at it, lest it caused him to heave again. Even the bitter, acidic smell made him shudder but, unless he threw up an organ, he had nothing left. After getting most of it down the drain, he lapped up some water from under the tap and rinsed out his mouth. After swallowing a few mouthfuls of the cool liquid his body, and stomach, began to relax. The pounding in his head remained, but ebbed enough to allow him to get on his feet and take a shower. He stood under the water for twenty minutes and gulped down more of it before he felt clean enough to get out.

Naked, Viorel lay back down on the bed as the day's light began to fade. It would be noon the following day before he felt well enough to go out and get some food inside him.

He was two days away from his appointed destiny with the cardinal.

• • •

Cardinal Costa was not about to change his habits because of a mere threat on his life. If anything, he followed his routine to the letter to allow the Swiss Guard, who kept themselves hidden quite effectively, an opportunity to capture whoever was behind the threat.

The cardinal had found that his secretary, Father Kevin, had been quite a resourceful soldier of The Brotherhood. With permission, Father Kevin had listened in when Costa had partaken in that quite enjoyable verbal jostling with the two cardinals and the Commander. After that episode, Father Kevin decided to have the commander followed for several days thinking it likely that his adversaries would take some form of action and, if so, most likely led by Commander Gallo. He had placed one of The Brotherhood's soldiers on his tail and soon had a report back about a visit to a private detox center in the outskirts of the city.

By claiming to be from the Vatican, and he was, Father Kevin found out a Swiss Guard had stayed there. Because the Church did not have any legal jurisdiction, the center refused to divulge the officer's name. Despite this, he still managed a short interview with the councilor of the Guard, and, almost by accident, found out about the picture of Cardinal Costa.

"I am very pleased with you, Brother Kevin," said Cardinal Costa as he sat behind his desk looking up at the secretary priest.

Father Kevin blushed as he stood in front of the ornate desk.

"All in the service of our cause," said the secretary priest in a low voice, his eyes downcast.

"Yes, yes, quite right," answered the cardinal.

"One more thing," added Father Kevin. "The councilor had said that the officer had something coming up soon, something important, at the next church holiday."

Cardinal Costa pondered for a moment and said, "Inform the Swiss Guard that you heard rumors of a possible attempt on a cardinal, but do not divulge anything else, not who may be threatened, who the perpetrator is, nor what organization he belongs to, or even when it might happen."

Cardinal Costa felt he did not need any more attention on himself.

"As you command, Your Eminence," said Father Kevin.

"Just tell them to be extra diligent in their duties the next several days," added the cardinal. "That should be enough of a clue, if they are not too stupid."

"Yes, Your Eminence," replied the priest.

"You can go," dismissed Cardinal Costa.

Father Kevin gave a slight bow and left the room, closing the door behind him.

So, the Protectors want to play games, thought the cardinal, as he leaned back in his chair.

He would use himself as bait to flush out his opponents, especially after the devastating losses in Malta.

The more Protectors eliminated the better, he thought.

But what a terrible price The Brotherhood of the Rapture paid. There were only eleven men left, and that included Father Kevin and he himself. To make matters worse, he lost a valuable commander. Gabriel, one of his most capable men and the most dedicated, and now he was gone, vaporized, along with any clues as to whether the Descendant went with him. It would be more than worth it if she was, but he didn't know for sure. So he kept the few of The Brotherhood that survived, searching – searching for any clues. There were no new trails, but he wasn't about to give up.

Master Costa would not stop until he succeeded in his life long quest of destroying the descendant of Judah the betrayer.

• • •

Per long held tradition, the Pope himself would say the mass on the day of Ascension. After the mass, he would lead a procession of cardinals, each with a large candle in hand, out to the square in front of the Basilica and lead the crowd gathered in two prayers. All this, to commemorate the day that Jesus Christ rose up into heaven.

With the mass scheduled for early afternoon Viorel headed for the square mid-morning just as the crowds started to gather. He dressed in a dark grey, almost black, single-breasted suit with a similar colored shirt and black military boots. The outfit considered standard issue for the Swiss

Guard on active duty in order to be discreet and not attract any undue attention from the public. His strategy was to appear on an official errand when he approached the guards at the doors to the Charlemagne Wing.

Carrying the telescope box his arm he reached the doors. Viorel smiled as he stopped in front of the two guards at the doors and placed the box on the ground before reaching for his ID.

"Hi, boys, how you doing?" he said casually, not making eye contact and looking bored.

The guard looked at Viorel's credentials and back to his face. "Weren't you here a few days ago?" asked the guard, wrinkling his eyebrows.

"Yup," answered Viorel. "Just got another delivery of equipment for the exhibition hall." He looked around routinely. "Looks like you got another busy one today," added Viorel, changing the subject as he took his badge back. "Not me, I'm done after this." He put his hands in his pockets as if he had nothing better to do, looked around for a moment and then up to the cloudy sky. "Looks like it's gonna rain. I'd stand by the doors when it starts, if I were you, that's what I used to do."

The guard's shoulders relaxed, Viorel proved to be one of them. The guard opened the door and stepped aside.

Viorel picked up the box and went inside. "Thanks buddy," he said. "I am gonna head out from the cathedral side when I'm done, so don't wait for me," he smiled, "and don't get too wet." The door closed behind him.

Viorel followed the same route as before. He got through the maintenance door and up the stairs but stopped short of opening the door to the outside. Since the pope and cardinals would be outside later that day, he knew there would be guards on the roof but stationed in such a way as to be hard to spot by the crowds and that's what Viorel counted on. From the guards' locations, in the nooks and crannies on the roof, they would not have a direct line of sight across the entire roof. Besides, they would be looking down at the crowd, not up.

To increase his chances even further, Viorel would crawl out on the roof only when his target came into sight. He figured his chances were fifty-fifty of getting spotted before he got off a shot. It was the best he could hope for and he also figured he had a ten to one chance getting away once he did fire.

Viorel looked at his watch and saw he had three hours before the cardinals came out. He crouched down next to the box and carefully opened it.

He took his time assembling the rifle.

•••

The weather remained overcast the rest of the day but the rain held back. The crowds gathered in the square and Viorel could hear the sounds of the moving, but well-mannered, throng.

According to his watch, the mass was just about to finish inside the church. Soon the pope would lead the cardinals outside to the square in front of the Basilica, coming out in single file, each holding a candle.

Viorel opened the door a crack. The elevation afforded him a direct view of the front of the cathedral and be able to spot the procession as soon as it came outside. When the cardinals gathered in front of the crowd and began their prayers of Ascension, Viorel would crawl out and quickly set-up behind the railing at the edge of the roof. With luck, the guards would not spot him until too late.

The increased murmur of the crowd told him the time had arrived. First, several priests came out holding a cross at the end of a long pole. Behind them came the pope in full regalia, hands held together in prayer and meditation. Behind the pope came the cardinals, white smocks over their red uniforms, each holding a lighted candle.

Despite his training, Viorel began to perspire, cold beads formed on his forehead and upper lip. A cold finger of sweat trickled down the center of his back as he peered out with one eye through the small slit between the door and frame.

The pope stopped in front of a microphone a couple of hundred feet from the railing that held back the throngs of the faithful. The row of following cardinals began to line up behind him, facing the crowd.

Viorel saw Cardinal Costa to the left of the pope. This positioned the cardinal closer to Viorel and decreased the margin of error though one hundred and fifty yards away. Viorel adjusted the scope accordingly. Under normal circumstances an easy shot for him, easy if he had a spotter and plenty of time to set-up. Neither which he had.

He loaded the magazine with three rounds. It held ten but he saw no reason to add more. He figured he had a chance to fire one, maybe two rounds if his luck held out. The third cartridge in case he had extremely bad luck in his aim and extremely good luck with the guards asleep on the job.

The Pope would say two prayers to the attentive crowd and Viorel planned to act during the second.

The pontiff put up his hands and made the sign of the cross with his right to the large crowd. The microphone picked up his high pitched but clear voice as the pope began his opening prayer.

"Let us pray
God our Father
Make us joyful
in the ascension of your Son Jesus Christ.
May we follow him into the new creation
For his ascension is our glory and our hope.
We ask this through our Lord Jesus Christ, your Son
who lives and reigns with you and the Holy Spirit,
one God, forever and ever.
Amen."

"AMEN," responded the crowd in one harmonious cry.

As the prayer rang over the crowd through enormous speaker strategically placed around the square, Viorel's heartbeat pounded loud in his ears so loud that he almost missed hearing the start of the second prayer, but when he did hear it, when sure it had begun, his promise to his friend and his training moved him into action.

"O Lord Jesus, I adore You," began the pope.

Viorel slid the magazine into the rifle.

"...Son of Mary, my Savior and my Brother..."

The door slid slowly open and he crawled out onto the roof.

"...for You are God. I follow You in my thoughts..."

Viorel rose up on one knee and rested the muzzle of the rifle on the stone railing.

"...O first-fruits of our race..."

He pulled the bolt back and a cartridge loaded into the chamber.

"...as I hope one day by Your grace, to follow You in my person, into heavenly glory..."

He looked into the scope, locked his view onto the row of cardinals and began to swing the rifle across, searching for Cardinal Costa.

"...In the meantime, do not let me neglect the earthly task that You have given me..."

Cardinal Costa came into view. Viorel froze and the crosshairs came to rest between the firm eyebrows of his target.

"...Let me labor diligently all my life with a greater appreciation for the present..."

Viorel looked at the face in his sights. His finger moved to the trigger. He hesitated.

He knew he took too long and lucky the guards hadn't spotted him already, that no alarm had gone out. In a way, it upset him that the guards hadn't spotted him yet. Under different circumstances, he would be reporting this as a gap, a fault, in the security measures in place.

"...Let me realize that only by accomplishing true human fulfillment can I attain Divine fulfillment..."

The prayer reached the end and the opportunity to fire quickly closing. He had to pull the trigger soon, but when he looked again at the face through the scope, a face that appeared so close, he did not see an enemy, he saw a priest, a representative of the church that he himself belonged.

Time and luck ran out for Viorel.

A bullet smashed into his left shoulder and the force of impact caused him to roll to the right and over his rifle. As he did so, his finger on the trigger squeezed involuntarily and a shot went off high over the procession and hit the side of the dome of the Basilica. Because of the silencer, no one in the crowd heard or saw a thing. Viorel did not hear the bullet that hit him either, it too from a muted weapon.

He looked up to see a guard running in his direction from the left, from where the shot came from. He quickly looked right and saw another guard running towards him. Both were in black and both had a scoped rifle with a silencer.

Part of him felt relieved.

It's about time, he thought.

They were still a couple hundred feet away and Viorel knew he had only a few seconds.

Down below, as Viorel looked on, he saw at least a dozen men in dark suits swarm the pope and surrounded him in a protective shield of bodies, cutting his prayer short. The men of the Swiss Guard quickly escorting the Holy See back into the Basilica.

A murmur rose from the crowd. All eyes locked on the stage, confused by all the commotion. The cardinals were herded in the same direction as the pope but there were too many of them and too few of the guards to provide any serious protection.

Viorel lay on his side, bleeding heavily from his shoulder wound. It felt numb rather than painful and he could no longer move his left arm. He reached for the rifle with his right arm and quickly wedged the butt between his legs, pulled the bolt back and loaded a second bullet into the chamber while the spent cartridge flew out. He had to try for one more shot.

His raised the rifle with his single hand. It felt heavy as he rested it on the railing, looking for his target. He felt another bullet go by near his face, the faint breeze almost cool on his now hot sweaty cheeks. Viorel looked again through the scope and scanned the moving faces of the cardinals.

The footsteps were getting closer. He heard them yelling for him to stop. He frantically scanned the back of the heads of the cardinals through his scope. He had to be sure before he fired. He stopped suddenly at a face looking up in his direction.

Cardinal Costa.

Viorel put his finger on the trigger, ready to fire. The cardinal stopped and ignored the shoving of the men around him. He had spotted Viorel and looked up directly at him, almost seeing him through the scope.

Viorel hesitated.

The man Viorel aimed at looked unafraid, unafraid of been shot, unafraid of death, almost daring him to shoot as he stood there in the open and not moving, an easy target. Viorel could almost feel the man's will reaching up at him, grabbing him by the roots of his being, by his soul. Just for a second, Viorel could not move, and he ran out of time.

A bullet entered Viorel's left temple and blew out the right side of his head. His body didn't even have enough time to convulse. He simply fell over onto his right side from the impact of the bullet. Dark red blood began to pool around his head. The Russian rifle lay next to him with his hand still on the grip.

One of the last things that Viorel sensed was not a thought or an idea, but more of a sense of relief, and a feeling of release from his mortal body and all of it weaknesses and addictions.

The guards, coming from opposite directions, got to Viorel at the same time. They looked down at the body and the spreading pool of blood.

"He seemed to hesitate on that second shot," said one of them.

They looked down and saw a cardinal standing alone and looking in their direction. Cardinal Costa had not moved the entire time while looking up defiantly.

"I guess it pays to be a cardinal," casually added the second guard.

The last image Viorel had, as the blackness quickly engulfed him, was of the old man when he uttered – "Life, and death, follows the path of least resistance."

CHAPTER FOURTEEN
DISCOVERY

"Dude, you're out of your mind. I aint going down there," said Fritz, the lanky, blonde, twenty-six year old research scientist recently appointed to the Austin campus of the University of Texas. He took a swig from his eighth can of beer in the course of two hours. "I'm gonna break my neck!"

"Chicken shit! It's not that bad," slurred Raza with a smirk on his face, at twenty-nine, the older of the two. The beer in his hand his tenth. "Look at me, my friend, I'm short and fat and I can do it, while you're a tall, fit German, and you're scared?"

"Yah, I'm scared," replied Fritz, his face contorted in a terrified smile and eyes wide. "That's a long way down and we got no breaks."

Both men, wearing football helmets that had seen better days, stood behind small, waist-high, steel workbenches fitted with oversized go-cart wheels. For body armor, they had duct-taped Styrofoam, front and back, sandwiched over their t-shirts and additional strips over their cargo pants. The Styrofoam acquired from packing material from just arrived boxes of new equipment.

They looked down the north side of Mount Locke, part of the Davis Mountains of the state of Texas, at the foot of the domed structure holding the Otto Struve 82" Reflector telescope, one of the three observatories that made up the McDonald Observatory Facility.

"Think about the honor of your family," said Raza, "and the honor of your race."

"My race, and family, will be reduced by one, if I try this," responded Fritz.

Raza looked up with blood shot eyes at his friend and co-researcher. "Better to sacrifice many for the honor of one." He leaned on his wheeled contraption and almost lost his balance as it rolled slightly away from him. The beer spilled onto his pants as he went to grab the table.

"You mean, better to sacrifice the one for the honor of the many?" corrected Fritz.

Raza looked up at Fritz with drunken dismay. "So why did yah ask?"

"I didn't."

"You didn't?"

"No."

Raza looked down at his beer as he tried to stop the world around him from spinning. With a confused look on his face, he stared back up at Fritz. "So what didn't you do?"

Fritz looked at Raza and then at the beer can. "How many of those did you have?"

"Not enough," answered Raza who guzzled down the remainder and celebrated with a long burp. "Alright," began Raza once again as he rubbed his hands together and positioned himself behind his cart. "Finish your beer and let's go."

Fritz didn't say anything, not because he felt powerless to argue, but because he wanted to show his friend he could do it. He looked at the man next to him. Raza didn't fit the stereotypical astronomer depicted so often in the media. Raza was a short, dark skinned man born in the U.S. after his family emigrated from India. Like Fritz, he got his doctorate from the University of Texas and now doing post graduate work in the McDonald Observatory a few miles from the small, rustic village of Fort Davis. Raza was as American as anyone can be. He embraced the university life, and everything that it entailed, with enthusiasm. That meant he could party with the best of them but at the same time dedicated to his chosen profession of astronomy.

Fritz had also just recently finished his doctorate studies and had joined Raza on his own post doctorate only a month ago. For the German, the last four weeks had been an intense period of research and observations, but today, the Sunday of the Thanksgiving long weekend, was a day to unwind and let off a little steam.

Fritz finished the last of his beer. The alcohol had been working its magic and it finally gave him the courage he needed for the so called "initiation sleigh ride" down the side of Mount Locke. Down the valley, the view looked intimidating, but at only a 45-degree incline and no less severe than a ski slope of moderate difficulty. To Fritz, who had never skied, it looked suicidal.

"Okay," began Raza enthusiastically, "When I count to three, we jump on the carts and fly down the hill."

Fritz dropped his now empty can of beer and wiped his sweaty palms on his 'armor,' building up his courage.

The countdown began. "One, Two, Three, Now!"

Raza dived head first on top of trolley, landed squarely on his chest and grabbed onto the sides in a futile attempt to control the steering, his feet dangling out in space behind him. Despite the Styrofoam, the not so steady landing on top of the cart knocked the wind out of him, but he managed to hang on as the cart started its travel down the slope.

Fritz wasn't as courageous. After a slight delay, he jumped on his cart butt first and held onto the sides of the cart to steady himself, his feet over the sides of the cart, riding horseback style.

Both men quickly picked up speed as they began to scream in a mix of panic and exhilaration, Raza slightly ahead of Fritz. The downward trip became a virtual obstacle course. The sandy dirt covered side of the slope littered with thorny shrubs, small trees and cacti, each capable of inflicting damage to the foolish daredevils. After a hundred feet down the slope, Fritz noticed Raza heading straight for a small cactus. Raza lowered his head and aimed the top of his helmet straight out like a battering ram, his eyes closed. The cart and Raza's helmet severed the plant in two pieces that flew in the air as the cart rode harmlessly over the remainder of the cactus. Raza looked up and opened his eyes in astonishment and a smile. Fritz noticed the other man's helmet now boasted a row of thorns, Mohawk style.

Suddenly and without warning, Raza's front wheels hit a boulder hidden from view just under the surface of the sandy soil. The cart tipped forward and threw the rider off. Raza became airborne. A few seconds later, Raza hit dirt and began to roll. If not for a well-placed bush in front of him, he would have continued several hundred feet down the hill and hit several cacti and even a tree or two. The gods were looking out for his friend, thought Fritz. The bush acted like a safety net and he came to rest within its embracing branches, suffering nothing more than a few scratches.

Fritz wasn't so lucky. His cart bucked like a wild horse but he managed to hang on despite the beating his ass took on the hard tabletop. His chin kept slamming against his Styrofoam chest-armor like a bobbing-head toy dog caught behind the rear window of a car in a Nascar race. Fritz managed only a hundred feet before he slammed into a bush. Unlike Raza, the bush was too small to catch him but not small enough for the cart. Fritz too became airborne while maintaining the same upright riding position with his legs wide apart heading straight for a cactus. Fritz slammed into it and the piece he straddled broke off. He now rode a torpedo-shaped chunk of the thorny plant. Flashes of Slim Pickens in the movie Doctor Strangelove flashed through his mind. When he finally hit the ground, the cactus went one way and he went another, rolling another fifty feet before finally coming to rest near the base of a tree.

Raza, recovered from his fall, ran over to Fritz still lying on the ground.

"Hey man, you ok?" asked Raza with a smile on his face. "That was some ride."

Fritz lay stunned for a moment. He moved his arms and felt no broken bones. He moved his legs and felt nothing broken there either but soon began to feel sharp stings between his legs. He managed to raise his head and look down. Dozens of thorns protruded from his inner thighs. He managed a meager groan as he realized his predicament.

Raza looked down and saw what had happened. "We're gonna have a busy afternoon getting all those out," he said casually.

"No shit!" answered Fritz. "What the hell was I thinking?" Looking up he added, "This is all your fault!"

"Take it easy buddy," said Raza. "You just proved you got balls."

"Balls, what balls? I think I left them skewered on the cactus back there!"

"Come on, give me your hand," said Raza reaching towards Fritz. "Let's head back to the house. I'll get a pair of tweezers from the lab along the way."

Fritz managed to get up slowly with hot pain emanating between his thighs. With Raza's help, he managed to make it up the hill, the carts forgotten somewhere below. Walking with his legs wide apart, he now truly felt like Slim Pickens.

•••

Jeffrey Baker got out of his vehicle and stretched his legs. He had travelled six straight hours to get to his destination and felt stiff all over. He was also relieved that the van made it without any major breakdown along the way. The lime green 1979 Volkswagen van looked its thirty years, but it served its purpose and got him where he wanted to go. It wasn't exactly a chick magnet though, but then, neither was he at five-foot-ten, skinny, sporting large framed eyeglasses and a face full of acne even at twenty-five.

He considered this newly appointed assignment at the Observatory the highlight of his doctorate in astronomy through Texas U. His professor had told him he would share living quarters, and scope time, with two other scientists also on post doctorate work. His pending meeting with his new roommates made Jeffrey a little nervous for he wasn't sure what to expect or whether they would like him.

At just after five in the afternoon the sky looked crystal-clear and free of clouds. At an elevation of 6,791 feet above sea level, the air felt cool, almost cold, but that did not surprise him since it was, after all, the month of November.

Jeffrey grabbed his duffel bag and headed for the sleeping quarters housed in a set of low buildings around the facility. He headed for the building and room number given to him by the registry office back at the university.

He noticed very little activity around the place. Not surprising since it was Sunday afternoon of the Thanksgiving weekend. Who were not getting ready for the nightly viewing at the scopes were either visiting families or down at the village of Fort Davis a few miles away.

Jeffrey found the room number but hesitated before knocking when he noticed a plaque attached to the door that read 'Watch the stars, and from them learn. To the Master's honor all must turn, each in its track, without a sound, forever tracing Newton's ground.' One of Einstein's many famous quotes and he smiled as he did a quick rap on the door before opening it. University etiquette didn't require waiting for someone to answer the door. If not locked, then the student didn't have a girl in the room, or a boy for that matter.

He entered while introducing himself. "Hi there, I'm Je..." Jeffrey Baker stopped short when his eyes focused on the scene. A tall blonde young man, with beer in hand, lay on one of the three single beds, his pants down to his ankles. Another man on his knees and bent down over his crotch with his back to the door. Both men raised their heads and looked over at Jeffrey as he stopped at the threshold in shock.

Jeffrey's words caught in his throat as both men smiled back at him and said, "Hi!"

Jeffrey backed out of the room and exclaimed meekly while closing the door, "Sorry, gents. I'll come back in half an hour."

A shriek of laughter burst from the two men in the room. "No! No! It's not what you think," began the dark man on his knees. "Fritz here got a bunch of thorns growing out of his inner thighs and I'm helping him remove them with a pair of tweezers." The dark man, whom Jeff assumed to be Raza, showed Jeffrey the tweezers in his hand.

Less embarrassed then a moment ago, Jeffrey headed back inside the room and smiled back. He looked closely at the prone Fritz. "Ooh, that's gotta hurt, man."

"Damn right it does," said Fritz. "I feel every single one that he pulls out."

"Shut up and drink your beer," said Raza. "It'll help with the pain. I'm almost done anyway." He bent down again and reached for the last few thorns.

"I'm Jeffrey Baker, the new guy assigned to your room," began the newcomer as he dropped his bag on the floor near the door. "You two must be Fritz and Raza."

"I'm Raza and he's Fritz," said Raza as he pulled the last thorn out of his companion's leg. He got to his feet and dropped the thorn in a paper napkin in his other hand. Jeffrey estimated there were at least a couple of dozen bloody thorns in that napkin.

Raza threw the napkin in the wastebasket and grabbed the iodine bottle and cotton swabs on the night table near the bed. "Here," he said as he dropped the bottle and swabs on Fritz's lap. "You can do this part yourself."

"I thought you were going to give me the full treatment," said Fritz with a smile as he grabbed the bottle. "That would really give Jeff something to think about." He was soon busy turning his thighs red with the antiseptic.

"So, Professor Tarnake sent you over?" asked Raza as he grabbed two beers and threw one at Jeff.

Jeffrey caught the beer, opened it and took a sip. "Thanks. Yes, the old man himself assigned me here."

"Working on your doctorate?" asked Raza.

"That's right. Looks like I'll be staying with you guys for a while." Jeffrey took another drink and added, "How about you guys?"

"Allow me to formally present ourselves to you," began Raza as he bowed to his new roommate. "I'm Razachandra Vishwanath. Just call me Raza. I'm doing some post-doctorate work." Raza shook hands with Jeff.

"Vishwanath?" asked Jeffrey. Before waiting for an answer, he added, "I recall a nice looking chick named Vandana Vishwanath at the University.

"How do you know my sister?" asked Raza angrily.

"Only by reputation," said Jeffrey in a squeaky voice, regretting what he said as soon as he said it.

"By reputation?" asked Raza, his voice rising. "What reputation?"

"I didn't mean it in a bad way," said Jeffrey, shrinking a little into himself. "I meant, in a hot way."

Raza looked at Jeffrey severely. "That's my sister, bud. What do you mean, hot?"

"Hot? Did I say Hot?" Jeffrey started to sweat and his cheeks flushed. "I didn't mean hot hot. I meant warm hot." Seeing that it did not have the desired affect he added, "More like lukewarm hot."

That did not appear to appease Raza either, who seemed to get even angrier.

Jeffrey became even more concerned, almost scared. "Hey, I'm sorry, man. I didn't mean it."

Raza looked at Jeffrey and then at Fritz. Slowly a smile began to appear on the little man's face and said, "Got you, buddy!" He slapped the surprised, and relieved, Jeffrey on the shoulder and added laughingly, "That's cool, man. I'm ok with it."

Jeffrey smiled back, took a sip of his beer, and sat down in the nearest chair. Raza was going to take some getting used to.

His laughter having spent, Raza continued with the introduction. "This is Fritz Zsiga, a classic example of the Arian race, otherwise known as a non-Jewish Caucasian of Nordic stock." Fritz threw his now empty beer can at Raza who easily ducked out of the way. "Shipped directly from Freiberg, Germany at age three, he's here working on his final thesis for his own doctorate but I'm sure you've heard of him."

"No. No I haven't, actually," said Jeffrey. "Should I?"

"You've never heard of Fritz?" asked Raza as he opened his beer and took a long drink.

Fritz continued applying the iodine without looking up. Jeffrey racked his brain for a moment but nothing came to mind.

"Fritz...Fritz Zsiga," said Raza.

"What's the big deal?" asked Fritz. "I've never said it was me. *You're* the one who found it on the internet."

"I got it from the teacher's assistant working for the professor, and after two years it is still on the internet," said Raza.

"Well that's no huge feat," retorted Fritz. "There's a lot of crap on the internet and it seems to last forever."

"Never mind what he says," said Raza waving him off as he looked over at his new roommate. "Sit down, Jeffrey, I got it right here."

Raza put his beer down and went to the message board near the door. He pulled out a thumbtack and brought over the papers it held up.

"Here we are," said Raza scrutinizing the papers. "Now drink your beer and listen up."

Fritz flushed as Raza began his narrative. "In Fritz's second year Chemistry class, the professor had handed out a test with a single question, 'Is Hell exothermic, gives off heat or endothermic, absorbs heat?'

"Most of the students wrote proofs of their beliefs using Boyle's Law, you know, gas cools down when it expands and heats up when it is compressed, or some such variant.

"Fritz, however, wrote the following: First, we need to know how the mass of Hell is changing in time. Therefore, we need to know the rate at which souls are moving into Hell and the rate at which they are leaving. I think that we can safely assume that once a soul goes to Hell, it will not leave. Therefore, no souls are leaving.

"As for how many souls are entering Hell, let's look at the different religions that exist in the world today. Most of these religions state that if you are not a member of their religion, you will go to Hell. Since there is more than one of these religions and since people do not belong to more than one religion, we can project that all souls go to Hell. With birth and death rates as they are, we can expect the number of souls in Hell to increase exponentially.

"Now, we look at the rate of change of the volume in Hell because Boyle's Law states that in order for the temperature and pressure in Hell to stay the same, the volume of Hell has to expand proportionately as souls are added.

"This gives two possibilities:

"One, if Hell is expanding at a slower rate than the rate at which souls enter Hell, than the temperature and pressure in Hell will increase until all Hell breaks loose.

"Two, if Hell is expanding at a rate faster than the increase of souls in Hell, than the temperature and pressure will drop until Hell freezes over.

"So which is it?

"If we accept the postulate given to me by Teresa during my Freshman year that, 'It will be a cold day in Hell before I sleep with you,' and take into account the fact that I slept with her last night, then number two must be true, and thus I am sure that Hell is exothermic and has already frozen over. The corollary of this theory is that since Hell has frozen over, it follows that it is not accepting any more souls and is therefore extinct, leaving only Heaven, thereby proving the existence of a divine being which explains why, last night, Teresa kept shouting 'Oh my God!'" Raza looked up at Jeff. "When the marked papers were handed back, Fritz got a perfect score!" He ended his narrative with a huge smile followed by a swig of beer.

Jeffrey gave out a laugh and finally said, "Yes, I heard of that one, but I didn't realize that such a distinguished person would be sharing the same room with me."

"Well, now you know," said Raza smugly.

Jeffrey looked at Fritz and said, "From his wounds, it appears that, sometime over the last few hours, he had attempted to ride a cactus of one form or another, and how did such a distinguished person end up in such a predicament?"

"Ask Gandhi sitting next to you," said Fritz.

"He ended up this way by not listening to me," explained Raza. "I told this Nazi youth to ride the cart face down but he decided to ride it like a horse."

"You did not say that at all, mini-Buddha," retorted Fritz. "You were too drunk to know what you did, or say."

"But I'm not the one lying there with my legs open, you big Krout."

"Given how hard up you are you'd probably jump me if you had a few more beers."

"Hard up? I'll have you know, I can be quite charming to the ladies, if I had the time."

Raza noticed his message machine blinking. "You expecting a call?" he asked Fritz.

"Can't say that I do. My folks are on vacation and not expected back for another week."

Raza went over to the machine and pressed the play button.

LAST DESCENDANT

"Hi there, it's Joanne," began a sultry female voice despite the tinny sound from the small speaker. "I'm on route and should be there by eight tonight. Can't wait to see you." The machine gave off a beep, sounding the end of the message.

"Great news! Joanne's in town," said Raza with a smile on his face.

"Who's Joanne?" asked Fritz.

"A strange woman who called my machine by mistake," said Raza in a deflated voice, "but it was nice to dream for a moment."

Fritz threw a pillow at Raza and missed. "Ah, shut up and throw me a beer, munchkin."

All three toasted to their newfound friendship.

•••

Jeffrey Baker spent the next week acquainting himself with his new colleagues and the observatory. He quickly discovered that his associates were the same socially stunted semi-geniuses as himself. With an IQ of 140, he had no qualms about his mental capacity, nor did he feel any arrogance about it. It remained a simple fact to him that, where he lacked in physical abilities, he made up for it in gray matter. Since his colleagues were also social outcasts, he felt a sense of camaraderie towards them, as they did towards him. Jeffrey did hold a bit of jealousy towards Fritz, though. The tall German had both the intelligence and the looks, but his Achilles heel was his social skills, he just could not function around the opposite sex. If an attractive woman even said hello to him, he'd stutter and blab out an unintelligible grunt, seemingly loose his motor skills and act like a moronic idiot, scaring off any would be prospect. As a result, the three men got along like peas in a pod.

As the calendar rolled into December, the carts remained forgotten down the hill and Fritz long since healed. When not at the telescopes, they poured over their findings and observations. Neither of the three actually worked on exactly the same thing but, interestingly enough, they still seemed to spend a lot of time together, both professionally and, of course, socially.

"Why astronomy?" Jeffrey's father had asked when his son had decided on his major years back. "Is this your way of looking for God?"

"Yes dad," replied Jeffrey, sarcastically, "and I'm specializing in searching within the center of our galaxy to see if He's there."

"And what if he looks back?" asked his father. Jeffrey was surprised at his father's wit at that moment for he always associated religious faith, religious fervor, which his father had, with lack of intelligence.

"You think that being religious means that you are stupid?" asked Raza, when one day Jeffrey shared his story with his new colleagues. "My friend, you have a lot to learn."

"Do you believe in God, Raza?" asked Jeffrey.

"Let me put it this way," began Raza. "Many academics believe that science re-affirms the existence in God, not denies it. For instance..."

"Here we go," interrupted Fritz. "The Book speaks."

"Shut up and keep working on your plans to invade Europe," retorted Raza. Turning back to Jeffrey he continued, "For instance, where do the laws of physics come from? Who, or what, decided on how matter should be structured? Who created gravity? Science can only confirm that these things exist, and mostly how they work, but it cannot explain why they are the way they are. Einstein said 'God is in the atom.'"

"I don't remember that quote," exclaimed Jeffrey and he thought he new all of Einstein's writings.

"Whoever said it, it was a good quote," said Raza dismissively.

Fritz interrupted again. "Einstein also said 'Two things are infinite: the universe and human stupidity; and I'm not sure about the universe.'"

"So you believe in God?" Jeffrey asked again of Raza, ignoring Fritz's outburst.

Raza smiled. "The answer is not that simple. We should be asking if there is a God and, if there is, what is God and does he even have a plan?"

"And your answers to those questions?" persisted Jeffrey.

"If I knew those answers, I would not be here at this observatory searching the skies every night," replied Raza. "No, my friend, what I call myself, and I've been called many things, is an agnostic wavering towards deism."

"I would lean towards the many other things to call you," added Fritz.

No one answered him.

"Deism?" asked Jeffrey.

"Deism," confirmed Raza. "Belief in a God who created the world, but has since remained indifferent to it. Doesn't care what happens to us. May not even remember we exist, or at least doesn't acknowledge it. As opposed to theism, what your parents would be described as believing: the belief in one God as the creator and ruler of the universe, without rejection of the biblical laws and revelation."

"So, according to you, God doesn't give a shit about us?" asked Jeffrey.

"That's putting it a bit blunt, but that is essentially correct," answered Raza.

∴

As the second week of December ended, Jeffrey had just completed some observations of which the results to him seemed strange, out of the ordinary, or at least, not what he expected. He spent the next couple of days pondering over them. The more he thought about them, the more they seemed extraordinary and he had to talk to someone.

Jeffrey went to dinner as he did every day, in the common room with his two friends. The discussion that particular night centered on whether the new server at the cafeteria was a real redhead or not. Raza and Fritz bantered back and forth concerning the color of her eyes and their relevance to her hair color.

"I am telling you, redheads don't have brown eyes," said Raza. "They have a tendency to be in the lighter colors or hues."

"Bullshit," said Fritz before he took a bite out of his burger.

Raza turned to Jeffrey. "Jeff, what do you think?"

"About what?"

"About what? Haven't you been listening?" asked Raza. He looked over at Jeffrey. "What's the matter, dude? You've been kinda quiet these last few days."

"Oh, I don't know," said Jeffrey. "My results seem kind of weird."

"In what way?" asked Raza.

Jeffrey didn't know quite how to explain it without sounding crazy.

Of course, they all knew the basics of the solar system and the galactic alignment. In the Solar System, the planets and the sun share roughly the same plane of orbit, known as the plane of the ecliptic. Likewise, within our galaxy, like all galaxies for that matter, the stars follow a similar plane referred to as the galactic equator, giving it the familiar wheel shape, or some like to describe it as a hurricane shaped structure. Every year for the last 1000 years, on the winter solstice, December 21, the earth, the sun and the galactic equator come into alignment.

"I have stumbled into something that appears extraordinary," began Jeffrey. "I have looked in all the literature, all the charts on hand, and I have found no reference to this."

"What?" asked Raza.

"Here's the thing," began Jeffrey. "On this year's winter solstice, December 21, Jupiter, Saturn, Earth and Sun all align with the center of the galaxy." He looked at his two friends and added, "The last time this happened was about 2000 years ago."

"Yes," interjected Fritz, "but this alignment has happened many times over the last few billions of years. If you calculate back, you will see this. It is inevitable."

"Correct," said Jeffrey. "But this time I have found something else." He shifted in his seat and continued, "Let me explain, on December 21, the Sun, Jupiter and Saturn will be aligned precisely to one side of the earth and the galaxy on the other side, but this time there will be an extra body between us and the center of the galaxy."

"Go on," urged Raza.

"I've discovered that there will be a pulsating star along the exact plane of axis to the center of the galaxy. I hadn't seen it till now because it had been hiding behind another star, but it is now just starting to emerge."

"That's great, dude!" said Fritz. "It means you can name the new star."

"There's more to it than that," added Jeffrey. "It appears that the pulsar has a very tight beam of light."

"That's nothing new," said Raza. "Pulsars are like the 'lighthouses' of the universe. They give off a beam made up of radio waves and/or light rotating at a set interval. The first one ever detected had been mistaken for a beacon emitted by some intelligence. Astronomers soon discovered that it was a common phenomenon. It caused quite a stir among the UFO fanatics for a while."

"This one is different," said Jeffrey. "This one does not rotate, and the beam will be pointing straight to earth, a tight beam and laser-like, of about a kilometer wide." He paused for affect and then added, "The beam of light will look exactly like a bright start, and will not be noticed by most people, but it will be there nevertheless, and it will sweep across the northern hemisphere. At exactly midnight on December 21, it will be pointing somewhere in the northwest part of the United States."

"What the hell have you been smoking?" mocked Fritz.

"I'm not shitting you," said Jeffrey. "It freaked me out when I first saw the evidence."

"You do realize what you are saying?" asked Raza.

"You are predicting a major religious event," answered Fritz, on behalf of Jeffrey.

"I am doing no such thing," responded Jeffrey knowing where Fritz was heading. "I am merely predicting an unusual astrological event."

"The hell you are," retorted Raza. "If any of the religious fanatics get a hold of this information, it will race through the internet like wildfire."

"We have to keep an open mind," said Jeffrey. "Don't look at it as a religious thing. There is nothing really that I have discovered that says it is. It merely points out that there is a major coincidence on that particular date."

"Bullshit!" said Fritz. "This could be the second coming of Christ."

"Or it could be the end of the world as we know it," added Raza.

"Or it could be just another astrological event," added Jeffrey.

Fritz and Raza looked at each other before they looked back at Jeffrey.

"You aint doing a great job convincing us, bud," said Fritz.

"Ok – ok, hold on," sighed Raza. "We gotta be scientific about this."

Raza got up and began pacing around, absently chewing on his nails. The few others in the common room looked up with mild curiosity but quickly went about their business when they saw whom it was.

"First we got to verify your findings and pinpoint the location," said Raza to Jeffrey. "Then we have to look at all the possibilities and come up with a most likely theory. Then we publish what we find."

"No way, man!" interjected Fritz. "If Jeffrey's calculations are correct, we can only do one thing." He paused and looked at the other two men.

"You're not suggesting what I think you're suggesting?" asked Raza.

"Yes I am," answered Fritz. "We go to ground zero." "And how are we supposed to do that?" asked Jeffrey. "We barely got five hundred bucks between us. We can't afford plane tickets and then rent a car to get there."

"We don't have to," said Raza with a smile. "We go on a little field trip with your set of wheels."

"A little trip?" said Fritz. "It's straight up the middle of the United States."

"It'll be an adventure," exclaimed Raza.

"My van barely made it here," said Jeffrey. "I doubt if it will get us where we want to go."

"Don't worry," said Raza dismissing the objection with a wave. "I know a bit about cars. We'll give it a once over before we head out."

"Hold it, hold it," objected Jeffrey. "How can you guys equate this to a Second Coming? The date of the event is December 21. Christ was born on December 25."

"Maybe the bible got the date wrong," said Fritz.

"Or maybe not," added Jeffrey.

"We'll find out, wouldn't we?" asked Raza. "One thing at a time, just like our professors taught us."

Raza sat down and returned his attention to his meal. "Finish up boys," he said. "We got a lot to do over the next few days."

●●●

The three men spent the entire night reviewing the data gathered by Jeffrey.

"Looks like you did your homework," said Fritz while his fingers were flying across the key board of one of the PCs in the lab.

"I'm disappointed you doubted me," said Jeffrey. "I would not have said anything until I felt sure, and even then, I had misgivings about telling the two of you. Now I'm going on some wild goose chase. I should've kept my mouth shut."

"Not like you, buddy," said Raza. "You'd be bursting at the seams if you tried to keep it to yourself."

Fritz stopped typing and looked intently at the screen. "Ok guys. Here's the coordinates of where the star of the new king will be pointing to."

"What?" asked Jeffrey.

"Never mind," said Fritz.

Raza and Jeffrey were looking over the German's shoulders. Fritz looked up the coordinates.

"Looks like we will be heading for Idaho," said Fritz. Our star will be aiming at a spot somewhere between the towns of Santa and Fernwood, Idaho, U.S. of A."

"Santa?" asked Jeffrey incredulously. "You must be kidding."

"Actually, it's sort of appropriate," answered Raza. "Santa actually means saint. Santa Claus should actually be described more accurately as Saint Claus, also known as Saint Nicholas."

"Great now we're looking for Santa Claus," said Jeffrey. "What do we do for an encore, look for the Easter Bunny?"

Raza looked at Jeffrey and said, "If you ever did bump into the Easter Bunny, it would probably beat the crap out of you."

"Take it easy boys," interjected Fritz. "Stay focused."

Jeffrey and Raza quieted down.

"The location is in some remote part of the forest in the area," said Fritz. "We'll bring along a portable GPS unit and it will lead us right to it."

"Any satellite maps on the internet?" asked Jeffrey. "We should be able to see the spot right here in the comfort of our lab."

"You trying to get out of the trip?" asked Raza.

"I already looked it up," said Fritz, not answering Raza's comment. "There's nothing there, but the pictures are a year old. Lots can change in a year."

"Have you figured out our route?" asked Raza.

"No, but let me just bring up a map site on the web and we can figure it out real quick," answered Fritz.

He typed in the directions calculator and the route popped up in a fraction of a second.

"Here we are," said Fritz. "It's roughly a two thousand mile trip."

"Two thousand?" exclaimed Jeffrey. "My van will never make it." He added, rubbing his eyes with one hand.

"Relax, dude," said Raza. "We will nurse it all the way there."

Fritz banged away at the keys again. "The computer calculated two days, but, considering our wheels, I'd not just double it, I'd triple it." He looked up at his companions and added, "Six days would give us time for eating, resting and deal with any minor mechanical emergency."

"That's still cutting it close, my friend," said Raza.

"Yah, I know," said Fritz. "Today is Friday, December 14th." He looked at his watch and added. "Or should I say Saturday morning, December 15th. We gotta leave tomorrow, Sunday morning, if we're going to make it there by the 21st."

"I think we better get a few hours sleep and begin our preparations," conceded Jeffrey.

Saturday was a blur of activity. They gathered up all that they thought they would need for the six day trip and threw it all in the van. Fritz, of course, brought the GPS and his laptop.

True to his word, Raza, worked on the van for most of that Saturday afternoon. He gave the engine a minor tune-up and oil change, and checked the rest of the fluids in the vehicle. His major concern was the poor condition of the wheels, which were almost bald.

"I told you it was in bad shape," chided Jeffrey. "I barely got here to begin with."

"Don't worry," said Raza. "We got a spare tire in case we get a flat. Besides, the wheel size is very common. We should be able to find some used ones along the way."

The three amigos pooled all their money and found that they had five hundred and twenty seven dollars of travelling money. They spent the rest of the evening approaching their other colleagues and begging for any amount of loans to help in their quickly planned 'ski' trip up north. Surprisingly, they managed to scrounge up another five hundred. Finally, they threw in all the food they had in their room into the van, stole a couple of cases of pop from the kitchen and headed out first thing on Sunday morning.

As the van slowly creaked down the mountain road towards Fort Davis, the young scientists looked like three smiling kids heading for their favorite fishing hole. Spirits were high, the sunrise appeared in a clear, cloudless sky, and they were eager for the road.

Fritz, sitting in the back, looked at Jeffrey in the driver's seat with Raza next to him and said, "You know gents, we could possibly be the 'three wise men' of the twenty-first century."

Jeffrey slapped the steering wheel and exclaimed, "I knew someone would say it! I knew it! I didn't want to bring it up because it would make this whole things appear nuts and now someone said it. Shit!"

Raza looked over and laughed. "So what, Jeff? Of course we are. We have all been thinking it since you first told us about the sign Friday night."

"You too?" asked Jeffrey in disgust. "And which of the Magi am I supposed to be?"

"That's a good question," began Raza.

"Oh no," moaned Fritz from the back seat. "The Book is at it again."

Raza didn't look over but continued, "Their names were Caspar, Melchior, and Balthazar, jointly known as the Three Wise Men, or the Three Kings."

He looked back at Fritz and added, "See, that wasn't so bad. Sweet and short"

"Thank God for that," said Fritz, looking out the window.

Fritz brought a map with the route clearly marked.

"So now we're kings," said Jeffrey slowly shaking his head. "We're broke, but we're kings none the less."

Raza smiled at Jeffrey and, with a slight bow, said, "King Jeffrey, it is an honor to be driven by such an esteemed royal entity."

Jeffrey felt like giving him a backhand but stopped himself. He knew it would only encourage Raza even more. He simply looked over in disgust and kept driving. Despite himself, Jeffrey looked forward to the trip. Whatever they would find at the end of their journey it would be an adventure.

"Instead of camels, we ride a Volkswagen," said Jeffrey.

Raza looked over and smiled.

The 'Three Wise Men' were on their way. If all went according to plan, the trip would take six days.

CHAPTER FIFTEEN
JOURNEY

The first day.

The trio followed the winding road 118 through hills and valleys within the Texas range. The grasses a dead yellowish color much like the surrounding area of the observatory. Apart from the blacktop they were on and the occasional wire fencing, the landscape remained much like in the days of the Settlers.

They did not take the van over forty miles an hour for fear of blowing one or more of the bald tires. This made for an interesting ride when the occasional eighteen-wheeler overtook took them with surprising speed. The resulting turbulence caused their 'hippie mobile' to swerve all over the road. The experience made Jeffrey have second thoughts about whether he made the right decision in agreeing to the trip.

They were still on the same road with no buildings in sight as the light of the day began to fade.

"I think we should pull over somewhere for the night," suggested Fritz.

"I was ready to stop hours ago," added Jeffrey, his eyes dry and red.

"Let's find a spot a few hundred yards off the road where we can camp out," said Raza.

They found an area flat enough to drive on and decided it to be as good a place as any. Jeffrey veered off and came to a stop when they felt they were far enough from the road. None of the three owned a tent so the van ended up as the de facto place for their sleeping quarters. They would simply curl up in blankets that they brought.

Fritz lit a fire close by to keep warm and cook their meal. The other two rummaged in the van for food and came back with canned soup and canned meat.

"I shouldn't have left you guys in charge of the food while I looked over the van," Raza said disappointedly,

"We're lucky we have anything that's edible," said Fritz.

"At least we didn't forget the can opener," added Jeffrey.

Suddenly they saw headlights turn off the road and point in their direction.

"Who the hell is that?" asked Jeffrey nervously.

The lights heading straight for them and, with the daylight almost gone, they could not see the make of the vehicle. None of them moved as a rundown Winnebago pulled up next to their van. If the three amigos rode in a hippie van, then this was the magic bus on an acid run. The entire surface of the motor-home completely covered with hand painted flowers, rainbows and green meadows. An old man who looked like in his seventies with long white hair jumped out of the driver's side while a woman of similar age jumped out of the passenger seat.

"How you doing, man?" asked the old man with a wide grin on his face as he approached the three men. He was a tall thin caricature of the 60s era with long, straight, pure white hair. He sported a thick long mustache that drooped down below his chin and dressed in bell-bottom pants and a multicolored flowery loose fitting long sleeved shirt. His companion, a woman, also thin and wearing a multicolored dress much like him but longer and down to her knees, her hair long, straight and pure white like her companion. She too smiled and didn't look threatening. The opened toed sandals they both wore completed the vision of the carefree hippy generation.

"Can we help you?" asked Raza in a cautious voice.

"Hey, it's cool man," said the old man. "Driving by, we saw your campfire light and thought we'd check it out. Mind if we join you at the warm and comfortable fire?"

"We're kind of a private group of guys, if you don't mind," replied Raza.

"Whatever you say," said the lady. "But we didn't come empty handed." She pulled out a large clear plastic bag. "We got a bit of fun that we thought you'd like to join in."

A bag full of weed, or what the Jamaicans call ganja. The three amigos looked at each other.

"Well I'm sure we can make some room," said Fritz the first to speak,

"There's plenty of space around the fire," added Jeffrey enthusiastically.

"How about some dinner?" added Raza displaying a wide grin.

"Let me introduce ourselves," began the man. "My name is Sonny and my old lady here is Chastidy."

Raza did the honors for the three amigos.

"My lovely young lads," began Chastidy with a slight frown. "Is that all you have for dinner? What will your mothers think? You wait here. I have some better things for all of you."

She threw the bag of weed to Sonny and disappeared into the motor-home.

"She's a good cook, my old lady," said Sonny as he sat down near the fire with the three men.

He reached into his pocket and brought out a sheet of rolling paper folded up neatly into a wallet size square. As he unfolded it, the three other men stared wide-eyed as it opened up to roughly the size of an 8.5"x11" sheet of writing paper. Sonny flattened out the creases and laid it carefully on his lap. He then reached into the bag, grabbed a handful of weed and gingerly sprinkled it onto the sheet of paper. The astronomers sat in awe as Sonny began to rollup over an ounce of the weed into an enormous cigar shaped joint the size they had never seen before.

"You've got to be shitting me?" asked Raza.

"Man, you gonna love it," smiled Sonny proudly looking up from his handy work.

"I already do," said Jeffrey, his eyes following every move.

The newcomer reached into the fire, pulled out a burning twig and began to light the humungous joint. He expertly dragged on one end as the fire lit the other. He stopped and held his breath in. With his eyes watering, he extended the joint to Raza sitting next to him and asked while trying to hold the smoke in, "Care for some?"

"Don't mind if I do, buddy," replied Raza.

He grabbed the joint with his entire hand and appeared at a loss on how to wrap his lips around it. He finally just simply opened his mouth and grabbed on with his lips. He pulled on it and a huge intake of smoke filled his lungs, the coughing fit he experienced like nothing he ever had before in his life. At one point, smoke seeped out from his tear-ducts.

"Hey man, passed that over," said Jeffrey, as Raza continued coughing between his legs.

Jeffrey was a little more cautious and managed to inhale just enough to avoid the same coughing reflex while getting a lung full of the sweet smelling smoke.

Fritz needed no stealth in his approach. He simply took a deep drag like the old man and held it in like a pro. His watery eyes the only betrayal to his controlled demeanor.

Sonny smiled as he saw the practiced methods of Fritz and said, "I see I have found a soul mate. I am glad we stopped by, man." He took the joint and took another drag.

"I see you boys started without me," said Chastidy coming out of the gloom in the direction of the motor home, her arms loaded down with an assortment of food stuff along with a couple of pans. "Hey honey, how about some for me."

Sonny handed the joint to her as she put down her burden. By the time that the group finished the smoke, the chicken stew simmered away and the soup was almost ready. They had a problem finding enough energy to get up but they soon managed.

"Ma'am," began Fritz while licking his spoon after doing the same to his now clean bowl. "That was, by far, the best stew I ever had."

"Thank-you, honey," responded Chastidy with a smile. Sitting next to Fritz, she patted him on his lap and added. "But don't call me Ma'am. Call me Honey, call me Chastidy, but don't call me Ma'am."

"Yes Honey Chastidy," said Fritz bleary eyed.

"You're such a charmer, big boy," she said smiling back with a twinkle in her eye.

Meanwhile, Raza, Jeffrey and Sonny lay flat on their backs gazing up at the clear and starry night.

"By God, that's so sick!" exclaimed Jeffrey as he stared at the countless points of light.

"What?" asked Sonny. "How can you say that? It's so beautiful!"

Raza curled up into a ball in a fit of laughter. Sonny could only stare over at the writhing man in bewilderment.

"No! No! Sick is a good thing!" explained Jeffrey, looking over at Sonny with blood shot eyes. "I mean that it is so beautiful, so cool, as you would say."

"Oh," responded Sonny, finally comprehending.

Raza eventually stopped laughing and looked over at the other two men. "I love you guys," he finally said. The other two now succumbed to a fit of laughter.

In the meantime, Chastidy had curled up under one arm of Fritz who now lay on his back near the fire with his head propped up by a log. They shared a regular cigarette and a beer. She reached down with her free hand and began to fondle him, but, despite her skills, he was simply too far gone to rise to the occasion. "Don't worry, honey," she said with a smile. "I have other ways that can even raise the dead."

She slowly slid her head down to attempt the resurrection as she took out her dentures and slid them into her dress pocket. A smile appeared on Fritz's face. As he began to respond, she in turn showed her approval with a groan. Before he got to the edge, she stopped just long enough to say in the sultry voice, "Honey, once you've spent, you're going to do me in kind, as good as I'm doing you."

She went back to work with even more fervor.

● ● ●

The second day.

Jeffrey slowly opened his eyes and a piercing light blinded him. The sun beat straight down on his upturned face. Raising his arm to shield his eyes, he looked around. He had been sleeping near the now smoldering fire, on the bare ground, fully clothed, with a blanket over him. He looked around and found Fritz also lying on the ground on the other side of the fire. He lay on his back, feet up on a log and arms out to his side and he too had a blanket as a cover. It appeared that someone had cared enough for their wellbeing to cover them up against the chill of the night. Jeffrey looked over to the van and spied Raza's feet protruding from the open back door.

Scanning the area where the Winnebago stood the night before, Jeffrey saw the spot empty. He slowly got up and looked around but it was nowhere in sight. Sonny and Chastidy must have left sometime during the night or the early morning.

Suddenly concerned about the stealthy departure, Jeffrey suspected that the old couple must have stolen some of their belongings before taking off. He took a quick inventory of things and found nothing missing. Not even their money stashed in the van's glove compartment.

Breathing a sigh of relief and with his two companions still sleeping, Jeffrey decided to start packing. While doing so, he thought about the now departed old couple. They were definitely a throwback from the 60s era of carefree and happy living. He felt a twinge of jealousy that someone could live in such a way, with little worries and no responsibilities, but if everyone began to live like that, the world would quickly revert to the dark ages. No, Raza thought. For someone to be like that there must be others to provide a support structure for the basic necessities of life. Or else, where would the wanderers get their food, gas and even medical aid when required? Besides, it seemed that they were either well off or made their living in the weed that they smoked last night.

Jeffrey walked over to Fritz and nudged him with his foot. "Wake up, buddy. We need to be on our way soon."

The German stirred and slowly opened his eyes. "Where are we?" he asked.

"Way behind schedule," replied Jeffrey. "Come on, get up and have something to eat. I'm making coffee."

Jeffrey had just turned to the coffee pot when he realized he had seen something on Fritz. He turned back to the German and caught sight of it. Teaching towards Fritz's lips, he pulled it out. Between his fingers, he held a white pubic hair and smiled when he realized what it was.

"Oh my God!" exclaimed Fritz wide eyed.

"What's the matter?" said Jeffrey still smiling. "Has your dick fallen off?"

"Oh my God!" repeated Fritz, as he grabbed his stomach looking as if he was going to be sick. "I can't believe what I did last night!"

"So what?" said Jeffrey.

"No, no, no!" said Fritz not hearing.

"You simply went foraging for some muffin last night," said Jeffrey, teeth now showing in his smile. "And it looks like you had your fill." He looked at the other man and added, "You want a coffee with that?"

"You little prick!" yelled Fritz. "Why didn't you stop me?"

"You gotta be kidding," answered Jeffrey. "I was way out there myself and in no condition to know what you were up to, no pun intended."

Jeffrey thought it through a bit more and lost some more of his smile as he tried to recollect what mischief he got into the night before. He played out what he could remember and began to relax again. "No, the *stars* are all that I got into."

"I need a coffee now!" demanded Fritz.

Jeffrey walked over to the boiling kettle and poured some in a Styrofoam cup as he said, "Relax buddy, as long as it felt good, then so what? I'm sure she has a smile on her face today."

Fritz looked around and saw the motor-home missing. "What happened to them?" he asked.

"No idea," answered Jeffrey. "Maybe she didn't want to break your heart if you saw her drive away and out of your life forever."

"Shut up and make some breakfast," demanded Fritz.

Within an hour, they were back on the road again and heading north.

The day remained clear but cool. The landscape gradually began to change as they headed farther north. The arid countryside, so prevalent in the south, replaced with more lush greenery. The traffic ebbed and flowed as they passed small towns along the way.

Eighteen-wheelers still made their hearts skip a beat or two as they overtook the smaller van that maintained a speed well below the limit. Otherwise, the day went by uneventfully.

Raza slowly came out of his stupor around the same time his stomach woke up at about noon. They stopped at the next truck stop and grabbed some fast food before moving on. He couldn't stop laughing when Jeffrey told him what had happened to Fritz.

Back on the road, Fritz said very little. Raza couldn't help but look over and laugh every once in awhile.

"You want another joint?" asked Raza mockingly.

"Shut up, little Buddha," answered Fritz.

"Relax buddy," said Raza. "You look like someone who's racked with guilt. You weren't exactly cheating on anyone."

"I know, I know," said Fritz. "What bothers me the most is that I actually liked it."

Raza laughed aloud. Fritz looked over and even managed a slight smile himself.

"Don't underestimate those gum jobs," said Raza. "I should consider getting one myself."

"You should," added Fritz, his mood lightening.

"Let's go visit your mother," said Raza.

"Bastard," said Fritz, in a better mood now.

By the late afternoon, they began looking for a place to rest for the night and they managed to find a secluded spot near a river. Once again, they built a small fire to keep warm and cook their meal.

"What do you guys think we will find when we get there?" asked Fritz, as they sat around the fire after supper enjoying a coffee.

Jeffrey shrugged and the first to answer. "Nothing, quite simply, nothing. Oh, maybe a deer or two and maybe even a few rabbits, but nothing else." He looked over at the other two men and continued,

"Unlike you guys, I don't see this as a religious pilgrimage, merely an astronomical event that coincides with a significant religious date. Man has done this too often in his short history on Earth. For some reason, we must always have a reason for something happening. Why can't it be that it simply happens, that it simply is?"

Jeffrey looked over at Raza and added, "Like you described yourself before, Raza, I would, most likely, be the same if I had any religious bones in me, that is, if forced out of me, then I'd say that I am a deistic. As you said, 'Belief in a God who created the world, but has since remained indifferent to it.'"

"You were listening?" asked Raza with a smile.

"I hang on every word," answered Jeffrey in a light mood.

"Good boy," said Raza. He looked over at Fritz and asked, "How about you, buddy boy?"

"What about me?" asked Fritz.

"What do you think is at the end of our rainbow?"

Fritz looked over and answered, "A life size golden Buddha with his arms outstretched as an invitation to his favorite follower, the mighty Raza!"

"Wouldn't that be something?" asked Raza. "The gold alone would be worth a fortune. We could really live like kings then."

"It figures you would say that," said Fritz.

"All kidding aside," said Raza, "what are you expecting we will find?"

"God only knows for sure," answered Fritz, "and I'm not saying that facetiously. Maybe the Messiah's rebirth, or maybe nothing, as Jeffrey said."

"Well, I've had enough," said Jeffrey getting up. "I'm going to crash out."

The night air felt noticeably colder as they were now further north and would continue to get colder the closer they got to their destination. That night they slept huddled together for warmth in the back of the van.

•••

The third day.

The day came and went as uneventful as before. They were surprised at how well the van held up to the long, daily drives.

They had reached the halfway point of their trip, just south of Salt Lake City. If everything went according to plan, they would traverse the lower part of Idaho the fourth day, into Montana the fifth, and back into the upper part of Idaho and to their final destination on the sixth and last day.

They decided to stop before they got to I-15 and into a more densely populated area where finding a camping spot would prove more difficult. The landscape barren and cold this far north and the trees void of any foliage. Just off the road and down a dirt path, they managed to find a cluster of pines that provided some cover from the cold northern winds.

The land around them looked like it had been harvested just recently and they hoped that the farmer would not discover the trespassers.

The three astronomers had just lit a fire when they heard a motorized vehicle approach from a cluster of pine trees nearby. A large farm tractor, over twenty feet high, came around and stopped near the van, the Volkswagen looked like a toy alongside the monster. The diesel engine coughed once and died as the cabin door opened and a burly black man in blue denim overalls made his way down the ladder.

"Howdy, lads. You are on private land, *my land*," said the landowner with a deep booming voice and a frown. He jumped down the last wrung and stood his full six-foot-four height.

Jeffrey took one look at the farmer and decided he wasn't a man to be trifled with. He saw a dark skinned, black man that appeared to be in his fifties with big hands and broad shoulders. His smooth, shinny, youthful face contradicted the white hair exposed under a John Deere baseball cap.

"Beg your pardon, sir," began Raza. "We've been on the road all day and are really tired and hungry. We were just looking for a quiet place to make something to eat and rest for the night. We didn't mean to trespass. We'll pack up quick and be on our way."

The farmer looked Raza up and down and asked, "You're Indian, aren't you, boy?"

"Not North American Indian," began Raza, "but a real Indian from across the ocean. The type that Columbus mistakenly thought he found."

"I know that, son, and that's what I meant," said the farmer. "I may not be a professor, but I'm no fool."

"Yes, sir," replied Raza averting his eyes.

"What's the matter with a motel room?" he asked. "They're cheap enough."

"Yes, sir," answered Raza now the defacto spokesman for the trio. The others were more than happy to let him take the lead. "But we're kind of short on cash and trying to save as much as we can for gas."

"Where you from, boys?" the large man asked, "And where you headed?"

"We're coming from the University of Texas," replied Raza. "We're students there and we're on a little trip up to Idaho to visit some friends."

"I see," said the farmer. "Well, I'm not going to risk your friends from Idaho hearing from you that folks in Utah are not hospitable. Pack up and follow me in the van to my home just up the ways." He reached into his pocket and took out a cell phone. "I'll phone ahead and let my wife know you're coming." He stuck out his large hand to Raza. "My name is Raymond King," he asked. "What's your name, boy?"

Raza grabbed Raymond's hand and shook it as best he could under the iron grip. "Raza Vishwanath."

All three shook hands with Raymond and introduced themselves.

"Grab your stuff and follow me in your vehicle," He said, calling his wife and climbing back onto the tractor. He led the way just as the sun began to set.

"We may have lucked out again," said Raza.

"Again?" asked Jeffrey feeling unsure of the situation.

"Relax, buddy," answered Raza. "He looks sane to me."

"He looks like your typical conservative American living along the bible belt," added Fritz.

"He certainly didn't sound like one of those hillbilly moonshiner type, did he?" asked Jeffrey not expecting an answer and feeling a little better about the whole situation. "Besides, he seemed more interested in you, Buddha boy."

"Nah," said Raza with a smile. "I think he's more into that milky, Arian, white skin of Fritz."

Five minutes later the two-vehicle convoy reached a large two-storey home a few hundred yards off the main road. To one side stood a large barn with a silo, on the other, another small structure that looked like a chicken coop.

Raymond drove the tractor up to the barn and killed the engine. Jeffrey drove the van to the front porch of the main house where a large black woman stood waiting for them.

"Hello boys!" she called out as they got out of the van.

Liandra King stood on her porch with her hands on her hips and her chin out as if daring the world itself to look her right in the eye. At six foot one and well over two hundred pounds, she looked like a perfect match for her husband. Her tight fitting blue jeans and loose blouse did little to hide her large but muscular frame and ample bosom. She looked like a woman who worked side by side with her husband and damned proud of it

"Looks like my husband was right," she said sporting a warm, wide grin of white teeth in her large dark head, surrounded by a mane of straightened but wavy black hair past her shoulders. "You boys look like such scrawny, little birds that even the buzzards wouldn't bother with."

"Hello ma'am," said Raza with his own warm smile and introduced himself and his friends.

The tall woman gave them all a bear hug and flick of their hair as if they just came back from kindergarten class and ready for some milk and cookies.

"My name is Liandra, boys," she said. "Friends call me Mama Li, and that's exactly what I expect you boys to call me."

"Yes ma'am, I mean, Mama Li," said Raza, correcting himself.

"Now, boys," added Mama Li, "it's a pleasure to have some company now and then, but before you step one foot in my house, you all need a bath to get the stink of the road off of you. My lord in heaven, boys, you could knock a buzzard off a shit wagon from twenty feet."

Raymond came within earshot of that last comment and chuckled as he got closer. He grabbed his wife around the hips with one large arm and gave her a surprisingly gentle kiss on the cheek.

"Baby," began Mama Li as she casually accepted the kiss, "you show these lads where the shower is in the barn and make sure there's enough soap for all of them." Turning to her visitors, she added. "Boys, you make sure you put on a change of clothes too or we will be sending your meals out to the barn instead of in my warm kitchen."

"Yes, Mama Li," piped the three young men. They were not about to argue against such an ultimatum.

"Come on, boys," said Raymond leading the way. "Grab your things and follow me."

With clean clothes in hand, they entered the large barn by the main doors. Raymond reached over to one side and flipped a switch, turning on the lights that flooded the entire barn. Over to one side stood several occupied horse stalls and a large shower area.

"This is where I wash down the horses and sometimes myself," explained Raymond. "There plenty of soap in the buckets by the shower heads. The water is not heated but I'm sure you boys can take it. Several towels are hanging on the hooks just outside the shower stall. I'll be back in the house. Turn off the lights on your way out." He made his way back to the entrance. "See you boys at dinner."

The soap felt gritty and the water cold enough to cause frostbite if they lingered too long, but, through gritted teeth, they managed to get themselves clean and dried without too much damage. They soon returned to the front door of the house where Mama Li stood waiting for them.

Come in, boys," she said enthusiastically. "Come in and make yourself comfortable."

They sat down at ready-set places at the kitchen table.

Though not large, the comfortable two-storey cedar-sided century home looked like a welcomed break from the outdoors to the weary travelers.

Raymond sat at the head of the table with a one-gallon jug next to him while Mama Li finished up with the preparation of the evening meal.

"Dinner consists of fried kitchen, potatoes, salad and homemade bread," piped Mama Li without looking up. "Ray, be a gentlemen and pour our guests a drink while you wait."

Raymond uncorked the jug and smiled as he began pouring a clear liquid into their large water glasses, "Drink up, boys. This will put hair on your chest, or burn it off, whichever comes first."

Jeffrey and Fritz hesitated as Raza took a quick sniff and a gulp of the clear liquid. Raymond looked on in anticipation.

Raza coughed and gasped for breath. "Good shit," he croaked between coughs.

Raymond lit up with a large toothy smile. "You bet your ass, boy." He took a large swallow himself and added, "Made it myself."

"Don't worry," said Raymond laughingly to the other two in response to their look. "I've been doing this for years. Not like you boys in university. It wouldn't make you go blind."

Fritz took a sip and looked up with a smile. "Not bad, not bad at all." He had another swallow.

Jeffrey took a drink and reacted much like Raza but gave a nod of approval.

All their bellies warmed with the drink as Mama Li brought over the large plates full of food and placed them at the center of the table.

"Eat up, boys," she said as she put down the last plate heaped with large slices of bread. She picked up her glass and gulped down half of it as she surveyed the table with pride, showing no reaction to the drink.

The four men helped themselves to generous helpings of the food and dug right in. Mama Li looked on and showed her pride and approval with a smile and a nod of her head

"My, it's nice to have some young people back in this house," she said.

"You have kids that have left the nest?" asked Fritz between bites.

"Had two boys," said Mama Li, her eyes misting over. "Both killed in the Afghanistan war back in 2010."

"We are sorry to hear that," said Raza as the three guests paused in their efforts at the food.

"Eat! Eat, boys!" she said waving her hand at the table. "Don't you pay no mind at a mother's memory. I am proud that they served our country."

"Amen to that," added Raymond. "They made fine soldiers and we're proud of them."

"As you should be," said Fritz.

"You are good people," said Jeffrey with genuine warmth. "Taking us in like this and knowing so little about us, we were even trespassing."

"Hush, honey," said Mama Li with a smile, obviously enjoying the compliment. "I'm sure your mamas would be happy that you are getting a good meal out on the road."

Mama Li made herself a plate and looked on with joy at the men around the table. Their attack on the food didn't diminish for some time. When all had their fill, they celebrated the end of the meal with another glass of moonshine.

"Ray tells me you boys are heading north to visit some friends," said Mama Li, more of a question than a statement.

"We're heading up to Idaho," said Jeffrey, carefully choosing his words, making no reference to the 'friends' Raza had mentioned to Raymond earlier. "We're hoping to get there by Friday in order to spend the weekend and the Christmas holidays up there."

"So you're not going to be hiding in a corner like so many other people will be doing on December 21st?" asked Mama Li in a sarcastic voice and sly smile.

"No, Mama Li," answered Raza answering her smile with his own.

"What will you be doing, son? Having a small party in honor of your arrival?"

"I'll tell you what we wouldn't be doing," began Raza. "We would be hiding in that corner you mentioned."

"December 21, is not the end," said Fritz, contributing to the conversation for the first time, "but a new beginning."

Fritz looked over at Raza and Jeffrey staring back at him. The eye contact did not go unnoticed by the big woman. "So you boys are not doomsayers but optimists?"

"None of the evidence that we saw showed any inkling that the Earth is going to be destroyed," explained Fritz. "Nor that the magnetic poles are going to reverse, or that any huge solar flares are going to be emitted by our sun and wipe out the atmosphere. They are, quite simply, ideas of crazies that are so prevalent on internet blogs these days."

"Those nut jobs have no real evidence to back-up their predictions," added Raza as he took another sip of the fiery liquid and winced as it went down. "They are simply people who are craving for attention and have found the internet a medium where they will be noticed, albeit only in electronic form."

"What you see here," began Fritz, as he waved to himself and his two comrades with his glass, spilling some of its content, "are astronomers with doctorate degrees."

"So you have looked?" asked Mama Li.

"Of course," replied Fritz, again he looked at his friends and, again, it did not go unnoticed, the moonshine taking effect. "No self respecting scientist would allow hearsay to go unanswered without proper scientific investigation."

Throughout the conversation, Raymond remained quiet. He merely continued to pour for himself, his wife and his guests, ensuring that no glass went empty for too long, especially his.

"But you boys did discover something, didn't you? It may not have been anything catastrophic or 'end of the world stuff,' but something." She leaned closer to Fritz and asked, "So what did you find?"

Fritz looked at Jeffrey who took a sip from his glass and asked, "You religious, Mama Li?"

Mama Li looked over to Jeffrey and answered, "I'll have you know that I am a proud member of our local church of Jesus Christ." She jutted out her chin with pride. "Both Ray and I are good Christians and raised our boys to believe in God and the Holy Bible. We go to church every Sunday and, sinners as we may be at times, try to follow the Good Word and be kind to our fellow man."

"Amen to that," added Ray.

"Here, here," said Jeffrey, sincerely.

"So why the question, honey?" asked Mama Li. "What did you find out?"

"We're not sure what we found," began Jeffrey. He actually wanted to tell someone, the thing too important to keep to themselves. He just had no idea how someone else would react but he would soon find out. "On midnight of December 21, this Friday, a bright star, one that has never been discovered before, or at least recently, will shine down, no, more like it will be pointing a tight beam of light, on a spot near the town of Santa in Idaho."

He paused for a moment to let it sink in. No one said a word.

Raymond took another drink and said, "Amen to that."

"We are on our way there to see what it will be pointing at on that very moment," concluded Jeffrey. He took another drink and waited for the reaction.

"My God, boy," exclaimed Mama Li, quietly. "You're telling me that Jesus Christ will return on that day?"

"We don't know," answered Jeffrey. "I can only tell you what we have discovered. As to what we will find, that remains to be seen. We have just enough money to get there and back, and whatever we find, it will be worth the trip, at least to satisfy our intellectual curiosity."

Mama Li sat staring at her guest for a few moments before she broke the silence. "You boys think you're the Three Wise Men from the Good Book!"

Her laugh echoed throughout the house so loud that it shook the windows. Before long, her husband joined in. The laugh became contagious. Soon, all five were laughing uncontrollably as if in agreement to how ridiculous it all seemed.

Tears were streaming down Mama Li's cheeks as she held onto her stomach in fits of laughter. "You white boys break me up," she finally managed.

In response, a new round of laughter suddenly broke out.

"Do I look white to you?" asked Raza, his face aglow with the room's gaiety.

The question solicited a new outburst from all.

"I don't know, boy," answered Mama Li, "but you sure act like one."

The laughter continued. Eventually, one by one, they became too spent to continue.

Finally, Jeffrey managed to find his voice. "You're right, Mama Li. It's a ridiculous suggestion, but it will be interesting to go and take a look anyway." He wiped his eyes on his sleeve and added with a smile, "At least we will see the light."

A terrible joke, but everyone broke out in a new fit of laughter. Fritz laughed so hard that he ran out to the porch to throw up

• • •

The fourth day.

Raymond rose before sunrise to tend to the animals. Mama Li got up soon after and began making breakfast, looking none the worse from the night before.

The three guests sprawled out on the couches in the living room, soon stirred as the smell of coffee waft in from the kitchen.

Raza and Jeffrey commented on how well they felt that morning as they walked back into the kitchen. Even Fritz said he felt no lingering after effects.

"That's the sign of a good brew," beamed Raymond as he came in.

"It sure is," added Raza.

"We don't want to take too much advantage of your hospitality," said Fritz. "We'll be heading out as soon as we've had some of your generous breakfast."

"Nonsense," said Mama Li. "You take your time, boys. It's good to have a noisy house again."

"Thank-you, ma'am," said Jeffrey. "You and Mister King have been so kind."

"Call me Ray, son," said Raymond in a light tone but with enough authority to allowed little argument.

"Yes, sir, I mean, Ray," said Jeffrey. The response brought out a small smile on the big man's face.

LAST DESCENDANT

They packed the van quickly. The dirty clothes they had on the day before had been washed, dried and pressed sometime during the night as they slept.

Mama Li handed a small piece of paper to Jeffrey and said, "Now, honey, that's our phone number on that piece of old paper and we want you to call us when you get there. We'd love to know what you find at the end of your journey."

Each hugged Mama Li as she gave them a kiss and a bear hug in return. Her eyes were moist as they turned from her to shake Raymond's hand.

Jeffrey was the first to bid farewell to Raymond. The big man held out his hand and the younger man took it. Jeffrey suddenly found a wad of bills in his hand. Raymond had handed him two hundred dollars.

"It's all I had on hand," said Raymond. "Mama Li and I would like you three to have it. It's not much, but it'll help pay for gas." As Jeffrey looked up at the big man, looking for words to gently decline the generous offer, Raymond added in a serious tone as if anticipating the reply, "Don't think about refusing our gift. You will insult Mama Li."

Jeffrey knew he had no choice and, besides, they really needed the money.

"Thank-you, sir," Jeffrey responded in a somber voice. "It has been a blessing to have known you and your wife."

The other two shook hands with him as well and got in the van. Raymond King had his arm around his wife as they started the engine and began to pull away.

Raymond called to them one last time. "You boys call that number if you get into any trouble, you hear?"

"Yes sir!" yelled Jeffrey as he turned the steering wheel to point the van towards the long gravel drive and out to the highway.

As the van made its way out, Mama Li went back into the house and straight on her computer. She would have a tale to tell to all her bloggers, and to the world of the internet.

The drive took them through the northern part of Utah. They stopped at Salt Lake City for quick lunch and continued north. The trio soon got to the state border and entered into the lower eastern part of Idaho where they continued north and were just south of the Idaho/Montana border when they decided to stop for the night.

The landscape looked bleak in this part of the state, trees sparse and the wind blew steadily across the countryside. They managed to find a small valley just south of the border but it provided little protection from the wind and cold. After eating a cold meal, the three amigos huddled in the back of the van under all their clothes and blankets in a failed attempt to keep warm. The morning found them still tired and cranky

•••

The fifth day.

They got back on the road without any breakfast and turned off at the first truck stop they came to and had their first hot meal since leaving the King residence. Back on the road, their route took them out of the belly shaped portion of Idaho and into Montana. The end of the fifth day spent much like the end of the fourth, huddled together in the back of the van trying to keep warm.

•••

Cardinal Costa got the news of a possible location the same day the three young scientists left the King farm.

Mama Li had posted the events of the previous night on her blog. The internet was abuzz with December 21st speculations, but the big woman proudly declared hers as the most original and, unlike all the other theories from many crackpots, backed up by three scientists.

Father Kevin had come running into the Master's office at the Vatican. He had failed to announce his entrance before opening the large doors, and Cardinal Costa had looked up from the papers on his desk in surprise as well as annoyance. His secretary had never done that before.

"I'm sorry. Your Eminence," said Father Kevin, breathlessly. "I think we may have found a clue of the Descendant's whereabouts."

Maybe God is finally giving us a helping hand, thought the Master. "Tell me what you have."

"A search on the internet has given us a hit about three young astronomers following a star, much like the Magi in the Holy Book. I looked into it, and there's some kind of galactic alignment that is to happen on December 21st. It appears that these three may have stumbled into something tangible. This star could be pointing to the Descendant and her spawn, Satan."

"Instead of Christ, it is pointing to the anti-Christ," added Cardinal Costa. "Of course, it would be an apt parallel. Where's the location?"

"In the United States, Your eminence, near some place called Santa, Idaho."

The Master thought about whom he could send to check on the story. They had investigated many dead-ends since May of that year but this one looked promising. He only had nine men left and all were scattered across the globe investigating various clues they had gathered during their search. With two days left, he had no time to recall any of them. It would have to be Father David and himself.

He made a quick decision.

"Book one of the Church's jets immediately to take us to the closest international airport to that location," ordered Cardinal Costa. "We'll rent a car from there and see what we can find out."

Cardinal Costa felt confident they would know one way or another very quickly. If the Descendant was still alive, she would be travelling with a large entourage of at least a dozen or more. He had been to America many times. The locals would easily remember newcomers to small towns and rural locations, especially if there were more than just a couple. He and Father Kevin needed only to ask the right questions to the right people.

"Small arms only this time," added Cardinal Costa as Father Kevin turned to go. They would need to travel fast, thought the Master.

He considered it a long shot but time was running out. With God on his side, the Master felt confident the way would be shown.

•••

The sixth day.

The final day of their journey. Friday, December 21.

The three astronomers woke up to a bright start of the day. The morning started sunny and the temperature hovered just above freezing. No snow on the ground yet and the countryside looked brown, almost dead, except for the clumps of pine and spruce trees scattered about.

Back on I-90, they re-entered into the northern narrow strip of Idaho and towards their final stretch south. From that point on, they would need to rely on the portable GPS unit Fritz brought along for the journey.

The day turned to late afternoon and close to dusk as Jeffrey turned the van off onto a dirt road per Fritz's direction. The path wounds its way through a thick pine forest. Yellow pine needles carpeted the ground and, other than pines, very little vegetation managed to survive the acidic environment.

A mile in, they spotted a 'No Trespassing' sign nailed to a post next to the path. Jeffrey stopped the van and turned the engine off. The quietness so deafening it made their ears ring.

"How far?" asked Raza in a whisper.

The sun had set and the gloom closed in on them.

"We're about a mile away from the epicenter," Fritz whispered back.

"Great choice of words," responded Raza.

Jeffrey just couldn't take it anymore. "WHAT THE HELL ARE YOU TWO WHISPERING FOR?" he shouted.

The two men jumped so high they hit their heads on the roof of the van.

"You bastard!" replied Fritz while rubbing the top of his head.

"Well, that really killed the mood," said Raza as he looked up at the underside of the roof. "I think I left a dent up there."

Fritz looked back at the GPS. The glow of the screen shining on his face as the early evening got darker.

"Keep heading on this path," he said to Jeffrey without looking up. "We're slightly southwest of the area but we're heading in the right direction."

Jeffrey looked up through the front window. "Looks like the night will be clear. We'll see the new star soon enough. It will get noticeably brighter as we get closer to the target area, much brighter."

The van's speed no more than a leisurely ten miles per hour as they came round a bend. Jeffrey slammed on the breaks, causing the van to skid on the dirt path for a few feet before coming to a stop in front of a wooden gate with a 'No Trespassing' sign on it. The three astronomers stared wide eyed in stone silence.

What shocked them was not the gate but the three men behind it with rifles at ready.

CHAPTER SIXTEEN
ENCAMPMENT

"They made me come here," cried Jeffrey. "It wasn't my idea."

"You coward!" retorted Raza.

"You were fine with it six days ago," said Fritz.

"That's before I knew there would be guns involved," responded Jeffrey staring out the window into the blackness.

The three astronomers rode in the back seat of an SUV with their hands cuffed behind their backs. The driver didn't say a word as he kept an eye on the three from his rearview mirror. A second man sat in the front passenger seat pointing a handgun back at the captives.

They soon arrived at a cluster of buildings, cottages really, built from materials gathered locally, the compound like a scene out of a Bonanza episode.

"I hope we haven't stumbled onto some kind of Jonestown waiting for the end of the world," said Raza as he spied the little community from the back seat.

"If they offer you a drink of Kool-Aid, don't take it," said Fritz. "Except for you, Jeff, you can have all you want."

"Screw you!" retorted Jeffrey.

The driver betrayed his attentiveness only by the slight smile on his face.

The SUV stopped in front of the main house entrance. Three armed men, standing on the porch and obviously notified of their arrival, came up to the rear passenger door. The guard, in the passenger seat came out, opened the rear door, and motioned for the prisoners to get out.

"Stand where you are," commanded one of the three new guards, as the vehicle drove off. Jeffrey assumed they were going to be shot on the spot when he spied the front door of the cottage open.

Father Sebastian came down the steps followed by Jonathan Koite and John Bernard.

"It appears we have company," said Jonathan, as he approached the trespassers.

"Yes indeed," added Sebastian.

John merely stood back and looked on without a word.

Sebastian took the lead as they looked over the three young men. "You do realize you three have trespassed on private land and that we have the right to shoot trespassers on sight?"

"Sir," began Jeffrey solemnly, "we did not mean to trespass."

"Did you not see the sign?" asked Sebastian in a serious tone.

"Yes sir, we did," answered Jeffrey, "but our curiosity got the better of us. We have come so far."

"You've come so far? Who are you and where are you from?"

Jeffrey introduced himself and his comrades and added, "We are astronomers from the University of Texas stationed at the McDonald Observatory, located in Texas."

"You are a long way from home," said Jonathan, "if that is your home."

"What is it you want?" interjected Sebastian.

Jeffrey looked at his friends and then back to the men around them. He figured he had nothing to lose. In a serious tone he said, "The star led us here."

Sebastian looked at the young man and didn't say a word for some time. Finally, he looked at one of the guards and said, "Take their handcuffs off."

Free of their shackles, the three trespassers rubbed their wrists and stood where they were. There was no point in running even if they wanted to.

To the guards Sebastian ordered, "Bring them to the guardhouse. We will be there in a moment." As they left, he turned to John and said, "Let's go see how Mariella is doing. You should be with her. I'll then go talk to these young men and find out what's going on."

LAST DESCENDANT

John, Sebastian and Jonathan headed back to the main house. As they walked over the threshold, they spied Mariella sitting in a rocker next to the fireplace. She looked full term by the size of her belly.

"How are you, my love?" asked John as the three men walked in.

Mariella turned around. "Well, if it isn't the three musketeers back from their little adventure." She looked up at her husband and finally answered him, "I'm doing just fine, babe. The water hasn't yet broken."

One of the Protectors, a surgeon, had checked her out that morning.

"The doctor said the baby had turned during the night," said Sebastian looking at her with adulation as he closed the door.

John went to sit down on the couch next to her.

"Don't I know it," said Mariella, looking down. "My whole stomach moved down and away from my ribs." She shifted in her chair as she held onto her stomach. "A bit of a relief, actually."

"It will be any day now," said Sebastian.

"Or any hour," added Jonathan.

Sebastian looked up at the tall black man and did not respond.

Jonathan walked over by the fire to warm his hands. "Did you send a message to Cardinals Leary and Peticlere?" he asked Sebastian.

"Yes. This morning, I had one of the men head up to Canada and send a telegram." Mariella looked up at Sebastian and asked, "So who are these three young men that we heard about on the two-way radio?"

"We'll find out soon enough," answered Sebastian. "I'm going to go and ask in a minute."

Mariella smiled. "They weren't exactly the angels descending from heaven blowing trumpets and declaring the coming of the Son of God that you men expected, were they?"

"We never said that," declared John with mild surprise.

She reached over and gently stroked his cheek as she smiled to him. "No, but I know what you men are always thinking."

Jonathan looked over inquisitively. "It's uncanny how you can do that." He then shrugged his shoulders and added, "I guess it comes with the territory."

Sebastian turned back to the door. "Jonathan, let's go and have a chat with our new guests."

"Yes, I think that would be a good idea," agreed Jonathan.

John remained behind to be with Mariella.

The two Seniors headed for the last cabin known as the guardhouse as it housed the members of the armed Protectors.

The three prisoners sat on a long wooden bench next to a picnic style table at the far end of the wall. Two of the Protectors stood guard with weapons ready while four others stood by the fireplace engaged in small talk. The place went quiet as the two Seniors walked in. Without saying a word, Jonathan went to stand by the fire and took out a pipe that he began to fill with tobacco. Sebastian took out a pack of cigarettes, took one, and offered the pack to the three sitting men.

"I don't smoke," said Jeffrey shaking his head.

Raza and Fritz shook their heads as well. Sebastian shrugged and lit his own.

"So," began Sebastian, "you said the star led you here." He took a deep drag from his cigarette. "Explain yourself."

Jeffrey explained his discovery and how a newly found pulsar was to shine at this very spot at midnight.

"So, a star will be pointing right here like a beacon?" asked Sebastian incredulously.

"Well, not quite like a beacon," continued Jeffrey, in his element now as every man in the place stared at him. "It's not like it will be visible all over the country. A layman will not even notice it if he is outside the cone of light. Only someone who knows what they're looking for will see it, but if you are within the said cone, it will shine with as much intensity as a full moon."

No one said anything as he finished. Sebastian looked at Jonathan, who showed no reaction, the entire explanation quite astonishing to Sebastian. When the team took off from Malta, they had not yet decided where to go, recalled the priest. After much discussion on the plane, they had finally decided to head for the United States and even then, they simply landed in New York, purchased several vans and headed out without any idea where they would go, exactly as planned. The reason, in the event that any one of them was captured they would not be able to betray the rest of the team's whereabouts. Not that any of the

Protectors would voluntarily give out the information, no amount of intimidation or torture would open their mouths. They most feared the drugs, truth serums and mind-altering chemicals.

It took the team almost two weeks before they found the place they liked and even then, by accident. At a coffee shop the small caravan had stopped one morning, a couple of the Protectors had overheard a Real Estate Agent talking to a client about several hundred acres of land for sale in Idaho. It ended up being exactly what they were looking for, isolated, large and no interference from local officials or neighbors, and now, to hear the location practically written across the heavens seemed incredible, while at the same time, a confirmation of what they were witness to.

"Who else knows about your findings?" asked Sebastian keeping his voice calm but sturdy.

"Did you tell anyone about your discovery and where you were heading?" added Jonathan.

"No one," answered Jeffrey. "We have been on the road since last Sunday and have stopped only to eat and sleep."

"What did you think you would find?" asked Sebastian feeling relieved.

"The end of the world, the return of Christ, we don't know," answered Jeffrey in a sincere voice.

"That's what we came to find out," added Raza.

"To tell you the truth," began Fritz, "since you're located right in the center of it all, we were kind of hoping *you* would tell *us*."

Jonathan began to chuckle and everyone looked his way. "What gifts do you bring, oh Three Wise Men?"

Everyone chuckled along.

"I would much rather prefer 'We Three Kings,'" answered Jeffrey with a subdued smile.

"Actually," began Raza, "The story of the wise men is told in the bible in Matthew 2:1 which says: '...Now when Jesus was born in Bethlehem of Judaea in the days of Herod the king, behold, there came wise men from the east to Jerusalem . . .' The Bible doesn't state how many wise men actually came from the east. It doesn't even claim these men to be kings; however, it is speculated they were at least learned men and perhaps even astrologers. It is also believed that the wise men came from the east by following a bright star that led them to Bethlehem."

Jeffrey picked up on Raza's enthusiasm and added, "There are several eastern religions that claim up to twelve wise men made the journey."

"We should have shot them at the gate," Joked Jonathan.

"At least they've proven that they are indeed wise, as well as annoying," added Sebastian.

"And don't forget astronomers, modern day astrologers," added Jonathan.

"All that's missing is the acknowledgement of our royalty," said Jeffrey playing along.

"Don't push it, son," said Sebastian seriously.

Jeffrey did not reply and immediately lost his smile.

"If you're the Magi, then where's the gold, frankincense, and myrrh?" asked a female voice from the door.

Mariella walked in, a proud display of a woman in full term.

"My God, that's Mary!" exclaimed Jeffrey in a whisper.

•••

The seniors had concluded the three young men were sincere and meant no harm but they still assigned two guards to stay with them at all times.

Word had gotten around to the rest of the men in the compound about the star and all were anxious for midnight to come. Just before the appointed time, everyone went outside.

Raza and Fritz looked up at the night sky in awe.

"You were right, Jeff," said Raza. "It's almost as bright as a full moon."

"Well, not quite as bright, but close enough," added Fritz.

Jeffrey felt mildly annoyed that his friends had misgivings about his calculations. "If you had any doubts, why did you come along?"

"Come along?" exclaimed Raza. "We had to force you to come!"

"Whatever," retorted Jeffrey. "The point is we are in the middle of something historic. No, more than that, this is a major event that mirrors what happened two thousand years ago and we are part of it." Jeffrey suddenly grasped the implication. "We will be remembered for all time."

"Is that all you care about?" asked Fritz. "Talk about having no piety. You are missing the big picture here, buddy."

"I get it, I get it," said Jeffrey with some impatience. "But I'm still human."

"Have you noticed that the color is not quite white," said Raza. "It's pinkish, almost red in hue."

Fritz looked around and said, "Yes, you're right. You don't notice it when you look straight at it, but it becomes apparent when you look around at everything it touches."

"It could be the earth's atmosphere," explained Raza.

"It's almost what the glow would be if mars appeared bright enough to cast shadows on Earth," added Jeffrey as he too noticed the color. It reminded him of blood diluted in water and he quickly put it out of his mind. He just didn't like the analogy.

Nearby, John and Mariella were standing side-by-side and holding hands as they also looked up at the bright star.

"It's indeed as bright as the boys had predicted," said John. "Almost like a police helicopter hovering too far for the searchlight to be of any use but betraying it presence."

"Old habits die hard, hey babe?" asked Mariella as she looked over at him. "Once a policeman, always a policeman."

John simply smiled.

Sebastian and Jonathan stood next to the couple. They also looked up at the beacon of light.

"My only regret is that my son, Marco, could not be here to share this with us," said Sebastian.

"He's in good company, my friend," said Jonathan without looking over.

No one responded.

Gunfire suddenly shattered the stillness of the night.

Ten Protectors surrounded Mariella in an instance. They were so quick that she didn't even have a chance to react to the shots or even before John could turn to her and offer his assistance. Two men quickly but gently picked her up as the whole mass of bodies moved in unison towards the large house. The rest of the twenty odd men had weapons raised ready to fire at any movement around the perimeter.

Sebastian had also reacted quickly at the sound and pulled out his handgun. Observing that Mariella was been quickly escorted away, he looked about him to see if anyone had been hit. Two men were down and it included Jonathan. Sebastian quickly went to check on his friend. He had been fatally shot through the temple and lay dead on the ground.

As the mass of bodies carrying Mariella moved towards the main house, more shots rang out from the woods outside the perimeter. Two men from the human wall went down but quickly replaced with two more. The others scattered about, began firing into the woods in a random pattern. Shouts rang out from the men who had seen the muzzle flashes from the snipers in the woods. The return fire became more coordinated. The Protectors did not hide themselves behind any walls or throw themselves on the ground. They ran towards the enemy without any concern for their own wellbeing. The casualties were high, but nothing could stop such a force. Before long the gunfire stopped. Protectors called from the vicinity of the original gunfire.

Under the glow of the red star, Sebastian ran over to survey the scene. He found two men, one dead and the other wounded. They had stripped the wounded man of his weapon and he now lay next to the body of his comrade.

"You bastards!" said Cardinal Costa as he lay bleeding from a bullet wound in the right shoulder and knee.

His companion, Father Kevin, lay dead next to him, shot multiple times in the chest.

"Cardinal Costa," said Sebastian, with a tone of surprise in his voice but quickly composed himself. "I shouldn't be so surprised, for it appears that you have confirmed what we always suspected, that you are the Master of the Brotherhood of the Rapture."

"Yes I am," said Costa with pride in his voice as he propped himself up in a sitting position by a tree trunk. He winced in pain caused by the movement. "And you must be one of the Seniors of the Protectors?"

"Alas, thanks to you, I am the last Senior," answered Sebastian without emotion. "My name is Sebastian, Father Sebastian."

"And a priest at that," said Costa. "How could you allow yourself to protect such a cursed lineage? Her line, she herself, will bring the end of the world!"

Sebastian wasn't about to be dragged into this argument. His friend lay dead and he remained anxious to find out the condition of Mariella, though he would have heard immediately if any harm had come to her.

"That, I'm afraid, is a matter of opinion," replied Sebastian.

"And the abomination?" asked Costa with authority. "Has God allowed me to rid her from this earth, along with her Satan spawn?"

Sebastian looked at the wounded man. Costa bled heavily from his wounds. Sebastian felt pity for the misguided man. He did not bother to answer him.

"Put a tourniquet around each of those wounds to stop the bleeding," ordered Sebastian to the closest Protector.

The man did as ordered without any hesitation. He ripped a couple of strips from his own sweater and tied them just above the wounds. Satisfied that the tourniquet slowed down the bleeding, Sebastian gave his next order. "Pick him up and bring him into the house."

"Gently," said Sebastian as he walked behind.

One of the men came up beside Sebastian.

"How's Mariella?" asked Sebastian.

"She's fine, sir."

"What's she doing now?"

"She's in the main house resting in the kitchen with her husband. She wanted to help with the wounded but everyone gently refused any help."

"How many dead and wounded?"

"Nine dead and four wounded. The dead includes Senior Jonathan."

That left thirteen able-bodied men, thought Sebastian, plus John and himself.

"How bad are the wounded?" asked the Senior.

"The doctor said they will survive. None of the bullets hit any vital organs but they will be out of commission for some time," answered the lieutenant.

Bringing the men into town to a proper hospital was not an option, concluded Sebastian. The attempt would invite too many questions from the doctor and local authorities, but it wasn't necessary, their doctor, also a Protector, more than capable to handle most injuries. They even had all the equipment and medicine necessary for most operations done in hospitals. They were, quite literally, self-sufficient.

"Put him in that chair over there," said Sebastian, as they entered the main house. "But leave him for the end. Take care of our men first."

The wounded were all located near an operating table. A generator at the back of the house powered the electrical devices

The Doctor worked on the most serious of the wounded. The others sat patiently in chairs nearby while being administered by other able-bodied men.

Mariella sat in the kitchen area. A half wall all that separated the kitchen from the living room where the wounded were been treated.

Costa looked around and spotted Mariella in the kitchen talking to John. His face turned to stone as he stared at her profile.

Sebastian noticed Costa's expression.

"Yes," said Sebastian to the wounded man, "she is alive and well."

"She carries the child from hell!" said Costa, venomously. "She and the child must be destroyed."

"Our organizations have been on opposing sides for two thousand years, Cardinal. Our predecessors, just like us, have insisted that they were on the right side, the side of God, the side of Jesus, and yet, one of us must be wrong."

"You, lecture me?" asked the cardinal.

Sebastian looked down at Costa and felt pity for him. "Do you really think that you know all there is to know? That you know God better than anyone else? Vanity is a sin in itself, cardinal."

Costa glared Sebastian. "How dare you lecture me? History itself is on my side."

"Is it? The written word in the Holy Book may support your opinion, your point of view, but written and rewritten over the centuries by men such as yourself. Because an idea is believed by the majority it does not necessarily mean it is the truth."

"Of course, you are implying that I am wrong and you are right," stated Costa. "You preach to me that the Bible is wrong, modified, changed, to suit our needs and support our beliefs. I pity you, Father Sebastian. For how can we believe in the words of the Bible but change it to meet our wants, our desires? Is that not self-defeating in itself? You have such a low opinion of us, Father Sebastian, and it is a wonder that you joined the Church to begin with."

The doctor had taken care of the other wounded and two men picked up the cardinal bringing him to the operating table.

"Just like you are accusing that the Bible has been modified throughout the history of the Church," continued Costa without interruption. "Likewise your journal from Marius Sestus could have been so twisted by your predecessors."

The doctor and an assistant cut away the clothing from the cardinal to get at the wounds as he spoke.

"You have read it?" asked Sebastian with surprise.

"Of course I have," answered Costa. "I am not a fool."

"Then you know that Judah was an instrument of Jesus and a vessel for his return?"

"I know what is says but it doesn't mean I believe it. The document could have been written by a co-conspirator or Judah could have lied all along."

Sebastian began to feel anger against the man lying on the table and it worried him. Did he have any doubts? No, it meant that he dealt with a cunning enemy.

"The journal had been written by a man who was a direct witness to the truth. It has survived to this day without any changes whatsoever."

Costa stopped a gas mask from being placed over his mouth and asked, "How can you be so sure, Father Sebastian?"

Costa relaxed and allowed the doctor to put him under. Sebastian also relaxed and the pity he felt for the man returned.

The cardinal will be witness to the momentous event, and he will finally see the truth, thought Sebastian. It is the only way.

The Senior went to check on Mariella.

"How is our new guest?" asked John as Sebastian came into the kitchen.

"He'll survive," answered the Senior. "How is Mariella?" he asked the mother-to-be, addressing her in the third person.

"A bit shaken, but I'm fine," she answered. "The water hasn't yet broken."

Sebastian looked at his watch. It had just turned one in the morning of December 21.

Mariella stirred. "I need to go to the washroom, again." She got up and took a few steps when she suddenly stopped and grabbed her belly. She looked over at John and Sebastian. "I think it's time." Mariella looked as a stream of water ran down her leg and onto the floor.

CHAPTER SEVENTEEN
ARRIVAL

The main house became a flurry of activity. The doctor and his assistant moved Costa to a cot and gently placed Mariella on the operating table. The technicians hooked her up to the monitors.

Sebastian ordered all the able-bodied men outside to stand guard. Only the injured, including Costa under the anesthesia, the doctor, his assistant, Sebastian, and John remained. Partitions placed close to the delivery table blocked the view to the injured men.

•••

Raza, Fritz, and Jeffrey paced the grounds under the watchful eye of the guards. They had escaped the short gun battle without a scratch, running for cover as soon as the first shots were fired and had lost their guards during the confusion. As soon as the Descendant was safe inside and the perpetrators nullified, the guards returned by their side.

"I guess all we can do now is wait," said Jeffrey.

"What else would you have us do?" asked Raza. "We all want to be here for this momentous event."

"I dunno. I just wish there was something we could do," said Jeffrey. "Be useful rather than be in the way."

Fritz sat nearby.

"That's really unusual," said Jeffrey as he looked up at the night sky once again.

The red star still shined down on the compound.

"Besides a red pulsar aiming a direct beam right at this spot?" asked Fritz sarcastically. "What could be more unusual then that?"

"A star that moves with the rotation of the Earth," answered Jeffrey, still looking up.

"What do you mean?" asked Raza.

"We should be outside the beam of light by now," replied Jeffrey.

"Yes, I see what you mean," said Fritz. "If the beam is only a kilometer wide, it should have passed us within a few minutes, seconds even, but it's still shining straight down on us."

"As if it's following along," added Jeffrey. He thought about it for a moment as all three looked up. "The only thing that can explain it is that the rotation of the pulsar has slowed down to the same speed as that of the Earth."

"What have you been smoking?" asked Raza. "That's ridiculous as well as impossible."

'Given what's happened in the last week, I'll believe anything right now," said Jeffrey.

Looking at Raza, Fritz asked, "If Jeff is wrong than what else could explain it?"

"I wonder how she's doing," said Raza looking back at the main house, ignoring the question.

"I'm sure she's fine," said Fritz. "If she wasn't, I think you would see a lot more activity. No one seems to be panicking around us. It's almost like we have a bunch of expectant fathers nervously pacing about."

"Yes, but they're all carrying guns of one form or another," added Jeffrey looking around.

Fritz smiled at him. "Well, I wouldn't worry too much about that at this point. I think they provide, even us three, some form of security rather than something for us to be concerned about. Once they saw we meant no harm, they relaxed a bit around us."

"I hope you're right," said Jeffrey.

"And if I'm wrong there's nothing we could do about it anyway," concluded Fritz.

LAST DESCENDANT

•••

Back inside the main house, Mariella began to feel the contractions. The doctor had instructed her to tell him when each one started and, eventually, the intervals became shorter.

"They are coming on much faster than normal," said the doctor.

"It goes without saying that this is not a normal birth," said Sebastian standing at a discreet distance.

"Don't worry, guys," said Mariella. "I can feel them start and stop, but I feel surprisingly little pain."

"Why am I not surprised?" asked John.

With a slight smile, Mariella looked up at her husband. "Relax, babe. Remember that I exist only for this very thing."

John smiled weakly back. "I haven't forgotten, and for that matter, I don't think anyone here has either. Sebastian is still expecting a choir of angels to proclaim the Second Coming."

"Night's not over," said Sebastian lightly, hiding his mixed anticipation and anxiety.

Before long, the contractions were less than a minute apart and beginning to get her attention, the labor pains coming on.

"She is fully dilated now," said the doctor.

Mariella looked up at the doctor and said with some annoyance, "I am right here. You don't have to talk as if I'm not."

"Sorry, Mariella," said the doctor looking up at her. "I'm just a little nervous."

"A little nervous is ok, it keeps one sharp," said Mariella. "Just make sure it doesn't cause you to screw up."

"Of course," said the doctor in a hurt voice. "You have my complete attention."

"I'm sorry, doctor," she said. "I'm sure you are doing everything you can. I'm just a little keyed up myself right now."

"Don't worry, my dear," interjected Sebastian standing nearby and overhearing the whole exchange. "I'm sure he understands completely."

"Absolutely," added the doctor.

The contractions were almost constant now.

"Get ready to push, Mariella," commanded the doctor. "Push, now!"

Mariella obliged. Beads of sweat appeared all over her face as she stopped pushing and caught her breath.

"The head is cresting," said the doctor. "Get ready to push again."

Mariella let out a small scream that made Sebastian's heart miss a beat. He felt powerless for the first time in his life.

The doctor took hold of the baby's head and said, "Hold it there for a minute, Mariella. The heads out, but I need you to stop pushing for a moment."

The assistant handed over a suction tube and the doctor cleaned out the baby's nostrils and mouth. The baby grimaced as if annoyed. The doctor handed off the device and, while holding the baby's head in both hands, said, "Ok, Mariella. Get ready for the final push."

The moment they were all waiting for.

John sat mute next to his wife. Sebastian stood still as a statue a few paces away and completely focused on the event. Costa had recovered from the anesthesia just enough to see the event but too weak to move.

The doctor turned the baby's head to the side and gave his final command to Mariella. "One – Two – Three – Now!"

Mariella gave one final push with all her strength. The newborn came out with arms and legs waving.

A boy, just like everyone expected.

The doctor pulled out the umbilical cord from Mariella and placed the baby face up on the table next to him. He quickly cleaned the baby with sterile sheets of cloth. The newborn had not cried but had simply gurgled with eyes shut.

The doctor tied the umbilical cord near the stomach and cut it with a pair of scissors and the baby opened his eyes.

•••

The baby had kept his eyes closed throughout the entire birth and subsequent escape out into the world. He didn't have to look around; he knew exactly what was happening and acutely aware of his surroundings.

LAST DESCENDANT

When the doctor made the cut, the newborn opened his eyes. The pain disappeared as quickly as it came, but it annoyed him. He looked right at the giant man above him, the man that pulled him out of the warm and comfortable place, the man that now caused him pain. With little effort, the baby reached up into the man's mind with his own. The baby pushed aside the awe and surprise that the man felt, and turned and looked through the man's eyes. He saw himself lying on the small table, looking so small and frail.

The baby shared the thoughts and emotions of the man. Both looked into the eyes of the little face on the table. The both saw the eyes were yellow and the pupils not round but vertical slits, like the eyes of a reptile. The baby felt the horror bubble up within the doctor and the newborn felt threatened. Before the man could react, the baby reached back into the man's mind, back into the lower part of the brain that controlled the body's automatic functions, and squeezed. The man's heart stopped in mid-beat and the doctor collapsed in a dead heap.

It surprised the baby at how easy that was. The man's mind had felt weak and primitive. The baby could have easily manipulated the man's mind, molded it to his liking, but he reacted with instinct to the perceived threat to the frail body that he now possessed in the physical world. He quickly learned an important lesson from this first experience. No matter how strong his mental capacity, his body remained weak and he must rely on the adults around him, at least until his body grew strong enough. He remained motionless to see what would happen next.

It took Sebastian a moment to come out of his stupor. He had seen the doctor collapse without saying a word. When he saw the man fall, his concern turned not on the doctor but on the baby. Sebastian unglued himself from his spot and ran over to investigate. As he reached the table, he soon realized with great relief that the Savior, the One, was safe. He wrapped the baby in a white clean blanket and picked him up with all the reverence he could muster. The baby had his eyes closed again and seemed to be napping but the movement of his arms told him he remained awake.

Sebastian complete forgot about the doctor and became enthralled in the moment. This was what he had been waiting for all his life, his destiny to witness, and why, after all these years, he remained alive and still sound of mind and body. The One had finally returned to the material world, to save Mankind from itself, and from the evil ways of the dark one, from Satan.

Sebastian closed his eyes and relished in the moment. Never had he felt happier in his life, never so fulfilled than what he felt at that very moment. The sacrifices he made, the death of his son, all washed away in an instant. He looked down, hoping that the Savior's eyes were open and expecting to see into the face of the Son of God for the first time in his life, well aware this would be the first time that anyone had looked at the face of Christ in over two thousand years.

The babies eyes opened and what Sebastian saw did not register in his mind right away; yellow reptilian eyes, much like that of a snake, the vertical slits, stared back at him. For a moment, Sebastian tried to understand why the One had such eyes. There was no mention of it in the Bible, nor in the journal of the First Protector, Marius. How could the men back in those holy days have forgotten to mention such a thing? Confusion and doubt began to set in.

The baby peered into the new man's eyes, but not yet into his mind. He saw a human much older than the last one, the one that broke when he squeezed. This time he tried to be more careful and not destroy a useful being, at least not all of them. As he continued to stare, he saw a shadow cross the man's face, much like the last one, and he recognized it for what it was. The baby reached up into the man's mind and saw what lingered there - doubt about the newborn. What registered the most were the eyes, the eyes of something not human and unholy. Realizing what caused such doubts, the baby found the spot in the old man's mind that held that vision, the sight of reptilian eyes, and squeezed.

Sebastian's vision suddenly changed. One moment he looked into inhuman snake eyes, and the next he saw normal human orbs. He thought of his mother's blue eyes and Sebastian quickly saw that the baby's eyes were also blue, the exact same blue. Once again, he felt confusion.

The baby squeezed again ever so slightly.

Sebastian shook his head. He felt remnants of a feeling of concern, of doubt, but try as he might, he could not think why he felt such a way. Was this not the Son of God, the One?

The baby squeezed a bit more.

Sebastian looked down at the Savior, the One, and smiled. Sebastian's moment had come, his life-long quest complete. Sebastian felt at peace with the world.

"Bring him to me," said Mariella.

Sebastian brought the baby over to her without hesitation. It took all his strength to hand the One to Mariella.

It took three attempts, but the baby had learned quickly, and it got easier each time.

The baby allowed the older man to hand his frail body over to the woman on the operating table. His senses recognized her as the female that carried him to term. Before she looked directly at him, he reached into her mind and gently squeezed. So good at it now that she did not even flinch when it happened. He looked directly at her and Mariella smiled as she looked upon him. His eyes shined an emerald green and with such intensity that she squinted against the brilliance. With reluctance, she gently moved his head to her breast where he began to suckle.

The baby fed on her milk, not just because of the natural instinct to do so but because he realized his body needed the nourishment to grow, to gain strength, until the day when he no longer needed others, when he could care for himself. As long as they were useful, he would allow these people to live.

Cardinal Costa had watched the birth of the baby and it actually did not surprise him when the doctor dropped dead on the spot, so sure of the origin of the newborn. In one sense, he felt happy that one more of his enemy lay dead but, at the same time, horrified that his predictions, his fears, were coming true. The baby was a monster, the beast, the dark one that would roam the Earth. Every fiber of his being compelled Costa to action. With no one paying him the slightest attention, Costa quietly rolled off his cot and onto the floor. His shoulder and knee screamed with pain. The anesthesia had completely worn off. He bit his tongue to keep in the groan and tasted blood. He looked over at the other injured men, all heavily sedated and unaware. Nearby he noticed the iron poker resting against the stone fireplace. If he threw it right, he might be lucky enough to hit the baby, he thought. He had to try. He couldn't just sit idly by and let such an evil creature live, and if he guessed right, it became stronger with every passing minute and he might not have another chance. Costa reached up with his left hand and took hold of the poker. He began to crawl on his side towards Mariella and the baby, pushing himself along with his left elbow while holding onto the poker.

The pain excruciating and the bandages on his right shoulder and knee were soon soaked with blood. He had ripped open the stitches on both limbs when he rolled off the cot.

He had managed to move several feet towards his goal. Amazed that no one had noticed his movements. Were they that enraptured with the creature, he asked himself? Whatever it was, it worked to his advantage. The closer he crawled the better his chance of success, however slim it might be.

As he fed, the baby sensed a presence, a strong presence, nearby. His mental tentacles could only reach so far, maybe a dozen feet or so, and he did not notice this new presence until just then. He felt it coming closer, and although the new being remained too far away for the baby to reach into the new mind, the edges of his reach managed to touch the surface. The baby felt the hatred that loomed below, the desire to do him harm. No, more than that, to kill him.

He waited patiently, and purposely kept the woman and the old man, who called himself Sebastian, oblivious of the new enemy on the floor. The man soon came within the baby's sphere of influence and, rather than destroy the man's mind outright, he thought of trying something different.

Something made Costa stopped crawling. His two good limbs no longer wanted to move. He tried again and failed. His senses remained, but the arm and leg refused to move to his command. Costa looked on in horror as his arm suddenly rose on its own accord. It still held on to the poker. Costa felt his hand grip the poker tighter and his arm muscles tense. The arm swung down with full force and hit his injured right knee with the end of the poker. Costa heard the snap of bone splintering before he felt it and his leg bent in a weird and unnatural angle. The searing pain reached his brain quickly. Costa began to scream as his arm rose again and came down hard once more. Try as he might, he remained powerless to do anything about it. With his knee crushed to a pulp, only flesh held the lower part of his leg to his body. He caught sight of the three men and Mariella, ready to plead for help, but they had not turned around at the sound of his screams, their attention fully on the child in the woman's arms.

His arm came up again and he looked in horror while his scream continued. Bloody spittle flew from his mouth. The third blow hit wood. The poker had gone through his knee and into the floor, severing the lower part of the leg.

The baby let go and the man dropped the weapon in his hand. With the danger nullified, he decided to finish it, not because he felt pity for this man, the feeling itself would have been completely alien to him, he simply wanted to test the limits of his powers for they increased with every passing moment. He reached in and squeezed, this time with much more force.

Costa froze in mid-crawl. His eyes bulged as his head began to swell. He looked as if to scream, but nothing came out. His eyes exploded from their sockets and blood sprayed from his ears. A fraction of a second later, his head exploded, sending flesh, brain, and bone spraying throughout the room. The headless torso remained up on its arms for a moment then collapsed. It twitched for a moment and lay still.

As an afterthought, the baby reached around and into the mind of the medical assistant and squeezed. The assistant got up and began to pick and dispose the scattered parts of the cardinal into a nearby pail.

The baby continued suckling on the woman's breast and relaxed his hold on the other beings around him. He let his mind wander around the room and he became curious of the only other able-body man in the room. He was a much younger man than the one called Sebastian. Like the others in the room, he made him oblivious of the carnage that had just occurred. The baby did not feel any association or connection of any kind to the man. He simply knew, felt, that the man had an emotional bond with the woman. This bond felt alien to the baby and he quickly concluded that this particular makeup, the feeling of sentiment within these beings, simply a part of their psyche. He felt this bond between the woman and the man to be strong and it made him curious. The baby, though physically very tired and drowsy, opened his eyes to get a good look at this new creature. He felt very tired for he allowed his mind, his thoughts, to register on the man's mind.

John had come out of his trance and looked upon his son suckling on his wife's breast. He decided it was time for him, as the father, to have a look at his son who lay partially hidden by the blanket that covered him. Gently pulling the blanket away from the bay's face, he peered down just as the newborn looked up at him.

John caught a glimpse of his son's eyes and they were not human, the revulsion overwhelming. He felt the baby's thoughts as a mind-numbing blow. The unfocused visions, evil and dark, like the very pit of hell.

John reacted instinctively and without thought. He reached for his sidearm, the same weapon every man in the compound wore to protect the Descendant, Mariella. In one swift motion, the gun in his hand and pointing at his newborn son.

No, it could not be my son, he thought. This Thing! - not human. Something else entirely.

He had to kill it! He had to protect Mariella from whatever it was! He aimed directly at the baby's head.

John hesitated.

A shot went off and the side of John's head blew off. Brain, bone, and blood sprayed throughout the room, some of it landing on Mariella. His head tilted over by the impact of the bullet and his body followed. It hit the floor like a bag of wet cement as his hand remained clenched around the unfired gun.

Mariella did not yet register what she had just witnessed and instinctively turned towards the direction where the bullet came from. Sebastian stood with his gun held in both hands, smoke emanated from the end of the barrel. The realization slowly seeped into her mind. The horror of seeing her beloved killed became too much for her. A scream caught in her throat, a deep, dark chasm began to well up from the pit of her stomach and threatened to engulf her.

The baby had heard the shot. Through his mind's eye, he had witnessed the entire event. He had felt the revulsion of the man that called himself his father and had detachedly watched the man's reaction. The baby wasn't concerned but rather curious. He could have stopped him any time. He could have even stopped the bullet from firing but he wanted to see what would happen and he wasn't disappointed.

He saw, to his satisfaction, that his manipulation of the old man's mind was indeed complete. It wasn't that difficult, he thought. The old man's instincts instilled in him from over two thousand years of breading, from one generation to another. The baby simply had to smooth over some of the wrinkles. He now had to deal with the caregiver woman. She had the nourishment that he needed. She remained too important to him to allow any damage to her, for now.

The baby reached up into her mind and squeezed.

Mariella looked down at her now dead husband and felt an intense hatred for what she saw. How could she have loved such an evil thing? He tried to kill her baby! If she had the strength, she would have gotten up and kicked whatever remained on the floor until it became a mass of blood and flesh, such was her revulsion.

"Are you alright, Mariella?" asked Sebastian unsteadily.

"Yes – yes, I'm alright," answered Mariella. She looked down at John's body with contempt and hatred. "How could that son of a bitch have tried such a thing? How could he have even thought it?" She looked up at Sebastian. "Thank you, Senior, you saved my baby's life."

"The One is all that matters," said Sebastian resolutely.

"Yes, the One is all that matters," echoed Mariella.

The baby smiled inwardly. It was getting to be very easy.

• • •

Raza, Fritz, and Jeffrey had been standing near the main house and had heard the single shot. They ran to the door and opened it before any of the Protectors. They did not expect what waited inside. John lay dead on the ground near Mariella with one side of his head blown off, the apparent victim of the single shot. Sebastian stood nearby with a gun in his hand. Their eyes widened in horror as they caught sight of the headless torso near the door and, finally, the doctor lying in a heap near the operating table.

Only Sebastian moved towards them, the assistant picking up body parts.

"I think it's time we leave," whispered Jeffrey. He did not wait for an answer.

The three men began running at full speed back up the path towards their van while the rest of the Protectors poured into the house.

The baby had sensed the three young men at the entrance of the house. His reach had increased but they remained too far to bend them to his will. He could have sent Sebastian or any of the other men under his control to get them, even kill them, but he did not see the point. Their minds told him what he needed to know. They were young and harmless – harmless in the sense that they would not try to kill him and if they talked, who would believe them?

No, the baby didn't bother.

He simply needed to squeeze lightly the minds of all the men that now came into the room. Bend them to ensure that they were committed to his wellbeing.

•••

Later that night, as he slept by the woman's side, the baby felt a new presence, a presence stronger than any that he had so far sensed. The new presence was not near, but far away, very far away. He reached and sensed more of it and for the first time in his short human life, he felt fear.

The presence felt like him, but not like him.

Like positive and negative, white and black, yin and yang, so was he to this new presence and he sensed that the new presence had just come into the world, much like him.

The baby calmed himself.

One day they would meet, but for now, they were both too young and weak.

And on that day, I will be ready, thought the baby. For I, The One, am ordained to rule Man for a thousand years.

•••

Made in the USA
Charleston, SC
04 April 2014